I0817766

GODS AND HEROES

WINDS OF FATE

GODS AND HEROES BOOK 4: WINDS OF FATE

Hardcover Edition

ISBN: 978-0-6484294-8-7

Brendan is not currently represented by any publishers or literary agents. He can be contacted at:
enquiries@brendanwrightauthor.com

Connect with Brendan:
Instagram: @brendanwrightauthor
Facebook: /brendanwrightauthor
Website: brendanwrightauthor.com

Cover art by Rebecacovers via Fiverr
Map designed by Renflowergrapx via Fiverr

This book is dedicated to the love of my life, Annabelle. You are my everything.

THEARA
THEARA
OROMUS
OLYMUS
OMAS
TARSIUS
Sitharkos
AKRILLUS
AROS
ANTEIOS
DYMEA
MARA
AMASEIA
AETHOS

ERMOOR
ERMOOR
SHANAKEN
SARNIA
AZAR
OMATUS
CARMERTH
TARSIUM
N
PANDEIA

Aerene

1750

Wind rushed through her hair, whistling and whooshing in her ears. Boulders the size of mountains towered out of the ocean, looming above her as she fell. The blue of her skin made her blend in with the sky above her, and her golden wings and hair shone like the sun itself. To anything below, she could be mistaken for a cloud, with the sun's rays shining through.

The water, a blue so deep it was almost black, sped towards her. When she was close enough to see the murky shapes of fish close to the surface, she spread her wings, and her fall broke into a graceful glide. Hunting was her favourite.

Her spearline, weighted perfectly for her, rested lightly in her hands. She glided close to the water's surface, looking ahead; waiting for the perfect fish. Some grew large enough that they were bigger than her, and some small enough to hold in one hand. Aerene could only hold so much while flying; but she wanted as big a fish as possible to bring back to Aelis. He didn't need the food, of course; but he couldn't leave the city.

Throwing her wings in a hard downward stroke, Aerene rose back into the air. Her eyes scanned the ocean constantly; she was Austris Aran, and their eyesight was even better than most of the birds of prey that hunted in the same areas.

"Come on," she said, staring into the freezing depths as she sped past, "come on."

There. She readied her spearline, twisted her wings to steer into a wide arc, and sped towards the fish she found. It was a lionfish, about a metre long. Lionfish were exotic-looking, colourful fish that were far less common than salmon and trout. Aerene had brought several to Aelis before, but the last was several decades ago.

Drawing her arm back, Aerene waited until the perfect moment to strike; the lowest point in her downward arc towards her prey, while the fish was still a few metres ahead of her. She exhaled and threw her hand forward. The spear launched from its sheath, the thin but almost unbreakable rope trailing behind it.

As her spear streaked into the water, Aerene sped past it above.

Now for the tricky part, she thought. Holding the spearline's rope in both hands, braced for the impact, she twitched her wings and started an upward glide. The line snapped tight, and Aerene started pumping her wings to gain height.

A loud splash came from below as the lionfish was ripped from the water. Pumping her wings as hard as she could, she pulled at the rope hand over hand, bringing the fish close. It fought like mad, twisting and throwing itself in every direction. Grunting with the effort, Aerene held the rope in one hand as she drew her dagger with the other. In one lightning-fast strike, she rammed the blade into the fish's head. *Aelis will be so happy,* she thought. Smiling, she flew back to the city.

Lining the outskirts of Austris Ara were a series of platforms for hunters to dive from. The city floated far above the ocean, above even the clouds. Diving off those platforms never failed to give Aerene a rush of exhilaration. What she loved more than that, however, was flying back up towards the massive floating city, and landing back on one of the platforms. As much as she enjoyed hunting, Austris Ara was home.

With the lionfish slung over her shoulder and her spearline packed and sheathed at her belt, Aerene headed for the royal palace. Prince Aelis rarely left the confines of the palace, though it was hardly a small space. *You could spend a night in each room in the building,* she thought, *and it would take years before you stay in the same room twice.*

She could have flown to the palace, of course; but hunting was exhausting, and the lionfish was her last catch from an entire day's work. Her wings needed the rest, so she walked instead. Austris Ara was as beautiful to walk through as it was to fly over. Gleaming white walkways spread in every direction, wide enough for several people. Trees and shrubs lined the paths. They were always neat, tended to by the Aethan people as part of their duties.

Aerene strolled through a residential sector for the Aethans, gracing some of them with a smile as they kneeled and stared. *Strange how they treat us like Gods,* she thought, *even after millennia.* Austris Arans were taller than the Omasi-born Aethans, and far more God-like. Blue skinned, with fine gold hair, bright white eyes and large golden wings, the Austris Arans were pure and ethereal beings next to Aethans.

The Aethans didn't actually worship the Austris Arans, exactly; both groups worshipped Aurath, God of Air. But the lowly Aethans were born to serve, and they played their role perfectly.

Aerene wasn't royalty. She could never lead the great city of Austris Ara; that was a matter of family line, and she wasn't born with royal blood. What she had been born with was a great deal of magic, so instead of wearing a crown, she wore the simple white robes of a priest-in-training.

Austris Ara floated above the clouds, which meant every day was a beautiful day; albeit colder than Pandeia's surface. Aerene took a deep breath as she approached the palace. The lionfish lay over her shoulder, heavy and cold. *Aelis is going to love this,* she thought, *he hasn't seen a lionfish in ages*.

Prince Aelis sat on one of the worship platforms on the edge of the palace's roof. He prayed every day, as each of the royal family was supposed to. They'd been friends for most of their lives, and whenever Aerene could, she prayed with him. On days that she hunted or trained, he knelt alone. As a priest-in-training, Aerene had to pray every day too; but the priests of Austris Ara had their own worship platforms separate to the royal family.

Worship platforms were simply a wide-open space, as high as possible and open to all of the Magic that filled the air above Pandeia. Austris Arans were said to be the most powerful of all magic users. *Because we're surrounded by magic constantly,* Aerene thought, *I'm not sure if that means we're actually more powerful than the others*. Aerene had never seen the other people of Pandeia; Austris Ara was created well before she was born, and floated into the southern skies shortly after it was built.

Aerene knelt next to Aelis. He didn't react at first; praying was a solemn occasion that every Austris Aran took seriously. She took the time to pray as well. She felt the air swirling around her, cold and electric. Silently, she called out to Aurath, God of Air, and as always, she felt its presence respond.

After they were done, she showed Aelis the lionfish. He laughed and held his arms out for it. When she dumped it into his arms, he gasped and stared at its colourful scales.

"It's so much bigger than I remember them being," he said.

"Well, most lionfish don't look like that. I searched for ages to find that one."

They walked back to Aelis' quarters together. Aerene was glad he only wanted to walk; her wings were still sore.

"So," Aelis said, "are you excited for tonight? If you got back from your hunt much later, you would've been late."

"What? What's happening tonight?"

He laughed at her, shaking his head.

"You get like this every time you hunt. The ceremony, Aerene. I'm being chosen tonight."

By Aurath, she thought, *I totally forgot!* Although the ceremony was two thousand years in the making, the date was only announced a month before. The high priest announced it after communing with Aurath. Aelis would be chosen, of course; the royal family was the closest to Aurath itself, and the last chosen Hero had been King Raellor. Prince Aelis' great grandfather, King Raellor had led the armies of Austris Ara against Sithares itself.

King Aethor was still alive, of course; but no one expected him to be chosen. At almost nineteen hundred years old, Aethor was past his prime. Though a great King, everyone agreed he would no longer make a great Hero.

Aelis, on the other hand, was young and strong. He took after his father in many ways, and many said he was fit to be Aurath's chosen, even though he was only three hundred and seventy years old. All of Austris Ara considered the ceremony to be a mere formality, Aerene included.

"When's the ceremony, again?" Aerene asked.

"In about half an hour," Aelis said, "I was just praying to prepare."

Damn it, she thought, *I don't even have time to change back into my robes*. The priests and priests-in-training never wore their traditional robes when hunting; instead, they wore tight-fitting combat outfits that allowed free movement and breathability for Air Magic use. Aerene didn't mind them, but the robes were far more comfortable, and made her feel like a real priest.

They walked together to the kitchens so Aerene could drop off the lionfish. Now that he'd seen it, its purpose was fulfilled as far as he was concerned. It would now be prepared by the cooks like any other catch the hunters and priests-in-training brought back to the city. After they dropped it off, they returned to the palace roof. *Just in time,* Aerene thought, *walking through the palace takes way too long*.

The ceremony was ready to begin when Aelis and Aerene arrived. It was held in the Air Temple, which lay in the centre of the roof of the royal palace. A wind chamber stood atop the temple as an alter to Aurath; it was the highest point in Austris Ara. Prince Aelis rushed to the centre of the chamber, and Aerene took her place with a handful of the other priests in training around the chamber's edge. High Priest Allor waited in the centre of the chamber, and when Aelis reached him, he raised his hands.

"Aurath has decreed that our Hero will be chosen today," he said, his voice carrying over the wind whistling through the chamber, "Sithares has risen, and the second War of the Gods will begin soon."

Aelis stood with his back straight, utter certainty lighting his face as he smiled next to the High Priest. He looked like a king in that moment. *Like a Hero,* she thought.

"Prince Aelis," the High Priest said, "Kneel in Aurath's Chamber, and say the prayer of Aurath."

He did, and even kneeling he looked heroic. Aerene watched him recite the prayer they were all taught from childhood, excitement filling her along with the rush of magic sweeping through the chamber's wind tunnel. When he was done, only the sound of wind was left. They waited, Aelis' face still confident.

"We pray to you, Aurath," the High Priest said, "that you reveal to us your chosen Hero for the war to come."

Aerene watched Aelis carefully, occasionally glancing at the High Priest. Then a crushing silence filled her ears; the constant whistling of the wind tunnel disappeared, but no one else reacted. High Priest Allor's gaze snapped to Aerene, his eyes wide. Aerene heard something, faint but loud compared to the utter silence it broke.

Aerene. I choose you.

All at once, the sound of wind came rushing back to her ears. A glow emanated from her skin, blue and white. The High Priest shook his head, staring into her eyes with a focus that unnerved her.

"The Hero has been chosen," he said, "Aerene. Step forward."

Shaela

1750

Shaela watched Prince Aelis praying before the ceremony. Though she was a royal guard, she'd grown fond of Aelis, beyond simply protecting him. He was a little immature, and more than a little arrogant; but for a prince, those were acceptable traits. Especially for one so young. She certainly looked forward to the prince gaining some maturity and perspective, but she knew that was most likely centuries away from happening.

Before Prince Aelis, Shaela worked as royal guard to his father, King Aethor. As one of Aethor's best and most loyal guards, she was assigned to Aelis from the moment he was born. Once he was chosen as Hero, Shaela would officially become the Hero's Guard; a role almost as important as the Hero themself. Shaela trained for the role her entire life. Her family, for generations, had been royal guards.

As Shaela watched the prince, Aerene appeared. She dragged a giant lionfish in her arms, and gave a nod of greeting to Shaela as she passed. Shaela nodded back; usually no one was permitted to approach the prince while he was praying, but the two were close friends. *She is one of his only friends,* she thought, *and sometimes, friendship is more important than protocol.*

They prayed a while in silence. After that, they spoke together, out of earshot of Shaela. She watched them walk together towards the kitchens. *Aerene is going to make him late,* she thought. They followed the same pattern quite often; Aerene would bring something back from her hunt to show him, and then they'd deliver it to the kitchens when he'd seen enough. Usually, however, there wasn't an important ceremony Aelis had to attend. *If he's late,* she thought, *I'll get the blame from Allor.*

The High Priest was a serious man. In all the centuries she'd known him, Shaela had never seen him smile. He took his duties seriously, but it was more than that; he took everything seriously. If Aelis showed up late to a ceremony dedicated to him, Allor would never let Shaela hear the end of it.

Shaela considered following them, making sure they came back in time. But Aelis wouldn't miss such an important event; she was certain of it. He'd been waiting his entire life for this moment. Aerene knew how important it was, too. Shaela remained at the temple, deciding to trust the prince to make the right decision.

As time passed, Shaela grew nervous. High Priest Allor arrived along with his priests-in-training. He shot a look at Shaela that said *why is he not here yet?* She kept her face blank, trying to hold her ground against the impatience emanating from Allor. *He'll be here,* she told herself, *he still has a little time before he's technically late*.

Finally, Aelis and Aerene rushed into the chamber, and Shaela sighed in relief. She looked at the High Priest; the impatience on his face didn't budge, and Shaela held back a frustrated grunt as he began the ceremony.

Aerene lifted off the ground, apparently unaware she was doing so. Her skin glowed. Her face was the picture of shock, her eyes wide as though they saw something Shaela couldn't.

"The Hero has been chosen," High Priest Allor said, "Aerene. Step forward."

Shaela's breath stopped. Her heart thudded painfully, and she glanced at Aerene before staring at Aelis. His face was a study in disbelief and outrage. His entire life, he'd been told he was the next Hero. It was all but a certainty. Now, his best friend in the world had been named instead.

No one expected it. Even Allor couldn't hide his shock.

Aelis stormed from the temple without a word. Shaela raced after him, though she wanted to see the ceremony finish. Aelis stalked through the royal palace, utterly silent but for the controlled rage that came through in his breathing.

"Listen," Shaela said, "I know-"

"No," Aelis said, "you don't."

"I'm sorry," she said, "but Aurath made its decision. It's… unfortunate, but there's nothing we can do."

"How could this have happened? I've been a devoted servant of Aurath my entire life. I'm the prince of Austris Ara."

"We don't have a say in the decisions of the Gods," Shaela said, "as much as we may want to."

"That means nothing."

"I'm trying to help," Shaela said, "I know this must be frustrating for you."

"Frustrating?" Aelis said, his voice taking on a deadly edge, "*frustrating?* I've been waiting for this my entire life. Everyone told me I'd be Hero. My father, High Priest Allor… You."

Shaela barely held back a sigh. It was true; she'd told him he would be Hero herself. She was trying to be there for him, but the truth was that she had no idea how he must have felt. *It's not my job to be a shoulder to cry on,* she thought, *it's my job to protect him. But how can I protect him from this?*

"I know," she said, "and I'm sorry. But Aerene is our Hero

now. It's done."

Aelis picked up his pace, all but running through the palace towards his quarters. Aethor would have snapped at his son, she knew it; the King was a great ruler, but had little patience for Aelis and his ego. Shaela didn't have the luxury of snapping at him, even if she was a little cold.

"She shouldn't be Hero," Aelis finally said, turning into the hallway that led to his quarters, "she's not even… she's nothing."

"Aurath clearly disagrees with you," she said, "you may not like it, but there's more to her than you can see."

Shaela didn't know Aerene personally; she only knew about her as part of her duties protecting Aelis. She'd learned a lot about the girl just to make sure she couldn't possibly be a threat to the prince. *Not that anyone really is a threat,* she thought, *being an isolated flying city means we have no enemies to protect against*. The throne belonged to Aelis' family for the entire history of Austris Ara; even before they'd built the flying city. Their rule had never been contested. The only people who had cause to potentially revolt were the Aethans, and even they seemed content to be ruled by the Austris Arans.

They reached the door to his quarters. The two royal guards stationed outside the door didn't budge. Shaela never went in there, unless there was an emergency. She stood facing Aelis, watching his expressions change as he processed what had happened.

Aerene rushed into the hallway behind them; Shaela stepped away as she approached. *The ceremony ended quickly,* she thought.

“Don’t destroy your friendship,” she said, “over a choice that wasn’t Aerene’s to make.”

Aelis didn’t respond. He stared at Aerene as she rushed down the hallway, his eyes glowing with rage and injustice. *I’ve done all I can,* Shaela thought, *for now*. Aelis would handle things as he always did; impulsively, and recklessly. *That might be the reason he wasn’t chosen in the first place,* she thought, *I think Aurath might have made the right choice*.

Aerene

1750

"What did you do?" Aelis said, his blue skin flushed and purple, "how could you have been chosen?"

"I... have no idea, Aelis."

"You need to commune with Aurath, right now. I'm the Hero, not you."

They sat in his quarters in the palace. Aelis stormed off the second the ceremony finished, and Aerene raced after him as soon as she could. She was as confused as him, but what she hadn't expected was the rage in his eyes when he finally looked at her again.

"How could you do this to me?"

"I didn't do anything!" Aerene said, trying not to shout, "Aurath chose, I had nothing to do with it. I didn’t even want this, Aelis, you have to believe-"

"I've been waiting for this my entire life, Aerene. You've ruined everything."

Aerene felt a sickening wave of anger rise up within her. *How dare he blame me for this,* she thought, *what choice do I have in the decisions of the Gods?* She'd been excited to see him named Hero, and he knew it.

"If I could shed the title of Hero," she said, "I would."

"So do it. Pray to Aurath, make it known the decision was wrong."

"Listen to yourself, Aelis," she said, "you want me to defy Aurath, just for your ego? Our God made a decision. We don't have the right to argue that."

He stood, abrupt and cold, and made his way to the doors. He opened them hard enough that they slammed into the walls, and pointed violently into the hallway beyond. The royal guards stationed outside the doors turned, watching and ready for trouble.

"Then I'll make a command I do have the right to make," he said, "you're banished from the royal palace, Aerene. Get out of my sight."

"Aelis, we've been friends for centuries," she said, frustration cutting through the pleading in her voice, "don't do this."

The royal guards glanced from her to Aelis and back again. Though they were sworn to protect and obey Prince Aelis, the chosen Hero was meant to be the highest authority in Austris Ara. It occurred to her in that moment how immense her responsibility really was, now that she'd been chosen. *I'm not a hero at all,* she thought, *what am I supposed to do now?*

"Aerene, if you aren't willing to give up being Aurath's chosen, you aren't welcome in the royal palace."

"I can't just *give it up,* Aelis. Why aren't you understanding this? I don't want it; I don't want to be the Hero. But I was chosen by a God. You might as well tell the sun to stop rising."

He stared at her, his eyes sparkling with undisguised hatred. *How quickly his loyalty changed,* she thought, *when he didn't get his way.* She could barely believe the way he was acting. In over three hundred years of friendship, they'd never once had an argument. *And now, he's kicking me out of the palace itself.*

The Hero must be selfless. Aelis thinks only of himself. He was never going to be chosen.

Aurath, she thought with wonder, *I can't believe I hear your voice directly.*

"Aerene," Aelis said, "get out. Now."

She stood, moving slowly towards the door. Her mind reeled; *everything is different now,* she thought. Her entire life had been turned in a whole new direction. *Why?* She thought, trying to focus the word towards Aurath, *why me?*

You are powerful. And you have the capacity to sacrifice yourself for the greater good.

Oh, well then. I hope it doesn't come to that. She couldn't help thinking it, but a pulse of subtle warmth spread through her body; it felt like Aurath was smiling at her. She left the palace, her mind and heart racing as she tried to imagine what her future would look like.

Shaela

1750

She waited outside Aelis' quarters. *He's not going to take long to blow up at Aerene,* she thought, *his ego is far too fragile.* Shaela was right; barely a few moments passed before the doors to Aelis' quarters were wrenched open. His finger thrusted aggressively out towards the hallway.

"-to make," Aelis was saying, "you're banished from the royal palace, Aerene. Get out of my sight."

Aerene tried to reason with him, but Aelis would have none of it. Shaela watched them argue, the royal guards beside the door watching Aerene intently in case a physical fight broke out. Aelis told her to leave again, and a strange expression flashed over her face. Then, abruptly, she walked away. She seemed strangely calm; as though Aelis' rage was merely a distant wind she could barely hear.

When Aerene was gone, Shaela looked at Aelis. He stood perfectly still, the rage on his face only growing as he looked back at Shaela.

"You banned her," Shaela said, "from the palace?"

"She took my life from me," he said, "she doesn't deserve to be here."

"She took *nothing*," Shaela snapped, "she was chosen by Aurath. Why can't you understand that?"

He stared at her, seething.

"I was meant to be chosen. Not her."

"Obviously that's not the case. You have no right to doubt the choices of the Gods."

Aelis scoffed and shook his head. *This is like trying to teach Air Magic to an Aethan*, she thought, *time and energy wasted for no good reason*. He'd never been easy to reason with, even when his mood was bright.

"You can't ban her," Shaela said, "the Hero is a higher authority than anyone in Austris Ara. Including you."

"I *can*," Aelis said, "and I have. She has no authority, Shaela. She has nothing. She doesn't deserve the title of Hero."

"So, you speak for the Gods now?" Shaela said.

A frustrated growl escaped Aelis' throat, strangled by the fury that emanated from him.

"Be careful, Shaela," he said, his voice shaking, "or I'll ban you, too."

"Have you spoken to your father?" Shaela asked, "I wonder what he has to say about this whole situation."

As she knew he would, Aelis balked at the mention of his father. The two were at odds constantly, and despite his old age, Aethor was one of the only people Aelis was genuinely intimidated by. When he was little, Shaela had threatened Aelis with telling his father any time he'd misbehaved; it always served to bring him back in line. Even at his current age, it still worked.

"He should have been at the ceremony," Aelis said quietly, "he chose not to be there, so it's none of his business."

"Aelis," she said, "you need to be reasonable about this. You have no right to ban Aerene from the palace. She belongs in the Hero's quarters."

"No, she doesn't!" Aelis all but screamed it, his face flushing once again to a deep purple.

Shaela sighed. Aelis caught it; his fury grew in response, until his eyes took on a manic sheen.

"*I* deserve it," he said, "I belong there. No one else. Don't tell me to be reasonable, Shaela. You have no idea what this feels like."

Shaela took a moment to calm herself; arguments with Aelis always escalated this way. She'd learned a long time ago to be the bigger person, to rise above his petty tantrums. *I have to be a source of calm for him,* she thought, *or he'll only grow angrier*.

"You're right," she said, "I have no idea what you're going through. Neither does Aerene. But neither of us chose this situation. We both want what's best for you. If Aerene could change things, she would."

Aelis scoffed again; Shaela wondered if there was anything at all she could do to calm him down. His friendship with Aerene was important. She was one of the only people he knew who wasn't royalty or staff.

"I can't be okay with this," Aelis said, "I just… can't. Even if she didn't choose it, my life's purpose is now gone. If I'm not the Hero, all the training and learning I've done my whole life was meaningless."

"You've trained to be King," Shaela said, "to rule all of Austris Ara when your father dies. Being Hero is a temporary honour, and a huge responsibility. Now you can focus on being the best King you can be."

For a moment, Shaela thought she'd convinced him; his shoulders dropped, and he let out a gentle sigh. He stared hard at the ground for a few breaths, then looked back up at Shaela. His eyes had taken on a bright shine; not just anger, but a steely dedication. *He'll never let it go,* she thought, *never*.

"I'll make a great King," he said, "that was never in doubt. But she took my only chance to be more than that. Aerene will be in history books as the Hero. She'll be studied, and revered. I'll be a footnote hidden under her accomplishments. Under her name."

Shaela's patience finally collapsed. She'd always tried to do what was best for Aelis, and he never saw it. He seemed intent to remain immature; Even most of the people agreed he would make an atrocious King. The staff that advised and served Aethor were going to do the same for Aelis; for that much, Shaela was eternally grateful. They were intelligent and wise, and cared deeply for Austris Ara. *As long as Aelis listens to their advice*, she thought, *things will be okay.*

"You could work *with* her," Shaela said, "and be in the history books together. The King and the Hero; a perfect team."

Aelis frowned, his lips pulling up into a snarl. He stared at Shaela as though she'd suggested he cut his own wings off. He shook his head.

"No matter what I do, she will always be Hero. No one cares about the King while there's a Hero in Austris Ara. It won't matter if I work with her… my name is diminished merely by existing at the same time as the chosen Hero."

His frown grew deeper, his eyes boring into Shaela's.

"I will never forgive her for this," he said, "never."

Aerene

1750

Rumours about Aerene's banishment from the royal palace spread throughout all of Austris Ara within hours. It was a scandal; the Hero was the highest honour bestowed upon any Austris Aran, and they were considered an even higher authority than the royal family. In the highest level of the palace, just down the corridor from the King and Queen's chambers, was the Hero's quarters. It remained empty until a Hero was chosen, but its position was right at the front of the palace, overlooking the major part of the city.

Even outside of not getting to use the Hero's quarters, Aerene's own quarters were now off limits to her. Priests and priests-in-training lived in the royal palace, in the west wing nearest the Air Magic Academy. *Now I'll need to stay in the academy itself,* she thought, *or in the barracks with strangers*.

Aerene was with Shaela now, at a small table in the barracks, talking about Aelis and Aerene's new role as Hero. Shaela sought her out after she left the palace, perhaps knowing that Aelis couldn't be reasoned with.

The barracks was austere to the point of being cold; Austris Ara's soldiers and royal guard were allowed no possessions of their own, except their weapons. They wore the same uniform each day, a blend of robes and armour for the perfect balance between protection and light weight.

"I still can't believe he kicked me out," Aerene said, "is he even allowed to do that?"

"Technically, no. I don't think so. The Hero is supposed to outrank the prince. And the King and Queen, for that matter."

She knew it was true, but she didn't feel like an authority figure. Growing up, Aelis and her were inseparable, and she saw him give orders effortlessly every day. He had a confidence she'd never felt in her life. *I'm not ready for that kind of responsibility,* she thought.

"I can't see myself giving Aelis orders," she said, "and even if I could, there's no way he'd listen to me."

"What about Queen Lorae?" Shaela said, "Aelis would listen to her, and she's reasonable enough to set her ego aside for the Hero's sake."

It was true; Lorae was a great Queen, who had garnered the respect of the entire city over centuries of grace and dignity. King Aethor was just as beloved, but he would side with Aelis in any argument; in public, at least. Aerene nodded, and gave Shaela a grateful smile. She was Aelis' personal royal guard, and had been since Aerene could remember. But she'd also known Aerene for just as long, and they both knew how unreasonable Aelis could be.

"The only problem now," Aerene said, "is how do I actually get to Lorae to speak to her?"

"I'll talk to her," Shaela said, her kind smile filling Aerene with warmth, "I'm not banished from the palace, after all."

Paca

1774

When the second outsider showed up, Paca and her people tried their best to ignore him. Before him, another outsider had tried to save them; that only angered the demons that kept them in Tyra. They knew now that the 'demons' were in fact simply people wearing ornate armour. But that didn't change anything after they forced the Tyrans back underground; so, they still referred to those keeping them as demons.

The demons were powerful, almost invincible, and after the first outsider, every Tyran was sure there would be no escape from them. Where there had been a spiritual feeling connecting all Tyrans as they kept the Wheels of Life turning, there was now a deep, seething rage. Rage, and a cold emptiness. Paca had believed in her mission with all of her soul, and now the jagged truth was laid bare for all the Tyrans to see.

We are nothing but workers for a whole world above ground; the word had spread rapidly to those who hadn't gone above, and all of Tyra mourned. Paca belonged to the group who'd stayed behind, which meant her only knowledge of that other world was based on the rumours that had spread in the aftermath.

Since then, turning the Wheels became ever more difficult. Paca was several dozen rotations into a shift, panting into the cold air and trying to imagine what life might be like for the people they served. She wondered if they lived in perpetual comfort. More than that, though, she wondered if there were things they had that she couldn't even dream of. What treasures must a world like that contain? She knew it would plague her mind for the rest of her cold, hard life.

Then, another outsider had appeared; the second in Tyran history. The Tyrans, desperate to avoid the wrath of their captors, ignored him as best they could. After he'd been in Tyra a while, with no consequences, they slowly warmed to his presence. He wasn't trying to force them above ground, like the last one. He didn't open the walls where the demons emerged from. Instead, he brought them food. He showed them new ways to build strength, new weapons. Most importantly, he brought them something each Tyran thought they'd lost forever; hope.

Though they were far too scared to dare another uprising, the outsider's training helped them understand how it might be done in the future. An unspoken agreement spread between the Tyrans after they'd trained a while; *Not now,* it went, *but someday. Someday, we'll rise above*.

The outsider's name was Zailen. He wasn't one of the people from above; he came from an entirely different world, one with giant plants and more natural light than any Tyran could have imagined. They couldn't communicate with him easily, but he eventually learned how to teach them little bits about his life.

Mostly, he taught them to fight, and to hone their bodies far more than their shifts at the Wheels ever could. Tyrans from all over the city visited to train and take weapons from the massive boxes he'd brought with him. He trained as many people as he could, working in classes of several dozen at a time.

Paca looked forward to each training session; it was the only thing that brightened her waking hours. Zailen trained them as groups for efficiency's sake, but every now and then he sparred one-on-one with whoever offered; Paca offered as often as he allowed. After her shift was done, she would sleep. After that, she could spend some time with him again.

Paca woke in the cold and dark, as always. And, as always lately, her first thoughts were to wonder what the people above felt as they woke. Once she rose, her focus shifted to Zailen. He would most likely be training others already, and Paca didn't want to miss out. Dressing as quickly as she could, Paca strode quickly through the hallways towards the room Zailen had chosen for training.

As she predicted, a small group stood before Zailen, running through an advanced series of moves he'd begun teaching. Paca recognised them, and joined in when she found the rhythm. Zailen nodded in greeting when he saw her; she nodded back, pleased that he'd noticed. She realised she'd forgotten the spear she claimed when weapons were first handed out; at Zailen's insistence when he first arrived, many weapons were kept hidden in case of future battles.

After the lesson, the small crowd melted away. Paca stayed behind, and Zailen nodded again. They couldn't talk to each other fluently yet, but they still spoke; he was beginning to pick up the basics of her language.

"Could we train together?" she asked, miming the actions along with the words.

Zailen nodded, and gave a brief answer in his own language.

"Okay," she said, "be gentle, though, won't you?"

Again, she mimed as she spoke, and Zailen nodded.

They stood several paces away from each other, both in a stance he'd taught her. She waited for him to move, but he stared at her instead. His gaze was mesmerizing, his eyes a strange dark colour she'd never seen before.

Paca leapt, taking even herself by surprise. Zailen saw it coming somehow, and swayed out of her path. They sparred without weapons, and Paca still hadn't become accustomed to some of the movements. She'd taken to the spear, and was used to more reach. Zailen, on the other hand, was a master with every weapon; and with no weapon, for that matter.

She threw attacks at him with fists, feet and knees. He dodged or blocked all of them. He moved with such ease, as though he barely had to try. Paca double her efforts, pushing hard through the exhaustion that already threatened. Finally, a punch connected with his side, and he grunted.

It was the only strike she managed to get past his defense. He got her multiple times, but he only ever struck gently, just to let her know he could have really hit her if he'd wanted. It showed her where her weaknesses lay, and she took note. She tried to make it so he only ever hit a spot once, but he was simply too fast. They fought for what felt like a long time, until both were sweating and panting.

Towards the end, Tyrans began crowding into the space, waiting for the next lesson. Paca heard them gasp and exclaim as she held her own against Zailen. They all knew he could beat her easily if he needed to, but Paca had learned more than most, and faster too, so they were impressed nonetheless.

They finally finished, and Zailen smiled and put his hand on her shoulder. He said something that sounded supportive, and Paca smiled back. She stayed for the next lesson, and picked up a few more moves to try against him when they next sparred. She looked forward to it.

Shaela

1750

After speaking with Aerene, Shaela went straight to the palace. Queen Lorae would take the side of reason. As much as the King was sick of Aelis' petty childishness, he always publicly defended his son. Lorae, on the other hand, never let personal relationships or public opinion sway her from acknowledging the truth.

Even the people know Aelis has no right to banish Aerene from the palace, she thought, *he cannot win this fight*. By acting out against the Hero, Aelis would only succeed in sullying his own name, and turning the people against himself. *He was so worried about people loving Aerene more than him, but the only reason they will do so is because of his own actions*. Unless the Queen intervened. She could overturn Aelis' order, letting Aerene back into the palace; and if Aelis played along, the people would see a temporary lapse in judgement rather than an immature feud.

Queen Lorae sat in the throne room, next to Aethor. Shaela approached them, forcing herself to calm down from her last conversation with Aelis. Luckily, he wasn't in the room. The King gave her an expectant look, his eyebrows raised as she stopped at the foot of the stairs leading up to the thrones.

"Shaela," he said, "what is it that brings you here?"

"I must speak with the Queen in private, your majesty," Shaela said, "about a personal matter."

"Involving my son, no doubt," Aethor said, annoyance darkening his tone, "very well. Lorae, would you like the room? Or will you walk with Shaela?"

Lorae glanced at Shaela, who shrugged. She didn't mind where the conversation happened, as long as the King and Aelis weren't there to hear it.

"We'll go for a walk," the Queen said, "I'll be back momentarily."

They walked together through the palace in silence until they reached a place with no people. The Queen turned to her with a patient smile.

"Aelis has-" she started, when Lorae nodded and held a hand up.

"He banned the Hero," she said, "everyone knows. And no, he doesn't have the right to do so."

"I knew the King wouldn't do anything about it," Shaela said, "unless maybe you spoke to him?"

Lorae laughed, nodding in the slow, graceful way she often did when talking about her son or husband.

"I've mentioned it to him already," she said, "he seems happy enough to dismiss it as Aelis being Aelis."

"But-"

"Don't worry, Shaela. I will speak to Aelis myself, without Aethor. As harmless as they seem to think this is, it's a grievous insult to Aurath and the Hero. We'll resolve it, I promise."

After speaking with Lorae, Shaela went to Aelis once again. He looked a little calmer, but Shaela wasn't fooled by that; Aelis held a grudge longer than anyone she knew. When he was little, one of the royal guards accidentally called him 'Aeli'; the prince still refused to acknowledge the man's existence, almost three hundred and fifty years later.

"Aelis," she said, "how are you feeling?"

He grunted, not bothering to look at her.

"Okay," he said, "as long as you're not here to talk about *her*."

"Her name is going to come up at some point, Aelis," she said, "you can't escape that."

"Then I'll make her name illegal."

"Aelis, listen to yourself. This is ridiculous."

"Ridiculous?" Aelis hissed, "I'm the prince of Austris Ara. This is my city. You're *my* royal guard, Shaela. This all belongs to me, even you. You have no right to tell me what's ridiculous."

In the centuries she'd spent looking out for Aelis, Shaela had never felt the urge to hit him; until now. Her hand balled into a fist on its own, and she even cocked it back before stopping herself.

Aelis flinched, and then a look of absolute rage flashed across his face. Air Magic pulsed around him, and for a moment, Shaela thought he was going to attack her. Instead, his eyes settled into empty pools of distant hatred; *he's about to disown me,* she thought, *act like I never existed, like the guard who called him Aeli.*

He turned from her, waving his hand in a lazy gesture of dismissal.

"Get out," he said, "now."

Shaela stood still for a moment, wondering how to turn things around again. Lorae was going to summon him soon, and if he was still in this mindset, even the Queen couldn't reason with him. She tried to find the right words, anything she could say to get him to understand. But before she could say anything, a servant tapped at the door to Aelis' quarters.

"Your majesty," he said, "the Queen requests your presence in the throne room."

Aelis looked straight at Shaela.

"What have you done?" he said, "you went to my mother, to try to overturn my command… is that it?"

Shaela didn't respond. There was nothing to say.

"You think just because she likes you, you can take every little problem to her," Aelis said, "but just wait until I'm King. What will you do then, hmm?"

Aelis strolled past her, his footsteps slamming into the smooth stone floor. Shaela followed a step behind, though she knew it would aggravate him. She needed to be there for the conversation, even if it made Aelis mad.

"When you are King," she said, "I will obviously follow your commands. I know it doesn't seem like it right now, Aelis, but I'm on your side. I always have been."

"Then act like it," Aelis said, "going against me like this, undermining me at every turn… that's not what a royal guard is supposed to do. How can I trust you to protect me, if I can't even trust that you'll listen to what I say?"

Shaela had no answer; she couldn't tell him that sometimes he was simply wrong. *I'm not looking forward to when he's King,* she thought, *the entire city will have to bend to his will, or face whatever punishment he deems appropriate*. For now, all she could do was hope he learned from Queen Lorae's example. *And,* she thought, *hope that King Aethor lives a long, long life*.

Paca

1774

Paca was working the Wheel of Life when Zailen disappeared. Even the people who'd been near him, all asleep, had no idea how it happened. But all of Tyra was awake shortly after, when a giant voice boomed throughout the halls and rooms of the entire city.

"The man who was among you has been taken. He is the last. There will never be another visitor to your pitiful little world. Any who defy us will die."

Panic followed the announcement. Paca had to keep turning

the Wheel, but her heart hammered painfully in her chest as the voice filled her head. *They were just here,* she thought, *and no one even realised.* Even if they weren't really magical creatures, the things they could do still terrified her. The deep, powerful voice was something they'd never done before, either.

When Paca finished her work, she went to the training room out of habit. Zailen hadn't been in there when the demons came, but it still looked barren; the demons took every weapon that had been left in the room. Her own spear was safe, hidden in the corner between her stone bed and the floor and covered by what little clothing she owned.

She sat in the training room, wishing Zailen was still here. *It's not enough they force us to work in darkness and cold,* she thought, *they had to take him, too.* She hoped, if there were ever another uprising, that it might happen while she was strong enough to fight.

After a while of simply sitting in silence, someone else entered the room. Paca glanced up; it was her friend, Quinta. Though younger than her, Quinta had learned almost as quickly as Paca.

"He's really gone," Quinta said, "isn't he?"

Paca nodded slowly, her eyes stinging. Quinta sat next to her.

"We can still train, though. He taught us enough that we can keep practicing."

"I suppose that's true. I still have my spear, too."

Quinta laughed, though it was gentle and subdued.

"I kept my sword hidden, too."

They each brought their weapons back to the training room. Nothing could replace Zailen's training, but Paca needed something to focus on now that he was gone. She still couldn't quite believe he'd disappeared so suddenly. *How did they even know he was here?* She thought, *and why did they let him stay so long, if they knew?* The demons worked in mysterious ways, there was no doubt.

Quinta stepped close and swung at Paca; she swept the sword aside with the blade end of her spear and twirled it in her hands so the butt end came around at Quinta's head. Quinta ducked just in time.

"You're getting better," Paca said as she swung the spear at Quinta once again.

Paca pressed the attack, pushing to move faster as Quinta dodged and blocked.

"I'm learning," Quinta said, grunting between words as she fought, "but you're not making it easy."

Paca eventually grew tired; not physically, as she did against Zailen, but tired of training without him. *It's just not the same,* she thought, *curse the demons for taking him*. He gave the Tyrans hope when they thought none could be found. He gave them weapons, and the skills to use them. But now that he was gone, there was no one to lead the Tyrans in an uprising; their training meant nothing without someone to guide them.

She motioned for Quinta to stop. For a moment, they simply

stood facing each other, catching their breath. Paca sat down, her mind swimming with thoughts of Zailen. *The demons must pay,* she thought, *all of them.* Quinta sat next to her, her expression echoing Paca's dark mood.

"Do you think we could actually ever succeed against them?" Quinta said.

"Without Zailen? I don't know."

She wanted to believe they could, but it was almost impossible. The first time they tried, they didn't have weapons; but from the accounts Paca heard, the demons had weapons and armour far beyond what Zailen had given them. *He knew how to defeat them,* Paca thought, *I'm sure of it. He wouldn't have come down here if he didn't.*

"Even if we could beat them," she said, "we have no way of opening the portal to above. We're stuck here unless they attack first."

"Zailen came here without opening a portal," Quinta said.

"We don't know that for certain. He comes from a totally different world… maybe his people know how to create their own portals?"

Quinta frowned. Paca wasn't sure she knew what she was talking about, but they couldn't rely on Zailen anymore, and wandering into the tunnels where he came from was a sure way to disappear. If they didn't know where the tunnels went, they couldn't use them to get to the surface.

"There has to be some way," Quinta said, "we can't live here forever now that we know the truth."

Paca knew she was right; ever since the attempted uprising, the Tyrans spoke almost constantly about gaining their freedom. The entire city hated the demons who kept them underground. She had no idea what life was like on the surface, but she deserved to know. All the Tyrans deserved to know.

The Tyrans who'd made it to the surface described powerful lights, warmth, and cleanliness beyond anything that could be found in Tyra. There was no dust up there, according to the rumours; no mud, no dank stone, and more food than the people could even eat. She didn't know how much of that was true, but at least some of it had to be.

"All we can do is wait," Paca said, "for the demons to appear again, or for another of Zailen's people to come to help us."

It pained Paca to admit it, but without a portal to the world above, there was nothing they could do. And the worst part was, until they could fight and defeat the demons, they were forced to live and work underground.

"Wait," she said, "we can't open a portal ourselves… But what if we make them open it for us?"

"What do you mean?"

"They attack whenever the Wheels stop turning."

Realisation dawned on Quinta's face. She nodded, a slow smile spreading over her lips.

"So, if we can get everyone ready, and convince them to stop the Wheels…”

Paca smiled back. It would be dangerous, especially without Zailen; but it was the only chance they had.

Aerene

1750

Queen Lorae had always treated Aerene as one of her own. When Shaela asked her to intervene, she invited Aerene to the palace immediately. Aelis was livid. Aerene and Queen Lorae sat in a side chamber off the throne room, and when Aelis arrived with Shaela, he didn't say a word to Aerene. His eyes grew wide when he saw her, and his teeth bared in a twisted snarl.

"Mother," he said, cold and short, "you wanted to discuss Aerene's banishment?"

"I wanted to discuss why you think you had the right to banish her," Lorae said.

Aelis scoffed, glancing between the three women as though they'd each slapped him.

"I am the prince of Austris Ara, the one who was meant to be chosen. She had no right to take that from me."

"Aelis, the chosen Hero does not choose themselves. It's out of our hands."

"The choice was wrong."

Lorae gasped, and Aerene's breath caught in her throat.

"You dare question Aurath?" the queen said, her voice low and dangerous.

"Mother, how are you taking *her* side? I was promised to be Hero. Her being chosen instead is all but treason."

"And you questioning the decision of Aurath is heresy," the queen said, "the Hero is chosen to lead us in the war of the Gods. She is above the royal family, and answers only to Aurath itself. Perhaps you need another lesson from High Priest Allor, to refresh your loyalty to Aurath."

He stared at the wall behind them for a long moment, his face dark as rage boiled beneath the surface. If Shaela and the Queen weren't with her, Aerene would have feared a physical attack from him. *I've never seen him look this angry,* she thought.

Aelis—and all of Austris Ara, for that matter—had been waiting for the moment he would be chosen for centuries. Before the ceremony, not a single person in the entire city doubted it would be

Aelis.

"Aelis," Aerene said, "I'm sorry. I really am."

The prince shook his head, not bothering to look at her. Everyone in the room knew his mind had not been changed. Aerene glanced at the queen; she stared at her son with no trace of lenience on her face.

"I'm sorry too," he said, though there was no such emotion in his voice, "but I just can't forgive you. This is all I've wanted my entire life. You don't deserve it."

Lorae stood, her wings spread and her mouth pressed into a thin line. She stared at Aelis. Shaela and Aerene glanced between the two, and Aerene knew without needing to ask that Shaela was as uncomfortable as she was.

"Aelis," the Queen said, "I don't care if you forgive her. But you will rescind her banishment, and publicly apologise. The Hero isn't just a warrior, or an avatar of the Gods. She is the true leader of Austris Ara, someone who will guide our city through the war to come."

The only indication that Aelis heard her was his eyes dropping to the ground. *Is he actually ashamed?* She thought, *or is this just more stubbornness?* Aelis had never acted this way before, but he was always stubborn. *It shouldn't have been surprising; he was told being the Hero was his destiny. I understand why he's so upset; I just wish he wasn't aiming it all at me*. Everyone else understood that it wasn't her fault; why couldn't Aelis?

He folded his arms, his jaw set and his eyes narrowed. Aerene could barely breathe. *He's never going to give this up,* she thought, *he'll hate me for the rest of his life*.

"Why don't you just make an announcement yourself?" he said.

"Because the royal family needs to be united," Lorae said, the coldness in her voice replaced by compassion, "and we all need to support the Hero. As servants of Aurath, that is our duty."

He shook his head slowly, a deep frown creasing his face.

"Aelis," Shaela said, "no one expected this. It's not anyone's fault, but we all need to accept the way things are. Aurath's word is law."

"If it was up to me," Aerene added, "I'd give up being Hero. You know I would. I don't want this, Aelis."

He looked at all of them, his frown only growing darker. *How did this happen? Why me? I never even thought about being Hero, much less wanted it.* Aelis was made for leading; it was in his blood. He was royal to his very core. Aerene would have been more than happy serving under Aelis both as the prince and as the Hero of Austris Ara.

I told you before. He was never going to be Hero. It was always going to be you.

It was only the third time Aurath had ever spoken to her, and the depth of power in the God's voice still chilled her to the bone. It felt endless, deep and ancient, more powerful than any magic Aerene had ever used. At the same time, hearing that voice filled her with strength and purpose, as though simply being spoken to by a God was enough to slowly transform her into the Hero.

Finally, Aelis sighed, shaking his head and looking at Aerene. There was still far too much cold in his eyes, but his face had softened.

"Fine," he said, "I'll take back the banishment. You can live here, again. I'll announce it later this afternoon."

All at once, the anger came back, and his face became a snarling mask.

"But we are no longer friends. You won't talk to me ever again, unless you absolutely have to."

Paca

1774

It took time to convince enough people to join in Paca's plan; but eventually, they had enough to fill one of the Wheel Rooms. Though the Tyrans were furious at the demons, they weren't naturally fighters. Zailen's training was the only reason Paca managed to convince them at all.

The portal always appeared in the same place: in the wall, near the far corner of the Wheel Room. At Paca's instruction, the Tyrans brought their weapons to the room. They placed their weapons on the ground nearby, so they could retrieve them as soon as they stopped the Wheel. A handful of Tyrans waited by the place where they knew the portal would appear.

For a while, they went about turning the Wheel as though everything was normal. Paca wanted to make sure everyone was ready. *I can't let the shift go on for too long,* she thought, *or we'll be too exhausted to fight*.

Along with the hundred workers who turned the Wheel, there were perhaps another hundred in the room, lining the walls, ready to attack. They all waited on her signal. *When did I become a leader?* she thought, *I never meant for this to happen*. Paca desperately wanted Zailen back in that moment.

Quinta had been a huge help, spreading Paca's plan and recruiting as many people as she could. If her plan worked, the Tyrans could actually see the surface; they could have their freedom. It felt so close, Paca couldn't help but try to imagine it.

"Almost," she said to herself, grunting as she pushed the Wheel's handle, "almost there."

She heard whispers throughout the room, saw the Tyrans shuffling impatiently. Taking a few deep breaths in a row, Paca gathered her nerves and cleared her throat.

"Okay," she shouted, "now!"

With a shuddering scream, the Wheel slowed to a stop. After the sound faded, an uneasy silence settled into the vast room. The Tyrans closest to the corner shifted into a ready stance, staring at where they knew the demons would appear. For what felt like a long time, nothing happened.

Finally, a slice of intense light broke the wall where they were looking. Paca turned away, squinting into the light to try to see the demons. As best she could tell, the portal never opened more than a crack.

Instead of a swarm of demons attacking, the light disappeared again. A brief moment of quiet confusion followed before a devastating explosion roared through the room, knocking Paca to the ground. Her head cannoned into the cold stone underneath her, and her mind fell away.

It couldn't have been long after the explosion that Paca woke again; chaos filled the Wheel Room. Screams and smoke were everywhere, bursting inside her head in time with the painful throbbing she felt. Pushing herself to her knees, Paca blinked through the smoke, trying to see the Tyrans around her.

There were dozens wounded, and at least several killed. Paca groaned as she stood, her back and head screaming in pain. *It's impossible,* she thought, *we can't win.* They hadn't even faced the demons directly; and they still lost. *Who knows what other weapons and magic they have up there*?

She really thought the Tyrans had a chance. Now she knew better; her people simply didn't have the power or the resources to win against the demons.

"Paca," someone said, "what do we do now?"

She took a few shaky steps towards whoever spoke. Someone grabbed her, holding her up just before she fell.

"I don't…" she said, "I don't know. We need the healers."

While shouts of 'Healers!' began filling the room and echoing down the tunnels, Paca glanced around. Quinta wasn't anywhere she could see. A hot, sick feeling spread through her stomach as she looked over the corpses near where the explosion happened.

Quinta's body lay next to two others. She was strewn at an uncomfortable angle, her eyes open and glassy. One of her legs was missing, the arm on the same side also gone; what was left made Paca's stomach lurch and heave.

"The Wheel," Paca said, "we need to keep the Wheel moving. They'll attack again if it goes still too long."

Tyrans got to work immediately; those who weren't wounded slipped into place by each handle and began their march. Shortly after, and almost slipping by Paca's notice, the healers appeared. They went about their work quickly. Paca sat on the bench that lined the walls, her head spinning and throbbing.

When the healers got to her, she was almost unconscious. They looked her over, asked her questions, and poked and probed her body where she'd landed after the explosion. Someone guided her gently to the sleeping quarters, and she slipped into a cold, empty sleep.

When she woke next, a slow confusion trickled into her mind; was it a nightmare, or had the explosion really happened? She tried to rise, and the question was answered.

"Ow," Paca said, groaning and grunting as she forced herself upright.

The room was empty. With a huge effort, Paca managed to get on her feet. Slowly, painfully, she shuffled through the tunnels to the healer's room. Little more than a storage room for the various potions and ointments healers made, there was nevertheless almost always at least one healer in there waiting to be summoned.

Paca entered the room panting and sweating, though more from pain than exhaustion. Without looking for the healer, she sat down on the small bench that lined one side of the room. Once she caught her breath again, she glanced around; there was no one in the room but her. *They must be tending to the rest of the wounded,* she thought, *I'll have to find them myself.*

Instead of getting up, as she knew she should, Paca sat where she was. The pain was too great, all over her body, to go searching for the healers on her own. Her injuries felt severe, and she'd passed out before the healers could do any real work for her. With a jagged, heavy sigh, Paca put her head in her hands, and waited for a healer.

Aerene

1750

High Priest Allor had been communing with Aurath for centuries. His role, now that the Hero was chosen, was to teach and guide her through her responsibilities. As the highest authority other than the royal family, the high priest was perhaps the most powerful person in Austris Ara. *Certainly the most connected to Aurath, anyway,* she thought.

All of Austris Ara took her side when Aelis banished her. He almost ruined his own reputation, and the public apology he issued didn't do much to repair it. As much as the people loved him, they were devout, and would have followed the Hero no matter who it turned out to be. Despite how brief her banishment was, the damage was already done; the people were talking about Aelis, and none had anything good to say.

Aelis seemed to be getting along well with Shaela and Queen Lorae again, but he remained cold towards Aerene. When she wasn't training or praying, Aerene spent more and more of her time with either Shaela or the high priest. The other priests-in-training were fun to be around, but Aerene didn't feel the same connection with them that she had with Aelis before the ceremony.

"Aerene," Allor said, his endlessly patient voice cutting through her thoughts, "focus. You're talented, but talent means nothing without practice."

"Yes, high priest," Aerene said, bowing her head, "I'll do better."

High Priest Allor trained her in more advanced magic than any of the priests-in-training were allowed to use. Her progress was slow, but Allor never lost patience with her, and she felt Aurath's presence through it all.

Allor was also an advisor to the royal family, which meant the only two people Aerene spent her time with were very close with Aelis. *It feels like I'll never get away from him,* she thought, *and he's going to hate me for centuries. Maybe even the rest of his life.*

Their training was mostly combat; she was supposed to be the Hero after all, and war was on the horizon. The Austris Arans were historically powerful warriors, but two thousand years floating high above the world turned them into hunters rather than fighters.

"Remember," Allor was saying, "just because air is everywhere, it doesn't mean you won't run out of magic if you're not careful. You still need to draw in energy to use it."

She took his advice, opening her body to the magic around her. It rushed in, filling her with energy. Allor nodded.

"You need to learn to be mindful of your magic intake just as much as your output. During combat, if you can't draw it in at the same time, it could mean your death."

Aerene nodded back at him, and prepared for the next demonstration. Allor always framed lessons in the same way; he would explain the theory of magic or the strategic value of a spell, and then immediately expect her to perform it. At first, he asked her each time. After a while, he started launching straight into a new spell after talking about it. Now he simply watched and waited until she showed him herself.

Breathing slowly, Aerene drew in magic and unleashed a simple attack spell at the same time. The attack withered quickly, and Allor didn't even bother blocking.

"If I'd attacked," he said, "you would be dead."

"I know. I've just never needed to do this before. It's difficult."

"Being the Hero isn't meant to be easy, Aerene. It's why we practice so often. You'll get there. Try again."

Shaela had to spend a lot of time around Aelis; she was his personal guard, after all, at least until she'd fully trained her replacement. But she visited Aerene whenever she could get away from him, and they talked about anything but the Prince. Both of them were intent on ignoring Aelis' childish feud.

Months had passed, months of hard work and training, and Aelis remained completely shut off to her. It was a difficult change, but Aerene was slowly growing used to his absence. *I need to be focused on becoming the Hero, anyway,* she thought.

"So, how's the training going?" Shaela asked, "are you a Hero yet?"

"Not even close."

"It's only been a couple months, Aerene. Besides, Allor is just about the best person who could be teaching you magic. No other priest-in-training gets that kind of attention from the high priest himself."

"He is a great teacher," Aerene said, "but the things he's teaching me are so advanced, it's going to take me ages to get anywhere."

"We haven't been summoned back to Aethos yet," Shaela said, "maybe it'll still be a while, and you'll have more than enough time to train."

I hadn't thought about that. She had no idea if the war of the

Gods would start again soon, or if it would be another hundred years. *Or if it's already started.* But that couldn't have been the case; *surely Aurath would have told me if the war was already started.*

You will know when the time comes.

Aurath's voice still unnerved her. It felt familiar and powerful, but in a strange way that she still wasn't used to.

"I'll know..." she said, frowning.

"What?"

Aerene shook her head, trying to laugh it off as nothing.

"Wait," Shaela said, "did Aurath just speak to you?"

"Well, yes. It's only happened a few times."

"By Aurath, that's amazing! What does it sound like?"

"I don't know. Powerful. Strange. I can't really describe it."

"It must be the best feeling."

It must be? Knowing that Aurath spoke to her was something that still baffled her; the knowledge that she held the attention of her God hadn't properly settled in her mind. *But the best feeling?* She thought, *no*.

"It's exciting, sure," she said, "but it's too odd to feel anything but confusing at the moment."

"I wish I could hear its voice," Shaela said, "I've been praying since I can remember. I feel Aurath's presence, of course, but it would be great to actually get a reply. Just once."

"Aurath isn't exactly chatty, you know," Aerene said with a smile, "it's not like I'm having full conversations."

"It's still more than every other Austris Aran gets, Aerene," Shaela said, "you should be grateful for that."

Paca

1774

Paca healed slowly. Even when she felt better, her body still felt stiff and tender. Working the Wheel of Life left her sorer than ever, and the hopelessness that spread through Tyra after the explosion made things even worse. Paca had never felt a total lack of hope before in her life; the Wheels used to represent a glorious purpose, and now were the symbol of their suffering. She used to wake with a sense of duty and honour, but now she woke with only a cold sense of dread.

A while after she'd healed, Paca woke to find two people

missing from their shared sleeping quarters. Tyrans lived by a strict schedule; it was rare that they diverged from their routine. Paca rushed to the Wheel room; her first thought was that with several people dead, the missing people must have changed their shifts to pick up the slack.

Tita and Sope. The two were friends, and Paca had grown closer with them after Zailen's visit. They took to his training with almost as much passion as Paca herself, though with noticeably less skill. They weren't in the Wheel room. Paca checked as much of the city as she could, even a few of the other Wheel rooms; Tita and Sope were nowhere to be found.

"Where are you?" she asked out loud, trudging down yet another tunnel, "you have to be somewhere."

She asked anyone who passed her in the tunnels. She called out their names when there was no one to ask. Finally, she gave up. The city was too big, and Paca didn't have the stamina she once had. *Maybe they moved to a different Wheel room,* she thought, *and different sleeping quarters*. Some part of her, deep down, knew it wasn't true, but she had to at least try to hope.

Her next shift passed slowly, in relative silence. The spaces where Tita and Sope usually worked were empty. Paca's breathing remained heavy, as though her lungs had shrunk to half their previous size. Halfway through her shift, the booming voice of a demon lanced into her ears; the Wheel faltered for a brief moment before the Tyrans wrestled back into rhythm.

"You were warned. Any who defy us will die. We have taken

some of you, and more will be taken. Until you learn your place, more of your people will disappear every day."

Paca couldn't sleep. Despite exhaustion from her shift, and searching for Tita and Sope for so long, sleep simply wouldn't come. Though the voice didn't specifically say they would kill the Tyrans they took, Paca couldn't imagine they'd survived. Even worse; Tita and Sope wouldn't be the only ones. More would be taken and killed, until the demons were satisfied that Tyra would never stage an uprising again.

There was no telling when the demons would be satisfied. In the meantime, more Tyrans would die every 'day'; Paca had no idea how much time one day was. All she could do was wait and hope no one else disappeared. After the first attempted uprising, Paca thought things couldn't get any worse; she was horribly wrong.

Near her own bed, Tita and Sope's beds lay bare. Paca couldn't help but keep staring over at the empty space where her friends used to sleep. *How many more will be taken?* She thought, *will we live the rest of our lives always wandering?*

Almost a dozen waketimes passed before two more Tyrans from her sleeping quarters went missing. *Is that one day, then?* She wondered, *or have they been taking Tyrans from other areas of the city?* Either way, Paca knew she couldn't stop them. She hated admitting it, but there were no options. All she could do was keep turning the Wheel.

Eventually, word from the other sections of Tyra reached Paca; people had indeed been disappearing all over the city. At least one Tyran had been taken every sleep-wake cycle. Paca felt sick just thinking about it; every waketime, more Tyrans were dead.

The time she should have been sleeping passed slowly, and finally it was time for another shift at the Wheel. Keeping pace with the other workers took almost everything Paca had. A dark mood settled over everyone in the Wheel room. Without a word, Paca knew all the Tyrans were thinking the same thing; *Will I be next?*

Riffolk

1778

Her face plagued him. Despite his work, his goals, his focus; she kept swimming into his head. He could still feel her energy. For a while, it had simply disappeared, as though she'd died. Then a couple of months later it came back. Distance seemed to have no effect; they couldn't possibly still be in Ermoor, and yet her energy still felt the same as it had when she was in the city.

It had been almost five years since she disappeared. His lab had been destroyed back then, partly because of Mara. Then, the Commander Mathys Corby had found him in the saferoom that branched off it. After that, he set up an even more secretive lab in the Twelve's private tunnels under Ermoor. But, slowly, he rebuilt the underground facility over time, and now was back to working in the familiar space.

Shortly after Mathys and Mara both disappeared, a fabricated story was released to the public about Mathys kidnapping him as part of a Shenza plot to destroy Ermoor. It was ridiculous, of course, but Mathys provided the perfect scapegoat, and the Ermoori public would believe anything their government told them. It had also given Riffolk the opportunity to paint Lord Commander Arthor Symond as a hero; thus cementing his place as Riffolk's right hand when the time came to go public as Ermoor's ruler. Until then Riffolk still ruled from the shadows by pretending to be the Twelve Crowns.

Mara. Despite the years, she was still there, lurking in his head through the connection formed by their shared magic. The feeling of magic in his mind was far too vague for Riffolk's taste; he needed to track her down properly. Sensing her presence left him unable to focus as much as he wanted to on his work. Fortunately, his current project was almost done, and it would help with the situation he found himself in; a magic detection device that would help him locate the other books of the Gods throughout Pandeia. *And it should locate her, too,* he thought, *so I can finally be rid of her*. He simply called it the Detector.

His blueprint was done, updated and ready to implement. There were only a few changes from his last design. He rarely needed many changes once he'd settled on a new design; a few small tweaks usually did it. The device would pick up on any large spike in magic, anywhere in Pandeia. Not only that, it would pinpoint the location where the spike happened.

Building the device didn't take long; when Riffolk designed a new invention, he knew the blueprints inside and out. It glowed in his mind, vivid and complex, the inner workings as clear to him as the blue sky on a cloudless day.

Most of a day after he started, the device whirred to life. A full map of Pandeia lay on a screen, with several other screens around it. Each screen had its purpose, but what Riffolk focused on was the map.

The device continued whirring, processing the information it received from the detection wand attached to the lab's roof. Riffolk had set the device's sensitivity low to begin with, as a baseline; magic was powerful, and there was no way to know how the device would react to extreme magic if it so happened to pick any up.

Nothing happened. Riffolk fiddled with the dials, altering the settings to try to pick up on something. He knew there was magic in Pandeia; the only problem was that if he set the device's sensitivity too high, it would pick up on the thousands of people who possessed magical ability. Even worse, the device could easily overload and be destroyed.

Finding a signal took almost as long as building the device had in the first place. Finally, colourful lights and beeps sprang to life on the device's control board. There were more than Riffolk expected;

the sensitivity was still fairly low, which meant only incredibly powerful magic would show up. The map had been designed with hundreds of tiny light bulbs underneath it, meaning any location would light up individually when the device detected enough magic there.

There were at least ten spots lit up on his map. Several locations made sense to Riffolk; the swamplands of Ermoor, where Taranos escaped to. His own lab, where the book of Taranos remained in his possession. The volcano of Omas, known as Sitharkos, which was a known source of Fire Magic. The rest were the locations of either the books of each God, or some manifestation of them.

Riffolk didn't care where the Gods themselves were; being touched by Taranos had been unpleasant enough, despite endowing him with Power Magic. He wanted the books. At the very least, they'd provide him with indispensable knowledge of the other forms of magic.

He selected the locations most likely to contain books; by process of elimination, as well as what he already knew of the Gods, he was able to determine where to search. As well as weaponry for his army, Riffolk had been developing more advanced armour and weaponry for use by his specialized teams. They were also trained far more than his standard troops. A team of a dozen men would be sent to each location; four locations that he'd decided should contain the other four books.

The teams were already put together, and had already been

briefed on the mission. They had no idea what they were retrieving, but even before Riffolk took control of the Twelve, Ermoori troops were terrified of failure. The soldiers would either bring the books back to him, or they would die trying.

After choosing the locations, Riffolk built portable devices that each team could carry with them to show where they needed to go. Just like his detection device, they showed co-ordinates and altitude, and contained a smaller detection module that would beep when the magic was nearby.

Finally, after months of hard work barely leaving his lab, he was ready. Riffolk prepared all of the equipment his teams would need, and summoned the Overseers; each Overseer had assigned their best men from their respective branches, and were entrusted with briefing and dispatching their team. When the Overseers arrived, Riffolk gestured to each of the containers in front of him.

"The time has come," he said, "your teams must depart as soon as possible. Remember, failure is not an option. The items must be recovered and returned to Ermoor. For the good of all."

"For the good of all," the Overseers said in unison, then promptly wheeled their equipment out of his lab. *Time to see what these elite teams can do,* he thought, *all that's left is to wait.*

Mattias

1778

Footsteps thumped from the corridor outside Mattias' quarters, and he turned in time to see Commander Rawley's hard frown.

"Mattias," he said, standing in the doorway, "Overseer Burnham wants to see you."

Mattias stood, feeling cold sweat already soaking the armpits of his military tunic. *It's been six years,* he thought, *they can't have found out.*

"Do you know what it's about?"

"Your experience during the Tyran uprising, I believe. Step to, soldier. The Overseers don't like to wait."

Memories of the guard tunnels bordering Tyra still plagued Mattias. Even after six years, the vision of a lethal shadow tearing his squadron apart never left his mind's eye. *The Twelve weren't lying,* he thought, *they're savages. Animals. They don't even move like people*. Sitting alone in his quarters, Mattias tried to bury the memories of watching his team sliced to pieces in front of his eyes.

All his life, Mattias heard constant announcements over the teleradios stationed at every street corner in Ermoor. Just like every citizen of Ermoor. The announcements, which occurred every hour, taught the Ermoori about Shenza, and about the Godless people of the rest of Pandeia. Mattias remembered always thinking that there must be *some* decent people out there; and that maybe the rest of Pandeia could be saved instead of destroyed. Ermoor's repeated attempts to enlighten Shanaken proved otherwise, and Mattias' personal experience with a Shenza showed him that destruction was indeed the only option.

He'd never been to Shanaken, instead being assigned guard duty in Tyra due to his age. Any Ermoori was lucky to be given Tyra duty; the Tyrans didn't even know they were captives, and never saw the guards. It was simply a matter of marching through empty hallways.

Until the uprising. Mattias was the only survivor of the guards on duty at the time, and he only lived by fleeing. The Overseers didn't know he ran away, and it was a horrible secret he'd kept to himself since. Ermoori soldiers were expected to give their lives protecting Ermoor, and to honour the one true God. Cowardice was akin to desertion, and desertion was a form of treason. The memory of a Shenza tearing his team apart was equally as terrifying to him as an Overseer discovering that he'd fled from battle.

Overseer Burnham was one of the military Overseers; there was one for each branch of the Ermoori military. Charles Burnham was the Overseer of the Tyran Guard, and had been for longer than Mattias had been alive. His office was on the top floor of the barracks, overlooking one of the training courtyards. Mattias had never been in an Overseer's office before; it looked like the comfortable living room or study of a mansion rather than the office of a military leader.

"Mattias Sterling?" the Overseer said.

"Yes, Overseer."

"You survived an attack by a Shenza savage, correct?"

"Yes, Overseer."

"How?"

Mattias hesitated. Lying to an overseer was a form of treason too. *No matter what I do,* he thought, *I'm committing treason.*

"It's okay, son," Overseer Burnham said, "you don't need to be humble. No other soldier survived that attack, you should be proud."

"I... just kept shooting," Mattias said, "it was wounded, and it disappeared."

"Did you hit it directly?"

"No. I don't think so. It moved too quickly."

"What did you learn about them?"

That they can't be killed by gunfire, he almost said.

"Wounding them barely slows them down," he said instead, "and they kill quickly."

Teleradio announcements often mentioned the cruel and sadistic practices of the Shenza, but from what Mattias had seen, they aimed to kill their enemies as quickly as possible. *They must save the torture for captives,* he thought, *survivors at the northern shore they take into the forests.*

"When they have to," Overseer Burnham said, "yes. But make no mistake, if they get the chance, they will take their time to make you suffer."

The idea of being captured by one of those monsters drove a shiver down Mattias' spine. He barely suppressed it in time, and Overseer Burnham gave him a calculating look.

"We're putting together a mission," he said as his face snapped back to a neutral expression, "one that cannot be allowed to fail. As someone who has seen the Shenza in action, and who has proven himself to be an exemplary soldier since, I volunteered your name to the Twelve Crowns."

"Yes, Overseer. Thank you. May I ask, what is the mission?"

He glanced at Mattias' Commander, who left the room without a word. After Commander Rawley's footsteps faded into silence, the Overseer finally looked at Mattias again.

"No one can know about this," he said, "it is to be kept absolutely secret."

"Yes, Overseer."

"Overseer Riffolk Hayne has built a device that detects... anomalies. One has been found in the northern mountains of Shanaken. It must be recovered and brought back to Ermoor, so that the savages of the forest don't misuse its power."

"I'm sorry, Overseer," Mattias said, "but what do you mean, anomalies?"

"Overseer Hayne was not specific about the nature of the item you'll be obtaining. All he said was the device will lead you to it. You are not to do anything with the anomaly except bring it safely back to Ermoor."

Mattias couldn't even imagine what Burnham or Hayne meant by anomaly. *Unless,* he thought, *it's possible they mean...* But he didn't dare finish the thought. The Twelve Crowns were adamant that magic didn't exist. But if it wasn't magic, what else could it be? The way the thing had moved when it attacked his team… it wasn't possible.

The Shenza had no technology. Ermoori had no need for animal or plant specimens. If it was a weapon of some type, the Shenza would have already started using it against the Ermoori. *Besides,* he thought, *why would there be something in Shanaken that the Shenza didn't know about in the first place?* As savage and animalistic as they were, one thing all Ermoori were sure of was that the Shenza knew the forests as well as Mattias knew his own quarters. If there was something there, something powerful, the Shenza would have known.

"You'll be part of a small team," Overseer Burnham was saying, "made up of others who have come up against Shenza and lived. All the rest of your team are soldiers who came back from the northern shore. You will follow their lead. Our armies have never been able to breach the forest by force, but a small group should be able to sneak in if you're careful. Especially climbing the northern mountains."

Mattias felt the blood drain from his face. *I'm going to actually go into those forests*. It had never been done, in the history of Ermoor. There would be no running away, no covering for cowardice. *I either succeed,* he thought, *or I die*.

Shaela

1778

Almost thirty years passed after Aerene was chosen. Aelis' grudge continued, and though Aerene lived in the Hero's quarters, they never spoke to each other. Shaela's life resumed more or less as normal; except that now she worked as Aerene's personal guard instead of Aelis'. It was a welcome change.

Living in a gigantic floating city meant that no external threats existed. Shaela's job was essentially to make sure no other Austris Arans dared approach Aerene without permission. It wasn't the most exciting life; especially compared to protecting Aelis. But still, Shaela settled into the daily grind of escorting Aerene between the Hero's quarters and the Sky Temple. They trained together, and ate together, and prayed together.

Then one day, for the first time since Austris Ara had been built, newcomers were seen on the horizon. A ship, its purpose clearly sinister, cut through the water far below them. Though the distance made it a little difficult to see fine details, the ship was undoubtedly heading straight for Austris Ara.

It was the first and only time Shaela knew of that Austris Ara might be visited by non Austris Arans. And it finally gave her something real to do. As the protector of the Hero and the royal family, it was Shaela's job to make sure the travelers weren't a threat. She let a fellow royal guard know and told them to pass the word around; the Austris Arans had to be ready in case the scout ship was a precursor to something bigger.

Shaela dove off the edge of Austris Ara. She carried her spearline, ready for whatever may come. The city floated far above the ocean; Shaela let herself fall until the water below her took up her entire field of vision. Then she threw her wings wide, and swept up into an arc that carried her high into the air again.

The ship slowly grew larger. Behind it, the water roiled in a plume of white foam. *I've never seen a ship before,* she thought, *but that's faster than anything should be able to move on the water*. She counted a dozen men, wearing a kind of armour she'd never seen before. They each carried weapons, and there were dangerous-looking gadgets attached to their belts and armour.

Whatever they're doing, she thought, *they're not looking for peace*. As she flew towards them, they noticed her; as she predicted, they reacted with aggression. The sound of explosions pounded through the air, and projectiles whistled past her head. *Those weapons are no joke,* she thought, *they're far deadlier than a spearline*.

Shaela began angling her wings, twisting through the air in evasive patterns as the warriors below her continued firing. When she drew close enough, she launched her spearline at one warrior and sent a wave of Air Magic at another. Both were hit; both died. As she soared past them, barely a couple metres above the ship's deck, she whipped her knee into the face of another warrior. Glancing back as she cleared the ship, Shaela watched the man plummet into the ocean, his face a mess of blood and bone.

Shouting rose from the remaining warriors, and Shaela readied her spearline for another attack. She flew in a sideways arc, swinging around to face the ship again. The warriors kept firing their weapons. As she approached a second time, Shaela formed a wedge-shaped shield of Air Magic in front of her. It worked to deflect the projectiles fired at her; she could have been hit multiple times despite her evasive movements.

The warriors never gave up; even as she killed them, she admired their discipline. *They have no magic,* she thought, *even if their weapons are powerful, they are as weak as the Aethans*. With about nine of them left, Shacla landed on the deck of the ship.

One of the warriors said something to her; Austris Arans spoke Oman and Kashenzakii, the language of the Shenza, but the people she faced looked Ermoori, and she didn't speak their language. *I've only read about these people,* she thought, *and even then, that was the Ermoori of more than two millennia ago.*

Shortly after speaking, the man flourished his weapon. Shaela gathered as much Air Magic as she could, and unleashed it in an explosive blast. The Ermoori were flung off the ship with such force that their screams faded into near silence before they hit the water. Under her feet, the ship itself cracked and rocked as her Air Magic smashed through it.

Open ocean surrounded the now broken ship for kilometers in every direction. *Even if they survived that blast,* she thought, *they won't live much longer without somewhere to swim to.* The ship wouldn't stay afloat long either; though it looked like a brilliantly designed piece of technology, Shaela's magic had rendered it more or less useless as a boat. She scanned the horizon in the direction they'd come from. *No more of them coming,* she thought, *though we'd best be vigilant.*

Satisfied that the threat was neutralized, Shaela cast her eyes over the ocean nearby one last time, then leapt into the air. The King and Queen should already have been told about the ship, but Shaela brought good news; it was a small, unprepared team, and they were destroyed. As far as Shaela could tell, they hadn't seen Austris Ara itself. The only exposure they'd had to the floating city was Shaela, and they had no way of telling anyone about that now.

Mattias

1778

Shanaken was undeniably beautiful, but an otherworldly darkness emanated from it that terrified Mattias beyond words. *Trees should not be that massive,* he thought, staring up at the tops of them as their tiny boat skimmed over the choppy water. He had to crane his neck to see, looking almost straight up.

They were far west of the northern shore that offered the only reasonable place to land; every surface before them was jagged rocks and cliffs that blended straight into the mountains. *The mountains we need to explore*. His team was small, as Overseer Burnham had said.

Still, Mattias had hoped for more than the dozen men he'd been given. It wasn't even close to a full unit; in the Ermoori military, a unit was fifty men.

Reaching the lowest outcrop of rock, they maneuvered the boat backwards to face out for a quick getaway, anchored and threw a grappling hook to climb up. Every man in the team looked as terrified as Mattias felt. In complete silence, they carefully scrabbled up the rock cliff. Each of them carried as many weapons as they could, and wore the latest stealth armour designed by Overseer Hayne.

When the last man was on the clifftop, they turned their attention to the device. It whirred, and an accurate map of Shanaken appeared on the small screen on its face. A red dot blinked on and off, several kilometres from their position.

"It's closer than I thought," Elias said, "we can reach that within the hour if we hurry."

"Then let's hurry," one of the others said, then hurriedly added "uh, Captain. Sir."

They were a brand-new team, and most of them had never met. Elias Radcliff was made Captain at the last possible minute, and none of them, Elias included, were used to addressing him as such.

Marching over the rocky, sloping ground wasn't as easy as Mattias hoped it would be, but they kept pace as best they could. Weapons out, staring in every direction, and ready for an attack at any moment, they rushed up the mountain.

The journey there took longer than an hour, requiring them to climb impossible mountains and massive rocks in tense, fearful silence. All twelve men were panting and sweating by the time the dot on their device came close to their position.

As they approached the anomaly, Overseer Hayne's device beeped and whirred. Mattias squinted at the mountain ahead of them; a slightly unnatural shape protruded from the ground, black as the sky at night. The closer they got, the faster the beeps became.

When the team was close enough to see what they were supposed to take, a low growl echoed from somewhere nearby. The team tensed, gathering into battle formation in a clumsy rush. Mattias couldn't tell where the growl came from, but their standard battle formation was an outward facing circle that covered every angle of approach.

The strange protrusion twisted up from the rocky ground, shiny and smooth like metal. In its centre, a hollowed-out enclave presumably contained the anomaly. *It's hard to tell if there's anything in there,* he thought, *it's so, so dark. Impossibly dark.* It gave off the same atmosphere as the shrine in the church of the one True God; cold, powerful, and intimidating.

Mattias knew Shanaken was a dangerous place; every Ermoori understood the dangers of a Godless, wild forest. But his worst nightmares paled in comparison to the monster that emerged from behind the black shrine.

It was huge, sleek, and bristling with claws and fangs that Mattias could have sworn were made from the same black metal-like substance as the shrine. A chilling intelligence burned from behind its pitch-black eyes, and its mottled green fur made it look like the forest itself come to life.

He tried to move, tried to fire his weapon, anything, but a pure, blinding terror turned his body to stone.

"Captain," one of the men said, "what is that?"

The Captain didn't answer. Two more of the monsters appeared, moving silently despite their size. They stood in a formation of their own; one remained by the shrine, the other two at the team's flanks. *Surrounded. By monsters*. Mattias had never known such terror in his life.

An echoing boom shattered the silence, and then everything happened at once. His body finally moved, and he did the first thing he could think of as the team fired their weapons; he raced to the shrine, shoved his hands into the darkness and snatched the heavy anomaly from its place. The monster roared, and Mattias ran, firing behind him as he did.

"Go, Mattias!" Elias screamed, hurling an explosive at one of the monsters, "we'll slow them down, get that thing to the boat!"

He ran faster than he thought he was capable of. Roars and screams chased him, and suddenly he felt like he was back in the corridors of Tyra, running from the Shenza. *Only this is much worse,* he thought, *these are actually monsters*. He didn't dare look behind him, but he could tell from the sounds that the monsters weren't following. *The team is doing their job*.

A small part of him, the same part that ran from the Shenza six years ago, felt a wave of relief at the fact that he wasn't staying behind to distract monsters. Their screams could still be heard as he ran. *It sounds like less men already.* All he could do was run and hope that he reached the boat before the monsters reached him. *By the grace of God,* he thought, *I hope those things can't swim fast.*

Sprinting down the mountainside proved to be far more difficult than rushing up the other way; he slipped and tumbled, smashing his shoulders and legs against jagged stones as he rolled. His body screamed at him to stop, to rest, even for a moment, but he climbed to his feet and pushed on.

By the time he could see the boat, Mattias heard no screams or roars. *Either everything is dead,* he thought, *or they're silently running after me right now.* The thought filled him with renewed energy, and he climbed down the cliff face so quickly that it was almost falling. Every part of his body burned with exhaustion and pain, but he threw the anomaly into the boat and leapt in after it.

Igniting the engine, Mattias pulled the accelerator lever. The boat sped forward immediately, and Shanaken began shrinking behind him. He stared at the rocky mountains, and saw a lone figure staring back. *That's not one of ours,* he thought, *that's a Shenza.*

When Shanaken was a thin line on the horizon behind him, Mattias finally inspected the item he snatched. It was some kind of massive book, but the cover was unlike anything he'd ever seen. *It looks like darkness given physical form,* he thought, *like magic.* The thought unsettled him almost as much as the ordeal he'd just survived; he knew magic wasn't real, and yet he was holding something that seemed to prove otherwise.

Laying the book on the boat's floor, Mattias tried to cast his thoughts as far from it as possible. He didn't allow himself to feel properly relieved until his feet touched the smooth streets of Ermoor once again.

Riffolk

1778

Almost two months passed after his teams left on their mission. Unknown to them, Riffolk had been tracking each team; he watched their progress every day. The team tasked with travelling to Omatus disappeared when they reached the Royal Palace. He'd heard many things about the current King of Omatus, and the deaths of the troops at his hand came as no surprise.

At almost the same time, the team in Tarsium was destroyed as well. The Tarsi were mysterious creatures, and Riffolk had only learned a little about them. Weapons seemed to work on them as normal, though they were much faster than Ermoori. They were also difficult to find when they didn't want to be seen; Riffolk surmised it had something to do with the magic they used.

Most frustrating to Riffolk was the team he'd sent south. They left Ermoor in a brand-new ship he designed specifically for long distance travel by sea. The signal Riffolk found was further south than any map he knew of. He designed the ship to withstand all weather conditions, even the worst storms and the biggest waves. Yet still, the ship was somehow destroyed. It disappeared, along with the team it contained.

The only team who succeeded was the Shanaken group. Riffolk watched them on his screens, alongside the other teams, as they raced ashore. They moved quickly, and even when the dots that represented each soldier began flicking out, they kept moving. Finally, down to a single soldier, the bright light Riffolk knew to be the book of Amalus raced back onto the boat and jetted away from Shanaken.

A while later, the book of Amalus lay before him; Shadow Magic was almost within his grasp. Experimenting on the Shenza who snuck into Ermoor yielded extraordinary results; but possessing the potential for the magic they used was a far greater opportunity. The only mystery that remained was how to gain the magic within the book's pages. Power Magic had come to him as a mistake; albeit one he cherished.

He'd be able to harness the magic that emanated from the book in some ways, using technology; but gaining magic from it himself was a different story. It would take more study, he knew, and plenty of research. But eventually, Shadow Magic would be his. And after that, the other types of magic. It was only a matter of time.

There were only three books left now; though his other teams had failed, he at least knew where the books themselves were located. Resources were of no significance to him. Whether people, money, or technology, he would spend as much as it took to take the three remaining books.

No one else that he knew of was looking for the other books; or even knew how to locate them. If Riffolk could obtain them, he'd become the most powerful being in all of Pandeia. *It's just a matter of time now,* he thought, *I have everything I need to take the books for myself.*

The biggest thing to consider now was reciprocity; The teams who failed had revealed themselves to Riffolk's enemies. Attempting to capture such important and invaluable items by force would provoke counter-attack. Riffolk anticipated an attack from at least one of the countries, and sooner rather than later. But his army was powerful, and the books in his possession were in the safest place in all of Ermoor. When the attack came, he would be ready.

Shaela

1778

As soon as she landed back in Austris Ara, Shaela headed straight for the palace. The city was abuzz with excitement about the strange ship. People stared at her as she strolled towards the palace, and she heard snatches of their conversation;

"… Moving faster than any other ship can…"

"… At least twenty of them…"

"… Using magical weapons…"

Shaela ignored them, picking up her pace. *I just hope Aelis isn't around when I get to the throne room,* she thought, *he'll only complicate things*. Knowing Aelis, he'd attempt to declare war on Ermoor or some such. Not that the King was likely to listen to that, of course; but being ignored only pushed Aelis into being more childish.

Lorae and Aethor both sat in the throne room when Shaela arrived. Aelis wasn't in the room; Shaela breathed a sigh of relief. Not surprisingly, Aerene sat with the King and Queen. The Hero assisted with ruling Austris Ara when not actively fighting in the war of the Gods, and Aurath hadn't yet advised Aerene that the war had begun. For now, her responsibilities were simply to train and liaise with Lorae and Aethor.

As soon as she entered the throne room, Lorae and Aerene both greeted her. King Aethor glanced up at her, and gave a noncommittal nod. Shaela reached the foot of the stairs and waited to be addressed.

"Shaela," Lorae said, "you have news of the scout ship?"

"They were Ermoori," she said, "about a dozen, heavily armed and looking for battle. They opened fire as soon as I came within range."

"Do you think they knew where Austris Ara was?" Aethor said.

"I can't be sure. But before I reached them, they were heading straight towards us."

The King frowned. Though she wanted to believe the Ermoori stumbled upon them by chance, no Pandeian people had ever come across them before. The King's concern was justified; the Ermoori had clearly discovered their whereabouts somehow, or at least the general direction to search in.

"What was the conclusion of your… meeting with them?" Aethor said.

"The threat is destroyed, your majesty," Shaela said, "none of the Ermoori survived."

For the first time in a long time, Shaela saw the King smile. The fact that it was the deaths of a dozen men that brought the smile to his lips sent a shiver down Shaela's spine. She didn't feel any remorse for killing the scouts, of course; but she didn't enjoy it, either. *Although,* she thought, *it did feel good to use magic in a real fight.*

"Good," the King said, "they have nothing to report to their people, then."

"What if they send more?" Aerene asked, "they were surely expecting that group to return."

"Then Shaela will destroy them, too," King Aethor said, "won't you?"

Shaela nodded; it was her job, after all. Aerene glanced at her; the look in her eyes broke her heart. *She thinks I enjoy their deaths as much as Aethor does,* she thought, *but there's no way to tell her I don't.* She made a note to speak with Aerene in private as soon as she could.

"How would you like to handle this, your majesty?" Shaela said, "are you satisfied that the situation is resolved?"

Aethor looked between the women in the room. There was no

doubt on his face, no uncertainty. *He's not looking for suggestions,* Shaela thought, *but he's still searching our faces… what is he looking for?* Aethor had never been the type to hesitate. He took advice from his staff, but whenever a big decision was laid at his feet, he always had an answer ready.

Shaela couldn't tell what the King might say; whether he would order an attack on Ermoor, simply let it go, or even move the city closer to the northern continent to watch over them. If he wanted the former, Shaela didn't know how to react. Starting a war with Ermoor when the war of the Gods still hadn't even started would be far too reckless. Moving the city north was unheard of; Austris Ara remained out of sight of the other countries since first lifting off from Aethos. Shaela only imagined that as an option because she knew Aethor well. He liked to know everything it was possible to know about a situation.

Finally, the King shifted in his throne and cleared his throat. The room was silent. Shaela's breath caught in her throat; Austris Ara had never been on the brink of war with any of the other people in Pandeia before.

"I'm sure they'll send more scouts this way," he said, "and we'll deal with them when they come. But our duty lies with the Hero, and Aurath. We will wait until we are summoned to join the Circle of Shadows and the war of the Gods."

Shaela breathed again. *Aelis never would have made such a rational decision,* she thought, *at least for the time being, we have a*

King who can rule properly. At almost two thousand years of age, however, King Aethor wouldn't live much longer. He still had his wits about him, but not many Austris Arans had ever lived beyond two thousand.

"Yes, your majesty," Shaela said.

Aerene beamed at her, and at the King. She was surprisingly comfortable around the rulers of Austris Ara; possibly because she'd spent most of her life as best friend to the prince. In the almost thirty years since becoming Hero, Aerene's casual presence and unconscious humility never changed. It was a breath of fresh air for Shaela, who had to deal with the King and Queen daily. Meeting with them felt far less stuffy with Aerene there to soften the strict atmosphere of formality.

After meeting with Aethor and Lorae, Shaela walked around the city perimeter. Aerene still sat with them, and royal guards stood at attention inside and outside the throne room; it was one of the only times Shaela could get away with being alone. *I hope the Ermoori learned their lesson,* she thought, *if they send more, we're going to war against them.*

Riffolk

1778

He'd been correct; a counter-attack had come in response to Riffolk's attempted stealing of the books of power. What Riffolk did not expect was the perpetrator of that attack; Kerberos, the King of Omatus himself. Riffolk respected—albeit begrudgingly—the fact the Kerberos didn't bother sending assassins or warriors to do his work for him.

His saferoom was destroyed. Prototypes, blueprints, and the book of Taranos were kept in there. All but the book was destroyed, leaving nothing but smoking debris. *Kerberos,* he thought, *has made himself a very powerful enemy.*

His priorities were set; the blueprints that had been destroyed needed to be replicated. *I need to work now,* he thought, *while I can, in case I've forgotten anything. And before I forget any more.* Snatching a pile of blank papers, Riffolk set to work. It was unlikely he'd forget his designs so easily, but Riffolk never left anything to chance.

As he worked, Riffolk recalled the details of Kerberos' attack. The man was precise, and intelligent. But he'd given Riffolk far more information than he should have. *He's not used to facing anyone as intelligent as he is,* Riffolk thought, *let alone someone even more intelligent.*

He knew two key things now; the first, and most important, was how to activate the magic within the books. The second was that Kerberos read the passages he needed to read from the two books in Riffolk's possession. *He is ahead of me,* Riffolk thought, *he possesses at least three forms of magic now.*

Riffolk stopped drawing briefly, glancing instead at the book of Shadow Magic. It lay on the bench where he worked, closed for now, but calling to him nonetheless. His work needed to be finished, and if he could he would rebuild his destroyed devices as well. After that, his saferoom needed repairing. Though he controlled all of Ermoor, much of his work could only be completed by himself. The other scientists weren't on his level; no one was. He had them do the work they could be entrusted with, and did the rest of it himself.

Kerberos flashed into his mind again. He represented complications that Riffolk wasn't certain he could overcome. The plan before now was to take all of Pandeia for himself. Kerberos had always stood out as a powerful threat to him, considering the man's reputation and history. But now, as well as commanding an army of Fire Magicians, the King of Omatus wielded several types of magic himself.

Omatus presented a problem for him; the city was built to withstand armies, and taking it would prove difficult even when Riffolk's army reached its full potential. He was a long way from that, but Riffolk still worried. *It will come down to the soldiers themselves,* he thought, *even Kerberos can't win against an entire army.* The soldiers, and their weapons and armour. Provided he could design and built the things he envisioned, his army would prove unstoppable even against magic.

Gaining the other forms of magic for himself was pivotal; Riffolk had already incorporated Power Magic into certain weapon designs, siphoning his own magic into technology that could retain it. If he could do the same with the others, there was no limit to the strength his army could possess.

For two days, Riffolk worked almost non-stop; not only recreating the destroyed blueprints, but writing up entirely new designs. Several of them would be useless until he gained the other types of magic, but the designs were impeccable. Different weapons to be used against different opponents. A weapon perfectly suited to each country, each race. Armour that would withstand every magic type. Riffolk saw it all laid out before him; an army so perfect that even the Gods could not stop him.

By the time he was done, even Kerberos would be unable to stand against him. He knew it was possible. It was just a matter of time. In Riffolk's experience, there was nothing he couldn't design and build. All he had to do was think it through.

His plans looked perfect to him. After the two days of work, Riffolk had even more designs than when he started; surprisingly, however, he found himself even more excited for the newer designs. All of them were weapons that focused on the magic he'd be gaining soon. He particularly enjoyed weapon design; something about the ability to take life filled him with a thrill that nothing else could replicate.

There was no real reason he couldn't read the Shadow book now; but once he began designing things, it became difficult to stop. Usually, Riffolk spent at least a week on new blueprints. Every now and then, however, he drew up plans which needed no alterations. They emerged from his mind, perfect and ready to build.

Repairs to the saferoom were next, and Riffolk did the best he could; but much of the damage was beyond even his capabilities. He salvaged what little he could, and sealed off the room. *Building another saferoom will be less effort than cleaning out and fixing everything in there,* Riffolk thought.

The prototypes were well and truly ruined. He'd have to build all of them again from scratch. Most of the factories in Ermoor were dedicated to either processing raw material or mass producing Riffolk's commercially available designs. His prototypes, on the other hand, were never produced in his factories. Especially the ones in his saferoom; they were more often than not confidential.

He took the pieces of his broken devices and set them aside. Though they were beyond saving, he could at least reverse engineer them by looking over their remains. Re-drawing his blueprints was a success, but some prototypes had been built without them. He kept space in his mind for all the technology he'd ever designed, but they were so complex and nuanced that many details could be lost if he wasn't careful.

After he was done with the saferoom, Riffolk launched straight into rebuilding destroyed technology. His lab contained everything he needed to build almost any kind of technology; storerooms attached to the building were full of all the material his factories produced, as well as everything mined from elsewhere in Pandeia. He kept spares of all his tools and appliances as well, and his underground lab contained just as much as the main one above it.

When he'd done as much as he could with the prototypes, Riffolk's focus returned to the books of the Gods, and his plans for the future. *I'll have those books sooner or later,* he thought, *and when I have them, I'll have Pandeia itself.* Kerberos, although he wanted to rule, lacked the ambition Riffolk possessed. If not for Riffolk, Kerberos might have been content with Omatus. But now that he knew

Riffolk's plans, his own could have changed.

He knows I won't be willing to share my rule, Riffolk thought, *and he knows I won't stop until all of Pandeia is mine. He's smart enough to know his only options are to take over Pandeia himself, or die fighting me*. Smiling, Riffolk thought about the challenges to come. An opponent like Kerberos was a rare thing, and Riffolk found himself looking forward to the fight.

Mattias

1778

Lord Commander Arthor Symond stood behind his desk, hands behind his back, staring at Mattias with cold intensity. Everyone knew about the Lord Commander losing his right hand fighting to save Overseer Riffolk Hayne; but he still kept it out of sight as much as he could. Rumours spread shortly after the incident of Overseer Hayne constructing a mechanical hand for the Lord Commander, but Mattias had never seen it.

"Mattias Sterling," Lord Commander Symond's deep voice wrenched Mattias from his thoughts, "I am honoured to present to you the medal of valour and bestow upon you the rank of Captain. For bravery and decisive action in the field, and for the success of your first mission as a stealth agent. Congratulations."

An officer next to the Lord Commander handed Mattias a decorative box with the medal inside. Though it would have been polite and proper, the Lord Commander made no move to shake his hand.

I'm a Captain? He thought, *what now? I don't know how to be a Captain.* He'd only survived the mission by running away, and grabbing the strange artefact had been a stroke of luck. The action of running towards that horrifying monster to grab the anomaly went against every instinct screaming in his mind. He still wasn't sure why he'd done it.

He was ushered out of the Lord Commander's office, and headed straight for the nearest tavern. No one told him what to do next, so he simply sat and drank. Ermoori ale was stronger than Omasi cider, though he usually preferred the taste of cider. Something in him craved a stronger drink, but he couldn't tell why exactly. A few days had passed since his return from the northern mountains of Shanaken; he hadn't slept a full night since.

Maybe the ale will help me sleep. He didn't believe it, but he hoped it was true. The low growls and cold black eyes of the monsters he'd faced were always lurking somewhere in his mind, returning whenever he closed his eyes. Every shadow in his quarters looked like a crouching predator in the dark of night, ready to pounce and rip his body to shreds. *So maybe I do know why I need a strong drink after all,* he thought.

As a Captain, he would be required to not only go into battle again, but lead others into the fight. *I'm not even sure I can look at Shanaken without passing out,* he thought, *how am I going to lead soldiers?* He never wanted to be a Captain. He never even wanted to be in the military; it was a family career, and he was never given any other option.

His promotion was effective immediately, but a new uniform wouldn't be made and delivered for another couple of days yet. *I have at least that long then, to still feel like a lowly soldier*.

"Another?" the barman asked.

Mattias nodded, swapping his empty glass for a new one brimming with cold ale. The tavern was in Dreadhold, right near the barracks, and its customers consisted entirely of military personnel. It wouldn't be long before most of the people inside would be required to salute him when he entered. *Not the kind of attention I enjoy,* he thought, *I'm already tired of being a captain, and I haven't even seen battle*. Sighing, Mattias drained the glass and nodded when the barman asked if he wanted more.

Riffolk

1778

Finally, Riffolk thought, *Shadow Magic is mine*. Waiting this long had been entirely unnecessary, but he liked to challenge his own self-discipline occasionally. Overcoming the obstacles he faced externally brought satisfaction, but beating the challenges he set for himself brought pride.

Now that he was finished with his other responsibilities, Riffolk stood in his secret lab with the book of Amalus open on his table. Energy emanated from the book, so strong it almost vibrated. He felt the same sense of apprehension he'd experienced when the book of Taranos first lay before him; only now he knew how to access the magic within.

If not for Kerberos, Riffolk would have been unwilling to attempt gaining more than one form of magic; it stood to reason that mortal beings had a natural limit to the magic their physical bodies could contain. But if Kerberos could do it, so could Riffolk. Besides, though he'd read much about magic since discovering its existence, he found nothing to convince him that people needed to confine themselves to one form.

The book of Amalus differed from the book of Taranos in one major way; Riffolk was able to touch it without any pain. When he first acquired the book of Taranos, Riffolk had to keep it in a fully enclosed glass tank to avoid the lightning that bound it. But other than a strange cold and the energy humming from it, the book of Amalus seemed harmless.

Riffolk read the entire book. The words didn't change anything inside him, and when he finished it, nothing had changed. He frowned, staring at the book. *Kerberos said reading it would bestow the reader with magic,* he thought, *I must be doing something wrong.*

He thought back to his encounter with Kerberos. Conjuring the scene vividly in his mind, Riffolk ran through the memory in every detail until he found the words Kerberos said.

"You have already read the prayers, yes?"

Riffolk's eyes flew open. *Not the entire book,* he thought, *just the prayers*. It explained why Kerberos hadn't attempted to steal the books; he only needed to read the prayers to recite later. *Perhaps he is more formidable than I gave him credit for,* Riffolk thought. He tried not to underestimate anyone, but it was rare for a person to possess more knowledge than himself.

Now he knew the prayer written near the beginning of the book was all he needed, the final piece fell into place. *Simply reading it is not enough,* he thought, *to gain its magic, the prayer must be read aloud.* Once it occurred to him, it seemed obvious. Prepared for another rush like the one he'd experienced when Taranos touched him, Riffolk read the prayer out loud.

The second he finished, a cold feeling of inexplicable darkness rushed over his body. He felt both light and heavy, trapped between two worlds that merged where he stood. His lungs emptied, his vision fading to nothing.

When the feeling passed, Riffolk's lab appeared again before his eyes. He still stood in front of the book, and though it felt to him as though hours had passed, he knew from the clock on his wall that he'd read the prayer only seconds ago. Strength and energy filled him. *No wonder the Shenza are such fierce opponents,* he thought, *fighting must be an easy task for a warrior who feels this way.*

He imagined how possessing all five forms of magic must feel. Riffolk had never been a warrior, but he was beginning to master offensive and defensive Power Magic. Sooner or later, as evidenced by Kerberos' bold attack on his lab, Riffolk knew he would have to fight. *One can't take control of a country without getting one's hands dirty,* he thought, *though the more magic I acquire, the easier those fights will be.*

Over the years, Riffolk had studied Shenza and their combat abilities. As well as capturing one for himself, he compiled reports from the military operations on the northern shore. He knew as much about them and their magic as it was possible for an outsider to know.

Focusing, Riffolk brought Shadow Magic to the surface of his palm. It pooled like liquid metal, black as midnight. He willed it to take shape, and it rushed to comply; a viciously sharp dagger materialised in his hand. Practicing with Power Magic had prepared him well; the control and focus it took to learn one form of magic was easily transferred to learning others. All it took to wield magic effectively was focus and imagination. Riffolk possessed an abundance of both.

The blade melted away, and Riffolk reformed it into a solid sphere. After that, he made it coat his hand and forearm as a thin, malleable metal armour. As a test, he took one of his cutting tools from a workbench. Its whining filled the room as he turned it on. Watching closely, prepared for pain, Riffolk touched the cutting edge to his hand. Sparks flew from the black liquid metal coating his skin; but there was no pain.

Satisfied, Riffolk moved on to his next test. Gripping a corner of the workbench loosely in his magic-covered hand, he squeezed. The thick metal bench caved under his hand as easily as if it had been fabric. He smiled. Power Magic was devastating as an attack; Shadow Magic was almost indestructible when used as a shield.

He had built armour using synthesized Shenza steel; though it was incredibly strong, it couldn't compare to the real thing. Now that he could conjure Shadow Magic himself, the armour he'd be able to create would be truly unstoppable. The only problem he foresaw was that mass producing armour using the magic within him would take a long time.

He knew from experience how draining magic was; but with Power Magic, Riffolk could draw energy from the electricity coursing through Ermoor itself. Shadow Magic couldn't be replaced anywhere near as easily.

Ideas raced through his mind; different ways to use less magic to achieve the same results. He had time; as much as he wanted to achieve his goals as soon as possible, his army grew stronger every day, and the longer he waited, the more weapons and armour he could create for his soldiers. *By the time I'm ready,* Riffolk thought, *I'll have the strongest army in history*. Smiling, he got back to work.

Mattias

1778

Weeks after his promotion, Mattias attended a training session with his men. It was the first real time he'd spent with his new team; the elite squad he worked with had all died in Shanaken. *That was a different thing,* he thought, *now I'm a leader. These men follow my orders*.

They ran through their movements as one perfect unit. *The training is even more intense than when I was being trained,* he thought, *why would these men follow me if I'm not even as well trained as they are?* He was going to have to train even harder than them.

Doubt gnawed at his nerves, growing as he watched the men train.

Lord Commander Arthor Symond believed that Mattias had what it took to be Captain of his own unit. Though he had yet to meet any of the Twelve Crowns, he'd been assured they felt the same. It was a strange feeling; the leaders of all of Ermoor showed more faith in him than he had in himself.

Overseer Burnham stood next to him, watching the soldiers train with a severe expression on his face. It was Burnham who recruited Mattias in the first place; *he had to have seen something worthwhile in me,* he tried to tell himself, *not just my luck in surviving the Shenza attack in the tunnels*. Mattias was still the only one who knew the truth about his cowardice. Everyone else still thought of him as a hero.

"How do you feel about your new unit?" Overseer Burnham said, "do they meet your expectations?"

Mattias tried to stifle a scoff; he had no expectations, other than for himself. Truth be told, the soldiers intimidated him. He was more worried that he wouldn't meet their expectations.

"They are impressive," he said instead, nodding in appreciation, "I'm sure they will fight well."

There would be a lot of training to come, he knew; Lord Commander Symond expected the best of his soldiers, and Mattias couldn't skate by on luck anymore. *I have to become what they already think I am,* he thought, *otherwise the world will discover I'm nothing but a coward*. Cowardice in Ermoor was akin to treason.

There was no choice but for Mattias to be a Captain.

"They will," Overseer Burnham said, "and with the new technology Overseer Hayne is developing, they will be unstoppable."

Mattias knew that they trained with an ultimate goal in mind; everybody did. But no one knew what the goal was. He wondered if Overseer Burnham knew. Riffolk Hayne must have known, and the Lord Commander too. Other than that, Mattias wouldn't assume anything. The Ermoori government kept more secrets than anyone could count; and the worst part was even stating that fact put one in danger. They tolerated no words against them, especially if those words were the truth.

Over millennia, Ermoor had sent countless soldiers to Shanaken as part of the exploratory forces. Missionaries, whose purpose was to civilize the Shenza and bring the One True God's love to them. This was different. The training was more intense, and the Overseers gave off a sense of cold focus that couldn't be ignored.

He wanted to believe things would continue as they always had; that the Ermoori soldiers would be deployed on the northern shore and fight to show the Shenza what real civilization looked like. But what scared him more than the Shenza, more than the nightmares that plagued him, was the fact that he had no idea what the future held.

Mattias stepped in next to one of his troops and joined the training exercise. He'd only managed a few movements before Overseer Burnham waved him away.

"Captain Sterling," he said, "let the troops train on their own.

Captains should not be training with their men… especially with drills."

Embarrassed, Mattias returned to his position next to Burnham. *At least none of my men mocked me for it,* he thought, *though that was hardly a good first impression.* Commanding a unit meant commanding the respect of the soldiers; if they thought of him as a joke, they'd never follow him into battle.

"You'll have your own training sessions," Burnham said quietly, "with other Captains. Your soldiers need to think of you as above them. If you train right next to them, doing the same drills, they'll believe they're equal to you."

Mattias nodded. He'd never been a Captain before, so he'd never needed to think that way; but it made sense.

"Don't worry, son," Overseer Burnham said, "you'll get the hang of it."

As he watched his new unit train, Mattias couldn't help but doubt Overseer Burnham. He knew the man meant well, but the bottom line was unavoidable; Mattias wasn't cut out to be a Captain. He barely handled being a soldier, back when all he had to do was follow orders.

The Overseers were another thing altogether. Instead of commanding units, they were in charge of entire sections of military and industry in Ermoor. They were intelligent, driven, and beyond question. It was the only reason Mattias endeavored to live up to the title he'd been given; the Overseers themselves believed he could do it, and Mattias could never have questioned their judgement. Not out loud, at any rate.

Mattias watched the training movements carefully. Many of them were moves he didn't know, though he was sure he could learn them. As the men completed each move, they gave a unified shout; it worked to intimidate Mattias, despite the knowledge that these men would do whatever he told them to.

Overseer Burnham stared at him expectantly, and Mattias cleared his throat. He'd forgotten that the man spoke, and was lost in his own thoughts. *He told me I'd get the hang of it,* Mattias reminded himself, *what do I say to that?*

"Yes," he said, "yes, I'm… I'm sure I will."

Riffolk

1783

Five years after he gained Shadow Magic, Riffolk decided it was time. Though the public never would have found out that there were no surviving members of the Twelve Crowns, the other Overseers and other high ranking government officials eventually could have discovered his secret.

The only option was to go public. He would become Ermoor's first solo ruler. The Twelve never showed their faces, or even appeared in front of the public; it meant he could make an announcement without needing to arrange false appearances from them. Riffolk had already gained control of all of the Twelve's resources and their communication channels. After his coming announcement, almost nothing would change but the public's perception. *That,* he thought, *and I won't have to hide behind letters and messengers.*

Before Riffolk took control, the Twelve was already controlling Ermoor's population through manipulation and propaganda. It was a system Riffolk greatly admired, and one he helped to make far more effective; his teleradio design ensured the Twelve's messages were heard on every street and in every home. Through the teleradio, he was able to tell all of Ermoor that a major announcement was to be made on the last day of the month.

He would have preferred to simply announce over the teleradio that he was Ermoor's new leader; but it wasn't an option. Such an unprecedented moment in history would have invited unwelcome questions if the appropriate ceremony wasn't observed. Despite their historic hatred of the spotlight, the Twelve had been nothing if not theatrical.

The Lord Commander was to lead the ceremony; as the Twelve's representative to the public, and the leader of their military, he possessed more authority than any other public figure. *At least as far as the citizens are concerned,* he thought, *not that it'll last much longer.* As soon as Riffolk became the sole ruler, Arthor would finally be seen as the right-hand man he was.

When the day arrived, Riffolk wore his traditional Overseer

jacket. He barely touched it except for his rare public appearances, and after this he would have a new one made to fit his station. He met Arthor at Rookfell Square. A massive crowd had already gathered, and Riffolk strolled up the stairs of the stage ahead of the Lord Commander, an easy smile on his face as he looked over the crowd.

Contrary to Riffolk, Arthor looked miserable as he stood near the back of the stage. His hands were grasped behind his back; ever since he lost his hand attacking Riffolk, he refused to show it unless he had to. The mechanical hand was a particular point of pride for Riffolk; it bothered him that Arthor hated it being seen by anyone other than himself.

"People of Ermoor," Arthor said into the teleradio amplifier, "you are gathered here today to witness history. The Twelve Crowns have recently made a monumental decision, and today they have allowed me to announce it publicly."

The crowd exploded in hushed murmurs; announcements such as this were rare.

"The decision of the Twelve Crowns is," Arthor continued, "that they will be stepping down as the rulers of Ermoor."

Stunned silence greeted Arthor's words. *If given a million years,* Riffolk thought with satisfaction, *none of them could have ever predicted this*.

"Taking their place," Arthor said, "will be Overseer Riffolk Hayne."

Arthor gestured to Riffolk; letting his smile brighten even

more, he stepped up to the podium to take Arthor's place.

"Thank you, Lord Commander," Riffolk said into the amplifier, "I have spoken with the Twelve, and they have bestowed upon me the new title of Prime Overseer."

Applause swept through the crowd; Riffolk had always been adored, and now they finally had a ruler they could name. *It's about time,* Riffolk thought, *having a public ruler benefits all of Ermoor, myself included.* He wouldn't need to cover his actions in a shroud of secrecy any longer. Everything he did was granted legitimacy by the mere fact of his title; his word was now law.

"Ermoor is entering a new age," Riffolk said, "an age of transparency and progress. No longer will your leaders pull the strings from the shadows. I will rule Ermoor out in the open."

Another bout of cheers spread through Rookfell Square. The people, if anything, adored him even more now. All things considered, he couldn't believe how easy it had been to get to where he was now. *It almost feels like Ermoor was always mine,* he thought, *and everything that's happened is merely a formality.*

The people kept cheering, and Riffolk raised his arms to them. *Ermoor was easy,* he thought, staring out at the faces of the people, *and the next step is Pandeia. May the Gods help anyone who stands in my way.*

As Riffolk basked in the glow of the cheers and applause, the crowd began chanting:

"For the good of all!"

Eliza

1793

He's dead. Mathys is gone.* The words didn't sound real in Eliza's head, as though they could only be formed in the midst of a nightmare. No matter how scared she'd been, before that day, Mathys had always been her hero. An unstoppable, invincible source of protection and love. Kerberos scared her perhaps more than any other person in Pandeia, but even after meeting him she'd felt safe with Mathys around.

It's up to me now, she said, *to protect my mother*. Even with her mind reeling, her mother's safety was one of her first thoughts.

The Circle's headquarters were in ruins, the building riddled with smoke and giant holes. Everything looked broken. The Circle itself was broken. Without Mathys, Eliza had no idea what to do.

Her mother took the news even harder than she did. After the first few hours, her screams and wails died down into complete silence. After that, she settled into a trance-like state, barely even blinking. Eliza felt the same way, but she had to be strong. *I'm all she has now. At least Mathys trained me,* she thought, *before he... Before this happened.*

Her power had grown more than she thought it would. With Mathys' help, she learned to control it and focus it. Her mother still couldn't quite control her own power, though she had trained almost as much as Eliza. But as powerful as Eliza had become, now that Mathys was gone she felt completely helpless.

They stayed in the meditation room at the back of the headquarters; Zeera refused to let them out in case they saw Mathys' body. Eliza tried not to think about what that meant. It wasn't just Mathys, either. Kerberos' attack left dozens dead, if not more.

Eliza couldn't believe the attack. In what felt like seconds, what was supposed to be the ultimate safe place had become a mass grave. Destroyed, or at least broken almost beyond repair, the Circle was now nowhere near strong enough to fulfil their mission.

A lot of the rooms where they slept were more or less intact. Another room was set aside for Lashek, who'd been badly wounded during the fight. The Tarsi were skilled healers, and they got to work almost immediately after Kerberos fled. There were more wounded, but the Circle had to prioritise Lashek. Mathys, irreplaceable though he was, technically wasn't one of the Heroes of the Circle. Even if he'd survived, Lashek would have been cared for first. It made sense to Eliza, but she still didn't like it.

What scared her most, though, was how truly dangerous Kerberos really was. *Mathys may not have had magic,* she thought, *but he was stronger and better than most of the Circle*. If Kerberos could kill Mathys along with dozens of Circle agents in minutes, the rest of the Circle didn't stand much of a chance. Lashek was one of their Heroes, and it was pure luck that he was alive at all.

"Eliza, Mara," Zeera said as she entered the meditation room, "the corridor is clear now. We have tidied your quarters, though they were mostly untouched by the battle."

Eliza helped her mother stand, walking with her gently to make sure she didn't fall. *She's barely even moving on her own.* She'd never walked so slow in her life, but finally they reached the room that her and her mother shared. Her mother dropped to her bed, and sat still again. Eliza sat on her own bed, rubbing her hands over her face. *What do we do now?* She thought, her mind and heart racing as fast as each other.

The next day felt no different to the day before. Zeera was a great leader; she managed to keep everyone from falling apart. It couldn't have been easy. While they waited for Lashek to heal, Eliza tried to focus on being there for her mother. *That's not easy either*, she thought, *she hasn't said a word since, and it doesn't look like she'll speak or move any time soon.*

"Mother," she said, keeping her voice as gentle as she could, "should we join the others for the morning meal?"

There was no answer, but Eliza pulled her to her feet anyway. She still moved slowly, so Eliza moved slowly as well. One of the meeting rooms was set up as a dining room; a table large enough to seat all of the Heroes and their companions lay in the room's centre.

When Eliza entered with her mother, the others greeted her with slight nods and grim smiles. Despite Zeera's best efforts, morale was at rock bottom. The food they ate was similar to what Eliza grew up eating; she'd grown up in Tarsium, after all. It was far more flavourful than what Mathys and her mother had cooked, however. *The Tarsi really know food,* she thought. Her mother had cooked her a few Ermoori meals over the years, and Eliza didn't enjoy a single one of them.

"Mother," she said, "eat something, please."

They sat in silence, Eliza trying to feed her mother as the others stared at their plates. Zeera must have already eaten; there was no plate or food in front of her. She simply sat with them, waiting with endless patience for the group to finish.

Her mother ended up having two small mouthfuls of food before Eliza gave up and finished her own meal. *As long as she's eaten something,* Eliza thought, *I'll feel okay.* The others finished shortly after she did, and all eyes naturally settled on Zeera.

"We do have a plan," Zeera finally said, "but we need to wait for Lashek to finish healing."

"What are we doing after he's better?" Eliza asked.

"We need to continue our mission to destroy Sithares. We can only do that in Aethos, where Sithares was originally captured."

"Can we even still do this? What about Kerberos?"

"I don't believe he will return," Zeera said, "he has what he wanted. I have dispatched several agents to try to take back the book of Asheilos from him. By the time we take it back, we will hopefully be in Aethos and Kerberos will not be able to find us until Sithares is destroyed."

Knowing Kerberos was out there terrified her more than anything. Under the fear was a boiling rage that threatened to consume her. As scared of him as she was, a big part of her wanted to hunt him down for what he did to Mathys. She wanted to hurt him almost as badly as she wanted to hurt the man in her nightmares, the blue-eyed monster who she knew was her father.

Arthor

1793

Lord Commander Arthor Symond stood in his office, using the silence to control his breathing. Riffolk had just asked him a question, but Arthor also wrestled against the voice in his head. It had plagued him for decades now, and though it wasn't as consistent as it once had been, Arthor still struggled with quieting it from his mind.

Overlooking the city and the ocean beyond it, the large window he stood in front of let in the faltering evening sun. Riffolk was behind him, awaiting his response. Arthor faced Hayne once again, hands clasped behind his back.

"I'm sorry, Overseer Hayne," he said, "it's a foolish plan."

"We have been working towards this for a very long time, Lord Commander. The plan will work."

"Sending all of our forces overseas? All of them? We'll be completely defenceless."

"While they will be entirely on the defensive. No one will have the time, the resources, nor the inclination to invade Ermoor. The war we bring to them will keep them far too busy."

"I'm urging you, Prime Overseer. Even just a single squadron."

"And I'm telling you, it's not necessary. A small administrative crew will remain to manage standard day-to-day functioning. As it's so important to you, Lord Commander, I'm ordering you to stay behind to oversee that they adequately protect our great city."

He should have seen it coming; disagreeing with Riffolk Hayne was a dangerous idea at the best of times. *I'm just lucky he hasn't had me killed yet,* Arthor thought, *though I'm usually careful to agree with him*. Arthor was now in a precarious position. Riffolk was giving him a warning, but at the same time providing him with the opportunity to gracefully bow out of their impasse.

"As you wish, Overseer Hayne."

A small smile twisted Riffolk's lips. His eyes didn't change; they pierced Arthor's own, unwavering and cold. In that moment, Arthor felt as though he was face to face with a powerful, wild predator. Like at any moment, he could be struck by an unseen claw, and die before he even realised he'd been hit.

Behind his back, his right wrist itched. Riffolk destroyed his hand years before, and had replaced it with a prototype artificial hand of his own design. Over the years, Riffolk provided him with upgraded versions. Though he was grateful, it felt to him like just another thing that put him under Riffolk's thumb. He flexed the mechanical hand, feeling it move with the left.

He still woke in a sweat most days, flashes of yellow lightning in his mind's eye. Riffolk had always made him uncomfortable, but after his experience discovering the Overseer's takeover of the Twelve, Ermoor's prized scientist terrified him. The population still had no clue of Riffolk's deeper machinations. To them, The Twelve had appointed him Prime Overseer of their own volition. As far as the rest of Ermoor was concerned, after that they had simply stepped down.

"How is your hand going, Lord Commander?"

He flexed it once again.

"Perfectly, of course. I've been adjusting the pistons as you showed me."

"I'm glad to hear that," Riffolk said, "I've been working on another upgrade."

There were rare moments when Riffolk almost resembled a human being. He ruled over all of Ermoor, and yet still found time to dedicate to Arthor's artificial hand. If he didn't know Riffolk better, he might have confused the effort for compassion. But he did know Riffolk; upgrading the hand was simply an intellectual challenge.

He might have even mangled my hand on purpose, Arthor thought, *just for a new project.*

"Thank you, Prime Overseer," he said.

A nervous-sounding knock echoed from his office door, and Arthor called for whoever it was to enter. Commander Eli Barton slipped into the room, casting a furtive glance towards Riffolk before addressing Arthor.

"Lord Commander," he said, "the soldiers are gathered in Rookfell Square. They're ready for you."

"Thank you, Commander Barton," Arthor said, "Prime Overseer, is there anything else you'd like to discuss before you depart?"

"Forgive me, sir," Eli said, "it sounds as though you're not coming with us?"

Arthor gave a pointed look at Riffolk. He knew the Prime Overseer would have foreseen the problem, but he wanted to make his point just the same. Arthor commanded respect and devotion from every man in Ermoor's military; without him, morale would likely suffer. Riffolk was a genius, but Arthor had decades of experience in battle.

“I have ordered the Lord Commander stay in Ermoor,” Riffolk said, his voice quiet, certain, and daring Eli to respond.

“I… I see,” Commander Barton said.

“You don’t agree with my order, Commander?”

Eli shot a look at Arthor, eyes wide. Arthor gave the barest of warnings; a slight shake of his head. The Commander looked back at Riffolk, head bowed.

“Apologies, Prime Overseer. I’m merely concerned about our men fighting without their Lord Commander.”

“They will be fighting for Ermoor, Commander. Besides, I will be there. They will be fighting with their Prime Overseer.”

Arthor watched Eli’s reaction carefully; genuine shock, and intimidation. It was as he’d feared, and perhaps something Riffolk hadn’t considered. *Riffolk coming along will be a surprise to the men,* he thought, *and they’ll be too scared of him to focus on the fight.*

“Of course, Prime Overseer.”

Riffolk’s face hardened, his eyes glistening with danger as he watched Eli. *He noticed the reaction as much as I did.*

“Leave us, Commander,” he said, “the Lord Commander and I have one last thing to discuss before we address the soldiers.”

“Yes, Prime Overseer.”

Commander Barton left as quickly as he could, almost running by the time he reached the door. Riffolk turned his deadly stare on Arthor, no trace of a smile on his face now.

"It seems the soldiers are more attached to you than I would have thought," he said, "I hope their discipline outweighs that attachment."

"They are the most disciplined soldiers in all of Pandeia, Prime Overseer," Arthor said, "you have my word on that."

"I do hope you're right. It would reflect very badly on you if they failed in their mission without you to hold their hand."

I'm not the one who volunteered to stay behind, he thought, *if they fail it'll be because of you.*

"As you say, Prime Overseer," he said instead.

"Now," Riffolk said, his subtle smile returned, "time to address our army. After you, Lord Commander."

Karak

1793

It was his one chance at redeeming himself in the Circle's eyes; bring the book of Sithares to Zeera. He'd failed. Thearans got their hands on it, and disappeared into the deserts of Omas. *It'll be almost impossible to find it now,* he thought. All the work he'd done infiltrating Omatus ultimately meant nothing. To Karak, the worst part was that it had been stolen by a random group of Thearans on the road between Omatus and the trading settlement of Tarsius. If it had been taken from him by Kerberos himself, or by some other powerful force, he could have lived with knowing it wasn't his fault. But a small group of Thearans? It was unforgivable.

His last conversation with Zeera, where he'd told her of his failure, still left a sour taste in his mouth. *No matter how hard I try,* he thought, *it seems I'm doomed to disappoint her*. At least his suggestion of summoning the Austris Arans had been met with enthusiasm; she'd smiled, and Karak saw plans forming in her mind.

Eventually, he knew, Zeera would have attempted to summon them anyway. They were a part of the Circle, after all. But bringing them to help search for the book meant their chances of finding it were significant.

Losing the book of Sithares wasn't the only tragedy that had struck the Circle; while Karak was away, Kerberos attacked the Circle headquarters. He'd caused irreparable damage to the building, grievously injured Lashek, and killed dozens of Circle agents. Not only that; he stole the book of Asheilos.

Karak was the one who sent him to Azar in the first place. It had been an attempt to help the Circle, and get himself back in Zeera's good graces. Instead, he was responsible for every setback the Circle had suffered through. *I'll never live this down,* he thought, *Zeera will never forgive me*. All he wanted was to be a part of the Circle again, to make up for all that he'd done.

Though a large chunk of the headquarters were damaged, Karak's quarters were fine. He sat, alone, thinking about all the ways he'd failed the Circle. His conversation with Zeera ended on a fairly positive note, but she'd still left the inn with a decidedly cold aura.

They'd walked back to the headquarters together in silence, Zeera pushing the pace until Karak could barely keep up.

When they arrived, Zeera disappeared. With no orders to follow and the headquarters in chaos, Karak had gone straight to his quarters. To get there, he needed to walk down the partially destroyed hallway where Kerberos staged his battle. *I was lucky to survive an attack from him,* he thought, remembering Kerberos almost killing him in Omatus, *he must have been holding back.* The damage done to the hallway made Karak's brief encounter with Kerberos look like child's play.

He never wanted to be anywhere near Kerberos again; but he knew the Circle would have to face the King of Omatus. As much as it terrified him, Karak knew he'd have to join that fight when it happened. Anything less would be viewed with derision by Zeera and the rest of the Circle.

"He's going to kill us all," Karak said into the silence, "and it's all because of me."

"You've always been a little overdramatic," a voice said from the doorway.

Karak gasped and shot a glance at the door; his cousin, Tolor, smiled at him. He walked in, stopping a few feet from Karak as he kept talking.

"It's good to see you, Karak. Been a while."

He nodded, smiling despite himself.

"It has. I wasn't sure I'd ever see you again."

"Same to you. Zeera certainly doesn't speak highly of you these last few years."

"And what would she say of you, Tolor?"

It was meant as a joke, but a heavy silence pushed between them nonetheless. Tolor stared at him, cold and calculating, the way Karak's father used to. As though his every action were being judged, as though his very soul was on display for approval.

"What happened, Karak?" he finally said, "to drive you so far from the path you could have followed?"

"I... don't know."

Karak sighed, trying to backtrack the journey he'd taken since last seeing his cousin. *How long has it been,* he thought to himself, *decades?* He could barely even remember living in Tarsium; it had been too long. The list of his mistakes was even longer. After such a long time trying not to think about them, Karak couldn't remember how his failures had started.

"You were such a promising agent, back in the day," Tolor said, "maybe even the best of us. Not very powerful, but resourceful and quick-thinking."

"That almost sounded like a compliment, Tolor. If you're not careful, I might begin to think you actually like me."

Tolor laughed. *Finally,* Karak thought, *a smile*. His cousin had always been a very serious man; it was no wonder he got along with Zeera. Tolor and Karak were about the same age, and growing up, they were constantly told Tolor resembled Karak's father more than

Karak did. When they were younger, the two cousins got along very well; as they grew up, however, Karak began resenting Tolor for taking his father's attention and pride.

"I do like you, Karak," Tolor said, "I just don't understand how it all went wrong. One day you were an agent, and the next... you disappeared."

“I’m really trying to focus on how to fix everything,” Karak said, “rather than the mistakes I made.”

Tolor nodded, though an unmistakable spark of superiority danced in his eyes. Anger fluttered in Karak’s chest, and the years dropped away; he felt like he was younger again, back when Tolor and he were going on missions for the Circle. His cousin always made him feel second best.

“Well,” he said, “what *will* you do, to fix everything?”

“I don’t know,” Karak said, “whatever Zeera asks of me, I suppose.”

“A good start,” Tolor said, his tone dripping with condescension, “and she wants to see you for just that reason.”

Karak’s eyes narrowed as he stared at Tolor. *Why is he so close to Zeera now?* Tolor hadn’t gone up in rank over the years, nor had he any reason to know Zeera’s thoughts or desires. *They couldn’t possibly be lovers,* he thought, *could they?* Zeera was widowed; everyone in the Circle knew about it, and since her husband died, she’d never shown any interest in pursuing another relationship. *Something else then. Are they simply close friends?* But with Zeera, nothing was ever simple. Karak couldn't help but think she was simply using Tolor to manipulate Karak; or to make him suffer for his mistakes.

"We best not keep her waiting, then," Karak said.

Mara

1793

The world felt cold and distant. Mathys had been her safety net, the one person she ever learned to trust. He'd been her Hero. His death didn't seem real. Every day, she awoke thinking she would see him again. And every day, her heart broke all over again. *It has to be a nightmare*. She spent every waking moment praying silently, ignoring the cruel world around her as she prayed; *let him come back. Give him back to me, please. I need him*.

She knew Eliza needed her. She was a mother, and her daughter's needs should have come first. But Mara simply couldn't function without Mathys. She'd been through so much, and Mathys was the only person who showed her any humanity, any kindness. He trained her, and made her strong. He understood her, gave her space and time. No one else in her life had ever been on her side; not her parents, her husband, or any of her friends. Even the magic she gained had betrayed her; she'd killed her uncle, and would destroy anything she came near if she used it without complete control.

Eliza was growing into a strong and capable woman, seemingly without Mara's help. When she was young, Mathys and Mara both trained her, and now that she was an adult in her own right, she learned and grew faster than Mara could have imagined. It should have been comforting; but knowing they were swept up in the fate of the entire world meant that Eliza's strength and bravery left Mara in constant terror.

She will fight anyone the Circle tells her to, Mara thought, *maybe even... Him.* She wasn't sure if they would ever meet again, but Mara desperately hoped not. Riffolk was a monster. She knew something dark and unstoppable lurked in his heart; assuming he even had a heart. There was still no knowing if he was aware of Eliza; but if he knew, she was in more danger than anyone else.

Mathys could have protected us from him, she thought, *but I can't.* When Eliza was little, Mara trained to the point of being a formidable fighter. But that had been a long time ago. Training back then felt good, but now even the idea of training made her hands shake. Especially since the only person she trusted to train her was gone.

Memories of her life in Saford plagued her; she saw Mathys teaching Eliza, and quiet nights by the fireplace. Saford remained the highlight of her life; though she still woke in a sweat most days, it was the only place she'd ever felt safe.

Since Mathys' death, each member of the Circle tried speaking with her. They tried including her in meals, and meetings, but she couldn't bring herself to focus on anything. All their efforts only served to make her feel guilty. She just wanted to not feel the way she felt. *I can't think straight anymore. It's all just... blurry.*

Eliza's patience knew no bounds. She spent time with Mara every day, even when they simply sat in silence. When Mara woke screaming from a nightmare, Eliza rushed to her side to comfort her. Nightmares plagued Mara every night, usually more than once. Lightning buzzed and crackled in her mind, and Riffolk's horrible face filled her vision.

Some nights, her nightmares had nothing to do with Riffolk. Sometimes, it was simply Power Magic itself. Or the monstrous form of Taranos lying dormant in its glass prison in Riffolk's lab. Occasionally, it was nothing but black, cold fear.

Zeera was supportive, but Mara saw past her polite smiles and kind words; she knew Zeera would run out of patience sooner or later. All Mara wanted was to be left alone, to not have the weight of the world in her hands. The Circle expected so much of her, and she couldn't have fulfilled their wishes even if she wanted to. Magic had felt incredible when she first used it; now, using magic was a source of nightmares and terror for her.

Even during the day, Mara experienced sudden waves of fear for no discernible reason. Most of the time it happened, there weren't other people around. Nothing specific occurred to cause panic, yet her body still lit up with sheer horror. If she saw Riffolk again, Mara was certain that she would simply die of fear.

She tried as hard as she could to think about anything other than the fear. It never worked; somehow, her heart kept returning to the same cold, black feeling. *When will this end?* she thought, *why can't I stop feeling this way?* No answer ever came to her.

Zeera

1793

Rubble still filled the hallway. The bodies of those who had been slain by Sithares' Hero were no longer strewn all over the floor, but she still saw them in her mind's eye. Zeera knew the wreckage would be cleaned soon enough, but for now, the building remained a shrine to Kerberos' destruction.

Their priority had been the wounded who'd survived. Lashek and many others were now recovering; but so many more were dead. Her mind reeled at the journey before them; even before Kerberos' attack, the odds had been against them. Now, it seemed all but impossible to defeat Sithares. With Lashek wounded, Mathys dead, and the book of Asheilos stolen, Zeera couldn't think of a way ahead.

The Circle must be kept whole, she thought, *everything else will follow*. Though he wasn't technically a full member, Mathys had been the source of inspiration and bravery for both Mara and Eliza. Without him, they needed someone to guide them on. Even aside from Mathys, Kerberos' attack was a huge blow to the Circle's morale. He was, in a very real way, the physical embodiment of Sithares. *If we couldn't stop him, what chance do we have against the actual God of Fire?*

Eliza and Mara withdrew after the attack, both physically and mentally. Zeera would try her best, but other than supporting them, the only thing that they needed was time.

"But we are running out of time," she said to herself.

Karak's failure scratched against her nerves also. *If our situation wasn't bad enough,* she thought, *the book of Sithares is out of our hands*. Their entire mission relied on having that book in their possession. If Karak hadn't let the book go, they still could have defeated Sithares despite Kerberos' attack.

She'd spoken to Lashek and Karak, as well as Mara and Eliza. Spirits were low in every member of the Circle. As the leader, it was her role to keep them together. To keep them focused on their mission. But at the moment, even Zeera found it difficult focusing on what they had to do. The conversation she had with Karak at least gave her some hope; as uncertain as the outcome was, attempting to summon the guardians of Austris Ara was at least something she could cling to.

The guardians hadn't been seen since the Circle defeated Sithares the first time. Shortly after Sithares was locked up in its magical prison, the city of Austris Ara had been built, and once it was done the Austris Arans floated away into the sky. For any other country, the Austris Arans would have faded into myth within a generation or two; but Tarsium had a long memory, and an even longer recorded history.

Why did Karak think of that before me? She thought, *I should have remembered them.* The summoning spell was recorded, along with the spells and equipment needed to vanquish Sithares, in the Circle Headquarters. Zeera knew where it was, though she never bothered reading it while researching how to destroy Sithares. It made sense to summon them; assuming they still existed.

No matter what else happened, they would have to go to Aethos. There was magic there. But more than that, Aethos contained the necessary infrastructure they would need to destroy Sithares once and for all. The last time the Circle captured Sithares, it was in Omatus. But Kerberos was king there, and the magical prison had clearly been compromised once already. As the ancient home of the Austris Arans, Aethos was the perfect place to defeat Sithares again.

Lashek had to heal enough before they travelled, but other than that, Zeera wanted to leave as soon as possible. It was something to focus on, something to keep the Circle moving. *I have to give them hope.*

She visited Lashek in the room her agents set up for him. He looked horrible, but much better than the day of the attack. Tarsi healing was the best in all of Pandeia.

"Lashek," she said, "how are you feeling?"

"Oh, I'm doing just fine," he said, "never felt better."

Despite the situation, Zeera smiled. Lashek's constant joking was beginning to grow on her.

"Are you up for travelling?"

He sighed. The spark of humour in his eyes dimmed slightly, and he looked at Zeera with exhaustion.

"Not unless there's no other option."

Zeera nodded, smiling gently and trying to be a soothing presence for him.

"I understand. We will need to travel as soon as we can, but we can wait until you have healed more."

“How are the others going?” Lashek asked.

“Morale is low. Mathys’ death will be difficult to move past. Not to mention the other setbacks.”

“So, everything is going perfectly, then?”

“Lashek.”

He shrugged, then grimaced in pain. As much as she was beginning to warm to his humour, he seemed unable to control it. *Even when he's clearly in pain*. She’d never met anyone who used humour the way Lashek did.

“We need to work together, Lashek,” she said, “the Circle is at its most vulnerable. Part of that is getting out of Azar, and part of it is focusing on our mission."

"So, all the pressure is on me to heal quickly, then?" he said.

"That is not what I said."

He laughed, but it quickly turned into a groan of pain.

"You're far too serious, Zeera."

"The situation we are in is serious," Zeera said, "this is no time for jokes."

"Alright," he said with a sigh, "I get it. I'll rest and heal as much as I can, and then we'll leave."

The conversation left her frustrated. Lashek was a pleasant enough man, and she enjoyed his humour most of the time; but they were in the middle of a disaster. When he made jokes so soon after such a tragedy, he came across as uncaring and dismissive. *I thought he was supposed to be a Hero,* she thought, *I know he is a good person, but he hides it a little too well sometimes.*

Zeera returned to her quarters, her thoughts rushing as she tried to figure out a way to fix their situation. In that moment, she felt utterly alone. The other Heroes were wounded and grieving, all of her agents were busy trying to clean up after Kerberos' attack, and every decision lay solely with her.

Yet again, Zeera found herself feeling as though she wasn't ready for leadership. Leading a team was one thing, but leading the Heroes tasked with saving the world… It became even more difficult when those Heroes didn't even want their roles to begin with. Mara was unable to even talk without panicking. Lashek couldn't be in a room without mocking everyone in it. Eliza had potential, but wasn't a Hero. There was no one else.

Why were they chosen, she thought, *if they don't even want to be here?* The Circle was falling apart, and it felt to Zeera as though there was nothing she could do to stop it.

Riffolk

1793

Riffolk stood on the stage at Rookfell Square once again. He'd been Prime Overseer for ten years now; ten years of upgrades to his weapon and armour designs, ten years of intense training. His army was ready.

Arthor was in front of him, at the podium. For years, the Ermoori people had been fed constant propaganda about the people outside the city. It worked to convince them the attacks on the northern shore were not only necessary, but to be celebrated. In the last ten years, Riffolk pushed the teleradio campaigns even further; more fear, more religion. Now that the time had come, Ermoor's citizens were excited to see his army off.

He gazed at the soldiers, taking in their glistening jet-black armour. They stood in perfect formation; their weapons held ready, backs straight and eyes trained on Arthor. Riffolk was particularly proud of the rifles; the technology allowed for two different ammunition types to be loaded. Two barrels, each with their own magazine. He developed bullets with Power Magic imbued in them, and Shadow Magic bullets as well. A switch on the barrel allowed for an instant change between ammo types.

On top of that, there were attachments that added functionality to his rifles as well. Net launchers, explosive launchers, and more. He'd built the rifles to be modular, and once he started designing attachments he kept coming up with more ideas.

Almost as impressive was the armour itself. His first iterations, worn by the elite teams tasked with stealing the books fifteen years ago, were strong. But back then, he didn't have real Shadow Magic at his disposal. It had taken a long time to perfect, but the armour was now well and truly indestructible.

Even better, at least as far as Riffolk was concerned, were the vehicles he'd designed. Warships lined the docks at Onyxport, each able to carry thousands of troops and travel at unprecedented speeds. Within the warships, ready for deployment, were tanks. A brand-new type of vehicle, tanks were like armoured and heavily armed carriages. They moved slowly, but what they lacked in speed they made up for with sheer firepower and indestructible armour.

Ermoor had been attempting to take Shanaken for thousands of years. Looking at his army, Riffolk knew, with a strange certainty, that this time would be successful. *Shanaken will fall,* he thought, *finally, it will fall to Ermoor*. Once they took Shanaken, the fall of Pandeia would follow shortly after.

He still thought about the other books of magic; they were hidden throughout Pandeia, some in places he knew, and all unreachable. He'd sent more teams to retrieve the books for a while, but eventually he developed a new plan; focus on his army and their weapons, and take the books as he swept through Pandeia during the war.

Arthor was to remain in Ermoor; he'd argued passionately, but Riffolk simply didn't have faith in his loyalty any longer. Over the years, the Lord Commander had begun to display signs of resentment. His erratic behaviour continued, though he was quieter than he used to be. For all the resentment he clearly felt, however, Arthor still followed orders; Riffolk held the man in the palm of his hand.

Though the Lord Commander was staying behind, Riffolk decided he wanted to be a part of the invasion. Partly to show his soldiers and his enemies what he was capable of, and partly for the satisfaction of taking Pandeia himself. But mostly, he wanted to be there when his soldiers found Mara. *She's mine,* he thought, *no matter where she is, I will find her*.

The woman had been in his mind since they were both touched

by Taranos. Her specific thoughts couldn't be read, but her emotions and her general presence never left his head. It was a constant reminder of her rebellion against him; not only had she attacked and escaped, she lived free with no consequences afterwards.

Shaking his head and returning to the present, Riffolk looked out once again at his army. Around the edges of Rookfell Square, the public stared at Riffolk and his soldiers. Even to the people they served, the soldiers of Ermoor were intimidating.

It's time, he thought, *for the rest of Pandeia to see what Ermoor can do*. Up until now, the other countries didn't need to worry about Ermoor; they'd only ever attacked Shanaken. Tarsium and Omas so far, instead of fearing them, had benefited from Ermoor's exported technology. But that was about to change.

"Give the order, Lord Commander," he said.

Arthor leaned in to the amplifier. Riffolk watched the soldiers remain perfectly still as Arthor spoke.

"Soldiers," Arthor said, "to Onyxport. Board the warships, prepare for battle. For the good of all!"

Mara

1793

Since seeing the destruction that Kerberos caused, Mara only grew more fearful of magic. The entire Circle had been thrown into chaos by one man and his power. When she was younger, her own magic was barely in her control, and that ended in death and tragedy. Even now, it took constant focus to keep her magic at bay. It flowed through her body, just beneath the surface.

What scared her even more than her own power was Eliza's. Mara's connection with Riffolk wasn't the only connection she felt; Eliza's presence lay within her mind just the same. As well as knowing what Eliza felt at any given moment, Mara also felt the power that her daughter held within her. Though Mara knew her magic was formidable, the thing that terrified her more than anything else was the fact that Eliza's magic made Mara's look like nothing.

Mara had been chosen as Hero. That fact sat with her, heavy in her mind, every day. Her thoughts clashed constantly; a part of her thought Eliza should have been Hero, and a part of her reeled at the notion that her daughter could take on so much responsibility and danger.

She knew that Eliza trained every day. That on its own was scary enough; but on top of training, Eliza wanted to be as active in the Circle as possible. It meant if she ever had the opportunity to take over Mara's role as Hero, she knew she would take it. If that happened, Mara would be safe; but Eliza would become a target, facing more danger and magic than Mara could even imagine.

After another training session, Eliza came to check on Mara once again. As usual, Mara sat on a chair, alone, in her quarters. Eliza sat on the bed, then gave Mara a kind smile. Her face, with its sweet smile, broke her heart.

"Please," she said, "can you… Can you stop using magic?"

Eliza's smile disappeared.

"What?"

"It's so dangerous," Mara continued, "I don't know how you're controlling it, but the risk is too high that you'll lose control."

"That's exactly what the training is for," Eliza said, "I get better at controlling it every day. I've been telling you for a long time now, you should be training too."

Mara shook her head, the familiar cold fear rising once again.

"I can't. Please, Eliza. For me, please just stop. I'm… I'm so scared."

"I know," Eliza said, "I'm scared too. But running away and shutting yourself in your room won't help anyone. Training makes me feel like I'm strong enough to handle things."

She won't stop until she dies for the Circle, Mara thought, *nothing I say will change her mind.* Panic exploded inside her chest. Eliza hadn't even given a second's consideration to her plea. She wanted to train, wanted to fight, and wanted to be a part of the Circle.

There was a part of her, something deep and indescribable, that knew something bad would come from the Circle. She couldn't shake the feeling that she was going to die. Or even worse, that Eliza would die. It felt so strong to her, so certain. She wished she could convince Eliza; that she could share the horrible certainty that lay within her.

"Eliza…" she said, unsure of how to state the rushing chaos of thoughts in her mind, "I can't explain it, but… I think if we go ahead with this, one of us will die."

"We're saving the world, mother," Eliza said, "I don't want to die, and I don't want you to die, but if it means we save all of Pandeia, isn't that a worthy sacrifice?"

"You don't understand," Mara said, "I don't know how, but I *know* something bad is going to happen. I know it."

"We can't know the future, mother. Zeera doesn't know what will happen. Not even Aerene and Shaela know what the future will bring."

She's not listening, Mara thought, *why is she not paying attention to my warning?* Her role as mother was to protect Eliza, but how could she do that if Eliza never listened to her? If she died, Mara would never be able to forgive herself. She had to convince Eliza now.

"You need to trust me, Eliza," she said, "please. Please, it will save your life. Please, stop training with magic. Let the Circle handle this situation themselves. They don't need you."

"They might not need me," Eliza said, "but you do. I'm training so that I can help you, mother. You're the one who can't handle the situation. If I left it to you, it's far more likely that you'll die, but if I'm there to help you, we'll survive together."

Mara's mind screamed at her, clawed at the edges of her thoughts. She felt hopeless, as though nothing she did mattered. Her daughter was a woman now; a woman who didn't need her. She was the weakest member of the Circle, and she couldn't even deal with her own thoughts, let alone the expectations of Zeera and the others.

Eliza was right; Mara couldn't help anyone, or handle anything. She needed to rely on Eliza and the Circle. Mara desperately wished it wasn't the case; but she knew as well as anyone what her limits were. She hated the way she was. What made her grateful, despite her sheer terror, was Eliza's strength. *All I can do,* she thought, *is hope and pray that Eliza will be fine*.

Karak

1793

Karak," Zeera said, "has Tolor informed you why you're here?"

They stood in one of the meeting rooms of the headquarters. The smell of smoke still tainted the air, and Karak tried to ignore it as Zeera watched him intently. Tolor, true to form, had told him nothing as they walked to the meeting room together.

"No," he said, "no, he did not."

Zeera shot a quick glance at Tolor, and a sharp jolt of petty victory flashed through Karak's chest. *You were supposed to tell me,* he thought, *but you couldn't help yourself.*

"I see," Zeera said, "no matter. I would have briefed you anyway."

Returning Karak's look with a withering stare of his own, Tolor smiled. *You thought I was in trouble,* his eyes seemed to say, *well, you're wrong as usual.*

"You and a small team of agents are to travel into the Omasi desert," Zeera continued, "as soon as possible. You will search for their Queen, take the book, and bring it back to me."

Karak kept his breathing even, refusing to so much as glance at Tolor. The mission was almost impossible; but in all fairness, Karak brought it on himself.

"Understood," he said, "how small is the team, exactly?"

"Four," Zeera said, then gestured to Tolor, "including you."

Tolor's face broke into a shocked scowl instantly, and Karak barely held his own reaction in check; outrage at first, then amusement at Tolor's indignance.

"Understood," Karak said again.

"Understood," Tolor stammered at the same time.

"The other two agents are already briefed," Zeera said, "and are waiting for you. Pack what you need, and be ready to leave within the hour."

Other than Tolor, the agents assigned to Karak's mission were relative strangers. He knew of them, but had never spoken directly to either one. The journey from Azar passed in silence, none of the four agents interested in getting to know the others. Tolor fumed as they travelled, his rage palpable even to the two strangers.

They reached Omas without incident; Karak couldn't help scanning the horizon for Thearans. To begin their hunt for the book, the group started at Tarsius. Backtracking from Karak's journey, then following the direction he saw the Thearans heading in, they headed off into the desert. Each of the four were disguised as Thearans; four wasn't enough to be considered a tribe, but it wasn't unheard of for such a small group to travel on their own. *The group that attacked me and stole the book was about that big,* he thought.

The desert stretched before them, endless and unforgiving. His team carried with them everything they should need, but no amount of supplies could make the journey through Omas' deserts easy.

"Where are we looking first?" Korra said, "do you have a lead?"

"They said they were taking the book to their Queen," Karak said, "Zeera said her name is Aella. She's usually based in Theara, but they travel to Sitharkos at this time each year. So that's where we're going."

Karak had never been to Sitharkos before. He wasn't looking forward to it; visiting an active volcano at its most volatile seemed like a stupid idea to him. But regardless of his feelings, Karak had to do whatever it took to set things right.

The journey from Tarsius to Sitharkos took a month. They walked as much as they could, and set up camp whenever they couldn't. By the time they reached the foot of the giant mountain, Karak could barely feel his feet. Smoke drifted not just from the volcano's mouth, but from the plateau next to it too; Aella's Thearans camping out.

"We just need to get that book," Karak said, "whatever we need to do to get it, whatever the cost."

Thearans wouldn't part with such a powerful piece of magic so easily. Karak knew they had their work cut out for them; the Thearans fought each other even when their mood was pleasant. He couldn't imagine what they were like when something they prized was stolen from them.

After a short rest, the team walked up Sitharkos' winding path. Millennia of Thearans visiting their sacred volcano ensured the path that led up the side of the mountain had been beaten to a hard, almost smooth surface. Though still a difficult path to walk, it was far easier than traversing the dunes of the desert.

As they reached the crest of the path, Karak heard voices reach them over the low wind. He expected as much, but there were less than he expected. *That can't be Aella's tribe,* he thought, *there's maybe a hundred people, at most.* According to Zeera, Aella had amassed an army to rival Kerberos', and now ruled the previously abandoned city of Theara. The group on Sitharkos' plateau was a small tribe, even compared to when most Thearans didn't belong to one of two huge armies.

They trudged out onto the plateau, and finally saw the group camping there.

"A small group, wouldn't you say?" Tolor said, "couldn't be the army of a Queen."

"I agree," Karak said, "I think we've made a mistake."

Just as he said it, a group of three Thearans noticed them, and headed straight for them.

Aella

1793

Last time I was here, I watched Athan die. It feels like it was a lifetime ago.* Omatus shone in the morning sun, the grey and black stone taking on a bright silver light. Aella stood at the head of her army, ready to move. *It's finally time to take back Omatus from him,* she thought, *and stop him for good.*

He'd been ruler of Omatus for two decades now. Aella couldn't even imagine the conditions its people lived in under him; Kerberos was ruthless and had no regard for human life. His only love was for Sithares. *I don't think he even knows that Sithares has abandoned him,* she thought, *but it's time he found out.*

Sithares had given her even more power than she'd ever possessed before. It was hers on the condition that she bring it to bear against Kerberos. *He deserves to die, for everything he's done.* Kerberos slaughtered innocents, burned farmland, and took a city as his home instead of living in the deserts like the Thearans should. The only home for Thearans was either the deserts of Omas or Theara itself.

What was more, Kerberos had taken her very soul, and the souls of his best warriors, in exchange for their immortality. Aella never agreed to that, and she knew most of the others hadn't either. *He will pay,* she thought, *with his own soul.*

"My queen," one of her warriors said, "with respect, what are we waiting for?"

"We're not waiting," she said, "I'm thinking."

The man stepped back at once, silent again and resuming formation. She knew they were as eager as she was to begin the attack. They all knew of Kerberos and his brutality. As Thearans, combat and warfare were an integral part of their culture; but never against innocents, and nothing like the violence Kerberos had inflicted on Omas.

When Aella was last in Omatus, it was to stop Kerberos from overtaking the city. She'd hoped to join forces with the Omati royal guard temporarily to defeat Kerberos and force him from Omatus. After that, she would have left the city too. Instead, the royal guard simply let him take Omatus, and his army had driven Aella out of the city. *Just after I watched him kill Athan.*

This time, there wouldn't be any surprises. She knew the royal guard and Kerberos' loyal tribe would fight against her. But they had a good idea of the enemy's numbers, and Aella had the element of surprise on her side. She was hoping the people of Omatus would rise up and join the battle too. If they'd seen even half of Kerberos' violent tendencies, they would be ecstatic to escape the man's control.

As much as Aella longed for battle, and though surprise was on their side, she still felt a deep pang of apprehension. *Even if they don't see us coming,* she thought, *breaching a city like Omatus will not be easy*. For a long time, she planned her attack against Kerberos.

She was a queen, but she still trained intensely every single day. When it came to combat against Kerberos directly, she was confident she would kill him. *I could have killed him already,* she thought, *sparring against him when I was part of his tribe*. He'd been disarmed, beaten and at her mercy. If anything, Aella looked forward to fighting him. *Getting to him in the first place is the problem*. Her warriors would do their best, and she had faith in them. *They will get me to Kerberos*.

Aella drew her swords; forged in Theara after she took the city under her rule to replace her Fire Blades, they were perfectly weighted to her. *But still no replacement*. She hadn't seen her Fire Blades since the last time she was in Omatus. They were lost during the battle, and she died escaping the city before she could get them back. *After I kill him,* she thought, *I'm finding those blades, and I'm taking them back.*

"Okay," she said, "it's time. Begin the attack."

By the time they reached the walls, the Omati were alerted to their presence. Aella's warriors swarmed the main gate, launching fireballs at the thick wood and over the walls as the Omati rushed to counterattack. The gate was far too thick to burn through, but the explosions of their fireballs dug out jagged chunks of it.

"Focus your magic on one spot," Aella shouted over the chaos, "where mine hits."

She launched her own fireball at the lower left side, and immediately after it connected, her warriors bombarded the same spot. The gate splintered and creaked. Slowly, the old thick wood caught fire. Most of her warriors focused on the tops of the walls, where the Omati threw spears and fired arrows down at them.

For what felt like an eternity, her warriors were pinned down under a constant barrage of arrows and spears. Screams rose up from behind her. She poured as much magic as she could into her hands and built a dense, seething fireball with it. The gate was beaten down, not fully broken yet but close. Aella launched her fireball with both hands, pushing the magic as hard and fast as it could go. It cannoned into the weakened part of the gate and exploded.

A jagged hole appeared, big enough for people to run through, and a cheer erupted from her warriors. They charged in without hesitation, and Aella ran in as soon as she could. Omatus opened to her, and she smiled as she settled into combat. *Now I just need to find Kerberos,* she thought, *and finally get my revenge*.

The palace was on the far side of the city, across the bridge. *He'll be there, I know it*. Her warriors knew the plan; keep the main battle near the gate, with a small force to follow Aella to the palace.

"My team," Aella said, "with me."

They joined her, twenty of her best warriors, and together they sprinted towards the palace. Omati rushed at them occasionally from the direction of the palace, but they were easily killed by her own magic. None of the Omati seemed to possess Fire Magic, which was unlike Kerberos; *he used to force everyone to pray and learn Fire Magic at the earliest possibility,* she thought, *it's strange that he wouldn't want his own guards wielding magic*.

The sounds of battle faded as her team ran towards the palace. *Hopefully, my warriors can keep the battle on that side of the city,* she thought, *at least long enough for me to get to Kerberos*. All she needed was a little time. *I hope you're ready, Kerberos,* she thought, *today is your last day.*

Karak

1793

"Are you joining our tribe?" one of the Thearans said.

"No," Tolor said, "we need to see the Queen."

The Thearans laughed.

"The Queen? You mean Aella of Theara?"

"Yes," Karak said, "do you know where she is?"

"We got here after they left. We've been following them a while, but they were too far ahead of us and by the time we got here, they were on their way again."

"Why didn't you join them?" Karak said, "if you saw them

here as they were leaving, you could have joined."

"Our leader decided it was best to celebrate on Sitharkos while the fires still raged. Besides, our scouts discovered they left to wage war on Omatus. We have no desire to live in a city. Aella is turning soft, just as Kerberos did before her. No true Thearan lives behind walls and under rooves… unless it's in Theara itself."

She's attacking Omatus, Karak thought, *why in the world would she want to do that?* Kerberos revealed himself to be the rightful King of Omatus, Atillus Argyris; his motivation for taking the city was clear. Aella possessed no such claim to the throne, and already ruled Theara. It made no sense to him.

"We need to leave," he said to the others, "now."

"Wait just a moment," the Thearan who spoke for his group said, "you show up here, mine us for information, and then march off? I don't think so."

"What would you prefer," Tolor said, "that we join your little band? No. We have work to do."

Karak tried to keep his face blank, but he couldn't help shooting a furious glance at Tolor. *He's going to get us killed,* he thought, *or at the very least, himself.*

The Thearans reacted with deadly smiles, drawing their weapons and settling into combat positions. They didn't bother calling more warriors to their side. Karak's team drew their own weapons; Tarsi often didn't fight using martial arts, but they knew how when they needed to. The Thearan weapon he'd been given by Zeera felt strange in his hands; heavy and inefficient.

"We can't do this, Tolor," Karak said, "we need to go."

"Thearans fight, Karak. It's what they do. This was always a likely eventuality, with these disguises."

He spoke loudly enough that the Thearans heard him. Confusion flashed over their faces; but it turned quickly to rage.

"You're Tarsi?" one of them said, "how dare you pretend to be one of us. Filthy frog. You're as good as dead."

All three of the Thearans rushed at Karak's group. Karak unleashed his blinding defensive spell; Korra did the same. Light and noise exploded between the two groups, and the Thearans called out in outrage and confusion.

Karak ran; they were close enough to the path that they'd be out of sight of the camp within moments. Korra and Tarok followed Karak, but Tolor remained behind for a moment, staring at Karak with furious disbelief. *It's as though he wanted to fight,* he thought, *as though he wants to show me he can be deadly.*

Tolor had always been boastful and competitive when it came to Karak. Usually, he could disregard it as petty pride; but they were on a mission, and in a serious situation.

"Tolor," he called, "come on!"

The Thearans were still blinded, but it wouldn't last much longer. With a scream of anger, Tolor ran to join the others down the path. Together, they ran as fast as they could; the tribe behind them, though nowhere near the size of Aella's or Kerberos', was massive compared to a team of four Tarsi. *We won't stand a chance,* he thought, *if they catch us*.

Tarsi could move fast; as soon as they were out of sight, all four agents shifted into animal forms that could sprint faster than any human. Though they made good time in animal form, the transformation was draining. Once they reached the desert, they shifted back.

Omatus was an even longer journey from Sitharkos than Tarsius. As they trudged through the desert, Karak shook his head. *We were so close,* he thought, *if we'd just gone straight to Omatus, we'd have the book by now*. Once again, Karak had failed. And now, for all they knew, a tribe of Thearans could be following them. *Tolor certainly insulted them enough,* he thought. Though that particular failure lay at Tolor's feet, it still stung the same.

They marched, camping whenever they needed to. Heat sunk into Karak's body so far it reached his very soul, burning him as he walked. The grey sand beneath his feet slipped and shifted, his every muscle aching just to stay upright. Evenings meant predators; as soon as the sun drew close to the horizon, the sand came alive with snakes and lizards. Tarsi were omnivores, and in ancient times they hunted smaller prey; but Tarsium was home to no natural predators other than the Tarsi themselves.

Korra, who possessed an affinity for shape-shifting, stayed in the form of an Omasi sand panther for most of the journey. She killed or warded off the dangerous animals that approached; the sand panther was a familiar sight in Omas, and snakes and lizards knew to avoid them. As well as protecting the group, Korra hunted for their food.

Though he accepted the spoils of Korra's hunting, Tolor seethed as he ate. *His pride is taking a serious hit on this mission,* Karak thought with satisfaction, *he must be used to leading teams, instead of being the one following.* Karak hadn't joined Tolor for a mission in a very long time; he didn't know how he usually operated.

Since Sitharkos, Tolor had said nothing to Karak. He spoke occasionally with Korra, mostly uttering a begrudging thanks when she offered food. *I wonder if Zeera is aware of his attitude problem,* Karak thought, *she wouldn't tolerate that kind of behaviour in anyone else.* Karak made a note to himself to tell Zeera everything that happened on their mission; especially Tolor's actions and words.

They travelled for what felt like months. Tolor's mood didn't change the entire time. Despite his simmering anger, Karak bonded with the other two agents; they got along well, and Karak came to appreciate their differing talents. Where Korra had a knack for shape-shifting, Tarok was a secretkeeper, and a historian; he knew perhaps as much as Zeera did. As well as knowing the secrets of the people of Pandeia, Tarok knew almost everything about surviving in the desert.

With Korra and Tarok, the journey was made far more pleasant. The distance between him and Tolor bothered him far less than it normally would have. Finally, Omatus came into view in the distance. Karak sighed as it slowly drew closer. *That's the easy part done,* he thought, *now to steal the book and get it back to Zeera before the entire world is destroyed.*

Mattias

1793

The ships that were designed for the invasion were incredible; fast, massive, and deadly. As they sped towards the coming war, the reinforced ship almost made Mattias feel safe. Almost. He'd survived one Shenza attack already, not to mention the nightmarish monsters guarding the book he'd stolen.

One of those savages had destroyed his squad in seconds. He couldn't even imagine what facing an army of them would be like. It was no wonder Ermoor hadn't breached the forest in the hundreds of years they'd been sending the exploratory force to Shanaken.

But things are different now, he thought. *At least, I really hope they are*. The technology they were bringing to Shanaken was capable of destroying their sacred trees; Prime Overseer Hayne promised them himself. Their weapons and armour were brand new, designed specifically for facing off against the Shenza. For the last fifteen years, Mattias had trained with his unit every day, learning how to use new equipment and weapons whenever they were released.

His armour was perfectly fitted to him, heavy but almost completely unbreakable. Though he could move more or less normally, the armour covered every inch of his body. A thin opening in the helmet's face allowed surprisingly good vision while still protecting the entire face. There were gaps in between the armour plates, but those gaps were incredibly thin and a strong but flexible material covered the skin in between the plates. It would take nothing less than a full-force lunge from a Shenza blade or a very well-placed shot with a powerful bow directly to the material to do any real damage. The armour itself was black, moulded to the shape of a man's body on the inside, with sleek lines and sharp angles on the outside. Mattias had no idea how the Prime Overseer achieved it.

He checked his rifle for the twentieth time; it was a marvel of engineering. Two cartridges stuck out of the butt end of the barrel, one glowing yellow and the other packed with jet-black bullets. A switch near his thumb instantly changed the active cartridge, and both fired through the same barrel. The yellow cartridge fired bolts of pure lightning, explosively powerful, and the black bullets were made of the same material as their armour, but hardened to a fine point; they could pierce almost anything. Each cartridge held ten shots, and every soldier carried reserve cartridges of both ammunition types.

The rifle itself was sturdy, made of thick metal and designed to be as simple as possible; there were very few delicate technological parts, and those were covered by the metal that made up its body. *They've been designed to withstand rainforests, to remain in good condition regardless of rain or anything else.* Prime Overseer Riffolk Hayne really was a genius. Mattias couldn't have imagine a more perfect weapon. *But will it be enough*, he thought, *to finally succeed against the Shenza?*

With his rifle and gear set, Mattias glanced at his unit. None of them looked scared. None of them even looked nervous.

Mattias knew he wasn't normal; cowardice was unacceptable in Ermoor. But being surrounded by such unwavering courage and devotion made him feel like a complete fraud. As far as his soldiers knew, he was a solid rock of authority and power. The Ermoori were nothing if not fanatical; their belief was steadfast and as unbreakable as their new armour. As their Captain, Mattias was the face of Prime Overseer Hayne and Ermoor itself, representing them for his unit.

The only problem was he didn't share their fanaticism. *I believe in God, of course,* he thought, *and in Prime Overseer Hayne. But how am I supposed to face actual magic and monsters and believe that Ermoor will succeed?* After fifteen years, Mattias had come to the conclusion that the book he stole was real magic. He'd never told anyone, but it couldn't be anything else. *The Shenza I saw in the tunnels of Tyra had to be using magic too,* he thought, *no human can move the way that thing did.*

When the attack came in the tunnels outside Tyra, Mattias had been nineteen; fresh out of training, and certain of Ermoor's superiority. Now he was forty years old, and the men in his unit were as young as he'd been back then. Certainty glowed in their features, the confidence of youth and faith. *They have no idea,* he thought, *the horror that awaits them.*

They knew about the Shenza, of course, but only from the announcements over teleradio every day. Godless savages, living in trees, who refused to be taught civility and faith in God. Animalistic, violent, and primitive warriors who must be destroyed to save the world. All of it was true, but seeing it in reality was far more terrifying than anything Mattias would have imagined just from the teleradio.

Even before he'd seen a Shenza in the flesh, Mattias had been scared of them. He was scared of a lot of things. Most of his fears he kept to himself, of course, but it still seemed to him that no one else was scared. All his life, he was told that fear was for the weak, that all he needed was faith. Faith in Ermoor, in the Twelve Crowns, and in God. Whenever he looked at other people, he saw their faith. He had always wondered if there was something wrong with him; if his mind was broken somehow, if that was why he was scared.

"Captain Sterling, sir?" one of the men said.

"Yes, soldier?"

"The boys and I were wondering. How many Shenza have you killed?"

Their eyes were all trained on him, bright and wide. Mattias frowned, wishing he could come up with a great tale of battle and courage for them.

"I haven't killed any."

He saw them deflate a little, as though their respect for him was based purely on the assumption that he'd slaughtered countless savages. Mattias gritted his teeth, pushing past the fear that tried to choke his voice, and added what he thought would help.

"Yet."

A spatter of laughter spread through his unit, and Mattias smiled as best he could.

"I have faced them, though. And worse. They are not easy to kill."

"We have the best weapons in all of Pandeia," one of the men said, "they don't stand a chance."

"True," Mattias said, "try not to kill more of them than I do, boys. You don't want to make your Captain look bad."

They laughed louder this time, with genuine good humour. *These are good men,* he thought as the warship sped towards their first battle, *I hope at least some of them survive*.

Danel

1793

Danel stood in the kitchens, watching his friends argue as he cooked the fish they'd caught that day. News and rumours flew throughout Shanaken nowadays, as well as older stories, and many arguments resulted among his group of friends.

"It couldn't be possible," Delaik said, his face flushed with passion, "there's absolutely no way."

"I'm telling you," Zel said, "it happened. I know someone who was on the city's edge when it happened; it was fifteen years ago. He saw Lashek racing towards the northern mountains."

"No one can steal the book of Amalus. No one. The Shenza don't even know where it is. How could anyone else even find it?"

"Ermoor grows more powerful every year," Danel said, "Didn't you hear about Zailen? He was captured and killed by them, and he was *Kaizeluun*."

"You think it was the Ermoori?"

"Who else? No other country would dare. Besides, no other country wants to destroy us."

"But no one in Ermoor can even use magic," Delaik said, "it's just not possible that they could have found the book."

"Maybe there's some kind of device that detects magic," Zel said.

"No way. It makes no sense."

Danel shook his head. Delaik had always been stubborn. His response to most rumours was the same; if it seemed implausible or unlikely in any way, he refused to believe it. Danel didn't know one way or another, but the concept of a technological device that could detect magic terrified him. *It's not even that unbelievable,* he thought as he flipped fish on the oven's hotplate, *the things Ermoori can do with their technology these days surpass magic*.

"If it happened," Delaik said, "the *Duulshen* would have let us know."

"They tell us nothing."

"Careful, Zel. They tell us what we need to know."

"Food's ready," Danel said, moving the fish onto the bench

where they sat to eat, "hopefully it's tasty enough that you'll stop talking badly about the great *Duulshen*."

Zel rolled her eyes, and Delaik grunted as he shoveled fish into his mouth. The group went quiet for just a few moments, and Danel ate his own fish too. Most Shenza knew how to cook, but all his friends left the cooking to him when they spent time in the kitchens together; he had an undeniable talent. His group of friends, himself included, were fishers, and though fishers were generally considered beneath *Daishen* and *Kaizeluun*, they all took pride in their work.

Although trials were required to be passed to become *Daishen* and *Kaizeluun*, all Shenza were fully trained warriors. Fishers simply spent more of their time gathering food than training or fighting, and were only called to battle in times of extreme danger. Fishers hadn't been called to the north shore—or any other battlefield—in centuries.

"You know," Zel finally said, "I *have* felt a difference since then. The forest is different."

"You don't even use Shadow Magic, Zel."

"But all Shenza are connected to the forest. Look me in the eye and tell me you haven't felt any change."

"I haven't felt any change," Delaik said.

Zel rolled her eyes again and shoved him. Lashana laughed and shoved Delaik from the other side. Smirking, Danel tried to ignore them and kept eating. When he really thought about it, there *was* something different about the forest. It felt not quite empty, but... quiet, somehow. Even through all the insect buzzing and animal calls, the birds singing and the gentle wind and rainfall; there was a somber quietness to it.

Danel had never met Lashek, but it was common knowledge that the Shenza was chosen by Amalus. He'd left the city to live on his own well before being chosen, and even after he returned to Shanaken he'd chosen to live out in the forest itself. *Obviously being blessed by Amalus protects someone from the forest,* he thought, *no other Shenza would dare live out there*. Even the *Duulshen* never ventured out, and they advised Shenza to only travel through the forest in groups, through the canopy.

"I think it feels different," Lashana said.

"Me too," Danel said without hesitation, "I can't describe exactly what's different about it, but it feels quiet."

"What, you can't hear all the birds anymore?" Delaik said, "you going deaf doesn't mean the book was stolen."

"It's three against one, Delaik," Zel said, "if anyone's wrong, it's you."

"I'm the only one being logical here."

Uncomfortable silence descended on their group, punctuated only by the natural sounds of the forest outside. Delaik was always the one to stop discussions; his mind was impossible to change. He was a great fisher, but it was the same stubborn mindset that allowed him to tirelessly catch fish after fish that made him infuriating to argue with. They'd been friends for a long time, but moments like these made Danel question that friendship.

"Logic isn't always flawless, Delaik," he said, "especially when it comes to magic. The book could have been stolen. We don't know for sure, but all of us except you have felt something change in the forest lately."

Delaik's only response was a short grunt. The others laughed, and Danel sighed and shook his head. *Once again, Delaik agrees with no one.*

Their fishing was done for the day, and now that their midday meal was finished, it was time to gut, scale, and store the fish they'd caught. It was the worst part of being a fisher, but after he was done, he would go with the others to bathe in the stream; and that was one of his favourite things.

"Let's get to work on the fish," Danel said, "and stop talking about something we can't even confirm happened."

"Finally," Delaik said, "something we agree on."

Zel laughed, and gave Delaik another shove. She always seemed the least bothered by Delaik's stubbornness, though she was the most vocal when it came to their arguments. Zel was by far the best fisher of their group. She had a way of knowing where they were before anyone could even see them, and somehow picking the best spots before even getting on the boat each morning.

"Alright," she said, "now that Delaik finally agreed to shut up, let's get some work done."

Aella

1793

Explosions rang out behind her as her team approached the palace. The bridge was behind them now, as well as a trail of dead Omati guards. She glanced back the way they'd come; black smoke billowed up from between the buildings near the city's entrance. *They're putting up more of a fight than I expected,* she thought, *I knew they would fight against intruders, but my warriors should be able to take them.*

Kerberos never took chances; she knew that. But he had no reason to believe he'd be under attack. Two decades had passed since they'd last seen each other. His guards would be well-trained, of course, but they shouldn't have been prepared for this. *All I can do is trust my warriors to handle themselves,* she thought, *and stick to the plan.*

They kept running towards the palace, Aella in the lead. As she got to the massive doors, they opened in front of her and dozens of Thearans in Omati armour poured out to face them. *Kerberos' tribe,* she thought, *there's no killing these warriors*. They would die, of course; they just wouldn't stay dead. And killing them in the first place wouldn't be easy. *Same with Kerberos.*

Rumours had spread when Aella still belonged to Kerberos' tribe of his sword. It wasn't a normal blade; no one had seen it being made and no one knew where he obtained it from. But the warriors in his tribe spoke of it often. They said it was a Soul Blade, forged by Sithares itself and gifted to Kerberos as a sign of his station as ruler of the Thearans and Son of the Fire God.

According to the rumours, it was one of the only weapons capable of killing an immortal for good. *It's not surprising Kerberos would want a weapon like that,* she thought, *he gave us immortality, and he has the ability to take it away*. If the rumours were correct, Aella's plan was to take the blade and turn it on Kerberos.

The Thearans rushed out of Kerberos' palace, and launched into combat without hesitation. Aella recognised a lot of their faces. Three of them leapt at her, and their familiar faces became meaningless as she descended into bloodlust once again. Fire Magic roared through her body, filling her muscles with strength and speed beyond even her lifetime of training could have provided.

Blades sliced the air around her, barely missing her as she danced. *I can't waste much time here,* she thought, *I need to conserve magic and strength for Kerberos*. She ducked underneath a blade and sliced the attacker's inner thigh, spinning to block another attacker. There was no way around it, she would have to kill them; they at least would stay dead for however long it took them to resurrect, and by then she would be on her way to the throne room.

Her blades cut quickly and precisely, slicing just deep enough to open her opponent's arteries at their most vulnerable points. In less than a minute, all three had been cut enough that they'd bleed out within minutes. To make sure her work was done, she shifted her focus to their throats.

Their attacks grew weaker as they bled, and Aella finished them off one by one; blocking with one blade and cutting their throats with the other. The rest of the attackers she left to her team.

She sprinted through the doorway, casting her eyes around for a way to the throne room. The inside of the palace was a mystery to her, but she remembered seeing the balcony where Kerberos killed Athan. *It could be seen from the bridge,* she thought, *so it faces the rest of the city.*

The palace was huge, its foyer cavernous. By comparison, the palace of Theara was barely even a building. It was designed for only the minimal number of people, the ruler and their advisors, to be present at any one time. Other than that, the Thearan palace was made in the same way every other building in Theara was; function and warfare far outweighed grandeur. In Theara nothing was ornate except the temple to Sithares, it was all built to withstand war and magic.

In Omatus, it was the other way around. Almost nothing Aella saw had a real purpose, beyond satisfying the ego of the city's ruler. *I never took Kerberos as the type to indulge in petty extravagance,* Aella thought, *maybe living in Omatus has made him soft after all.* She wouldn't take chances when it came to fighting him, but it seemed his priorities might have shifted now that he lived in luxury.

Aella reached the top of a staircase and sprinted down the hallway in the direction the throne room should have been. She was most of the way down the hallway when she finally saw the throne room's entrance. The doors were almost as large as the palace's main doors, and just as ostentatious.

She sprinted the rest of the way, drawing Fire Magic to the surface and feeling it flood over her skin. A couple of metres from the doors, she leapt into a flying kick, launching a wave of fire at the same time. The doors exploded inwards, and Aella landed in a combat stance with her swords drawn.

The throne room was packed with Thearan warriors. They were ready for her. Kerberos sat on his throne, a satisfied smile on his face. Though he'd made himself King, he wore no crown. He wore the same clothing he always had, and his muscles remained as taught and toned as ever. *Being a king didn't make him soft then,* she thought, *and he wasn't so careless as to leave himself unguarded.*

He knew his own strength, but he was clearly still as careful as he'd always been. *Kerberos was never one to take chances.* The warriors around her waited, discipline keeping them utterly still. Aella waited too, staring at Kerberos.

"Did you really think it would be so easy to kill me?" Kerberos said.

"I hoped so, yes."

He laughed, genuine humour warming his usually cold voice. His eyes never left hers, and the warmth in his laugh didn't touch the lethal intent that glowed from them as he stared at her.

"You only made it this far because I let you. Omatus is mine, Aella."

"Only for as long as you live," Aella said, "and today is your last day. Whatever the cost, I *will* kill you."

Kerberos laughed again, but this time there was no warmth in it at all. He nodded, but otherwise didn't move. *I'm going to have to kill everyone in this room if I hope to face Kerberos directly,* she thought, *so much for conserving magic.* The same satisfied smile spread across his lips, and Kerberos' golden eyes narrowed.

"You are welcome to try, Aella."

Arthor

1793

Three days after the army departed, Arthor felt something he didn't recognize at first; peace. For the first time in a very long time, he had nothing to do, no one to answer to. And it took him that three days to realise part of what was happening; he hadn't heard the voice at all since Ermoor's military left their shores. The voice in his head felt like his own.

Arthor sighed, watching the smoke of his cigar tumble through the Rookfell Pub's stale air. There were maybe a dozen patrons, all close to Arthor's own age, all high-ranking government or military officials; Overseers, Governors, and non-active Commanders. All of them knew him, but out of respect they each kept their distance.

He sat at the bar, three empty glasses and an ornate ashtray in front of him. News of the invasion would come after the men reached Shanaken, but until then he had nothing to do. Some of the men sitting in a booth on the other side of the room were men he'd trained with in his early days; he gestured them over. They looked nervous, but they sat next to him nevertheless.

"Lord Commander," Havelock said, "I'm surprised to see you here."

"Not as surprised as I am to be here," Arthor said, chuckling as he greeted the others.

Commander Zachariah Havelock was impeccably dressed, his face clean shaved, his hair oiled and dark. Though only five years younger than Arthor, he looked less than half the Lord Commander's age. *He barely looks any older than when we trained together*, Arthor thought. His green eyes sparkled with intelligence, though the man was nothing compared to Riffolk. He was loyal, and honourable. Arthor had always liked him.

"I take that to mean our Prime Overseer gave you orders to stay behind?" Havelock said.

"That's right. Apparently, I am of more use here, protecting Ermoor."

"If Prime Overseer Hayne says it, it must be so."

I have to be careful, Arthor thought, *any words against Riffolk are treason.*

"Of course."

Overseer Byron Hawke sat to Arthor's other side. He ordered a drink and lit his own cigar.

"Have faith, Lord Commander," he said, "Ermoor will prevail, and our Prime Overseer will return with all of Pandeia under his rule."

"Oh, undoubtedly," Commander Marsh said, "and what in God's name will we all do then?"

Clarence Marsh, another Commander, was a couple years older than Arthor. Where Havelock apparently hadn't aged, Marsh looked at least a decade older than he was. One glance told him why Commander Marsh hadn't been ordered overseas.

"There is always a need for soldiers," Havelock said, "and weapons."

A deadly smile pulled at his lips, and he fixed his eyes on Arthor's.

"I trust you don't share Commander Marsh's dread about our future, Lord Commander?"

"Not at all. Prime Overseer Hayne will take care of us, I have no doubt."

That much wasn't a lie, at least; Riffolk would never disband his means of control. The Ermoori military was guaranteed to last, and those at the top would benefit most. Riffolk was as close to evil as a man could get, but he kept his word.

"Let's drink to that, shall we?" Overseer Hawke said.

They each took a swig. Commander Marsh lit a cigar, leaving Havelock as the only one not smoking. *Maybe that's why he still looks so young,* Arthor thought. They drank in silence for a moment, Arthor thinking about what his life would be like after the invasion.

Commander Havelock waved the smoke out of his face and raised his eyebrows at Arthor.

"Do you have an estimate, Lord Commander," he said, "for how long the war might last?"

"The Prime Overseer and I have spoken about it at length," Arthor said, "we both have our theories. It's not my place to say."

A subtle smile crept across Havelock's face. *He's testing my loyalty with every sentence*. Someone like Commander Havelock would use any means necessary to propel himself to the top of the command chain. If he trapped Arthor into saying anything even remotely insubordinate, he would go straight to Riffolk with it.

"I wonder if he might change his mind," Havelock said, "about keeping you here. If the war drags on longer than expected, that is."

"Whatever the Prime Overseer decides," Arthor said, "is what will happen."

Danel

1793

The great forest of Shanaken teemed with life. Every Shenza felt at home among the giant trees and magically shaped buildings in the canopy. But Danel loved being out on the ocean even more. The air flowed easier, with a crisp and clear bite, and the water's constant motion felt just as full of life as the deepest parts of the forest.

Shenza fishing boats were designed for a small team to work together. They used nets, of course, but most Shenza preferred to hunt the fish down with arrows or spears. Each team of fishers used at least one spotter, and the rest were tasked with catching.

Burning on the horizon, the sun rose as Danel and his team waited for fish to start appearing. The early morning air was still cold, but Danel had been a fisher for most of his life. *I don't mind the cold,* he thought, *I just hate waiting for the fish.*

They sat together, each staring into the water as the sky overhead brightened. Zel held her bow, an arrow already nocked to the string. A puff of mist rushed from her mouth as she sighed. Danel looked out to the horizon; the sun was high enough now that a line of blinding reflected orange light led from it all the way to the boat.

"Wait," Lashana said, "can you guys hear something?"

"Yeah," Zel said, "what is that?"

"I've never heard it before," Delaik said.

"It sounds almost like the war horns," Danel said, "but it's a different sound."

"Oh no. Oh, no."

"What's wrong, Zel?"

"I think I know what it is. That's the emergency alarm. Calling all Shenza to war. Even fishers."

Zel was right. They rushed to shore, then ran as quickly as they could through the trees towards the northern battlefront. When they reached the southernmost hub, they found it completely deserted. The next three were just as empty. When they reached the last hub, closest to the north shore, they finally saw the last group of Shenza waiting. Several dozen *Kaizeluun* organised the rest of the Shenza into groups, talking them through battle plans.

Danel saw smoke rising up from the north; deep, roiling black smoke that painted a picture of death and despair. A *Kaizeluun* motioned for him to join the nearest group. His friends were guided to other groups; he watched them go with a pang of fear. *Something tells me I might not see them again,* he thought. Ermoor had invaded Shanaken countless times; but this was the first time Danel ever heard of every Shenza being called to war.

"We'll be staying here," the *Kaizeluun* in charge of his group said, "as the final line of defense against the Ermoori if they break through the tree line."

"That'll never happen," someone said, "they've never been able to breach the forest before."

"You haven't seen their forces now," the *Kaizeluun* responded, "it's unlike anything we've seen before."

"We can still beat them back, can't we?"

The *Kaizeluun* frowned, staring at all the Shenza before him. A low, deep rumble rolled through the forest. Danel's eyes snapped towards the battlefront; a huge wave of black smoke swept up through the sky. The *Kaizeluun* glanced in the same direction, then shared a meaningful look with his fellow *Kaizeluun*.

"We hold here," he finally said, "until the forest is breached."

They waited, watching the skies above the northern shore as smoke billowed up from explosions and fire. Whenever the breeze quieted, faint sounds of screaming and cannon fire drifted to the waiting Shenza. Danel rested his hand on the hilt of his *Shenzuun*; though not as powerful as the shadow blades of the *Kaizeluun*, the blades of the majority of Shenza were still imbued with some Shadow Magic. Through the blade he'd forged, he felt the life around him, and a soothing cold certainty settled into his chest.

"The Ermoori might not breach the forest, right?" a Shenza near Danel said.

"They won't," another said, "the forest protects itself. Even the Shenza can't go where we shouldn't."

"It sounds like they have some serious firepower. I'm not so sure the forest can stand up to that."

"It takes more than a few cannons to take down the great trees of Shanaken. Ermoor has nothing that could get close."

Danel gripped his *Shenzuun*, trying to keep his heartbeat steady as the Shenza began shouting at each other. *Waiting is hard enough*, he thought, *without having to listen to such dark talk.*

"Enough," the *Kaizeluun* said, glaring at the entire group, "whatever happens is the will of Amalus. Our job is to protect Shanaken at all costs. We will do that, or we will die in the attempt.

It's that simple."

He sounds so calm, Danel thought, *the* Kaizeluun *really are the best of the best*. His words quieted the waiting groups of warriors, and once again the sounds of battle echoed through the forests. *There is nothing to do but wait. Either the Ermoori suffer another defeat, as they have countless times, or we fight for Shanaken.* All Shenza were fully trained for battle, but they were passivists at heart, and Danel had never enjoyed the idea of real combat.

He'd lived through more than one Ermoori invasion, and so far, had never been called to battle. *Nor even seen an Ermoori with my own eyes*. Rumours and tales spread through Shanaken after every attempted invasion, telling of the Ermoori soldiers in impenetrable armour, with devastating hand-held cannons, destroying everything they could see. When Danel was young, the tales sometimes kept him up at night. Now, standing and waiting to possibly face them himself, he doubted he would ever sleep soundly again.

Hours passed in tense silence, the forest whispering around them as distant screams blended with rumbling explosions. A far more horrifying sound reached them, and though none of them had ever heard it in their life, they each knew exactly what it was. A deep, sharp crack, followed by immense creaking, and finally a crushing impact that shook the platform on which they stood. The Shenza stared at each other, shocked disbelief and fear etched into every face.

It's happened, Danel thought, *the Ermoori have felled one of the great trees. They're breaching the forest.*

Aella

1793

A ragged breath escaped Aella as she lashed out at another warrior. She blocked a thrust at her neck, countered, and swayed under another attack. She'd killed at least a dozen of them now, but at the cost of too much magic. *At this rate I won't be able to face Kerberos by the time I've killed his warriors,* she thought.

Her own warriors never appeared in the throne room. She thought they wouldn't have any trouble fighting through the palace to join her; but apparently, they'd run into more of Kerberos' army somewhere along the way. *He really was more prepared than I gave him credit for,* she thought, *he's been waiting and ready for this fight since the day I left.*

She snatched glances at Kerberos when she could; he hadn't moved since the fight began. Instead, he simply stared at her, watching and analysing her movements. *Every second I fight his warriors is valuable to him. I can't do this anymore*. There was no way to win.

Summoning a surge of Fire, she unleashed an explosion around her that knocked the warriors to the ground. She dropped to a knee, breathing hard, and looked at Kerberos. His smile broadened as he regarded her exhaustion.

"Coward," she said, spitting the word out like a curse, "if you were a warrior and not a King, you would have faced me yourself."

"When you attack a King," he said, "you must be prepared to face his army. You should have planned better."

His warriors were on their feet again, weapons ready and pointed at her. They closed in, and Aella sheathed her blades. *They've trained hard,* she thought, *probably directly with Kerberos, given how skilled they are*.

"Your army has most likely been defeated by now, too," Kerberos said, "I have been preparing for this day a long time, Aella. My warriors are perhaps the best trained force in all of Pandeia."

Aella sighed, bowing her head as memories of her death filled her mind. Kerberos and his army had defeated her twice now. *And this time,* she thought, *He'll kill me with his Soul Blade*. When she died the first time, it felt like an eternity before she was resurrected. In reality, it couldn't have been more than a few hours. She couldn't imagine going through that for an *actual* eternity.

I can still fight my way out of this, she thought, *I just need to choose when to make a stand.* Now wasn't the time; she would have to let herself be captured and hope Kerberos didn't plan on executing her too soon. *I need time to build up more magic, and I need to get him alone*. If he decided to execute her here and now, there was nothing she could do.

"Make sure she is shackled properly," Kerberos said, "the way I showed you. Then leave her to me, and go to assist with the capture of her army."

They affixed a thick pair of steel shackles to her wrists, and another to her ankles. Then every warrior swiftly left the room, until it was only Kerberos and Aella. Finally, he rose from his throne, smiling.

"Why?" Aella asked, "just tell me why you had to take Omatus. You're Thearan, and you had the biggest Thearan army since the age of Heroes. Why would you destroy all that farmland? Slaughter innocents? And then take this walled-in city just to sit on a throne like some fat Omati lord?"

He frowned, staring down at her with something akin to pity in his eyes.

"How do you not know by now?" he said, his voice low, "I thought the queen of Theara would have heard. Do you not employ spies to gather information about your enemies?"

"I've never stooped to spying, Kerberos," she said, "when I fight, I fight honourably."

Kerberos nodded, the pity vanishing from his face.

"That you do," he said, "and look where it got you."

Rage boiled in her chest, and she screamed as Fire burned within her. But within her it stayed; her magic was still too low to attempt fighting him.

"Omatus was always my goal, Aella. It is my birthright. I am Atillus Argyrus, oldest son of King Thorinos Argyrus."

Aella stared at his dark skin, his golden eyes and bright white hair. *How is that possible?* He was clearly pure blood Thearan; anyone could see it at a glance.

"I don't understand," she said.

"No," Kerberos nodded, "I did not expect you would. I needed Sithares, and the Thearans, to take this city. All I ever wanted was for Omatus to be as great as I knew it could be. And now it is."

"But you led our tribe for *decades*," she said, "living in the desert as one of us. You never mentioned Omatus even once."

"I am a very patient man."

Aella shook her head, trying to fit the pieces together. *He has to be lying. It's just a trick. He's manipulating me somehow.*

"It does not matter now, either way," he said, "Omatus is mine, and under my rule it has flourished. I understand your need for vengeance, Aella, but I want you to see what I made of this city before you try anything more."

"You forced an entire city of innocents to live by the laws of Sithares," Aella said, "and you think showing me will change my mind? Have you gone insane?"

Instead of answering, Kerberos sighed. He looked at the doorway that led out onto the balcony where he'd killed Athan. Another surge of fury ripped through her chest as she remembered watching his body fall in the distance.

"You could have beaten me, you know," he said, strolling towards her.

This is my chance, she thought, *already. I haven't built up any magic, but we're alone and I can take him if I'm careful.*

"I know," she said.

"If," he added, a smile pulling at the corners of his lips, "I had not picked up several more... talents."

He gestured towards her, and shadows began forming in front of her eyes. They wrapped around her arms, moving like smoke. From there they snaked over her shoulders, her neck, and over her chest and stomach, until everything but her legs and head was covered in tendrils of shifting black.

Once she was covered, the shadows solidified into a cold hard metal, locking her in position so all she could do was walk. As soon as the metal settled onto her skin, her body became cold. The cold spread through her until she felt no fire within herself at all, no magic she could summon to fight or escape.

"How is this possible?" Aella asked, her voice wavering as the cold continued spreading, "this isn't Fire Magic. And you're no Shenza."

"Fire Magic was only the beginning. I am learning far more than you could ever imagine."

By Sithares, she thought, *how much more powerful is he?* Using Shadow Magic barely seemed to take any focus for him. *Like it's second nature*. If he possessed any other magic, and if he could use it as easily as Fire and Shadow, Kerberos would be almost unstoppable.

Suddenly, being alone with him turned from opportunity to certain doom. *There's no way out of this,* she thought, *I'm completely at his mercy*. Her army was captured, though she knew they wouldn't let themselves be taken without a fight. And now, if Kerberos wanted to kill her, there was nothing she could do about it.

Just to be certain, Aella tried to summon Fire Magic. She focused on heat, seeing the flames in her mind's eye, and tried to force the image into reality. But nothing happened, and the cold seeping into her from the black metal cage on her skin sunk deeper still.

"To your feet, Aella," Kerberos said, "I have a special place waiting for you."

“You’re not going to kill me now?” she asked.

“Would you like me to?”

She shut her mouth, impotent rage boiling within her body. *He’s enjoying this far too much,* she thought, *he can’t even stop himself from smiling*.

He led her through the hallways of the palace, down stairs, and through more hallways. It wasn't long before she was lost. They turned into yet another hallway, and Kerberos stopped her with a hand on the shoulder.

"I am sorry," he said, "but some secrets must be protected, and no one knows of this place but me."

Before she could reply, he pulled a sack over her head and pushed her forward once more. His hand stayed on her shoulder, tipping one way or another to guide her through more hallways. She followed his direction as best she could, trying not to fall or walk into anything. Below the cold that suffocated her body lay a deadly, burning rage. *I don't know how I'll do it,* she thought, *but I will kill him.*

She heard a low creak as a door swung open, and Kerberos pushed her forward. A horrible cold, worse even than what came from her magical shackles, settled over her. Where there had been a vague glow behind the fabric over her face, there now was only pitch black. And worst of all, a deafening silence filled her ears.

"What's happening?" she tried to ask, "where are-"

But she cut herself off; she couldn't hear her own voice. When she spoke, only that deafening silence could be heard. Aella tried to turn around, but Kerberos' hand dug into her shoulder and held her in place. After a moment that felt like far longer, he finally pushed her forward again. A tiny glow began to filter through the fabric, and as she walked forward her footsteps slapped against the stone beneath her feet.

I can hear again, she thought, *I don't know what that was, but I never want to be in that room again*. Kerberos pushed her a little further, then spun her around and gave her a gentle shove. She fell back, grunting as she landed in a chair. He pulled the sack off her head, regarding her with his cold, golden stare.

"You will stay in here until the trial," he said, "and before you waste time and energy trying, there is no escape from this room."

Without another word, he walked through an ancient looking ornate door, and disappeared into silence.

Mattias

1793

A red glow washed over the men in Mattias' unit; *we're about to come ashore*. Their faces still emanated pure faith; not even the knowledge that they were minutes from death swayed their certainty.

"Weapons ready, boys," Mattias said, "remember to stay in formation off the ramp."

Rustling and clacking filled the cold metal room as his men checked and double checked their weapons. The red glow pulsed off and on. They were one of hundreds of units in the initial attack wave, each unit made up of fifty men. His unit took up an entire room in the warship. Each warship contained enough space for a full fleet of ten tanks, and an entire battalion; two thousand soldiers.

The ship rumbled and swayed, and then collided with the sand of the northern shore with a massive thump. If they'd been standing, they would have fallen from the impact. As soon as the ship settled, the ramp swung open and the doors between each unit's room slid open at the same time.

"Go, go, go!" Mattias said.

His men moved without hesitation, leaping to their feet and sprinting through doors until they reached the ramp. Every unit behind them and in front moved simultaneously, like a giant machine.

Sunlight blazed down onto the beach, and Mattias ran out with his men to see the shore covered with Ermoori soldiers. As ordered, his men stayed in formation as they ran off the warship's ramp. At first, there were no Shenza to be seen. The trees towered over them, silent and ominous.

A soldier screamed somewhere nearby, then another, and before Mattias could react, chaos erupted on the beach. Clouds of shadow materialised from nowhere in the midst of their soldiers, and suddenly the Shenza were upon them. Gunfire exploded all around him, and all he could hear was explosions and screaming.

He saw a shadow and fired at it. A spray of blood flew from it, but the shadow disappeared before he could fire again. His men kept formation, facing the trees and sticking close together. They fired at anything that moved, and Mattias felt a strong surge of comfort; his unit fought well, and for that brief moment their certainty became his.

Reports of previous battles were full of countless Ermoori deaths. Mattias saw soldiers falling, but nowhere near the amount he'd come to expect. Many of the Ermoori who fell actually returned to their feet, though most were wounded. He took the time to look properly at the soldiers around him; though there was plenty of screaming, very few soldiers were dying. As the battle raged, however, he saw more and more Shenza bodies fall to the sand in ruined heaps.

"For Ermoor!" someone screamed, and then "for God!"

A cheer rose up, and the battle raged on. The Shenza kept coming, fighting viciously until their last breath. *They really are like animals,* he thought. A few of them ran together towards a unit near his own, and Mattias pointed at them and shouted.

"Soldiers, to your right! Fire!"

His men responded, and in seconds the Shenza were cut down in a wave of gunfire.

"Yes!" one of his soldiers said, "I hit one, did you see that, Captain?"

"Good shot, soldier," Mattias said, "eyes forward, they're not all dead yet."

A cloud of shadow formed directly in front of him, and Mattias felt a sharp thump on his chest. He glanced down to see a pitch-black sword blade pointed directly at his heart. The Shenza holding it glanced down too; Mattias' armour was unscratched. He looked into the Shenza's red eyes, smiled, and fired his gun point blank into its face. Blood exploded over a few of his men, and they cheered.

The battle raged for hours. Finally, the Shenza retreated to the tree-line, and another cheer rose up from the Ermoori. They set up in formation over the entire shore, and tanks rolled down the warship's ramps. No one had ever seen them in action before. They moved over sand with no trouble, driving between units of soldiers into position facing the forest.

Before any orders were given, a thick cloud of black arrows and throwing blades rained down onto the beach from high up in the treetops. Thousands of them, thudding into the sand and the Ermoori soldiers like deadly hail. Most Ermoori had shields, but their armour was impenetrable against the blades of the Shenza anyway.

"Fire into the trees," Mattias said, "at the top. Even if you can't see them, you might get lucky."

He aimed his own gun, near the tops of the trees, at nothing in particular. Other units followed suit, and once their gunfire was focused on the trees the rain of blades slowed down.

"Tank cannons are ready," the Captain of the tank unit said, "prepare to fire."

"Soldiers," another Captain shouted, "cease all fire."

Mattias' team lowered their weapons, staring up at the trees. Almost immediately, another wave of arrows and blades flew from the trees and fell towards them. Mattias felt one smack his shoulder armour and bounce off. A scream rose from one of the other units as a Shenza blade found its way between armour plates.

Then a deafening boom erupted and the top of a tree exploded in flame and distant screams. The tanks fired one after another, and the forest canopy lit up like a gigantic bonfire. The screams stopped, and Mattias glanced down. Hundreds of Shenza suddenly sprinted from the forest along the beach again, hurling throwing blades and brandishing their pitch-black swords.

"On the ground," Mattias shouted, "in front! Fire!"

Several of the tanks maneuvered to aim at the forest floor, but hundreds of Shenza were already too close. Still, their heavy cannons fired into the tree trunks directly, burrowing shallow holes in the ancient hardwood. Even with their sheer power, the trees barely shook.

The Shenza reached Mattias' unit; their blades flashed faster than his eyes could follow. His unit reacted with a volley of gunfire, shouting battle cries and cheering as the Shenza died. One of his men died, his screams merging with those of the Shenza. The battle raged, viciously, and it was all Mattias could do to keep from fleeing. But they died in droves, hundreds of them falling still, as only a few dozen Ermoori died.

It's never been this way around before, he thought, *I've read the reports. A hundred of our men normally die for every few of theirs.* Even Mattias, coward that he was, couldn't help but feel hopeful for the battle's outcome. *I might even survive this.* He fired at a Shenza approaching his unit; the shrieking savage died before he could scream, his head exploding in a mess of blood and bone.

Half of the tanks were now firing at the canopy, and the other half firing at the forest floor. After the wave of Shenza were culled, the tanks kept firing at the trees. They concentrated fire on one tree, and when it finally fell, a huge cheer rose up among the Ermoori. It was the first time in history that one of the giant trees of Shanaken had fallen.

For a moment after the tree fell, not a single Shenza appeared from the forest. The tanks moved their fire to the tree next to the one that fell. If they could make a space big enough for the tanks to fit through, the Shenza still in the forest stood no chance.

They waited, checking their weapons as the second tree began creaking and swaying. Every now and then a throwing blade would streak from the trees into the Ermoori, and the soldiers fired at the spot from which it came. Finally, the second tree fell. Another cheer rose, every single soldier adding their voice. The tanks lurched forward, and Mattias gestured to his team. *Here we go,* he thought, his heart racing, *for the first time in history, the Ermoori are going into the Shanaken forests.*

"Okay men," Mattias said, "into the forest."

They cheered, and he ran along with them towards the

towering Shanaken trees. There was no way to tell where the Shenza were. *They might be just beyond our vision, or they may have retreated further in*. Still, Mattias clung to the hope he'd felt earlier, and jogging next to one of the tanks made him feel protected.

He stepped through the tree-line into a cold, dark new world. It felt like leaving the warm barracks on a freezing rainy day. Constant rustling, animal calls and other sounds surrounded them, sounds he'd never heard before all mingling into a low cacophony that screamed danger from every direction.

The tanks moved slowly, and had to stop to fell trees too often to maintain speed. Mattias and his unit kept their eyes and weapons moving all over the forest. They all knew an attack would come, from somewhere in the twilight of the forest. It was an entirely different battleground, an environment the Ermoori had never fought in before. He began to doubt their choice to enter the forest, and just as he did, his men screamed all around him.

Aella

1793

She couldn't tell how long she spent in the tiny room where Kerberos left her. Despite essentially being a prison cell, it was cosy; quiet, filled with gentle light, and old looking furniture sat against the walls. Aella had to admit to being taken aback. *Of all the places he would keep me locked up,* she thought, *why would he want to put me in a room like this?*

No sound reached her from outside the room, not even through the walls. There was no way to know where she was in the palace, or where her warriors were. *No way to coordinate an escape,* she thought, *all according to Kerberos' plan.* She glanced around again; there weren't even any windows in the room. Kerberos had obviously cast some Fire Magic spell she was unfamiliar with.

All I can do is wait, she thought, *he's given me no other option.* He could have killed her if he wanted to; Aella knew that now. But he didn't, and it was unlike him. *He mentioned a trial,* she thought, *but what does he gain from that?* Kerberos ruled with total, ruthless authority; the man Aella remembered wouldn't have bothered with something as trivial as a public trial.

"What do you want, Kerberos?" she asked the silent room, staring at the ancient door he'd left through, "what do you want?"

But for days, Kerberos only brought her meals in silence. The black metal shackles Kerberos conjured around her remained, and she barely moved. Aella could only track the time that passed by the meals Kerberos brought her. The soft light in the room never changed, and Aella slept badly; if at all.

“Your trial is soon,” Kerberos said the next time he appeared, “I hope you are prepared.”

What felt like an entire day later, Kerberos appeared from the ancient looking door, covered her head with a sack again, and led her through the palace. Again, she couldn’t tell where the room was. Endless turns and long corridors pushed beyond her ability to remember.

She heard the crowd before she was led out the front doors of the palace. A deep groan and creaking echoed through the entrance hall, and then the noise of the crowd tripled. Aella kept her steps as dignified as possible without being able to see where she walked. Kerberos shoved her up a few steps onto the dais where public announcements were made, and finally removed the sack from her head.

"This," Kerberos said to the crowd, "is Aella, Queen of Theara. Her people attacked our great city, with the intent of taking it for themselves."

Shouts and jeers rang out at Aella. *Why are they taking his side?* she thought, *he may be their ruler, but surely, they see he's a monster.*

"Although she waged war on us," Kerberos continued, "I do not believe she should be executed. This trial will determine her guilt, and the appropriate punishment. Justice must be fair to all."

This cannot be Kerberos, Aella thought, *he's never been this interested in justice*. But the people of Omatus hung off his every word, and she saw nothing but awe and admiration in their faces. All she could think was that Sithares had corrupted them all.

"I am Queen," Aella said, speaking loud and clear, "your laws don't apply to me. If you insist on holding a trial, I demand it be held in Theara, according to Theara's laws."

Another wave of jeers greeted her words. Kerberos' expression didn't change as his eyes scanned the crowd and Aella herself. She saw the same iron will in his eyes that had always been present.

“You came to Omatus,” he said, “and you attacked the King. You committed an act of treason in my city. There will be no escape from justice.”

More cheers rose from the crowd, and Aella shook her head. No matter what she said, she’d already lost. She just had to hope whatever punishment Kerberos came up with wasn’t too awful. He knew that she would come back if he killed her; but he also already publicly dismissed execution. At this point, he could announce almost any punishment, and simply take her back to the secret room; once imprisoned there, he could do whatever he wanted without anyone in Omatus knowing. *Either way,* she thought, *Kerberos wins.*

Kerberos turned back to the crowd. He looked over all the faces, taking in everything. Aella couldn’t believe no one else saw the endless depths of rage and violence within those eyes. For a long moment, he simply stood and stared at the people in the crowd. He took one last look at Aella, and gave a small, barely visible smile.

“Aella,” he said, “there were countless witnesses to your crimes. We all know you are guilty. All that remains is your punishment.”

The crowd buzzed with excitement. In their faces, Aella saw a thirst for blood she’d only ever seen in Thearans during battle. If it weren’t for Kerberos feigning mercy, today might have been her last.

“As King of Omatus,” Kerberos said, “I sentence you and your warriors to twenty years imprisonment, as well as service in the arena.”

This time, the cheers were deafening. Aella winced at the sheer volume of the crowd as they screamed and chanted Kerberos' name.

"I will not sentence you to death," he continued, "but if you should die in the arena, it will be in the service of Sithares, as all things should be."

Aella felt no fear of dying in the arena; it was unlikely, but even if it happened, at least it would mean she had the chance to fight back. What she did fear was imprisonment; being forced to live in a tiny room, with nothing but daily meals and Kerberos' impassive face staring at her. It was no way to live, least of all for a Queen.

Her warriors faced the same sentence; she had no idea what the conditions of their imprisonment were like, but there was no way Kerberos had enough of those strange rooms to keep all of her army. *They might be able to escape,* she thought, *if their constraints aren't as binding as mine*. It was a slight chance, but a chance nonetheless. Aella had to hope that she could get away somehow.

"I refuse to be kept like some common criminal," she said under her breath, watching the crowd cheering for her punishment, "I will get out, and you, Kerberos-" she shot a look at the giant man, "you will die."

Arthor

1793

News of the invasion reached Arthor a few months after Riffolk and his army left Ermoor. As their battle plan dictated, they were attacking Shanaken first with all of their strength. He knew Riffolk would remain on his warship until victory was assured; one of the key differences between him and Arthor. *And one of the reasons he can't inspire the same loyalty and morale that I do*.

Arthor sat at his desk, the heavy silence settling back in after Riffolk's recorded message stopped playing. A few years ago, the

Prime Overseer developed a method of sending voice recordings over vast distances without any cables. The setup was large, and expensive, but Riffolk had no lack of money. He'd built one for his own house, one for his lab, one for Arthor's office, and one for his warship; now that the war was properly underway, messages came to Arthor's receiver at least once a week. Riffolk never asked him to respond, and gave no orders. He only gave basic information, just what he determined Arthor needed to know.

The months that had passed were uneventful for Arthor; no voice in his head, no orders from Riffolk. His home was empty, his office quiet. Decades of planning had gone into the invasion, and before that, Arthor dedicated his time to training and leading battalions of men. With all of that gone, and the invasion underway without him, Arthor felt directionless for the first time in his life.

Without the voice in his head, Arthor's thoughts slowly settled into a comfortable familiarity. It felt the same way he did when he returned home after being at Shanaken's north shore for months on end. Along with that familiarity came a sick feeling; *how long has it been since I was truly myself?* How many decisions had that voice made for him? Decisions that resulted in dozens of deaths, or hundreds; maybe even thousands.

Where did that voice even come from? He'd always thought it was some part of himself, but in its absence, he finally realised it was nothing like him at all. He'd lost – or given up – so much in his life for the military, and at the time it felt like the right thing to do. For the last twenty years, he'd focused so much on how to take over Pandeia. And, as with his life before that, at the time it felt right. Now, left alone in Ermoor, everything about the war felt horrible. Everything about his entire *life* felt wrong.

I haven't just been manipulated by Riffolk, he thought, *I was controlled by the voice in my head, too. Unless... Riffolk somehow made that voice?* If any man in Ermoor could do that, it was Riffolk. Arthor had no idea anymore. The voice could be anything, or anyone. *Maybe I just went insane.*

He left his office, Riffolk's last message repeating in his mind. *Almost like the voice,* he thought. The night was cloudy and dark, and there were puddles on the stone of the street as he left the building. Once again, as he so often did lately, Arthor headed straight from his office to the Rookfell Pub. Only a few people sat around the room, fat clouds of smoke drifting lazily above them.

Arthor sat at the bar, as he always did. Thaddeus, the bartender, nodded in greeting. He poured Arthor's favourite drink without a word passing between the two men. Arthor was almost finished his first drink before he finally spoke.

"Thaddeus," he said, "have you ever been scared you've made the wrong decisions in life?"

Thaddeus poured a second drink for him, raised his eyebrows, and looked intently at Arthor.

"You alright, Arthor?" he asked, "usually people don't ask questions like that until they've had at least a few more of these."

Thaddeus was perhaps the only person in Ermoor who would have called him by his first name, except for Riffolk. *And Ellie,* he thought, *but that was twenty years ago*.

"I think I am alright," Arthor said, "for the first time in my life, in fact."

Thaddeus whistled, pouring a third drink before Arthor even picked up the second.

"Well, if being Lord Commander is that terrible, I suppose I'm glad I'm just a bartender then."

Arthor laughed, a genuine laugh, for the first time in decades. He finished the second drink in one long gulp, and picked up the third. Thaddeus was good company, and if he hadn't known better, Arthor would have considered him a friend. The thought made him realise he didn't actually have any real friends. *For all the power and authority the Lord Commander wields,* he thought, *I don't have much to show for it*.

Riffolk. Everything came back to him. *He took everything that should have been mine. Everything that being Lord Commander should have meant, Riffolk destroyed.*

"If you're not involved in the mission overseas," Thaddeus said, "does that mean you're, sort of… on vacation?"

"I suppose, yes," Arthor said, "of a sort. Though I have no idea what to do with spare time."

"I'll never understand the problems of Ermoor's elite," Thaddeus said with a theatrical sigh.

"Well, what would you do?"

"I would travel. I've heard great things about Azar, and even better things about Sarnia, even though they're not believers. Since our missionary forces are over there, with any luck they'll be worshipping properly in no time."

"Travel is not the best idea at the moment, Thaddeus."

"Why is that?"

Arthor sighed. The public had no idea what the invasion was really about. As far as they were concerned, Ermoor was simply spreading the word of the one true God through Pandeia. Turning Godless savages into proper civilized people. *I have to be careful.*

"You've never seen Tarsi," he said, "or Shenza, or Thearans. Have you?"

"No, of course not."

"Well, they're called Godless savages for a reason."

Arthor didn't believe that. The Shenza were vicious opponents in battle, but they fought honourably, and they only fought to protect their own land. But, as much as he disagreed with it, some of the Twelve's – and now Riffolk's – lies to the public were necessary.

"Good point," Thaddeus said, "I suppose I'll have to wait until the missions are successful."

Danel

1793

Shortly after the first tree fell, what was left of their initial defenses returned to the city. The Shenza were grim, silent and exhausted. Most were wounded, some badly enough that they wouldn't last another day.

"What's happening?" someone shouted, "how are they doing this?"

A wounded *Kaizeluun* near Danel shook her head in response.

"They have new weapons," she said, "new armour. They're unstoppable now. Shadow Magic does nothing against them."

Her voice was low, quiet; she sounded as though she'd run out of hope, and was merely waiting for the Ermoori to take everything else from her. It was almost as heartbreaking to Danel as the sound of the great tree falling.

"What do we do now?" Danel said.

"There is nothing we can do."

"They're bringing the fight into the forest," another *Kaizeluun* said, "so we use the forest as our battle ground. They have no idea what they're walking into, but we've lived here for thousands of years."

Danel nodded, picturing the Ermoori trying to trudge through the brutal forest floor among predators, venomous insects, and other dangers.

"It's a good plan," he said, "by Amalus, the forest on its own will kill off a lot of them for us."

Laughter rose to meet his words, though it was half-hearted and quiet. *I wouldn't have reacted much either,* he thought, *if someone else spoke*.

"But they can level the forest," the wounded *Kaizeluun* said, "even if it kills some of them first, you haven't seen what they're like now. The forest will slow them down... it won't stop them."

"Then we fight," the first *Kaizeluun* said, "from the trees, from the shadows. We strike quickly and disappear, before they can aim their cannons."

A low cheer rumbled through the crowd, quiet but stronger

than the laughter from before. Danel added his voice too, nodding and trying to hide his panic. Shenza were supposed to be calm, in control at all times. Connected to the forest and to life. Despite being surrounded by his fellow warriors, and by the overflowing life of the forest, he'd never felt less calm in his life.

Gradually, more Shenza appeared from the north shore, each telling stories about the Ermoori pushing further into the forest. When most of the Shenza returned, they finally realised how many had been killed. Danel's vision blurred as the *Kaizeluun* returning reported thousands of deaths.

"I know this doesn't look good," a *Kaizeluun* named Lenai said, "and the Ermoori have never been this successful in their attacks. But I've seen them in the forest. They don't know how to fight among the trees. We have the advantage, and we can turn this around."

Lenai was a legend, almost as well-known as Elana in her day, and Lashek now. By all accounts, she wasn't quite as powerful as Elana, but she'd passed her trials to become *Kaizeluun* with flying colours. If anyone could lead them to victory, it was Lenai.

She split them into groups, and told them her plan. The Ermoori were also split into groups, she said, though they were much larger than hers.

"They can only travel slowly, and they need to fell trees before they can continue on, which slows them down even more. As far as I can tell, they've split into two or three large groups, with indestructible metal vehicles at the centre of each. It's those vehicles which take down our trees. We need a way to stop them, but for now, our best bet is to take out as many of their soldiers as we can."

"But how?" someone said.

"Their armour is strong," Lenai said, "and covers them from foot to head. But there are gaps. Use bows, and aim for the eyes. It won't be easy, but if we use the forest and the Shadows, we can strike quickly and retreat before they see us. Use bird calls as signals, line up as many targets as possible, and strike all at once."

Listening to her speak, Danel felt both dread and a desperate, burning hope in equal measure. Victory looked almost impossible based on what she reported of their strength and power, but her plan was good.

The Shenza who weren't able to use much Shadow Magic, like Danel, would take up ranged attack positions hiding in the trees. *Lucky I'm a good fisher,* he thought, *if I can hit a fish through murky water at dawn, I can hit an Ermoori through the trees*. He was good with a bow, and most other ranged weapons. Now it was time to see exactly how good.

Mattias

1793

Standing on the beach with his unit, firing into the trees, Mattias had felt as safe as he could have mid-battle. Now, he felt more terror than he ever had in his life. The monsters he'd seen in the northern mountains; he knew they were out there right now, possibly hundreds of them. *Not to mention the Shenza*, he thought.

They were in the trees above his unit, appearing like shadows and vanishing in a cloud of black smoke. The tanks did their best, and the soldiers themselves fired in every direction; but the tide was turning already. *I thought we could win this,* he thought, *but if the battle keeps up this way, we're done*. Inside the forest, the Shenza became invisible and a hundred times deadlier.

Mattias ordered his unit to stick together. *Less space between us means less room for those savages to attack.* They crowded together, firing up into the trees and trying to watch every angle of attack.

The bright white corridors outside Tyra flashed into his mind. Suddenly he was watching his men slaughtered in front of him, sliced to pieces in seconds, as he ran the other way. The strobing alarm lights blending with fresh blood on the floor, forming a sickening pink wash over his vision as he bolted for safety. He screamed, firing round after round into the trees, seeing nothing but mottled green leaves.

An arrow exploded through the neck of the man in front of him. Mattias couldn't remember the young man's name, but his desperate eyes met Mattias' as he turned, begging wordlessly for some kind of salvation as he choked and wheezed through his own blood. He grabbed Mattias, falling into him as he clawed at his neck. The man died clutching onto Mattias' armour, his face turning paler by the second until it was almost completely white.

More screams filled the forest, and Mattias dropped the man to keep firing his gun. He saw shadows appear and disappear again before he could aim. In the sunlit beach, they didn't have many places to hide; but in the forest, everything was darker and constantly moving. It was a formless void of chaotic life and danger, and they were now trapped in it. Surrounded by invisible enemies.

The tanks fired continuously, aiming for the tree trunks and any Shenza that appeared in range. Each tank contained not just the main cannon, but two turrets that fired standard handgun rounds, at a much faster rate than the guns Mattias and his unit carried. The turrets would do no damage to the massive trees, but against Shenza they were brutally effective. *When they actually hit one,* Mattias thought.

One of the unit Captains nearby shouted an order, and Mattias almost laughed out loud. *Of course,* he thought.

"Yes," Mattias said to his own men, "group two, guns down. Start using the nets!"

Prime Overseer Hayne had provided the Ermoori army with many different weapons and equipment. Among them was an electrified net launcher. There were also proximity-triggered explosives that could be shot from the same launcher.

"Groups three and four," he said, "explosives, up into the trees."

Each unit contained five groups; ten men per group. He gave the orders almost without thinking. *Maybe I am a good leader after all,* he thought as his men reacted instantly. Dull thumping filled his ears as the launchers went off around him. For a few moments, nothing happened. Then half a dozen explosions rocked the treetops above them, and the brief screams of the Shenza were cut short as they were torn to pieces. His men cheered.

"More explosives," Mattias ordered, "create a perimeter

around us. Make them hurt if they come within a hundred yards."

They cheered again, and fired their launchers at every tree trunk and branch in range. A few more explosions echoed from above them, before a tense stillness settled over the forest. *They've realised the explosives are traps*, he thought, *hopefully the anti-tampering technology Overseer Hayne promised works*. He had no reason to doubt the Prime Overseer, but the Shenza were cunning in their own way.

Who knows what they can do, he thought, *with those black swords? Not to mention their magic*. No other Ermoori would have admitted it, but the Shenza *had* to be using magic. They appeared and disappeared in flashes of smoke; *what else could possibly allow them to do that?*

Still, the Prime Overseer promised them his technology would work against the savages, and he was never wrong. All they could do was fight for Ermoor, and pray to God that Overseer Hayne's weapons didn't fail them. In tense silence, Mattias and his men waited for the next attack.

Aella

1793

After the public trial, Aella's thoughts refused to settle. *He's playing some trick,* she thought, *he has to be. Manipulating everyone. He was a monster, there is no way he changed this much.* Though her memories weren't always reliable, the vision of Kerberos killing Athanasius would never leave her. The burning farmland he left in his wake on his way to Omatus still plagued her as well. *That's Kerberos,* she thought, *not this imposter.*

But all the people of Omatus had cheered for him; he had their full support. None of them looked like prisoners, or victims of tyranny. They were healthy, happy, and the city itself was not only clean but beautiful. For so long, Aella held an image of Kerberos' hateful actions in her head like a bonfire, keeping her rage alight and pushing her towards his well-deserved death.

Except, she thought, *maybe he is exactly who he says he is.* It was possible that Kerberos really did love Omatus as much as he said he did. His actions were horrifying, regardless of the outcome; Aella was still intent on killing him. But he was truly loved by the Omati, and there would be no justice for him here. *They only see what he has done for them, not what he did to all those before.*

A long time had passed since Kerberos took the throne. More importantly, Sithares abandoned him during that time in favour of Aella. *Maybe without Sithares' influence,* she thought, *he shed some of the brutality he used to have.* The thought didn't bring her any comfort; exactly the opposite, in fact. *Sithares is in my head now. What if I turn into what Kerberos was?* She didn't feel like that could happen, but Sithares was a God, and there was no way of knowing the plans of the Gods.

The door into her strange little prison opened, and Kerberos emerged. He stood in front of her for a long moment, simply staring at her. She was still manacled in the black magic he created, unable to move except to stand and take small steps.

"I want you to know that I do not intend to kill you unfairly," Kerberos said, "there is no trickery here. The sentence was honest, and if you win in the arena, you will keep your life."

"But I will remain imprisoned?"

"Yes. You attempted to assassinate a King. Be grateful you were not already executed."

So that's his plan, she thought, *he won't kill me outright, but he won't let me go until I die in the arena anyway.* So much for no trickery. To the public, it would seem like she was simply one of the other arena warriors, fighting for the glory of their King and their God. It would be seen as a good thing, and Kerberos would be seen as merciful towards his would-be assassin.

"Forgive me for not feeling too grateful," Aella said, "it's not like you've given me any chance at freedom."

"Omatus has become a civilised city," Kerberos said, "it is far greater than it used to be, in every way. It can only thrive as it does if the law is upheld fairly. I show mercy at every opportunity, but some crimes cannot be forgiven."

They stared at each other, neither willing to concede their point. Kerberos smiled, though there was a lethal edge underneath it. He returned to the door, and glanced back at her.

"Your first battles will be held tomorrow," he said, "I am looking forward to it."

Despite the cold black metal holding her in place, Aella had slept well that night. *Perhaps I'm getting used to it,* she thought, and then shuddered. Kerberos took her from the small room and led her through countless hallways once again, with the same hood over her head to stop her seeing the way.

Eventually, the sound of a massive crowd echoed through the stone hallway, quiet at first but growing until it was deafening. Kerberos took her hood off and the metal holding her still swept off her body at the same time. In front of her, a cage door separated her from the arena beyond. Thousands upon thousands of Omati screamed and roared in the sunlight, ready to watch her die.

"I don't suppose I'm fighting you?" Aella said, unable to stop the sharp rage she felt escaping with her words.

"No," Kerberos replied, "not today."

"Who am I to fight, then?"

"You will see."

A cold wave swept through her stomach, deepening as the crowd screamed louder.

"It seems your opponents have arrived."

"Will I at least have weapons?" Aella said.

"They are out there now. Be quick, or your opponents will gather them all."

The cage door opened, and Aella strode out into the arena. Her swords stuck out of the sand ahead, close to the centre. She sprinted towards them, and then saw her opponents on the opposite side. A group of about two dozen of her own warriors. Her heart fell, dropping to the bottom of a deep pit that opened in her stomach. *He is evil after all,* Aella thought, *forcing me to kill my own people.*

She reached her swords, picking them up and holding them loosely as she stood facing her warriors. Refusing to take a combat stance, she simply looked at them as they approached. They looked wary, as though they believed she would fight them as easily as she would their enemies. But as much as she encouraged combat in Theara, she never would have slaughtered more than twenty warriors in one go. *Surely, they know this is Kerberos,* she thought, *and not my doing.*

But no matter what they thought, there was no way around it; either she would die, or they would. Kerberos' royal guards surrounded the arena, outnumbering Aella and her warriors twenty to one.

"I didn't want this," she said to them, "but we don't have a choice."

Several of them nodded, sympathy and injustice glowing from their eyes. The rest continued to fix her with wary stares, weapons ready. The heat coming off the sand in waves filled her with energy, and the sun shone down on her in full glory, directly above. If there was ever a situation in which she could have killed Kerberos fairly, this was it. But of course, he knew that too, and he would never face her in a fair fight.

Sighing, Aella finally settled into a ready stance. Her warriors approached slowly; every one of them had seen her fight. They knew they were walking towards their own deaths, but they approached anyway, and did it together as a team. Aella felt a swell of fierce pride, quickly swallowed by fury and grief. *If they'd been with me when I reached the throne room,* she thought, *most of them would have survived, and Kerberos would be dead.*

Aella glanced up at the King's seat; a large balcony set halfway up the tiers of the arena with its own throne positioned in the middle overlooking the combat. Kerberos was already there, staring down at her with satisfaction. Her rage boiled over, erupting as Fire swept over her entire body.

As the Fire overtook her, her warriors became unknown enemies, simply targets to destroy. Relief flooded her along with strength and power, and she settled into the joy of combat. She heard nothing but the screams of the crowd and the screams of her enemies as they fell. She saw nothing but fire and blood. She felt nothing but joy and power; and, distantly, Sithares laughing in the back of her mind.

Danel

1793

Danel perched on a branch in the pitch black, staring hard into the mottled darkness. He could see at least three Ermoori, though he wished for the magic of the *Kaizeluun*; they could see in the dark as well as he saw in broad daylight. Danel's group were in position, waiting on Lenai to give her signal. He had to keep distance from the Ermoori, though it made them harder to hit; they'd somehow set up invisible traps in the treetops that exploded when a Shenza came too close. Even *Kaizeluun* couldn't see the traps.

His bow balanced perfectly in his hands; an arrow already

nocked. He'd picked his target, and though the Ermoori armour was now impenetrable, there were gaps and weak spots. *Smaller than a fish,* he thought, *but still a target I can hit*. He would have preferred to attack during the day, but they were staggering their attack times and positions randomly, and Lenai had insisted on the dead of night for this attack.

A bird called somewhere in the trees, and almost immediately after that a slightly different bird call rang out; *the signal*. Danel drew his hand back, pulling the arrow string tight. He took aim, for the thin strip of pale skin between neck armour and helmet. *Five seconds after the signal, we strike together,* Lenai had said. Danel counted, then loosed his arrow and drew another without checking his kill.

Screams rang out in the ugly language of the Ermoori, and chaos erupted through the forest. Their powerful weapons flashed and boomed, sweeping the trees with waves of deadly metal faster than even the *Kaizeluun* could see. The Ermoori screamed and shouted at one another, giving orders and relaying information.

Danel fired arrow after arrow into the soldiers below him, killing at least two before their weapons began aiming in his direction. He dove behind the trunk of the tree he was in, flinching as the metal projectiles aimed at him thudded into the branch he stood on seconds before.

He saw his fellow Shenza fall too, but they were holding their own against the Ermoori far better than he'd first thought. *Those vehicles really are invincible though,* he thought, *there's nothing we could throw at them that will do any damage.*

As soon as the tide turned, the Shenza bolted. Danel leapt from one tree to another, keeping a tree trunk between him and the Ermoori at all times. Usually, the Shenza fought until the last warrior; but Lenai had specifically told them to leave after their attacks lost momentum and the Ermoori began fighting back.

The Ermoori were getting closer to the northern hub; it didn't take Danel long to get back to their meeting point. Lenai arrived last, breathing heavy and looking exhausted. For a long moment, they sat together on the platform facing the northern shore. Their numbers were diminishing.

"They've taken some losses," Lenai said, "but we need a way to destroy those metal vehicles, or we'll never win."

"We're taking far more losses than them," someone said, "and they're still coming. How can we possibly win?"

"Has anyone noticed any weaknesses in those vehicles?"

"There are none. They can level our trees, move over the forest floor, kill hundreds of Shenza, and can't be stopped."

"What if we get one of them to fire their cannons at another?" Danel said, "our weapons do nothing, but what if their own can pierce that armour?"

Lenai looked at him, a vicious smile spreading over her face. Murmuring started up among the Shenza around him, and all at once a new sense of purpose filled their eyes.

"It's not going to be easy," Lenai said, "but I think we can do it."

They spent a little while deciding on a plan of attack, but couldn't find one that didn't put them in a huge amount of danger. At the end of the day, the only way they could get a tank to aim at another tank was by using themselves as bait. They would have to kill off as many soldiers as possible so that the target wouldn't take fire from anything other than a vehicle.

There's almost no chance this actually works, Danel thought, *but we have to at least try, or the Ermoori will destroy the entire forest.* The battle was already getting away from them; now they had a mission that could win or lose it in one go. *Even if it works,* he thought, *we have to repeat it for every vehicle.*

It was Danel's idea. The enormity of the risk pressed down on him, forcing the air from his lungs as he watched Lenai give instructions. *If this fails,* he thought, *it will be my fault.*

"Okay," Lenai said, "are we all ready?"

A low chatter filled the forest air as the Shenza agreed. They split into their groups and stood ready, staring at Lenai as she waited for the moment. Finally, she breathed in deeply, cast her eyes over the warriors in front of her, and gave the order.

"Let's go."

Mattias

1793

They travelled deeper into the forest, at an excruciatingly slow pace. The Shenza remained out of range, and out of sight; but their attacks decreased as well. Mattias hoped that the threat of explosives would keep them at bay long enough for morale to rise again.

Above and around them, the forest loomed close, as if it would attack them itself. Though the Shenza attacked less often since the explosions, Mattias still found himself trying to look in every direction at once. Even without the immediate threat of Shenza attacks,

Shanaken was a terrifying place to be.

Animals could be heard, and insects, every moment of every day. Rain came and went at more or less the same frequency it did in Ermoor, but there was much more of it each time. Mattias and his men became used to the constant damp, and the constant noise.

Whenever an attack did come, his men reacted instantly, and they were able to fight off the Shenza quickly most times. They only did so by remaining ready at all times; even at night, most of them either couldn't or wouldn't sleep. Occasionally, an explosion shattered the darkness and relative quiet of the forest as another Shenza found one of their traps. Other times, gunshots roared suddenly to life near Mattias as a soldier spotted one of them in the trees. A few times a day, Mattias whispered orders to his men to fire randomly into the trees; it would keep the Shenza alert and fearful.

Days passed, and eventually the passage of time felt blurred and surreal. They ate when they could, and rested when they could; but every other waking moment was spent holding their weapons, staring up into the trees. Every shadow could have been the enemy, every slight movement the precursor to another attack.

Though Mattias prayed that he would never see them again, one of the monsters attacked his unit. He wasn't sure how long they'd been there, but as far as he could tell it was several weeks in. It came without warning, and faster than he could have imagined. They were digging trenches, building a better defence and a place to sleep, when it struck.

Mattias wasn't aware of what happened at first; a grunt and a thud came from somewhere near him. He snapped into combat stance immediately, but couldn't find the source. Then somewhere beyond the trees, still too close for comfort, a scream split the forest's ambient noise in two. Mattias recognised the voice; it was one of his men.

"Oh God!" the man screamed, "oh God no, ple-"

His screaming cut off as suddenly as it began, and Mattias and his men stood in silence, their guns pointed at where the noises had come from. Almost a minute later, a giant monster emerged silently from the leaves, a stomach-churning look of rage in its eyes.

"Fire!" Mattias shouted.

Gunfire exploded all around him. The monster was hit dozens of times in seconds. For a moment, it looked as though it would leap at them, tear them all to shreds before they could kill it.

It did leap, letting out a deafening roar as it did; but the sheer wave of Ermoori gunfire was simply too much. Mattias knew they had been killed before, with the help of a squad of highly-trained, elite soldiers. He knew it was possible, albeit incredibly difficult. But numbers counted for a lot against such beasts, and it died before it reached them. Prime Overseer Hayne had improved the power and accuracy of Ermoori weapons tenfold, and Mattias felt a stab of victory as he stared at the dead predator.

Morale grew considerably after that; an uneasy cheer even went up through the unit. But Mattias wasn't satisfied. *I'm losing men fast,* he thought, *we need to win this war soon.*

They dug trenches alongside the tank as it moved slowly, caving it in behind them as they went so the Shenza couldn't surprise them from underneath or behind. It was hard work, and they had to remain ready for an attack at all times even while digging.

Since they killed the monster, no more attacked them. The Shenza still appeared, and fought viciously, but the monsters seemed to have given up. *At least, for now,* Mattias thought to himself, *I won't believe we're really free of them.* Every now and then, Mattias heard a low growl from somewhere deep in the forest.

His unit were working on the trench when another attack came. This time, one of his men screamed while they were still in view. The men reacted without hesitation, laying cover fire into the trees in every direction until they could locate the attackers.

Mattias looked for the soldier who was screaming; he lay on the forest floor, holding his leg with one hand and flailing to crawl away with the other. Mattias ran to the young man, intending to drag him into the trench to get him away from the Shenza. He grabbed the soldier and pulled; but he was stuck.

"It's..." the man gasped, "it's not the Shenza, sir. This thing grabbed me."

He looked closer, and finally saw it; a thick vine was wrapped around the soldier's leg, squeezing and pulsing as the young man screamed again. His leg snapped, twisting to an angle that made Mattias' stomach rise into his chest, hot and painful. Desperate, Mattias aimed his gun at the vine and fired. It blew apart in chunks of viscous green and red, and Mattias dragged the soldier as quickly as he could into the trench.

"Stand down," Mattias said to the rest of the unit, "there are no Shenza."

The soldier, whose name was Tobias, breathed in ragged gasps. His eyes were screwed shut, his teeth gritted, and sweat poured from his pale skin in waves. Mattias held his hand.

"Tobias," he said, "you'll be alright."

The young man didn't react; just kept breathing raggedly with his eyes shut tight.

"You'll be okay, I promise," he repeated.

Mattias looked closer at Tobias' leg; the vine was still wrapped around it. He pulled it off, having to tug with far more strength than he predicted, and Tobias screamed again. Once it was off him, the vine curled into a tight ball, still pulsing with inhuman strength.

"Damn this forest," Mattias said, "damn it to hell."

Tobias died the next day. His skin had gone so pale by then that he almost seemed to glow whenever snatches of sunlight hit his skin. They buried him in the trench when they moved on, taking his rations, ammunition and weapons and shoving dirt over him in their wake.

A little while later, another soldier screamed as they walked, and Mattias turned to see him clawing desperately at his own face. The man dropped to his knees, his screams turning more and more feral as his skin turned a sickening, mottled purple. Again, there were no Shenza attacking; instead, Mattias saw a brightly-coloured plant hanging at roughly head-height near where the soldier had collapsed.

The plant's flowers were spined, and were so violent-looking that they almost resembled ornate weapons. One of the spines protruded from the soldier's face, a network of black and purple veins spreading from the point where it buried in his skin. By the time Mattias noticed, the soldier's screams had lapsed into silence, and the man was dead.

Danel

1793

Each large group of Ermoori contained several of the powerful vehicles they used to fell trees. They moved side by side, with soldiers walking alongside and behind each. Danel waited in position above one of the vehicles, listening out for the telltale thump of the Ermoori explosive traps. Though they were almost impossible to see until it was too late, the Shenza realised they were shot from the ground and made an unmistakable—albeit quiet—sound when they hit the trees and branches.

The Ermoori had figured out early on that firing their traps all throughout the trees stopped Shenza from being able to attack easily. Their tactics were evolving by the day, and their technology was beyond what Shadow Magic and Shenza weaponry could counter. It was a nightmare.

Danel was tasked with taking out as many Ermoori as he could, while Lenai brought attention from one of the vehicles to herself. She would try to draw its cannon fire, then subtly put herself between two of them. After that, all they could do was hope for the best. He had faith in Lenai's abilities, of course; she was *Kaizeluun*, and a legend in her own right. But the plan was clumsy at best, and relied on the Ermoori firing blindly at whatever target they could find without thinking about what might lay behind it.

It's not completely out of the question, he thought, *but they'd have to be pretty stupid to fall for it*. Either that, or have absolutely no compassion for their own troops and vehicles. Danel had heard of the Ermoori cannons on the north shore firing indiscriminately into the battle, taking out their own men as much as their enemies. It was part of what inspired his idea. But now that they were positioned and ready for the plan, he was doubting its success.

Lenai was close to one of the vehicles now, he knew she was. He couldn't see her, but they all knew the plan. They waited for her signal, Danel holding his bow ready. The Ermoori were always on alert now, but they had no idea an attack was coming. *If this works,* he thought, *we can try to destroy all the other vehicles they have. It'll give us the advantage we need to win.*

He waited, holding his breath without realising. Lenai finally gave the signal, and he shot for his first target. A strangled scream rose from the soldier, but Danel moved on. There was no time to double check everything, and a wounded soldier would be just as bad for the Ermoori as a dead one. *It might even slow others down,* he thought, *if they try to save them.* Danel took no joy in killing, just like all the Shenza. But it had to be done.

Most of his arrows simply bounced off their armour, and several hit non-lethal points; but he took out as many as he could, and wounded some too. Their armour was almost impenetrable; there were barely even any seams or gaps. He aimed for the neck as much as he could, but even then, the gap between the helmet and armour was all but invisible.

Shenza screams and Ermoori screams melded with the explosions of Ermoori cannon fire. Lenai appeared right in front of a vehicle, and leapt aside just as its cannon fired. She stayed close to its line of fire, swaying and diving to avoid the smaller guns as the cannon swiveled to aim at her.

Danel watched, enrapt as Lenai moved like a liquid shadow among the Ermoori. One of them, standing behind a tree nearby, took aim for her. Danel drew and loosed his arrow first, and it bounced off the soldier's helmet, shoving his head into the tree with enough force to knock him out. His heart raced as Lenai came close to being hit dozens of times within seconds of appearing. *She can't avoid being hit for long,* he thought, *even with most of the soldiers distracted and some wounded, those vehicles are doing more damage than any soldier could.*

Travelling slowly to a point between two of the vehicles, Lenai danced and spun. Danel tried to keep doing his job, but her movement was hypnotic, and the sheer danger of her mission squeezed the breath from his lungs. She reached the point she was supposed to, and the vehicle aiming for her fired its cannon. The deadly projectile flew past her, slamming into the vehicle behind her and exploding in a massive cloud of fire and smoke.

The Shenza cheered, but their victory calls died on their lips as the smoke cleared. Danel stared at the second vehicle, frowning as he examined its armour; *not a scratch,* he thought, *how is that possible?* Lenai turned as she heard the Shenza stop celebrating. She saw what Danel had seen, and her face fell in defeat.

Now behind her, the vehicle fired another cannon round directly at Lenai. From the waist up, the legendary *Kaizeluun* exploded into a mist of vaporised meat and bone. Her legs fell gracelessly to the forest floor, twitching and pooling blood onto the decaying leaves. Silence followed the attack, and Danel knew the Shenza were disappearing back into the forest. He followed suit, trying not to picture Lenai's death as he ran back to the city. *That's it,* he thought, *they can't be stopped. That was our last chance.*

Mattias

1793

How long has it been? Mattias thought, hunched down in one of the trenches they'd dug out for themselves. *Certainly, longer than weeks. Months?* It was hard to say. This deep in the forest, time seemed to move differently. They could never completely see the sun, and Shenza attacks came at random intervals. Besides, their trenches were covered over with makeshift camouflaged panels that emulated the forest floor. They spent most of their time in complete darkness, waiting for another attack.

As well as random attacks from the Shenza, the massive

predators had begun attacking again. So far, Mattias' unit killed five of the monsters. In return, only four of his men had been killed. *Thank the Prime Overseer*, Mattias thought, *his weapons are the reason we're alive*.

Two of his men sat next to him; Ernest Hammerman and Gabriel Wyndham. They were much younger than him, but even just the time they'd been in Shanaken had aged them considerably. *This is a whole new kind of war,* he thought, *deep in enemy territory, with no end in sight*. Previously, when the Ermoori reached a point of defeat, they merely bailed from the northern shore in a blaze of cannon fire and explosions. Now, there was nothing they could do but keep fighting.

"How long since the last attack?" Ernest whispered.

"Who can say?" Mattias said, "it feels like a day or so to me."

"I think it's only been about ten hours," Gabriel said, "we've had two meals since then."

Mattias shook his head. He couldn't remember the last meal they'd had, let alone how many there were since the last Shenza attack. But Gabriel was always observant. Mattias had no idea how he kept facts like that straight in his head, with a war raging all around them.

"Even if it's ten hours," Mattias said, "so what? They're not attacking at regular intervals anyway."

"There has to be a pattern."

"Why? The lack of a pattern helps them keep us off guard. If we can anticipate their movements, we can counter."

His men went quiet. They'd all learned a lot in the last few months, or however long it had been. Especially Mattias. He wouldn't have recognised the man he used to be. He'd never spoken to soldiers who returned from the northern shore before, except briefly to the Lord Commander; but having gone through it himself, he finally understood war. *It's nothing like the teleradios in Ermoor say,* he thought, *that's all just meaningless words. They make it sound like a great adventure, like killing Shenza is a game*.

They had portable teleradios now, though they were reserved for commanders. The handheld devices provided a direct link to Overseer Elmstone; the Overseer of the Shanaken exploratory force. Mattias had overheard his Commander, a man called Rewyn Liford, conversing with the Overseer. It sounded as though Overseer Elmstone didn't care about any casualties they suffered, as long as they finally took Shanaken. Though he wasn't completely shocked, Mattias was disappointed.

Ermoor is so perfect, he thought, *so beautiful. Why do we need Shanaken too? The Shenza have proven they will never see the light and worship the one true God. Why don't we just leave them to their wild jungle and live in our beautiful city?* He understood wanting to bring civil society to a country of savages, and teaching God's way to the rest of Pandeia to save their souls; but the war on Shanaken didn't feel like that sort of mission any more.

"Want to take bets on when the next attack will be?" Ernest said.

"Three hours," Mattias said.

"Within the next hour," Gabriel said at the same time.

"Who's timing? Do we even have any working time pieces?"

"I'll keep count," Gabriel said.

"Martin," Ernest said, "are you in?"

"Put me down for five hours," Martin said.

Now we just need to wait, he thought, *the worst part of that game is it doesn't distract from the waiting.* The units had become closer than families, and games to pass the time were common in the trenches. Mattias didn't own any dice, but they were passed around the units sometimes.

"Anyone have any dice?" he said to his unit.

"Amon took them a few hours ago," Gabriel said, "group three have them I think."

"We really need more dice. Can someone tell the Commander to make sure they send a bunch of dice in the next supplies shipment?"

The second wave of troops had arrived recently, along with a shipment of ammunition and rations. Supply shipments were supposed to be coming regularly, and rumours consistently spread about the kinds of supplies that might be included. Games, women, bigger guns, more tanks; speculation never ceased. So far, the only supplies they'd received came with the second wave of soldiers, and there was no actual confirmed supply shipment coming. *But hope and talk are keeping these men going,* Mattias thought, *and me too.*

While the first wave of troops dug in and held the ground

they'd gained, the second wave were pushing further into the forest. *Poor men,* he thought, *they're the ones getting killed now.* The Shenza attacked his unit every now and then, but their tamper-proof explosives and impervious tanks meant that their casualties had more or less stopped. Being hidden away in their underground trenches kept them out of range of the Shenza's deadly throwing weapons and arrows too.

"Would Commander Liford even listen to a request for dice?" Ernest said, "he doesn't strike me as the type of man who'd put up with his soldiers playing games."

"We're fighting a war for them," Martin said, "the least they can do is give us some dice."

An explosion shattered the relative silence above them, and all at once chaos descended upon them again.

"Damn," Mattias said, "Gabriel's got it. Within the hour. Weapons ready boys, let's go kill some shadows."

The tanks began firing immediately, and Mattias led his men to one of the hatches that opened out into the forest. They waited for an opening, listening for the Shenza leaping and running over the forest floor. The hatch above him thudded a few times, then went still.

"Go, go," Mattias said, "up and out!"

They sprinted up into the forest, casting their eyes everywhere. Mattias glanced at the tanks first; the gunners inside watched the forest constantly, and when they fired it was usually accurate. He followed the angle of a turret, and found a small group of Shenza pinned down by its fire.

"There," he said to his unit, "a group of them, fire!"

His men turned to the small group of Shenza, and opened fire without hesitation. Pinned down by the tank, with nowhere to go, they were cut down by Mattias' men in seconds. The Shenza usually attacked in groups of a dozen or less, and they'd just taken out four in one go. The rest were picked off by the explosive traps they'd left, and by the tanks, and suddenly the attack was over again.

Mattias heard the familiar static of a teleradio connection coming from the nearest tank; it had been a while since they heard word from the Overseer. He waited, ordering his men to keep watch around the forest. Finally, as he knew would happen, the tank hatch opened and the tank Commander emerged.

"We've received word that the canopy city has finally been abandoned by the Shenza," he said, "orders are to push ahead and weed out the last pockets of resistance."

Danel

1793

It's time, The *Duulshen* had said, *time to abandon the fight. Disappear into the forests. We will move to a place on the Eternal Mountain, where even the Ermoori cannot reach us. Those who wish can follow. The rest of you must escape to Tarsium.* In any other situation, the announcement from the *Duulshen* would have been met with outrage and arguments. But the Shenza had seen their enemy. They knew there was no hope. It would take a while, but their escape plan was the only way the Shenza could survive.

Small groups of Shenza Danel didn't know decided to stay in

the forests; they would fight to their last breath, causing trouble and giving the appearance that the Shenza weren't gone. Danel couldn't believe their bravery; they knew their actions would lead to death, and they knew they couldn't possibly win. But still they fought, to give everyone else the chance to escape.

Eyes downcast, silent and exhausted, the Shenza evacuated their home for the first time in living memory. They each took as much food as they could carry, as well as potions and a store of the amassed wealth of Shanaken. The *Duulshen* controlled all of the resources of their people, and shared them equally among those in need.

The first two hubs were already abandoned, the Shenza moving all their resources to the southernmost hub. From there, they could move to the southwest shore and then to Tarsium. Many followed the Duulshen to the Eternal Mountain. Danel hoped they were safe from the Ermoori. He decided to go to Tarsium, but there were hundreds, if not thousands, of Shenza trying to do the same. At best, it would take months to transport everyone.

Danel took a pouch of coin, a bag of food, a few potions, and restocked his quiver with arrows. Then he joined the crowd heading for the south west shore; the port between Shanaken and Tarsium, where all of their trading was done. *If the Ermoori really wanted to destroy us,* he thought, *they would have hit the southwest shore*. The second he thought it, he prayed to Amalus they wouldn't find Ermoori waiting for them when they arrived.

Let us get to Tarsium in safety, he prayed, *let no more of our people die*. He didn't dare hope the prayer would be fulfilled; *the way things are going, hoping for the best is just naive*. Danel would usually have thought of himself as optimistic; but his ability to see a bright future had been as utterly destroyed by the Ermoori as Lenai was.

Distant explosions echoed through the forest as they made for safety, broken occasionally by the crash and rumble of another falling tree. *How far have they come now?* He thought, *have they reached the city? Are they destroying it too?* He couldn't fully comprehend the depth of grief filling his heart at that moment. *And rage*. The Ermoori had been trying to take their forest for thousands of years; *and for what? To build another lifeless city? Fill it with empty people who don't care about life or nature?* There was no sense to any of it.

They kept a fast pace through the forest, running over branches and leaping between the trees. It would take a while for them to get to the southwest coast, but the Ermoori moved far slower. *They may take the forest,* he thought, *but they'll never catch us now*.

"I can't believe this is happening," a Shenza said next to him, "how could they do this?"

"They built weapons that can tear the forest apart," Danel said, panting as they ran, "I think they've been planning this for a long time."

"Will we ever get the forest back?"

Danel tried to think of some way it was possible. *Surely there's something the Duulshen can do, from their place in the Eternal Mountain,* he thought. But as hard as he tried to think of something, anything, that could help, nothing at all came to mind.

"I don't know," he said.

Riffolk

1793

The attack on Shanaken was progressing much as Riffolk predicted. He stayed on his warship, continuing research and design work while his soldiers took the forest. His research now focused on magic; the work he'd done on weapons and armour had gone as far as he needed it to, and now he wanted to understand magic fully.

In the years between first gaining Shadow Magic and launching the invasion, Riffolk had sent several more teams to retrieve the books; they never returned. But now that his army was at its peak, no one could stop him from taking what he wanted. He would find the books, and read them. It wouldn't matter if Kerberos already possessed every type of magic; Riffolk would too, and he would build even more weapons using the new magic for his army to wield.

When Riffolk owned the world, there would be nothing to stop him pursuing the knowledge he craved. Magic-imbued places and artefacts in each country would be available to him for study and experimentation at no cost other than the war.

He planned to install Governors to administrate each city, and an Overseer for each country. With the day-to-day running of Pandeia left to trusted officials, Riffolk could focus entirely on science. The world thought his current technology was incredible; but they still had no idea what Riffolk was really capable of. Even Riffolk himself wasn't entirely sure what the limits were; magic was a far more complex topic than he first realised all those years ago.

Riffolk's research so far was already beyond his expectations. The more he discovered about magic, the more he needed to learn. Most of the texts on magic were kept by the Tarsi; one of the only publicly known facts about them was their incredible knowledge of history. After the war he'd have access to their knowledge, but until then all he could do was source ancient texts from other places. He still discovered much more than he'd expected.

One discovery stood out far above the rest; it was possible, though the specifics still eluded him, to become immortal. The best he could do was a reference to the possibility upon possessing all five types of magic. There were also ancient spells, but they involved making deals with the Gods, and Riffolk wouldn't have trusted a God to simply hand over that much power to a human.

His research showed that other than specific spells, and the selection of what they called 'Heroes', the Gods actually had no choice in who obtained magic. Reciting the prayer gave anyone magic, and the Gods could do nothing to stop it happening. In fact, the Gods were merely sentient manifestations of natural, elemental forces. Beyond that, they were nothing.

Every day, as well as his research, Riffolk received reports of the war effort. He gave orders to his troops, and sent his own reports back to Arthor in Ermoor, via the long-range teleradio installed in his warship.

Once Shanaken was his, Riffolk planned to join his soldiers on the battlefield in Tarsium. For one thing, he wanted the book that he knew was kept somewhere under the ground. But as well as that, Riffolk suspected that Mara was in hiding somewhere in Tarsium, and he wanted to find her himself.

Arthor had been of the opinion that Riffolk staying on his warship during the invasion of Shanaken was a grievous mistake. He'd said it would lower morale among the troops, and create a disconnect between Riffolk and his men, damaging the chain of command. The man was a good Commander, and he had a point; but Riffolk's authority wasn't that fragile. His men would have followed him even if he'd stayed in Ermoor and sent orders from his lab.

Though Riffolk kept the Lord Commander updated, Arthor barely sent him any messages in return. It was clear the Lord Commander despised Riffolk. *Let him stew in his own hatred for a while,* Riffolk thought, *by the time the war is won, he'll have no reason to be so bitter*. Riffolk planned on appointing Arthor as the Overseer of Ermoor, after all; for all his resentment, the Lord Commander was unwaveringly loyal to Ermoor.

In the years before the invasion, Riffolk adapted the technology he used to create the Detector to create a second design; instead of detecting any strong sources of magic, it tracked specific pieces of technology Riffolk built. Each piece was attached to the armour of his Captains and Commanders; with them in place, Riffolk could track the movements of his entire army across the map on the device's screen.

The teleradio system he built for his army was more complex than the one in Ermoor too. There were multiple two-way channels, that connected Riffolk with different ranks. By switching channels, he could speak with the Captains, or the Commanders; by adjusting the device further, he could isolate specific soldiers to speak with just one person at a time. He rarely spoke with the Captains or individual soldiers, of course; but the option was there.

It was the most efficient strategic network that had ever been created. From the other side of the world, Riffolk could see and interact with his entire army. He knew everything that happened on the battlefield within seconds of it happening. Facing any other army in Pandeia, Riffolk had the advantage.

He watched his army progress through the forests. There was no way to track the enemy, or Riffolk would have done it. But seeing his own men was enough. He spoke with them, strategising as they reported their surroundings.

Despite their impenetrable armour and powerful weapons, many of his soldiers died in the forests. Riffolk was surprised to learn that a lot of the men who died weren't even killed by Shenza; the forest itself was deadlier than he ever gave it credit for. Not just predators, but deadly species of plants as well.

Though Riffolk had tried, there was no way to make the armour flexible; in between the indestructible plates was fabric, and though it was strong, it was an unavoidable weakness. He had no doubt that on open ground, where his men could maintain formation, they would suffer far fewer casualties. But the forest was its own opponent. If taking it down meant he lost a few hundred soldiers, it was a price Riffolk was more than willing to pay.

Arthor

1793

Almost a year after the invasion began, the alarm on Arthor's message receiver went off. Riffolk's cold, calm voice drifted from the machine as Arthor leaned against its console.

"Lord Commander," he said, "I am pleased to announce that Shanaken has been taken. As we agreed, I will leave a battalion here to retain control, and the rest of our forces will move on to Tarsium."

Things are moving faster than I thought, Arthor mused, *Riffolk is better at motivating the men than I gave him credit for*. A part of him couldn't help but feel outraged that Shanaken fell without him leading Ermoor's forces. *I've spent most of my life serving Ermoor's military, and our greatest victory was achieved without me.*

"I will send another message after this," Riffolk continued, "to be relayed through the teleradio to all of Ermoor. I will send it to my own receiver, it connects directly to the national teleradio system. Ask my servants to let you in to my lab."

No doubt Riffolk's message to the public will be nothing but lies, Arthor thought, *but at least it's still something positive... isn't it?* He'd been looking forward to it for so long, but without the voice or Riffolk here, and without being actively involved, Arthor was beginning to doubt everything. *Do we even need the rest of Pandeia?* Ermoor was a beautiful city, clean and advanced. Despite Riffolk, despite the voice in his head, and even despite losing Ellie all those years ago, Arthor was grateful to live in Ermoor. Now that he'd had time to really think, expanding their empire felt entirely unnecessary.

It's all just power, he thought, *and ego*. Riffolk wanted the world, and he would take it. Their expansion had nothing to do with God, or with sharing knowledge and civilisation. *I just hope the other countries are improved by Ermoor's influence*.

Arthor left his office, calling for a cart as it approached. It was another rainy day, and he had no desire to walk through the rain to Riffolk's estate. He wasn't looking forward to being at Riffolk's house again; Arthor had always been uncomfortable with the idea of servants, and didn't keep any of his own.

The cart pulled up at Riffolk's main gate. Arthor was waved through as the gate opened; Riffolk's staff knew him well. He followed the head of staff of Riffolk's servants, Lucius Scarborough, to another cart; Riffolk's lab wasn't on the same property as his mansion. The scientists working at his lab let no one in but their own, unless authorised by Lucius or Riffolk himself.

"Lord Commander," Lucius said, his voice clipped and proper as usual, "I trust your day is pleasant?"

"As pleasant as it can be, Mr. Scarborough."

"Lucius is fine, Lord Commander. No need for formality with a mere servant."

Arthor had never heard such words spoken in such an arrogant tone. Lucius had a knack for exuding an unwavering self-importance despite his standing. As much as Arthor disagreed with the concept of servants, Lucius' attitude still occasionally bothered him. *Riffolk is arrogant too,* he thought, *but at least he's a genius*.

Lucius sat across from Arthor in silence as the cart glided over Ermoor's smooth streets. Arthor was happy with the silence; Lucius didn't exactly make decent conversation. When the cart arrived at Riffolk's lab, Arthor leapt out and strode to the door. He had to wait for Lucius to authorize his entry either way, but walking beside the man any longer than he had to was not an appealing option.

"The teleradio announcer is just off the main lab," Lucius said, "down the hall. One of the assistants will guide you. Go to the announcer, play Riffolk's message, and come back here. Nowhere else in the lab, understood?"

The day I'm given orders by a servant of Riffolk's, Arthor thought, *is the day this city crumbles.*

"I will do as the Prime Overseer commands," he said instead.

The lab door slid open, revealing a young man in a white coat waiting for him. Arthor left Lucius outside and followed the assistant. He'd been in the lab before, but his visits were few and far between. The stark, shining white of the halls always shocked him.

Arthor stepped up to the announcer machine, following the assistant's instruction carefully. The message Riffolk sent him privately contained a password, and he entered it when the assistant told him to. After a few more buttons were pushed, Riffolk's message waited behind a blinking red light as it prepared to play through every teleradio speaker in Ermoor.

"Okay," the assistant said, "that's it. The message will play on the next scheduled announcement. Thank you, Lord Commander."

"Anything the Prime Overseer wishes," Arthor said.

"For the good of all," the assistant returned, "and I'm sorry if Mr. Scarborough was a bit strict. He's always like that when he visits."

"Well, yes. I'm not particularly impressed with the way he speaks to his superiors."

The assistant gave him a look; it seemed to say he wanted to tell Arthor a secret.

"What is it, son?" Arthor said, "spcak plainly."

"Well, sir, it's just that… if you needed to visit again, we have authorized visitor badges."

"Prime Overseer Hayne never mentioned that."

"They're not given out very often. But for the Lord Commander, I think it's appropriate."

A bright warmth spread through Arthor's chest; *I'll finally have some freedom*, he thought. With Riffolk gone, he already felt lighter, but having access to the Prime Overseer's lab allowed him the ability to possibly discover some of his secrets. *Riffolk thinks he knows everything that no one else knows,* he thought, *well not for long*.

"Thank you, son," Arthor said, "you're a good man."

The assistant disappeared for a moment, returning with a black disc on a lanyard. He handed it to Arthor. Without hesitation, Arthor put the lanyard around his neck and tucked the card under his military uniform. *Lucius can't see it*.

"No one knows about this but you and I, son," Arthor said, "and we're going to keep it that way."

"Yes, sir."

Arthor left the lab, once again subjected to Lucius' company. The cart took them back to Arthor's office, and Arthor left without a word to Lucius. From the building that contained his office, the roof gave a view of most of Ermoor. Arthor stood near the edge, looking out over the city as Riffolk's pre-recorded message began.

"Attention, citizens of Ermoor. It is my great pleasure to announce that our brave missionaries have converted the Shenza.

Those who refused to believe have been destroyed, and the rest will live under Ermoor's rule. For the first time in history, Ermoor's borders have expanded. Today will henceforth be known as the First Day of Unity."

Even from the roof, Arthor heard distant cheers. Coloured lights and fireworks spread through the city. After he re-entered the building, a swirl of chaos greeted him as Commanders and Officers celebrated. Arthor overheard snippets of victorious conversation:

"Finally, those savages got what they deserve."

"God's light will cleanse those filthy animals."

"I hope they can actually understand the scriptures."

And, through all of the violent and horrible sentiments barraging Arthor, one sentence kept being repeated;

"For the good of all!"

Eliza

1794

Lashek healed slowly, and Eliza existed in a cold haze as she waited to leave for Aethos. Her mother still barely spoke. Eliza visited Lashek every now and then, when he was well enough to talk. As defeated as he was, he seemed more upbeat than any of the other Circle members. Their conversations helped Eliza get through the rest of the time they spent in Tarsium.

The attack by Kerberos had come near the middle of the previous year. Eventually, Lashek healed enough to leave his bed. He could walk, albeit slowly, and he began joining them for meals. A little while after that, in the beginning of the new year, Zeera called for their attention at the end of a meal.

"It is time. We need to leave this place."

They packed everything they could carry, with help from the Circle agents, and then they were off. Zeera organised passage on a massive ship; it was large enough that they could board without drawing any attention. Other than Kerberos, there was no telling who might be keeping an eye on the Circle. Eliza didn't believe anyone would be able to spy on them if they didn't want it; Zeera seemed to know everything that happened at all times.

It was Eliza's first time at sea. The boat they boarded was part of a regular trade route that swept up the west coast of Omas. Smaller ships travelled up the Alpheus to trade with the farming villages and Omatus, but ships like the one Eliza sat in now could handle the open ocean. Aethos, being the southernmost city along Omas' coast, was to be the ship's first stop. Until then, Eliza would have to get used to travel by boat.

Her mother had travelled from Ermoor to Tarsium before Eliza was born, but other than that she'd never set foot on a boat either. Despite that, and how ill Eliza felt, her mother remained as withdrawn as ever. The entire trip, Eliza felt almost completely alone. Zeera and the other Circle members were there, of course, but they left Eliza and her mother to themselves.

I should be the Hero, she thought one day as they sat silently together. *She can't handle this. Even when Mathys was training me, all three of us knew I was stronger than my mother*. She didn't want it in a selfish way; completely the opposite. Eliza wanted to be chosen as Hero only to take the responsibility off her mother's shoulders.

She'd started praying every night, kneeling on the swaying ship floor in front of her bed: *Taranos, please release my mother from your service. Please, make me Hero instead. I'll give you anything. Everything*. Every night, her prayers went unanswered. Mathys and her mother never spoke directly to her about Taranos or their time in Ermoor; but she'd overheard a lot of things over the years.

After joining the Circle, she'd learned even more about Taranos and the Gods. There was still a lot the adults kept from her, but they were gradually trusting her with more information. She also understood the magic that belonged to her and her mother. *I'm far more talented than mother is at using it, too*, she thought. *And I'm a better fighter. I need to protect her*.

The Circle was going to destroy Sithares. It would take a huge amount of magic; her biggest fear was that her mother would crumble under the pressure; or even worse, that she might be hurt or killed somehow.

The truth was, she didn't know what dangers they faced. It sounded as though there wouldn't be any fighting, just some kind of magic spell. *If that's all it is, maybe mother really can handle it. But I'll still need to help her back to normal before that*.

Holding her mother, Eliza tried to avoid swaying with the ship's movement. Nothing stopped her stomach from lurching, but she couldn't help trying.

"Mother," she said, "say something. Do something, please."

Creaking and water lapping at the ship were the only sounds she heard. Just like the days before this one, all she could do was hold her mother and wait.

Each meal, Circle agents brought food to the cabins. It had been almost a week now, and though her mother was just as quiet as the day Mathys died, she was at least beginning to feed herself. The last meal they shared, Eliza hadn't even helped lift the spoon to her mother's mouth. There was no telling how long it would be before she was back to normal, but any progress was great as far as Eliza was concerned.

Whenever her mother slept, Eliza ventured out to the deck. She couldn't stand the swaying, but the view was beautiful. Sunlight shone from the water in jagged streaks, especially at sunset. There was a strange smell to sea air that she still wasn't used to, but it was refreshing compared to the stuffy cabins. *If mother is better soon,* she thought, *I'll bring her out here and show her the sunset.*

It wasn't until near the end of their trip that things finally changed. Eliza woke up one morning to see her mother already sitting up on her own. She was blinking, her eyes bright with real awareness. Eliza rushed to her side, battling to keep her hopes from soaring.

"Mother? Are you alright?"

"Eliza," she said, "where's Mathys?"

Mara

1794

If not for the fear coursing through her body, Aethos would have been a beautiful city. Instead, it felt to Mara as though the city loomed over her, waiting until she walked into the temple where they would live before it destroyed her.

When Zeera began talking about a summoning spell, and described the Austris Arans, Mara almost passed out; *she wants to summon powerful magical beings here,* she thought, *to join this horrible fight*. It was exactly what she feared; more magic, more warriors, more danger. No matter how terrified Mara became, something worse always seemed to come up.

After Zeera told the Circle about the Austris Arans, Mara sought her out privately. By the time she found her, Mara's heart pounded in her chest, and her hands shook violently. Sweat poured from her skin, dampening her clothing until it stuck uncomfortably to her. Thoughts and feelings raced through her mind, too fast and chaotic to make sense of.

"Zeera," she said, "we're in trouble. I don't think this… this summoning spell…"

She couldn't find the words. Her heart beat so fast, she thought she would die if it kept going. The edges of her vision clouded into a cold white blur. Zeera stared at her, waiting.

"We can't do this," Mara finally said, "it's too dangerous."

Zeera's eyes narrowed a little. For a long moment, she simply looked at Mara.

"Mara," she finally said, "The Austris Arans are the guardians of Pandeia. Why would summoning them to help us make our situation more dangerous?"

Mara's hands were still shaking. Her stomach felt cold, as though she'd swallowed a chunk of ice. She could vaguely feel herself swaying, the panic that flooded her body making her dizzy.

"More magic," she said, "means there will be more fighting."

She barely managed to get the words out without stuttering. The conversation was playing out the same way it had with Eliza; though Zeera cared for her, she wasn't listening, and didn't believe

Mara.

"Either way," Zeera said, "there will be fighting. There will be death. I am sorry, Mara, but that is unavoidable. The Austris Arans are perhaps the most powerful beings in all of Pandeia, and they are on our side. With them fighting for us, and with their Hero in the Circle, there will be far less death."

She couldn't make sense of it; Zeera simply refused to consider her words as anything other than baseless fear. *Why will no one listen to me,* she thought, *when I know that something horrible will happen?* It seemed to her as though the Circle wanted to die. Why else would Zeera, and her own daughter, completely ignore her warnings?

"Zeera," Mara said, "please. *Please*. Don't do this, I'm begging you."

Mara wanted to say that she'd seen something, that there was a cold certainty inside her that could not be denied. If they kept on this path, there would be death and tragedy. Whether that meant they failed, or they won; either way, the cost was too high. She knew it, but no one else could see it.

Through her panic, words failed to come out the way she intended. If she could put her thoughts and fears into words properly, they'd see what she saw. They'd understand. But no matter how hard she tried, she simply couldn't articulate what was happening in her mind.

"I know it's scary," Zeera said, "and I am sorry. But this is a fight we cannot avoid, Mara. Sithares has risen, and we must defeat it. If we don't, all of Pandeia will be destroyed."

"I… I know," Mara said, "but I just… can't. It's too much. It's going to be bad, Zeera. We're going to die, I know it."

It was as much as she could say; words just wouldn't come. She knew exactly what she wanted to say, but she couldn't.

"I understand," Zeera said, "I know the feeling. Trust me, Mara, I will do everything in my power to make sure we all get through this. It is my role for the Circle, after all."

Mara shook her head, tears welling in her eyes as the fear grew to a point she couldn't control. It didn't matter what Zeera did; there was going to be death. The rest of the Circle might have been comforted by Zeera's protection, but Mara's fear was limitless.

Zeera

1794

Once Lashek was mostly healed from Kerberos' attack, the Heroes and Circle agents left Azar for Aethos. Zeera had spent the time learning all the magic she would need to perform. The spells were complex, and would require every Hero of the Circle. Not just the spells they needed to destroy Sithares, but the summoning spell that would call the Austris Arans to Aethos.

Tarsi were powerful magicians, but it was common knowledge among the secret keepers that magic in ancient times was far more potent. Learning spells that were created thousands of years ago bordered on impossible. *At least the Heroes are powerful,* she thought, *and if the Gods are on our side, we stand a chance*. In ancient times, the Gods were known to grant their magic to Heroes in situations of emergency. A Hero's magic came directly from their God anyway, but usually it was a fraction of the magic that existed within that God.

The journey itself was uneventful, if a little unpleasant. Zeera focused on the magic she had to learn. She needed to know it completely before there was any hope of teaching the others. *What makes it impossible,* she thought, *is that the spells can't actually be practiced.* They could learn the theory, but performing the spell would have to wait until they arrived in Aethos. *It means when we try it, there's no telling how it'll go.*

Aside from that, Zeera's main concern was Mara. *She won't speak, she barely eats, and I haven't seen her use magic in a long time.* Certainly not since Mathys died. Getting Mara to practice and perform the magic required of the Circle posed perhaps an even bigger challenge than the magic itself.

Travelling to Aethos with the Circle gave Zeera a new sense of purpose. She knew what their mission was, and she knew how they planned on fulfilling it; but being on their way felt far better than simply thinking about it. She could now at least begin to hope that the Circle wasn't broken. They were together, and with Lashek feeling better, morale was slowly building.

She hadn't told the others much about what they were going to do in Aethos. The Heroes were aware of their overall mission, of course, but she didn't quite know how to tell them about Austris Ara. To the small number of people in Pandeia who'd even heard of them, the Austris Arans were merely myth. Legendary beings who were seen as simply stories. She had no doubt the Ermoori didn't know of their existence at all.

When they arrived, a handful of her agents stood at the city gates to greet them. The Omati who lived in Aethos were unlike any other people who lived in Omas; they were peaceful, humble, and possessed a surprising knowledge of history. They were more than accommodating to Zeera and her Heroes, and understood a little of their purpose.

The Queen of Aethos, Alexis Spiridon, emerged shortly after their arrival. She was accompanied by several dozen other Omati, mostly royal guards. They met each other in the city square, the central common area where a massive statue of an Austris Aran rose above the people.

"Greetings, visitors," the Queen said, "it is an honour to have you in our great city."

Zeera bowed her head.

"The honour is ours, your highness," Zeera said, "thank you for hosting us in our hour of need."

A man stepped in to speak for the Queen. He wore rich, ornate clothing, and no armour; Zeera placed him as an advisor or some such.

"Our temple has been set aside for your use," he said, "as well as all of the attached rooms. We can accommodate for any needs you may have. I'll give you a tour, and then we will organise the rooms as you need."

The Omati were efficient and hard-working. They set up each training room to reflect the Hero who used it, and organised the closest room to each as that Hero's sleeping quarters. Zeera's sleeping quarters were flooded, and her training room contained several tubs of water so she could use her magic.

Within the temple itself, an area had been prepared in the centre, on a circular pedestal that sat above the rows of concentric seats covering the rest of the floor. In its centre, a stone podium had been placed that left space for each Hero to stand around it. This would be where the Circle performed not only the spells that would destroy Sithares, but the summoning spell to bring Austris Ara back.

Zeera needed the others for the summoning spell, but only because it would take more magic than any one person possessed in the modern age. It had been designed for one person to cast, but Zeera didn't believe any one of them could have done it now. The Heroes of the Circle were more powerful than she'd ever hoped; but even they would have struggled to cast the summoning spell on their own. Eliza was particularly powerful, despite not being Ermoor's Hero. She wasn't sure what caused that power, but there was something different about the young Ermoori girl.

She stood at the podium, preparing herself for the magic she would need to perform. As soon as the others were settled in, she planned on calling them to the temple. All they would need to do was repeat after her and join hands; their magic would flow into her, enabling her to cast the spell properly.

It will happen today, she thought, *I need the Guardians here as soon as possible*. If they appeared soon enough, their Hero could assist in destroying Sithares. The Austris Arans were documented as being incredibly powerful, even more so than the ancient magicians of the rest of Pandeia. With them on Zeera's side, their chances of succeeding against the God of Fire grew exponentially.

Later that day, the Heroes gathered in the temple. The mood was sombre, though an air of determination shone through their small group. She'd spoken to them each individually about the Austris Arans, and though there was a lot of confusion, they understood the need for Pandeia's Guardians eventually.

Mara had been the most difficult to persuade; but then, she was against their entire mission, if only out of fear. Zeera understood, but she couldn't give Mara anything other than the advice to push on regardless of her fear. She'd only agreed to be involved if Eliza could be nearby for support.

The podium stood ominous in front of them, its stone cold; it buzzed with ancient energy, something Zeera hadn't noticed when she stood in the room alone earlier. *It can feel that the Heroes are gathered,* she thought, *the magic has been sitting inside it since the last time... and it remembers.*

She knew the spell. Before they got started, she explained it to the others. On the podium, Zeera placed the ancient scroll that contained the spell, along with a Tarsi magical artefact; a gem that focused and honed any magic that it came into contact with. Zeera told the others what the significance of the podium was; another one just like it lay in the Sky Temple in Austris Ara. It would react to the summoning spell, thereby calling Austris Ara back to Aethos.

Zeera sighed, looking into the eyes of each Hero.

"It is time," she said.

Karak

1794

The walls of Omatus loomed over them. Karak's heart raced as memories of the city flashed through his mind. Kerberos beating him to a pulp and throwing him out the palace window; snatching the book of Sithares and barely making it out of Omatus. Though he'd lived in the city a while, returning filled him with an ominous sense of dread he couldn't shake.

"There has been a battle here," Karak said, "look at the damage on the doors."

"They're practically destroyed," Korra said.

"I can't hear any fighting," Tarok said, "there's no way to know who won. Could the Queen have left already?"

"We would have seen her army," Karak said, "it's even larger than Kerberos', from what Zeera said."

"All we can do is search for the book," Tarok said, "that's the mission. It doesn't matter who won this battle, what matters is who has the book."

Karak knew where the book had been. The secret room within the royal library was the perfect place; it was where Sithares had been captured originally. After that, it was in Kerberos' quarters. Now, it could be anywhere; it was likely Kerberos would keep it as close to himself as possible, of course, but it was stolen once from his quarters already. *Even he's not arrogant enough to keep it in the same place,* he thought, *surely*. Karak wasn't even certain Kerberos would have the book again; Aella might have taken control of Omatus. If that happened, she could have hidden it anywhere; or even secretly sent it back to Theara.

"I have some ideas," Karak said, "but first, I think we need more information. I say we split up, and find out what's happened in Omatus. How we proceed will depend on who's on the throne."

They set a plan and left each other, branching into different directions within the city. Karak went first for the royal quarters; if Kerberos was still in control, the book wouldn't be there. But if he wasn't, there was a chance Aella wanted to keep it close. And either way, seeing the room would tell him who sat on the throne.

The others were gathering information the old-fashioned way; simply asking the citizens for the latest gossip. Most of what they needed to know was public knowledge, and with the Tarsi disguised as Omati, there was no reason the people wouldn't talk to them. According to Zeera, a huge amount of the secrets and knowledge possessed by the Tarsi had been gained simply by asking the right people.

As he approached the royal palace, Karak shifted into the form of a cat. *It worked for me last time,* he thought, *why not again?* The first time he'd infiltrated Kerberos' quarters, he'd almost been killed. But all he needed now was a quick look. *If I can confirm who lives in that room,* he thought, *I should be able to narrow down our search for the book.*

The rooftops of several buildings nearby offered a partial view into the royal quarters. Karak couldn't quite gather the courage he needed to actually enter the room. Instead, he stood on the roof of one of the buildings, peering at the doorway. Though he was still in cat form, Karak couldn't help but feel exposed. There was no way Kerberos would know it was him; but the man still terrified him nonetheless.

He stood on the rooftop for almost an hour, until movement within the room finally caught his eye. His heart sank as Kerberos walked past the doorway. *What happened to Aella,* he thought, *and her army, for that matter?* Though signs of battle covered the streets, things had calmed down to the point where Karak might have believed the battle happened weeks ago. His group saw no army on their way to Omatus. *They have to be somewhere here,* he thought, *even a man as ruthless as Kerberos wouldn't slaughter an entire army.*

Now, Karak had to find Aella. She wasn't Omatus' new ruler, of that he could be certain. But he refused to confront Kerberos, or even go near him; and other than Kerberos, Aella was the only person who would know where to look for the book. The team made a plan to meet up after they'd gathered the information they needed. Taking one last look at Kerberos with a sigh, Karak headed back to their meeting place.

"Aella didn't succeed in taking the throne," Karak told them, "Kerberos is still King."

"Yes," Korra said, "and Aella is imprisoned somewhere secret. Her warriors are being kept under the arena."

Somewhere secret, Karak thought, *the room in the royal library. It has to be.*

"They fight every day," Tarok said, "even Kerberos fights most days."

"Our priority is still finding the book," Karak said, "I don't believe he would keep it in his quarters… that's where I stole it from. There was one other place he would have kept it, but I believe he's keeping Aella there now."

“So, we still don’t know where to look?”

“I’ll talk to Aella,” Karak said, “you three, keep digging for information. Infiltrate the soldiers’ ranks, they might know something.”

The group muttered acknowledgement and departed once again. Tolor, yet again, said nothing. *At least he’s following orders,* Karak thought, *even if he doesn’t want to*. After the other three left, he took a moment to prepare for the rest of the mission. At some point, they would have to steal the book. Kerberos, if he wasn’t guarding it himself, would no doubt have his best warriors watching over it. *We’ll be lucky to get out with all four of our lives,* Karak thought, *even getting near the book will be dangerous*.

Speaking to Aella was most important to him now. He needed to know what happened, in more detail than the citizens could give. By Zeera’s accounts, Aella knew Kerberos well. If anyone could tell him where Kerberos might hide something that valuable, she could.

Shifting into an Omati form, Karak wandered towards the royal palace. *Aella will be kept there,* he thought, *all I can do is hope Kerberos doesn’t show up while I’m there*. When he got close enough, he shifted into his cat form once again, and slipped into the royal palace unseen.

Aella

1794

Whenever she wasn't fighting in the arena, Aella remained imprisoned in the secret room Kerberos set aside for her. She still had no idea where it was located within the palace; he was vigilant with covering her head whenever he brought her to and from it. He also cast the Shadow binding spell around her arms and torso every time. Life for Aella became a blur of meaningless repetition; sitting in silence, fighting for her life, eating a small meal.

Sithares still lurked in her head. She felt its malicious

presence, stoking the fires of her rage and pushing her deeper into hatred. Kerberos barely said a word to her the entire time. He simply watched her when she fought in the arena, and went about his business in silence when he brought meals or checked on her in her cell.

She needed Kerberos to die. Down to her core, in the deepest, truest part of her; she *needed* him to die. Even if he ruled Omatus fairly and well, the things he'd done to gain the throne were monstrous. She knew Sithares pushed him into it, in the same way Sithares was pushing her to murder him; but her rage was justified. Kerberos' actions could never be justified.

There would come a time, she knew, when an opportunity would present itself. When she would be able to escape and fight. And even with Shadow Magic on his side, Aella thought there was a good chance she could win. For what might have been a year, Aella waited with as much patience as she could muster. The entire time, Sithares whispered in her head to escape, to attack and murder Kerberos. To take her revenge. *I will,* she thought, *I just need time*.

Her arena battles were the only time she could be herself. Kerberos only forced her to fight her own warriors the first time; other than that, she mostly fought the volunteer Omati who joined in for the glory of Sithares and their King. It meant she could let loose, fighting and killing in a whirlwind of Fire and rage. Sithares' voice echoed in her head during those battles, its deadly whisper filling her thoughts with violence.

In the times when she was locked within the secret room, time passed slowly, and Aella had nothing but her fractured memories and Sithares' voice to occupy her. Though she couldn't hide it from her God, she grew to hate Sithares almost as much as Kerberos. It never left her alone, and she was sure that if it kept going, she would eventually lose her mind.

Finally, when Aella felt her mind starting to slip, something different happened. Her days of maddening repetition ground to a halt as the door to the secret room opened to reveal someone other than Kerberos. A tarsi man stood in the doorway, staring at Aella with his huge silver eyes. He glanced back the way he'd come, then approached her. *Is this some trick of Kerberos',* she thought, *or have I finally gone insane?*

"Hello, Queen Aella," he said, "my name is Karak. I represent an organisation that seeks to save the world from Sithares. We need your help."

This pathetic creature is lying to you. The world can only be saved by being cleansed. There is no stopping the Fire.

"How exactly do you think I can help you?" Aella said, forcing herself to ignore the voice in her head.

Karak smiled, a sad and tired smile.

"We need the book. I know you have it."

Aella nodded to the Shadows that bound her.

"Does it look like I have anything on hand right now?"

"Good point. But if I free you, you could obtain the book again, yes?"

The book stays where it is. None but the chosen shall touch it.

Aella sighed, lowering her head and willing Sithares out of her head. She knew it wouldn't work, but it didn't stop her from trying. The truth was, as much as she owed Sithares her life, Karak was her only option to gain her freedom back. Sithares hadn't done a thing to help her since the attack on Omatus. All it had done was whisper to her; feeding her rage.

"Can you free my warriors, too?" she asked.

"I can try," Karak said.

Karak told her all about the war of the Gods and the Circle of Shadows. By the time he was done, Aella knew what she needed to do. The Circle of Shadows was her best chance to kill Kerberos; not only that, but they had the potential to destroy Sithares itself.

You would not dare. If you turn against me, as Kerberos did, I will make your brief time within my kingdom feel like nothing.

Her mind was wrenched back to the inferno she endured after death. The memories were as scattered as any other, but she still felt the pain vividly enough. Screaming had filled her mind in that evil place. Some of the screaming was her own, but most of it belonged to something else. Something inhuman. Searing pain had become her entire world.

In her sleep, she still occasionally dreamed of Sithares' realm. She couldn't remember if she'd seen anything there, but Fire had taken up most of her vision. The second time she died, the pain and horror hadn't been any easier to endure. Somewhere, vaguely, she'd been aware of Sithares' presence there. Its laugh rang out through the Fire and screams, somehow even worse than the pain itself.

"You can't torture me if you're dead," she whispered.

A white-hot wave crashed through her mind, blinding and deafening her. With it came pain that sliced into her thoughts, robbing her of everything but its intensity. Aella almost passed out, but held on through the sheer power of her will. Sithares' rage was endless, colossal, and in that moment, pointed entirely at her.

She glanced up at Karak; he still awaited her response. After their talk, he'd asked her again if she would help the Circle by giving them the book of Sithares.

"Yes," she finally said, doing her best to ignore the thrashing screams of Sithares in her head, "I'll help you. But there are some complications.”

Karak

1794

As he predicted, Aella was being kept in the secret room. There were no guards, which surprised him, but he supposed Kerberos had kept the room's existence secret even from his own warriors. When Karak crept into the room, Aella stared at him with suspicion. Not shock, or fear, or even confusion.

Karak introduced himself, and asked for her help. After a moment's consideration, Aella agreed; in exchange for helping to free the rest of her warriors. He was shocked at how eagerly she agreed to help. *I thought the Thearan Queen of all people would hesitate more about helping others get the book.* Her suspicion didn't lift immediately, however, and she demanded more information.

"We are called the Circle of Shadows," Karak said, "and we're dedicated to saving Pandeia from Sithares' Fire. Our organization has existed for thousands of years, and now that Sithares is back, we're working to destroy it once and for all."

She nodded slowly as he talked, but otherwise didn't react. Every now and then, she flinched, as though a loud noise exploded next to her ear that Karak couldn't hear.

"Ever since the Gods existed," he continued, "they have fought each other. As elemental beings, it's in their nature to clash. But where the other Gods seek only to maintain balance, Sithares desires destruction. It will not stop until all of Pandeia has burned to ash."

"And you think you can stop the God of Fire?" she said.

"Yes."

Karak didn't bother elaborating; Zeera could explain everything far better than him. All he had to do was get to the book. *But Aella desires freedom,* he thought, *and she clearly wants Kerberos and Sithares both dead.* It meant they had yet another potential ally. The last time Karak sent a Thearan to the Circle, it ended in tragedy; but this time he sensed something different. Aella was trustworthy, something deep in his core knew it.

"The Circle has been devoted to stopping Sithares for millennia. We've done it before, and now we're putting plans in place to kill it forever."

He saw a spark in her golden eyes; and just like that, he knew she would join them. But he had to ask, outright, just to be sure.

"So," he said, "will you join us? Will you help me find the book?"

"Yes," she said after a long pause, "I'll help you. But there are some complications."

"Such as?"

"Kerberos is too powerful to fight head on, even for me. He's keeping the book in his quarters, under constant guard, and whenever he's not busy he's in that room himself."

"I see," Karak said, his stomach twisting as memories of Kerberos' quarters filled his mind, "well, he can't beat an entire army, can he?"

Aella's expression told him the opposite. An image of the ruined hallway in Azar crept into his mind; and the number of dead and wounded people Kerberos had left in his wake.

"Alright," he said, "so no fight, then. Let's focus on getting you out of here, then we'll think of how to get the book."

There was no way Karak knew to break the Shadows that bound Aella. Not even Fire could do that. *If it could,* he thought, *she wouldn't have been bound in the first place*. It occurred to Karak that he might have to simply bring Aella to Aethos as she was; Kerberos had at least left her legs free for easy movement. Besides, the *Duulshen* Zeera invited to consult them was still with the Circle, as well as Lashek. Between the two of them, they had to be able to remove Shadow Magic from Aella.

He couldn't have bound her warriors, he thought, *especially if they're meant to be fighting in the arena*. Getting the Thearans out from their cages was perhaps the easiest part; smuggling Aella out of the royal palace with Shadow Magic covering half her body would be almost impossible. All of Omatus knew her face by now, he was sure of it.

"I may need to come back," he said, "getting you out of here won't be easy. I need to plan with my team."

"Feel free," she said, a lethal note of impatience cutting through her voice, "I'll either be here, or fighting for my life in the arena. So take your time."

"Wait," Karak said, "you fight in the arena too?"

"Yes. Kerberos insists it's fair, but he keeps pitting more and more warriors against me. He'll keep making me fight until it kills me."

"But while you're in the arena," he said, "Kerberos removes the Shadow Magic?"

Aella's eyes narrowed; Karak couldn't tell what the expression meant.

"Yes," she said, "he does. As much as he wants me to die, he'd never blatantly cheat in front of his people."

"And your warriors are imprisoned at the arena themselves, yes?"

Aella nodded. Karak smiled.

"I have an idea."

Mara

1794

"It is time." Zeera looked at each of the Circle members.

Before they started the summoning, Zeera had told them what their part was; they didn't need to directly use magic, or really do anything, except allow their magic to be used by Zeera. It was the only reason Mara agreed. That, and Eliza being nearby for support.

Knowing she wouldn't need to actually use magic somehow failed to silence the fear she felt. Standing before a podium that emanated raw power left her feeling as though they were about to sacrifice something. As though they were making a mistake. Zeera had explained how the spell worked; they would need to join hands after Zeera constructed a spell that would absorb each of their magic, and then she would cast the actual summoning spell while they were connected.

They stood together, holding hands, and Mara battled the fear that surged through her heart. Zeera cast the spell. Lashek, still not completely steady on his feet, kept swapping between looking at Zeera, Eliza, and Mara.

When Zeera's absorbing spell was complete, she crushed it in her hand; it glowed and sank into her skin. Almost instantly, Mara felt a *pull*. Something inside of her was being dragged out through her body. She knew it was her magic, being used by Zeera, but the feeling was still somehow wrong. It only grew worse, dragging at her very soul, until suddenly it stopped.

The podium buzzed with energy, almost glowing. Mara's body almost gave out; it felt to her like the spell had not only taken her magic, but her strength and will. All that kept her standing was the hands that held her own; Lashek and Zeera. After what could have been an hour or a moment, Zeera gently let go of her hand and stepped away. Mara's hand snapped to the podium itself for balance, but its humming unnerved her.

"It is done," Zeera said, "the guardians should now be aware of our need for them."

"How long will it take for them to appear?" Lashek asked.

Zeera shook her head, a slight frown darkening her features.

“I have no idea,” she said, “we can only wait.”

“You told me…” Mara started, and then forced herself to continue, “you told me we would die without them.”

“Wait, what?” Lashek said. Mara ignored him.

“You told me that summoning them was necessary for the safety of all of Pandeia. How can you say that if you don’t even know when they’ll come to our aid?”

“They have been gone for millennia, Mara,” Zeera said, “No one knows where they are, or how long it took to get where they are. That does not mean their importance is any less serious.”

Lashek stared. Mara felt another panic attack rising up from the depths of her fear. She was against summoning incredibly powerful beings before she knew how badly the Circle needed them; knowing they might not even show up in time made all the terror inside her so much worse.

Zeera left without another worse, as though the matter was resolved. Lashek and Eliza watched Mara; they both knew how scared she was, and in that moment, they shared her fear.

Lashek

1794

The summoning spell left Lashek drained. He had to draw his *Kaizuun* just to get the strength he needed to walk back to his quarters. As always happened when he was alone, Lashek's thoughts settled on the war.

Shanaken was finished. So many Shenza were dead, and countless trees had been felled. The home that meant so much to every Shenza was quickly becoming a wasteland. Lashek knew his role as Hero was important, but no such knowledge would ever get rid of the guilt he felt at not being there to fight with his fellow Shenza. He felt like a coward, hiding away from the fighting to join the Circle in casting some spell.

You are no coward, Lashek.

He started, his heart pounding for a short moment until he remembered Amalus' voice. But even a god could not convince Lashek to get past the guilt that coiled in his chest. All he wanted was to fight against the Ermoori, to bring the Shenza back to Shanaken. He knew the threat posed by Sithares; but in that moment, he didn't care. Killing a god who threatened all of Pandeia didn't seem a worthy prize for the cost of his home country.

He hated the original Circle for merely trapping Sithares, instead of killing it as they should have. They had the power and the knowledge to destroy the Fire God, and simply… decided not to. And as a result, Lashek's entire country was being razed to the ground.

"These guardians better be worth it," he muttered to himself.

Word of the war came in regularly, and Lashek had listened in a daze over the months he was healing after Kerberos' attack in Azar. None of it had felt real, but the heaviness that settled over him during that time never left him.

Hundreds died between each Circle messenger delivering news, and each time Lashek grieved in an unending fog of physical pain and restless sleep. Now that he was mostly healed, the full weight of Shanaken's loss was properly hitting him. It no longer felt unreal, or clouded by pain and troubled sleep. He had to fight against rage as it boiled away in his insides like a wounded wild beast.

To add insult to injury, his body *still* ached from Kerberos' attack. The giant man had moved almost carelessly as he broke the Circle to pieces. Lashek was lucky to be alive, though it didn't feel like luck to him. He might not have been able to admit to anyone out loud, but Kerberos scared him more than Ermoor and Sithares combined. He commanded more magic than anyone else in Pandeia, and did so with an ease that was inhuman.

Lashek sighed, his thoughts racing around in circles; Shanaken's fall, Kerberos' attack, the guardians. He didn't know how Zeera could remain so calm, so assured. *Maybe Asheilos knows something Amalus doesn't,* he thought, *and I'm just not aware of how we could possibly win because Amalus doesn't know either.*

You cannot know, yet. There is still a journey ahead of you, Lashek. You have a pivotal role to play, but if you know too much before your time, your fate will not come to pass.

It was something, at least.

"Not exactly comforting," he said, "but I'll take it."

He wondered if the other gods were as cryptic as Amalus. *No wonder being a Hero is such a difficult task*, he thought, *half the job is blindly following Gods who give nothing but riddles*. If Lashek were a God, he would dispense with the games and simply tell the Hero exactly what to do.

Amalus said nothing more to him, and his thoughts returned to the war. The Ermoori had always attempted to take what didn't belong to them, but this war felt… different. It was a legitimate, full-scale invasion. According to the reports, they were attacking with weapons unlike anything that had ever been seen before, and their armour was almost entirely impenetrable.

Even if there's some way to win, he thought, *the chances of that happening are almost zero. I really hope Amalus actually knows what it's talking about.*

Zeera

1794

She didn't know what to expect; but after the summoning spell, nothing happened. Drained of magic and energy, Zeera retired to her quarters. The other Heroes did the same. For days, the Circle waited for some sign that the Austris Arans were coming.

It took her almost four days to recover from casting the spell. Four days of resting and meditation, submerged in the water that filled her sleeping quarters and absorbing the Water Magic around her. She knew the others were recovering too. Lashek would be ablc to gain his magic back within the training room set up for him; but Zeera wasn't sure how Mara could recoup her Power Magic. Aethos didn't use the technology that filled Ermoor and Tarsium; though there were a few devices in use, none of them would be enough to grant her more energy.

Zeera had studied magic most of her life. She knew that it regenerated slowly on its own, even without exposure to the source; but she also knew that magic provided benefits other than its normal usage. When a person's magic was at capacity, they had more energy, and felt physically better. With their morale so fragile, Zeera needed any advantage she could get.

She called for the advisor, Platon, who appeared within the hour. In any other city of Omas, a royal advisor would be pompous and self-important; but Aethos was a different city altogether, and its people were more than happy to serve the Circle.

"How much Ermoori technology do you have in Aethos?" Zeera asked him, "and how much of it can we set up in the quarters of my Ermoori companions?"

"We don't have much, I'm afraid," Platon said, "but I can organise to have more brought here. What is it that you need?"

"Anything with a powerful energy source," Zeera said, hoping she was right, "and small enough to stockpile in one room."

He disappeared shortly after their conversation, and Zeera was left once again to her own thoughts. Even after they recovered all of their magic, they would need more training and preparation to successfully cast the spells needed to destroy Sithares; *much* more training. Considering how difficult the summoning spell had been, Zeera was worried they simply didn't have what it took. *The original Heroes of the Circle never would have imagined how weak magic has become,* she thought, *otherwise they would have destroyed Sithares themselves, instead of simply locking it up.*

Not for the first time, Zeera wondered why the founders of the Circle didn't destroy Sithares. They had the power, and the knowledge; and they definitely had the motivation. The Tarsi had perhaps the most thorough knowledge of Pandeia's history; but some things were unknowable. Her only theory was that the Circle didn't want to be responsible for Fire Magic completely disappearing from the world. But there was no proof that a God's magic would stop existing if the God itself died. It made sense to her, but she knew it may not be the case.

So many things were happening now that the ancient Tarsi couldn't have predicted. Zeera felt the weight of their expectations on her shoulders; the Circle was in her hands, as was the fate of all of Pandeia. The worst of it was waiting; Austris Ara remained an unknown, and the timeline in which the other Heroes could regain their magic. Not to mention they still didn't have the book of Sithares. *All I can do is wait,* she told herself, *even if it hurts, for now, things are out of my control.*

Aerene

1794

Aerene shot through the sky, plummeting towards the ocean. It was a cold day; freezing winds threatened to throw her off course as she streaked towards her prey. Her wings twitched as she readjusted to the gusts hitting her. *As much as the cold air brings in magic,* she thought, *it's terrible for hunting. I couldn't fly in a straight line if my life depended on it.*

Without having to find something to impress Aelis, hunting took far less time. Though normally a reminder of his absence and refusal to befriend her again would have upset her, she was willing to take any excuse to finish hunting earlier. Her net, which hung from a jutting rock on a nearby cliff face, was almost full already. *I'll be able to return after one more fish.*

A large fish swam close to the surface near the cliff. *Probably too big,* she thought, *but I'll manage*. Its tail flicked occasionally, turning it in different directions as it searched for food. Aerene readied her spearline as she approached, praying for a lull in the wind. She knew Aurath didn't respond to such inane prayers, but it was such a deeply ingrained habit that she barely even realised she did it.

She rushed towards the fish, straining her wings to stay on track. Pulling her arm back with the spearline poised for attack, she waited for the perfect moment. *Now*. She threw her arm forward and watched the spearline streak towards her prey. A sudden gust blew it off course. *No,* she thought, and extended her arm towards the flailing weapon.

Magic flew from her hand, snatching the spearline and rocketing it towards the fish again. It speared the fish right through its head, and Aerene grabbed the line as she flew past it. She had to send a column of air rushing up under her wings just to pull the fish out of the water. After decades of practice, using magic while focusing on other things had become second nature.

Lugging the fish to her net, Aerene hauled it up by the line until she could drop it in. Then she perched on the small outcrop above her net and caught her breath. Her wings throbbed, sore and tired.

She technically didn't need to bring so much food back; in fact, she didn't need to hunt at all. There was an entire class of Austris Aran hunters who did this every single day. Priests-in-training only hunted to learn the basics of combat skills, and to teach themselves humility. *It's difficult to think too highly of yourself when you finish the day exhausted and smelling of fish.* As Hero, and no longer a priest-in-training, Aerene never needed to hunt again a day in her life; but she understood the value of humility, and she would have hated herself if she ever turned out to be as smug and arrogant as Aelis.

Her net bulged, precariously close to overflowing. It wouldn't break; Austris Aran rope was stronger than most of the bladed weapons in the rest of Pandeia. *The only problem with unbreakable rope,* she thought, *is it's too tempting to carry way too much.*

Stretching her wings, Aerene sighed and readied herself to carry the net. *One more flight, then I can get some rest.* She'd spent the entire morning training with Shaela and High Priest Allor. Then an hour praying to Aurath. Now, after a couple hours hunting, she was ready to sleep for a full night.

"Here we go," she said with another sigh.

Grunting, Aerene yanked the net off its moorings and tied it to her belt. Even standing, it weighed her down. She took a few deep breaths, grabbed two handfuls of the net to steady it, and spread her wings. It took a huge effort and a fair amount of magic to get her off the cliff and into the air. Once she was flying, she held her wings steady and focused more on forcing a constant swell of Air Magic from underneath her.

As Allor had taught her, she drew in magic at the same time she spent it, creating a cycle of perpetual wind that shot her through the sky. Though it was slightly easier than flapping her wings, she still felt them losing strength the longer she flew.

By the time Austris Ara came into view, Aerene heard the deep booming of war horns. Her shock almost sent her crashing down to the ocean far below. *The horns haven't been used since they were first made two thousand years ago,* she thought, frowning as she shot towards the city.

No sleep for me then, she thought, *I'm sure there'll be some sort of ceremony to mark this*. Her sarcasm died quickly as she realised the implication of hearing the ancient horns. *Either Austris Ara is under attack, or...* Aurath's voice appeared in her mind, clear and powerful despite the wind rushing past her ears. As it spoke, her fears rose, and a horrible dread settled in her stomach, heavier than the bulging net that weighed her down.

We are summoned. The War of the Gods has begun.

Karak

1794

The arena. It was perfect; the only time Aella and her warriors were in the same place, unbound, and Kerberos was guaranteed to be there too. Any other time, Kerberos might reappear in his quarters at any moment.

His team were positioned in the arena. Two of them were disguised as Thearan guards at the main gate, and one disguised as an arena master at the inner gate. The inner gate was all that stood between the battleground of the arena and the rest of the building.

Members of the public came in through the main gate and were guided up the stairs to the seats. Warriors came up from underneath the arena, emerging just inside the inner gate and organized by the arena master into teams.

Their plan was simple; wait until Aella and her Thearans were all at the arena, being watched by Kerberos, then steal the book. After that, the disguised arena master just had to open the inner gate. Then the guards would open the main gate. *Simple,* Karak thought, *but that doesn't mean easy.*

An escape from the arena was only the beginning; Omatus itself was a fortress. Kerberos' army would protect the book with their lives, and every one of them wielded Fire Magic. Assuming the escape worked perfectly, Karak still had to lead his team and Aella's army through the city. *Aella is a warrior Queen,* he thought, *she should be able to help with that part, at least*. Her army wielded Fire Magic, too. Karak had to believe they stood a chance.

While the other three agents in his team were disguised and in place in the arena, Karak crept to the royal quarters. As long as they knew Kerberos was nowhere near the book, Karak could steal it. He knew how to slip past guards, but Kerberos was another matter.

In his cat form, Karak stalked across the royal palace's rooftop. The guards would be stationed outside his door, in the corridor. Provided he was quiet, he'd be able to slip in and out without anyone knowing he was there. *My biggest concern,* he thought as he neared the balcony, *is whether Kerberos kept the black metal box.*

Built by a master blacksmith for Karak to steal the book the first time, it stopped the Fire from touching his hands. But Kerberos didn't need it, and nor did any Thearan. *If he threw it out, I'm in trouble.*

Karak dropped silently onto the balcony. He glanced out at the buildings nearby; he knew he could be seen if anyone were watching. Satisfied that no one was, he shifted into his natural form. He'd dragged a satchel with him across the roof. Now, he opened it, holding it ready. *In and out,* he thought, *waste no time, make no noise.*

He still couldn't quite believe Kerberos kept the book in his own quarters, after Karak already stole it from there. *I was wrong,* he thought, *he really is that arrogant.* Breathing slowly, evenly, Karak prepared himself to complete his mission. *Kerberos is distracted,* he thought, *he'll never know I was here. It'll just be one moment, and then I can run.*

Stepping through the doorway, Karak saw them too late; four Thearan warriors, in full armour, weapons at the ready.

"Oh, no," Karak said.

"Kerberos said someone would be back for the book," one of the Thearans said, "I didn't believe him. You're not brave, you know… For coming back. You're just stupid."

Karak's shoulders dropped, the air rushing out of his lungs. *This is it,* he thought, *this is the end.* He cast his eyes around the room; the chest was where it had been last time. As the Thearans approached slowly, flanking him, Karak tried to calculate a way to take the book without being killed. One of the Thearans stepped between him and the chest.

“I may be stupid,” Karak said in Oman, “but we’re going to win eventually. It’s only a matter of time.”

With that, he unleashed the blinding spell he’d become so used to casting. As soon as the flash of light and sound exploded through the room, Karak bolted for the chest.

Sharp pain lanced through Karak’s shoulder as he ran. He gasped at the intensity of it, and a quick glance down showed the tip of a spear plunged through his body. Karak dropped to his knees and glanced over his shoulder, back at the warriors; *one of them must have covered his eyes*, he thought, *I’ve never seen anyone react so quickly to that spell.*

The other three Thearans were incapacitated, still blinded and shouting. Karak crawled for the chest, his mind racing. *I need to get the book,* he thought desperately, *that’s all that matters. I get the book, or we’re all dead.*

He almost reached the chest; but the Thearan who’d covered his eyes got him first. The warrior slammed his foot down on Karak’s calf, pinning him in place. Then he wrenched the spear out of Karak’s shoulder. Karak screamed, but it was cut short as the spear stabbed into him again; this time in his other shoulder. The razor-sharp spearhead crunched into the stone below Karak, burying deep.

Again, the Thearan yanked his spear back. Karak turned onto his back to face his attacker, trying to ready another spell. For a moment, the Thearan smiled at him, holding his spear above Karak’s head like an executioner's axe. *I can't get the book,* he thought, *there's no way. The only chance I have is to escape with my life, and try again later*.

The warriors he'd blinded had calmed down; their vision would return any second. Karak knew what he needed to do. He'd completed the spell in his hand just as the Thearan above him raised his spear. Waiting until the perfect time, Karak unleashed the spell once again; this time, the Thearan above him caught it full in the face.

The second the spell worked, Karak shifted into his cat form again. He couldn't have timed it better; the spear came down despite the Thearan being blinded, and just barely missed Karak as it smashed into the stone behind him. He twisted, pushing past the pain that exploded through his mind and body.

Karak ran for the balcony, his shoulders screaming. The only thing that kept him moving was the knowledge that if he stopped, he would die. Pain crashed through his entire body, overwhelming his thoughts until all that remained was panic. *Move,* his mind said, *move until they can't find you.* He got to the balcony and leapt as hard as he could, barely making it onto the roof.

Limping on the four legs of his cat form, Karak forced himself to move to the other side of the roof. Even if the Thearans could follow him up there, they'd take too long to see him. Still, he pushed himself further. He still had to make it out of Omatus with Aella and her warriors. *If I can't get the book,* he thought, *I can at least bring Zeera an army.* It wouldn't make up for all his previous failures, and certainly not for leaving the book behind; but it was the best he could do for now.

Mara

1794

Mara went back to her quarters after the summoning spell was done. She felt no better than she had after she tried convincing Zeera not to summon them in the first place, despite Zeera's attempts to reassure her. Sitting alone on her bed, hands shaking, Mara didn't even notice Eliza walk into the room. When she spoke, Mara jumped and uttered a squeal.

"Mother," she said, "are you okay?"

She could do nothing but shake her head; her entire body shook even worse than before. *Such a small scare,* she thought, *and my whole body goes crazy*. Even worse, she knew Eliza didn't believe her when she spoke about the tragedy to come.

Eliza sat next to her again. She put her arm around Mara's shoulders, pulling her close. As she had before, Eliza let the silence settle between them. Perhaps her favourite thing about her daughter was that she never put pressure on her to talk. She was also the only one who understood that just because she was tired, it didn't mean she wasn't terrified.

"We're going to make it through this," Eliza said, her voice gentle, "I'll be here with you, and Zeera will too."

Zeera told her everything about the conversation we just had, she thought, *even though it was meant to be private*. Eliza was her daughter, but that didn't mean she wanted to share everything with her. Zeera's role was leader of the Circle, and Mara only wanted to talk with her because she made the decisions about summoning Austris Ara.

"What are you so afraid of, mother?" Eliza said.

"I'm… just scared. The leader of the Ermoori is a horrible person. If he comes anywhere near us, it… It won't end well. I can't stop thinking about him."

It was true; her nightmares were getting worse, and even during the day his face was never totally gone from her mind. She knew he wanted to kill her. He wanted everything; she felt his rage and his relentless drive in the depths of her mind. He was going to hunt her down, and if he found out about Eliza, he was going to kill them both.

"We're going to win the war," Eliza said, "as long as we fight together."

"You don't know that."

Eliza smirked, her eyes sparkling.

"Just like you don't know that things will turn out badly. Mathys taught us to be prepared for the worst, and at the same time to hope for the best. That's what I'm doing now."

She was right. Mara couldn't have admitted it, but she agreed with Eliza. Still, it was far easier to say than to do. With her mind in utter chaos, and her nights full of nightmares, it was almost impossible to hope for the best. She knew Riffolk was coming for her, and she knew he was powerful. Even scarier, he was the most intelligent man in Pandeia. There was nothing he couldn't do once he set his mind to it.

"You don't understand," Mara said, "even Mathys was scared of Riffolk."

Eliza's face twitched, changing slowly from gentle warmth to genuine concern. It was the first time Mara felt like Eliza took her fears seriously. Mathys had been afraid of almost nothing; Eliza worshipped him, and to hear that he had fears must have been shocking.

"Why?" Eliza said, "what scared him so much about some ruler of a city he left?"

Mara shook her head. She felt Riffolk's presence, and as far as she knew he felt hers too. Talking about him was too risky.

"Stop," she said, "stop talking about him. He'll know."

Eliza looked at her with undisguised pity; seeing that look on her daughter's face brought tears cascading down her face again. It felt to Mara as though she spent most of her waking life crying. Mara just wanted Riffolk out of her head. He lurked there all the time, his emotions spiking within her mind, clashing against her own.

"Okay," Eliza said, "okay, we'll stop talking about him. We don't have to talk about anything you don't want to."

For a while, Eliza simply held her, rubbing her back gently as she sniffled and tried to breathe evenly. They sat that way, comfortable silence falling between them, until Mara's fear began to build again.

"I just…" she said, "you need to stay away from him, okay? Whatever you do, if he ever comes near you, you run away."

"Okay," Eliza said.

"Promise me, Eliza. Please."

"Alright, alright," she said, "I promise. I will run away if he comes near me."

Karak

1794

Karak was badly wounded. He rested as long as he could, using the magic within his body to heal. But within hours, he knew, he'd need to be back at the arena. Their plan allowed for Karak to get to and from the royal palace with spare time to sneak around whatever security Kerberos might have put in place. If he'd succeeded, he would have been able to disguise himself and make his way to the arena through the streets. But now, getting to the arena would be its own challenge.

He limped through a narrow alley, blood soaking through his

clothing. The brief rest he took worked wonders to heal him, but the spear had gone completely through his body. No amount of Tarsi healing could fix his wounds in such a short time. *Just get to the arena,* he thought, *healing will have to come later*.

Shifting into the form of an old Omati woman, Karak exited the alley into the street. His clothes were dark, and though it didn't hide the blood, it was at least something. As an old woman, Karak's limping would attract less attention. His satchel hung from his hand, making his shoulder scream despite the fact it was empty.

Their plan was to fight their way out of the western entrance. As Karak walked, he realised how much more walking he'd need to do. *The others will need to move fast when they leave the arena,* he thought, *I'll only slow them down*. The decision settled in his mind before he consciously thought it, and he changed direction. *I'll have to meet them at the entrance*. He knew they'd understand; Aella even suggested it as their back-up plan in case things went wrong. *If you fail,* she'd said, *we can't wait around for you. If you're slower than us, we'll try to meet you at the entrance. Otherwise, you'll just have to make your own way to Aethos*.

He took his time, moving through the streets and alleys slow enough to match his appearance. Even though he didn't have the book, drawing attention to himself was the worst thing he could do. *I need to get out of here alive,* he thought, *if there's any hope of redeeming myself later*. He still wanted to be the one who retrieved Sithares' book for Zeera; *I'll either take it,* he thought, *or I'll die trying*.

When the city walls were in sight, a cluster of explosions rocked the ground beneath his feet. They came from behind him, towards the arena. Karak spun; smoke came roiling up from somewhere in the city, and distant shouts echoed through the streets.

Karak kept moving. *I need to get to the entrance before they reach me,* he thought, *they'll be moving quickly*. The shouts grew louder, and Karak grunted with pain as he pushed himself to move faster. More explosions shook the stone street. As he pushed himself further, the smell of smoke reached him.

The entrance appeared before him, and Karak let loose a ragged sigh as it came ever closer. *Almost there,* he thought, *I just need to make it past the wall*. Guards were posted inside and outside; as an old woman, he shouldn't arouse suspicion. But there was always a risk; especially if a battle suddenly broke out within the city.

Explosions and shouting rang out so loud and so close behind him when he reached the entrance that all four guards were already in a combat stance, facing in at the chaos. When they saw Karak shuffling towards them, their only reaction was to wave him towards the entrance.

"Get out," one of them said, "there's danger coming this way."

The old woman disguise worked even better than he hoped. *I didn't even have to talk,* he thought, *and I can get out without raising any alarms*.

Footsteps pounded the street behind him; the Thearans were so close now. The guards all but shoved him through the entrance.

Karak couldn't help but utter a scream as they jostled him, his shoulders exploding in searing pain. From the other side of the wall, Karak looked back into the street; the Thearans fought viciously, Fire Magic roaring to life through the air.

As Karak watched, Aella and her Thearans destroyed the guards. They launched fireballs at the entrance, blowing massive holes into it to allow their army to escape faster. Chunks of stone and Fire flew at Karak; he let his disguise drop as he ducked to avoid the debris.

"Karak," Tolor said as he ran through the entrance, "there you are. We were beginning to worry about you."

"Let's just get out of here," Karak said, "can you organise to steal a cart, or a camel? I need some help to keep pace with everyone."

Tolor glanced at Karak's shoulders, his mouth set in a grim line.

"That can be arranged. We need to move quickly, though… Kerberos' warriors are close behind us."

"Any sign of Kerberos himself?"

"Not since the arena."

Karak nodded, and Tolor disappeared to find transport. Thearans swarmed out of the entrance, running west as Aella had told them to. He watched them streaming past him, wishing he could fall in beside them. Thankfully, Tolor wasted no time finding a camel-drawn cart; he returned shortly after he left, urging the camels faster.

"Get in," he said as the cart drew close, "let's go."

Karak stepped into the cart, sharp pain lancing through his wounds as he pulled open the door. Tolor pushed the camels on again, and the cart picked up speed. The road was rough, and Karak bore through the pain as the cart bounced and swayed. *Now for the hard part,* he thought; *telling Zeera that I failed once again.*

Lashek

1794

For the first time since Kerberos' attack, Lashek was able to perform his *Zuunshai* properly. It felt as great as he remembered, but at the same time, it felt strange. His body was rigid and sore. He ran through it several times, feeling his muscles gradually loosen as he did. Tarsi magic helped him heal much faster than he otherwise would have, but Shadow Magic was the source of his strength and speed.

Now that he was healed, he could use Shadow Magic again without hurting himself. *I can finally get back to training,* he thought,

I feel like I've lost a lot of magic. He knew magic didn't work that way, but he still couldn't help worrying.

Aethos was an interesting place to Lashek; it seemed to be a blend between Tarsium and Omatus. But the Circle made a new headquarters there, and each member had plenty of space and rooms for training.

After his *Zuunshai* was done, Lashek sat down in the dirt. Zeera had prepared a garden room for him, with plants that breathed life and magic into the private space. It meant he could stretch out and connect with Shadow Magic in a greater way. The magic around him still felt muted compared to being in the forests of Shanaken, but at least it was something.

Zeera spoke to the Circle about the magic they would have to perform, and Lashek couldn't help but feel daunted; his ability to use magic was diminished more the further he got from Shanaken. *And Aethos is about as far from home as I can get.* On top of that, though he'd healed, he still felt weak. *I need training.*

He sought out Eliza; he would train with everyone, but Eliza was always warm and welcoming to him, and she was powerful. *I'm going to have to really push myself,* he thought, *if I plan on being strong enough to help the Heroes.*

Eliza was wandering through Aethos' streets. Lashek found her by wandering himself, and by the time he came across her he was exhausted. He called to her, and was thankful when she ran to him.

"Lashek," she said with a bright smile, "how are you feeling?"

“Tired. Sore.”

She nodded, her smile dimming a little. When they’d first met, a cold tension sat between Lashek and the Ermoori, particularly Mathys. But Eliza had grown up in Tarsium, without the hatred of the Ermoori towards Lashek’s people. She was kind, and had no preconceptions about the other countries in Pandeia.

“What do you think of Aethos?” Lashek said.

“It’s not as nice as Tarsium,” she said, “but I like it.”

“Have you seen the training rooms?”

Eliza smiled, a wicked spark lighting up in her eyes.

“Yes, of course.”

“Would you like to train now?”

She grinned wider and nodded, her brightness giving Lashek a slight wave of energy.

“Let’s go,” he said.

The training room was large, round, and designed for multiple people to be able to fight. It was perfect for magic; its size meant they had space to focus on each other rather than trying to avoid destroying the room.

Lashek held his *Kaizuun* loosely, its blade angled toward the ground. Eliza stood across from him, taking a combat stance he recognised from watching Mathys train. Her hands flashed with electricity, her eyes steady and focused. *I'm in trouble,* he thought, *she looks like she's in her prime, and I'm barely walking*. He felt far better with his *Kaizuun* in hand, at least.

Eliza was perfectly still, balanced and ready. *She won't move until I do,* he thought, *just like Mathys*. His movements had been efficient; he'd only moved when absolutely necessary, and focused on weaknesses in his opponents to bring them down quickly. Eliza was an intelligent and enthusiastic learner, and Lashek knew she was as formidable as her former teacher. *Maybe even more so*. Where Mathys used technology and strategy, Eliza had magic at her disposal.

He raised his blade, stepping into a wide stance. Watching her, trying to gauge her strategy, Lashek waited as long as he could. Eliza didn't move an inch. Finally, he gave a heavy sigh, steeled himself for the attack, and leapt.

Shenza, especially *Kaizeluun*, moved faster than possibly any other warriors in Pandeia. It was a testament to Mathys' training, and Eliza's skill, that she leapt to meet him before he could react. He'd expected her to remain on the defensive at least until after the first move. But halfway through his leap, her foot appeared and connected with his chest.

Lashek thudded to the ground, shoving himself back to his feet as he glanced around for Eliza. His body already felt as though it had been beaten over and over again, though the fight had barely begun. He grunted as he stood, and forced himself to settle back into the heightened awareness that his *Kaizuun* brought.

There. His instincts told him Eliza would come from behind and to the left, so he dove and rolled out of the way. A bolt of lightning exploded right beside him as he rolled. *I didn't see that coming,* he thought, *what happened?* His *Kaizuun* should have warned him. *Eliza shouldn't be able to move and react this quickly*.

He spun out of his roll, swiping his blade at an angle to send a razor-sharp Shadow streaking towards Eliza. Without hesitation, she jumped into a horizontal flip that carried her over the Shadow, missing it by barely an inch. In mid-air, halfway through her flip, another lightning bolt erupted from her hands. Lashek couldn't get out of its path fast enough, so he did all he could think to do; brought his blade up in a defensive block.

The lightning connected with his *Kaizuun* and exploded. Sparks rained down over Lashek, filling his field of vision as shockwaves rushed up his arms. Eliza was on the floor; the explosion her lightning caused had shoved her violently before she landed. Taking the moment, Lashek rushed at her.

She was on her feet before he reached her. Lashek ducked under a high kick and slashed his *Kaizuun* at her ankles. Eliza dodged effortlessly and returned with a barrage of punches to Lashek's stomach and chest. He managed to block a number of them, but she simply moved too quickly for him. *That's going to bruise,* he thought.

He attacked as much as he could, but with Eliza's speed, he was forced to attempt blocking or dodging more often than not. *She's got me cornered*. He stole a few seconds by slamming his knee into her stomach and shoving her away from him, then activating a shield spell on the back of his forearm. *That should help against lightning,* he thought, *hopefully*.

It did; but barely. He blocked two massive lightning bolts in a row, both of which exploded with brutal force, before the shield shattered. Pieces of Shadow Magic thudded into the dirt floor, before disappearing in a hiss of smoke.

Lashek once again took up a combat stance, but Eliza stood casually, the fight forgotten. She smiled gently at him, and gestured for him to sit with her. He frowned, taken aback; she usually trained for far longer.

"You need some rest, Lashek," she said, "I want to help you train, not kill you."

Karak

1794

Karak's injuries healed slowly. Sitting in the cart allowed him to focus all his energy on healing, and for that much he was grateful. His team had all dropped their disguises; Aella made sure all her warriors knew the Tarsi were on their side.

The cart contained small windows on each door, and Karak stared out at the horizon during their journey. To the north, Sitharkos loomed like a gigantic predator. Smoke billowed up from its jutting peak, black as midnight. It wasn't unusual to see smoke coming from Sitharkos this time of year, but Karak couldn't help a small gasp escaping as he took in the view; a vast black cloud hung above Pandeia, spreading even as he watched. The smoke spread over the horizon, sneaking towards Aethos, towards Shanaken and Ermoor. *Spreading, Karak thought, like a plague*.

Though the Thearans were used to traveling on foot, the journey was still long. Once they were far enough away from Omatus, they slowed their pace to conserve energy. Tarok and Korra visited him, applying healing potions to his shoulders to help. Karak owned his own potions, of course; but he'd used most of them up in Omatus before meeting the others.

As they traveled, Karak thought about the book. *Kerberos takes no chances,* he thought, *if we go back again, we'll need an army with us*. After one unsuccessful attempt to steal the book, Kerberos left four warriors watching it at all times. After the second, Karak knew it would be even more difficult to get anywhere near it.

Zeera is going to kill me, he thought, *I just hope bringing Aella's army to her softens the blow*. There had to be a way for the Circle to retrieve the book. *If we can successfully summon the guardians*, he thought, *they'll be able to take it*. He was certain. Whether the guardians themselves would appear after being summoned was another matter.

Several days into the journey, Aella visited him in the cart. She sat across from him, looking every bit as confident and lethal as Kerberos himself.

"Karak," she said, "how are you doing?"

He shrugged; the only answer was obvious.

"Not well," he said, "healing slowly."

"I'm sorry you didn't get the book. I would have helped, if I could."

Karak believed her; she was the kind of woman who meant every word she said. Still, it meant little to him after the mission had already failed. He didn't blame her, but such platitudes were hardly helpful.

"We'll need to try again," Karak said, "so does that mean you'll join us for the next attempt?"

Aella smiled.

"I may have a more important role to play in your Circle, Karak," she said, "we'll have to see."

Karak sighed; it was true. Zeera would find something for Aella to do, and Karak would be forced to attempt to steal Kerberos' book on his own. *Or with a small team again,* he thought, *though we've proven a small team doesn't stand a chance*.

Aella left the cart again, and Karak was alone with his thoughts. His shoulders had healed to the point that bumps on the road didn't ache quite as badly, but he could still barely move. *I'm not even sure Zeera will give me time to heal,* he thought, *before she sends me back to Omatus*. If he wasn't healed, he was doomed to failure. Even at his best, stealing the book for him approached impossible.

They followed the Alpheus west. Karak's pain stuck around, even as he healed. The ground grew rockier the further west they went;

Every bump of the cart was worse than the one before it. He'd never wanted to sit still so badly in his life. *I didn't think I'd ever hate traveling by cart,* he thought, *but it's still better than walking*.

When Karak worked for the Circle, travel was a regular part of his responsibilities. Most of the time, traveling as a Tarsi agent was easy; they could look like anyone, speak any language, and brought with them all the currency they'd need. But now that he was wounded, travel was the last thing he wanted to do. Last time he'd been in Omatus was the same; he'd been badly injured and had to travel on camel-back to Tarsius.

Korra visited him one day towards the end of the Alpheus, where it twisted up into the mountains. At first, she didn't say anything, just sat roughly in the seat across from him and smiled.

"Korra," he said, "how is travel going out there?"

"As well as can be expected," she said, "the Thearans make excellent travel companions. Other than the constant fighting and shouting, of course."

Karak nodded. Thearans fought everyone, even their own people. Most in Pandeia called them savages, but the Tarsi had a better understanding of their culture. *We had to understand them,* he thought, *to understand Sithares*. Without understanding their enemy, there was no guarantee of destroying it.

"Has Tolor relaxed?" he asked.

"No, not at all," Korra said, "anyone would think he was the wounded one. He's been sulking ever since we left Omatus."

"At least he found the cart for me fast enough. I wasn't sure he would, until he appeared with it."

Korra laughed, nodding as a spark of humour lit up her silver eyes.

"I wouldn't have bet on it either," she said, "though he does tend to do the right thing… when it counts."

Karak fell silent; memories of Tolor drifted through his mind. He'd certainly never done right by Karak, that he could remember. *Then again,* he thought, *we've never really been in a situation that required it. Except for the cart*. Though Tolor seemed able to focus on the job when he had to, he exuded a sense of resentment and rage that anyone could have picked up on.

"Do you think Zeera will be happy with her new Thearan allies?" Karak asked; his mind kept returning to Zeera, regardless of what he tried to focus on.

"It's not a bad consolation prize," Korra said, "but honestly? No. No, I don't think she'll be happy to see you return without the book."

Korra had always been truthful; it was one of the many things Karak respected about her. As much as the truth hurt, Karak already knew Zeera's reaction would be less than ideal.

"At least we have more of an army gathered for when the Ermoori reach us," he said, "even if Sithares is still around when that happens."

"If Sithares still exists by the time the Ermoori get to Aethos,"

Korra said, “it won’t matter how many people we have. Sithares needs to die as soon as possible, Karak. There is no other option.”

For the rest of the journey, Karak tried to plan out another mission to steal the book. He knew Omatus well, and Kerberos better than most. He knew where the book was, and what to expect when he reached it. But no matter how many different approaches he imagined, the plans in his head all ended the same way; with Karak dead by Kerberos’ hand.

Zeera

1794

Zeera stood at the entrance to Aethos, staring out at the horizon with fear and dread in her heart. In the distance, thick black smoke swallowed up the air in an endless cloud. *Sithares is gaining strength,* she thought. With every week that passed, the God of Fire grew more powerful. *We need that book,* she thought, *now*.

When she'd sent Karak to find the book of Sithares, Zeera knew there was a chance he'd come back empty handed. But he didn't; he came to Aethos with Queen Aella of Theara. At first, Zeera was taken aback, but when she saw the army of Thearans marching behind the Queen, hope and excitement rushed through her body in waves. *Even if the Austris Arans never show up,* she thought, *an army of Thearans increases our chances to find the book tenfold.*

Of course, there was the matter of trust; would these Thearans be willing to betray their God and destroy the book once they found it? Would their Queen? Would they fight alongside the other people of Pandeia against the Ermoori? There was no telling. But they held the book of Sithares, and therefore the Circle's only chance at destroying the God of Fire. Karak had to have convinced them it was the right thing to do, or they never would have come to Aethos in the first place.

The Thearans entered Aethos without ceremony. There was no greeting, no celebration. They simply walked in, and made their way to the barracks that Platon set up for them. All the other people who lived in Aethos, Omati and Tarsi alike, stared at them as they stalked through the city streets. Zeera couldn't help but notice Karak didn't come to see her when he arrived. A small pang of apprehension shot through her; he only avoided her when he had bad news.

Once the Thearans were settled, Zeera went to see Aella. The Queen sat in her quarters, cleaning her armour in silence. Zeera remained in the doorway, waiting until Aella acknowledged her presence. She cleaned and polished meticulously, and only raised her eyes to look at Zeera when she was finished.

"Zeera?" she asked.

"Yes," Zeera said, "I represent the Circle of Shadows."

"Karak told me about the situation. I'm sorry, I don't have the book with me."

The revelation sent a wave of hot sickness through Zeera's chest and stomach. She wrestled to keep her face still. *Karak failed after all,* she thought, *and he thought an army would suffice as a consolation prize*. Zeera sat next to Aella.

"Do you know where it is?"

Aella nodded, her mouth a hard-set line. Her eyes glowed in the dim room, a bright, glittering gold that somehow showed rage and calm at the same time.

"Kerberos has it," she said, "it was with me when we attacked Omatus. I believe it's in the royal bedchamber, or possibly in the throne room."

It made sense to Zeera; despite the loyalty of his men, Kerberos would take it upon himself to guard such an item.

"I say we use our combined strength," Aella said, "and go back to Omatus now. Kerberos won't expect it. He doesn't know how many warriors are gathered together in Aethos."

"We cannot do that, your highness," Zeera said, "the Ermoori are spreading further throughout Pandeia every week. We need to stay here. I will send a small group of Tarsi. They can remain undetected, and take the book without Kerberos even knowing."

"You underestimate him. A handful of Tarsi don't stand a chance against Kerberos."

Zeera watched Aella closely; her bright eyes hadn't changed. She needed to know what kind of Queen Aella was, and what kind of person. The information she'd received from her agents in Theara over the years was minimal; it seemed she was a fair and just ruler, but Queens and Kings could be anyone behind closed doors.

"What do you hope to achieve here, Aella?" Zeera asked.

She took her time responding, frowning and staring at nothing.

"I want Kerberos dead," she said, "for all that he's done to me and my people. And I want Sithares gone."

"Why would you want your God destroyed?"

Again, Aella hesitated. A long, drawn-out sigh escaped her, and Zeera tried to discern the thoughts that lay behind her captivating golden eyes. She came across as genuine; but there was a restraint, a sense of utter control, that crept from her like heat from the sun. Zeera couldn't help but be reminded of Kerberos.

"Can I tell you something," Aella said, "that no one else can know?"

"The Tarsi are nothing if not secret keepers."

Aella breathed slowly, inhaling and exhaling three full times, before continuing.

"Sithares has betrayed Kerberos. It's inside my head now, and I believe it has chosen me as the new Hero."

"I didn't think that was possible," Zeera said, "unless the current Hero dies?"

She shook her head, looking at Zeera directly.

"I don't know how the Gods work, Zeera," she said, "Kerberos decided he preferred being a peaceful ruler, apparently, over bringing destruction to the rest of Pandeia. His loyalties lay with Omatus. As much as I hate to admit it, he is a great king. But Sithares wouldn't have it. I was full of rage and vengeance, and that's all Sithares needs to connect with someone."

She stopped a moment, breathing carefully again. Her eyes remained fixed on Zeera's.

"Zeera," she said, "I want to destroy Sithares because it's in my head, and I'm afraid. If it gains more control, I'll end up just like Kerberos."

Zeera couldn't believe it. Decades of research had taught her that the Gods couldn't simply assign another Hero by choice. Her only theory was that Sithares had grown far more powerful than anyone realised. *Maybe its sheer power, the massive level of magic it has amassed, means it can do things no God has done before*. It was perhaps the most terrifying thought Zeera had ever experienced.

"You're willing to fight against Sithares," she said, "even if it means you lose Fire Magic? Even if it means you die?"

Aella smiled. It was a tired, awful smile that looked to Zeera like the loss of hope.

"I've died before, Zeera," she said, "I don't look forward to it, but if that's what it takes to get Sithares out of my head, then that's what I'll do. Besides, with Sithares gone, it may mean my soul ends up in some other afterlife. One far more peaceful than what Sithares gave me."

"If you had to choose between killing Kerberos and helping us destroy Sithares," Zeera said, her voice barely above a whisper, "which would you choose?"

She stared at the wall, the same sad expression on her face. Zeera watched her eyes, seeing the spark of strength and power they contained. But stifling that spark, dulling the glow of her presence, was a deep sadness. It filled her gold eyes like water in a pool, as though she'd lived a thousand lifetimes, and each had been filled with misery. *Another Hero I am unable to help,* she thought, *though she at least has a reason for wanting Sithares' destruction.*

"I would…" Aella said, and then sighed again, "I would help to destroy Sithares."

Lashek

1794

The day that the Queen of Theara arrived in Aethos, Lashek was certain the Circle would be destroyed. As far as he was concerned, Zeera made the same mistake twice; inviting a Sithares-worshipping murderer to join the Circle of Shadows. It was ridiculous to him that Zeera would try to compel a servant of Sithares to help them destroy the very God they worshipped.

He watched her every chance he got. By appearances, she was genuine; but then again, Kerberos had appeared genuine too. The biggest difference was that Aella brought an army with her, an army of Fire Magicians who all worshipped Sithares. It meant if she did intend to betray them as Kerberos had, it would turn into its own war. With Sithares and the impending threat of invasion from Ermoor, it was a war no one could afford to fight; let alone one they were likely to win.

The Thearans were infamous for fighting everyone, even their own kind, over nothing but sport. He didn't know much of their Queen, but any ruler of such a volatile group of people couldn't be trusted. Besides, though the Thearans fought each other, there was no certainty that Aella and Kerberos weren't working together.

The only thing holding Lashek back from arguing the point with Zeera was that she knew a lot more than he did. It frustrated him that she never told the Heroes as much as she knew. At some point, she would have to share her knowledge; Lashek just hoped it was sooner rather than later. Until then, he tried to stay quiet about his distrust of Aella, as long as nothing too suspicious happened.

Lashek was healing much faster now, and with training his strength came back. He no longer felt stiff and store, and he spent most days up and about. Aethos reminded him a lot of Tarsium, and he even grew to love it; for what it was. *If I survive this cursed war,* he thought, *the first thing I'll do is go back to the forest.*

He trained a lot now, and he spent a lot of time in the training room Zeera made for him; even when he didn't train, he enjoyed being surrounded by soil and plants. Amalus didn't speak with him often, but he felt closer to it in that room. Unlike any of the other training rooms, Lashek's had no roof, so that the trees and plants could benefit from the sunlight. It helped his connection to Shadow Magic, as well.

Every now and then, Lashek's dreams turned to the fateful day of Kerberos' attack. He would fight as hard as he could, but Kerberos always won. Every time, Lashek woke panting and covered in sweat. His body ached after every one of those dreams; as though Kerberos had beaten him once again, somehow.

As soon as he felt as strong as he'd been before Kerberos' attack, Lashek began training harder than he ever had before. Eliza pushed him to his limits and beyond; she fought faster and more intensely than anyone Lashek had ever seen. Zeera helped him learn the subtleties of magic. With her help, he began practicing spells he never thought possible; he learned how to create a platform of Shadow that could levitate objects, and how to immediately draw every spec of light from a room.

He communed with Amalus, and through the God of Shadow he learned even more. *Why didn't I ask about magic earlier?* He thought to himself, *I could have been practicing this years ago*. But the past was over, and Lashek focused on the magic he'd finally learned. Through Amalus, and with Zeera's help, he learned how to turn himself into an actual, living Shadow.

It was like the Shadow version of Kerberos' magic; he'd

become covered in flames, without being burned. In that state, Kerberos was invulnerable to blades and any physical attacks. Similarly, Lashek's Shadow state rendered him untouchable. He could pass through walls, become invisible, and launch devastating magical attacks. The only problem was that it ate through his magic reserves, and he could only maintain it for a short time.

Practicing magic became Lashek's priority. He tried to hold his Shadow state for as long as possible each day, and each day the time improved. He trained against Eliza, and surprised her with it. He still lost the fight; but for one brief moment, he almost had her.

He didn't know what would happen first; destroying Sithares, the Ermoori invasion, or Kerberos appearing yet again for vengeance. Even more, he couldn't tell which would be worse. But with every passing day, he began to feel a little more confident. His dreams about Kerberos grew less frequent, and eventually stopped; by then, he'd forgotten about them entirely.

Aerene

1794

Austris Ara floated through the sky, perpetually moving between a handful of landmarks in the Southern Ocean. Its movement was familiar and comforting to every Austris Aran. Now, for the first time since it drifted south two thousand years before, the floating city headed north for Aethos.

Aerene prayed every day, not just as part of her duties, but for guidance from Aurath. She heard its voice only occasionally.

Her quarters—the Hero's quarters—were spacious and luxurious. *My rooms are bigger and better than Aelis'*, she thought, *I wonder if he knows that*. She hoped not; it certainly wouldn't help things. They'd spoken, very briefly, a few times since the war horns boomed. He was intent on being as cold as possible.

For all the magic that kept Austris Ara afloat and moving, the city still moved slowly, and getting to Aethos would take a while. Aerene hoped to get through to Aelis before they arrived. *Even if only a little*. She didn't have much hope, but Shaela and Queen Lorae both agreed it was worth trying. *Why is it on me?* She thought, *why can't it be his responsibility to grow up and let go of this?*

The prince's quarters were only a couple dozen metres from her own. He stayed in there most days, unless he had a reason to leave, and the guards outside the doors glared at her whenever she passed. She stopped in front of them, and glared right back, until they shuffled uncomfortably. As loyal as they were to Aelis, they knew their ultimate loyalty was to Aurath's chosen.

"I need to speak with Aelis," she said.

Neither guard reacted for a moment, and Aerene almost unleashed a blast of Air Magic out of pure spite.

"Now," she added, raising her eyebrows at them both.

Finally, they stepped aside, and Aerene pushed the heavy doors open. Aelis wasn't in the main room. She went to the balcony, and found him staring out over the city.

"What do you want?" he said.

"You know what I want, Aelis. To let this go. To be friends again. Everyone else has adjusted, and accepted it. Why can't you?"

He stared, his face blank and his eyes distant. There was no telling what thoughts lay behind his cold white eyes. The tiniest hint of a frown angled his eyebrows, but other than that there was no emotion whatsoever. Aerene stared out at the city too, trying to control her impatience.

"There's nothing more to say," he said.

"Aelis. When the King and Queen die, you will rule Austris Ara. Right now, you're the only one who's still fighting this. If you're made King and you haven't won the people over, Austris Ara will become a mess. You need to do what's right for the city."

"When I'm King," he said, "what's right for the city is whatever I say."

Aerene scoffed at him, shook her head, and left him there. *Maybe I just need to give him a few more decades,* she thought, *but at this point I can't see him ever changing.*

Shaela sat in the main chamber, watching Aerene walk back towards the door.

"How's the Prince today?" she said, a dry smirk on her face.

"Stubborn and difficult."

"Same old Aelis, then?"

She stood as Aerene reached the door, and matched her pace.

"We're getting closer to Aethos every day now," Shaela said, "when we arrive, you might need to order Aelis to stay in the palace. We can't present a disorganised leadership to the Circle of Shadows."

She knew it was true; Aelis would only argue against

everything Aerene had to say. He would undermine her at every opportunity. *As much as I don't want to be the Hero in the first place, I can't have Aelis make me look like I lack authority.*

Like it or not, Aerene was the representative for all of Austris Ara. Aethos—and all of Pandeia for that matter—hadn't seen Austris Arans in millennia, and none of them lived that long. *We've passed into myth and legend,* she thought, *as far as they're concerned, we may as well be the Gods and Heroes of ancient times.*

"Giving him that order publicly will cause just as much trouble," Aerene said, "he'll do everything in his power to fight it."

"Better he fights it from the palace than in Aethos, in front of the Circle."

Mara

1794

After she spoke with Eliza, Riffolk appeared in her mind even more. It was as though he felt his name on her lips, as though he owned even her thoughts. When they were married, she felt like his property. At the time, Mara believed that was just how marriage worked. After Mathys saved her, she'd seen a whole new world; a world of freedom, where her life was no longer controlled by Riffolk or the scriptures of the One True God.

Now that she'd spoken to Eliza, and mentioned his name, that feeling of freedom slowly left her. Riffolk was going to take all of

Pandeia eventually, and when he did, there would be nowhere for Mara to hide. He'd own her again, the way he did before she escaped. It was that, or death.

She feared sleep now. Every time she closed her eyes, Riffolk was there. *He knows I'm afraid,* she thought, *he knows, and he's enjoying it.* As well as his evil face, and the crackling Power Magic she associated with him, Mara's nightmares began showing the future Pandeia that might come to be. In them, Riffolk sat on a throne, smiling in satisfaction as the people of Pandeia bowed down on their knees.

Mara tried convincing herself that they were merely dreams. In daylight, she could almost believe it. But a part of her, a part that couldn't be denied, knew they were more than that. Whether he achieved it or not, that future was exactly what Riffolk wanted. If it was possible for him to rule over Pandeia, he would do anything to make it happen.

In her nightmares, Riffolk was unstoppable. He was like a God. All he had to do was gesture, and the world bent to his will. Mara couldn't move, unless it was to do his bidding. The people around her, her friends and family, looked like empty shells. Their eyes were glossed over, their mouths slack. Riffolk's soldiers were the same, emptied of everything but rage and discipline.

Every night, it was the same thing. The Circle was broken, its mission never completed. Riffolk on a throne, smiling as he pulled the strings. Ermoori soldiers marched through every street, their eyes scanning everything. Every country had fallen, every army shattered against the unstoppable force of Riffolk's technological power. There were no Heroes in this world; they were dead or conquered, forced to serve.

Sometimes, Mara's nightmares showed the invasion itself. Aethos being overrun by Ermoori soldiers wielding devastating weapons, destroying anyone who dared oppose them. They killed thousands, and even the might of the Circle and its Heroes was crushed under Ermoor's heel.

No one listened to her when she talked about the nightmares. She didn't blame them; she had no evidence that what she was saying was the truth. Sometimes, she wasn't even certain herself. But when Riffolk's dark presence sliced into her mind, even during the day, those were the moments she knew. That was real. If she could show Zeera what it felt like, if she could share the rage that bubbled away in the corners of her thoughts, Zeera would believe her.

Mara wondered if a connection like the one between her and Riffolk existed between other people. None of the other Heroes had ever mentioned anything like it before. If she could get rid of her magic, and that connection, she would. She would do anything to have peace.

Before he died, years ago, Mathys had taught her to still her mind. He taught her that emotion was the enemy of both combat and success. Back then, Mara was able to gain control with focus and training. Now, however, her mind simply wouldn't comply. It was as though something had snapped; some connection between her thoughts and feelings that allowed her to push emotion down. Instead, Mara was now at the mercy of any feeling that surfaced in her mind.

Even if she could control her emotion, there was nothing she could have done about her dreams. She couldn't tell if Riffolk was influencing her dreams on purpose, or if his presence in her mind made them worse; but whatever the case, she knew they had something to do with their connection.

Riffolk was certainly the type to give her nightmares, if it was within his power to do so. If for no other reason than pure enjoyment, he would have caused her any pain he could. Mara understood that much, at least; if she was able to, she would have caused Riffolk pain too. She didn't even know how to learn something like that; Riffolk was at least smart enough to figure it out on his own.

Most nights, Mara lay awake, staring at the ceiling, too terrified to let herself go to sleep. Even so, Riffolk's face still swam up into her consciousness. She couldn't have stopped him if she tried. Her nightmares were becoming so frequent and so intense that they were bleeding into her conscious mind as well.

Mara would have given anything to see Riffolk dead. She wasn't sure how much of that desire stemmed from the hatred boiling up from Riffolk's presence, and how much was her own. If she was honest with herself, she didn't even care. Whether the fault lay with Riffolk, or if her need to see him dead came purely from her own genuine desire, when he died it would be satisfied.

She wasn't even sure if killing Riffolk was possible. In her dreams, he was untouchable. When she lived in Ermoor, he seemed the same way. Even when she gained Power Magic, he'd been several steps ahead of her. Mara was powerful, but Riffolk's intelligence meant that magic became yet another one of the things he could do perfectly.

In her nightmares, he was everywhere at once, powerful and all-knowing. Although she couldn't move, and despite seeing him on his throne, she somehow knew he was behind her too. Even if she ran, he would be at the end of every hallway, behind every door. He simply could not be escaped. In reality, she knew he couldn't do that; but a part of her had no idea what he was capable of now. If Kerberos could gain multiple types of magic, what was stopping Riffolk from doing the same?

Mara had no idea how intelligent Kerberos was, but she was certain Riffolk was capable of far more than the Thearan warrior. Knowing it was possible that Riffolk could have become even more powerful since she last saw him only served to drive her fear ever higher. Even before he gained the ability to use magic, Riffolk was perhaps the most dangerous man in Pandeia. With several types of magic at his disposal, as well as the entire army of Ermoor, he would be truly unstoppable. Mara already had her doubts that the Circle could destroy a God; to her, even that seemed more likely than defeating Riffolk. If he set his sights on the Circle, they were doomed.

Eliza

1794

Eliza was eating an afternoon meal when the Thearans arrived in Aethos. They were led by a Queen, a muscular woman who exuded the same dangerous energy as Kerberos. She moved gracefully, carefully, the way Mathys had. *I'm glad she's on our side,* Eliza thought, *if she actually is.*

The Thearan Queen's name was Aella. She took the Ermoori threat as seriously as Zeera did, and she hated Kerberos with a burning passion that matched Eliza's own. *I wonder what he did to her,* she thought, *if he killed someone she loved, the way he killed Mathys.*

Zeera welcomed the Thearans with open arms, bringing Aella into the Circle immediately. They held a meeting after Aella's army had settled in.

"We are glad to have you with us, Aella," Zeera said, "and hopefully now we have more of a chance."

"My warriors are dedicated and powerful," she said, "we all have cause to fight against the Ermoori."

"And to destroy Sithares?" Lashek said, his tone suspicious but careful.

Aella regarded him with polite detachment. She smiled, though it was cold and forced.

"Yes, and to destroy Sithares. I hope its death won't mean my own, or even that of my magic. But either way, it is intent on burning all of Pandeia to the ground. You don't need to be suspicious of me, Shenza. We have the same goals."

Lashek didn't look convinced, but he dropped the issue. The other Circle members seemed happy with Aella's words. *Especially Zeera,* she thought, *I think she's too excited to have the opportunity of getting Sithares' book to make good judgement about Aella.*

"Our next step is obtaining the book," Zeera said, "and then we will plan for the battle against Ermoor."

Aella nodded, the same cold smile on her face. Eliza saw death in her eyes. Mathys' eyes held the same deep darkness, though all her life he'd been a gentle and kind man. On a face she didn't know, that darkness was terrifying.

"The book is still in Omatus," Aella said, "I told your agent where it is. It won't be moved from there until we take it."

"Yes," Zeera said, "I just hope it can be retrieved in time. The Ermoori will breach Omatus before long."

"Why don't they just fall back now?" Aerene asked, "before they're weakened by an attack and have to flee?"

"Kerberos is far too confident in his ability to hold the city," Aella said, "he won't flee unless there is no other option."

"Do you think he can actually defend Omatus against the Ermoori?" Lashek asked.

"My warriors couldn't take it from him," Aella said, "but we don't have the technology and weapons the Ermoori have. I'm not sure."

"There's no way they can," Mara said quietly, "the Ermoori can't be stopped. I'm not even sure we'll win with all of Pandeia on our side."

Zeera shot a glance at Eliza; *she shouldn't be talking like that,* it seemed to say. *As though it's my responsibility what she says,* she thought.

"Mother, please," Eliza whispered, "we'll win. I promise."

Her mother went silent, eyes pointed down at the ground. She was pale, her mouth turned down into a thin frown. Eliza saw bright fear glowing from deep within her eyes. *She's seen Riffolk in person,* she thought, *she knows him. She knows Ermoor.* As much as she thought her mother was simply scared of him because of her past, a small part of her couldn't help but feel that same fear.

"Either way," Zeera said, "the plan is for our people in Tarsium and Omatus to come to us, to join together and break the Ermoori when they come here."

"It's a good plan," Shaela said, "even if the Tarsi and Shenza are weary, the Ermoori will be too. By the time they reach us, they will be exhausted. Meanwhile, we've all been resting and training, and most of us haven't been through months and months of battle."

"But all the reports we've received indicate the Ermoori don't seem to slow down," Lashek said, "whatever they're doing, they can do it a long time without tiring."

"Our allies are doing all they can to wear the Ermoori down," Zeera said, "I believe it's working. Besides, most of their travel so far has been either slowly slogging through forests or just sailing over the ocean. Their only way to Aethos after Omatus is on land. They're too big a force to travel down the Alpheus, and they would be too vulnerable approaching Aethos by sea."

Eliza began to see Zeera's point. The Ermoori had moved from battle to battle, barely getting time to rest, but facing a new army each time. After that, they would have to march through the Omasi desert. They would be overheated, exhausted, wounded; weakened. *Maybe we* can *do this,* she thought, *maybe we really can defeat them.*

Zeera

1794

After their conversation, Zeera invited Aella to train with her. Though Aella's controlled nature occasionally reminded her of Kerberos, there was an earnest aura around the Thearan Queen. She really did want Sithares destroyed; Zeera had no doubt of that at all.

Now it was time to see what she could do; both with magic, and in combat. Zeera knew what Kerberos was capable of, but if she were to put any real trust in Aella, she had to know what the Thearan Queen's limits were. Her sources confirmed that Aella was powerful;

but she wouldn't know until she saw for herself.

As well as organizing quarters for Aella and a barracks for the Thearans, Platon set up a training room for Aella. It was previously a storage room, the walls and floor made from Omasi stone, with plenty of space inside. Where the Circle had training spaces close to their quarters, Aella's was attached to the makeshift barracks.

Zeera and Aella stood across from each other, Aella with a short sword in each hand and Zeera with nothing but the waterskins on her belt. She would have preferred one of the water tubs that lay in her own training room; but the waterskins were better than nothing. Besides, at least for the first sparring session between them, Zeera wanted Aella to feel like she was on her own ground. The training room was entirely hers.

"You really don't want a weapon?" Aella asked, "this will hardly be a fair fight."

Zeera pulled the stoppers from her waterskins, feeling magic call to her from the water within.

"The Tarsi don't usually use weapons," Zeera said, "just magic."

She'd barely finished the sentence when Aella launched herself into the attack. *So fast,* Zeera thought, *and she's not even using magic yet*. Zeera dove to the side, reaching with her mind into the waterskins. The water reacted to her thoughts instantly, rushing out in a thin line and gathering into two perfect spheres.

Aella was already attacking again when Zeera came out of her roll; her foot flashed at Zeera's head. Zeera ducked, barely avoiding the hit, and aimed a kick of her own at Aella's stomach.

They fought the same way for a few minutes, Aella ignoring her swords in favour of kicks. Zeera kept her magic to a minimum, using it for extra protection when she couldn't dodge; at her command, it froze solid instantly in a thick shell along her arm or shin.

Finally, Aella's blades came into the fight. She began slicing at the ice shields Zeera used, though the razor-sharp metal only barely chipped shards off the solid ice. Within seconds, any ice that had been chipped off melted and flew back to Zeera's shields. Once she noticed this, Aella began a new attack; Fire Magic blossomed to life in her hands as she threw her swords to the side of the room.

"I've never fought a Tarsi," Aella said, a wicked smile on her face as fire danced in her hands, "let's see what you can do."

Two fireballs lanced out from Aella, twisting in the air around Zeera. One streaked towards her from the left, and she lost sight of the second. She leapt, thrusting her ice shield down as she flew over the first fireball. A deafening hiss came from the ice on her arm as it slammed into the fire; then the fireball exploded.

Zeera was thrown up and off course, twirling wildly in the air as she fought to locate the second fireball. She saw it just as she landed on the ground in a barely controlled roll; Aella was holding it until the right moment. Just as she saw it, the fireball screamed towards her. The whoosh of fire filled her ears. Desperate, Zeera formed a blade from her remaining ice and launched it at Aella's arm. As she hoped,

Aella was too focused on her magic to notice a direct threat; the ice sliced into her arm, deep enough to draw blood instantly.

Without hesitation, Zeera pulled blood from Aella's cut, drawing enough to form another shield. It wouldn't freeze, but Zeera pushed on and formed it into a solid sphere, launching it at the fireball.

This time, the explosion was even larger; Zeera was blown off her feet. She cannoned into the wall behind her, bright spots of light filling her vision. Vaguely, she was aware of Aella forming two more fireballs. *There was so much magic in the first two,* she thought, *they would have been enough to level a building. How does she have more?*

Again, Zeera was reminded uncomfortably of Kerberos. Fire Magic was known as the most destructive magic, so the destructive power harnessed by Aella wasn't a complete surprise; but the sheer amount of magic she commanded blew Zeera away. *She may even be more powerful than Kerberos,* she thought, *we are lucky to have her on our side*.

"Stop," she called, her voice failing as she got to her feet, "I think that's enough for me."

Aella's face twisted into a frown of frustration, but it quickly dissolved into concern as she let the fireballs disappear in a rush of smoke. When she saw Zeera could stand on her own, she glanced down at the cut on her arm.

"That was… interesting," she said, "I had no idea Water Magic could do that."

"Every magic type can be used in surprising ways," Zeera said, massaging the soreness from her neck, "it just takes a little creativity. And a *lot* of training."

Aella laughed, nodding.

"I wonder what else I could do with Fire Magic," she said, "if I really thought about it."

"That is a frightening thought," Zeera said, though she kept her tone light, "you are already far more powerful than anyone I have seen. Possibly including Kerberos."

Aella's eyes grew dark. The sadness Zeera had seen earlier came back to her then, and she suddenly looked ancient.

"I know," she said, without pride or bravado, "if he'd fought me himself, without an army between us, he would be dead right now."

"I think he knows it, too." Zeera said softly, "otherwise he *would* have fought you himself. Kerberos takes no chances."

Eliza

1794

The first time she watched Aella train, Eliza was filled with a deep and uncomfortable dread. *This woman is even more powerful than Kerberos*, she thought, *if she wanted to, she could kill us all*. It wasn't even just her magic; her combat skills were beyond anything Eliza had ever seen before. Aella trained against Zeera, and Eliza watched their fire and water collide in hissing explosions all around the training room.

In between magical attacks, the two traded blows and dodges. Zeera barely kept up with Aella's attacks. Eliza's training with Mathys allowed her to watch and analyse Aella's combat style. It was flawless.

I thought Queens were supposed to be like lady versions of Kings, she thought, *not lethal warriors*. She'd never heard of a real Queen before at all, of course, but she knew there were Kings in old times in Ermoor, and they spent their time sitting on a throne and giving out orders. *She moves like a Thearan version of the Spectre of Ermoor,* Eliza thought.

Growing up, her mother never let Mathys tell her about the Spectre. But he ended up telling her one day after she asked endless questions about his life in Ermoor and why he knew so much about combat and weaponry. To his credit, he evaded the questions for as long as he could. But even when she was younger, Eliza had a will as strong as steel.

Aella ducked under Zeera's kick as easily as taking a step, a look of vicious joy painted on her face. She fought the way Mathys had; efficiently and with extreme precision. Her attacks were more violent, her movements sharper, but other than that Eliza saw an uncanny resemblance.

"She's incredible," Lashek whispered to her, "isn't she?"

Eliza nodded, staring as Aella spun around another kick and launched a kick of her own that slipped between Zeera's defence and connected with her ribs. Zeera was thrown to the ground, and Aella settled perfectly into a combat stance.

"She should have been Sithares' Hero," Lashek said, "instead of Kerberos."

Just like me, Eliza thought.

"It definitely would have made things easier," she said, "if she was on our side from the beginning, Kerberos' attack in Tarsium never would have happened."

Lashek grunted in agreement, then went quiet. He glanced down at his leg; he still walked with a subtle limp. His wounds were severe, and though he'd healed a while ago, the reminder obviously made him uncomfortable.

Eliza left, thinking about Aella and Kerberos. How one of them should have been Hero, and one of them shouldn't. She thought about how *she* should have been Hero. *What do the Gods base their decisions on? There has to be a plan*. Her mother was an amazing woman, but she simply didn't have what it took to be a Hero. Everyone knew it; even she knew it. And yet, Taranos had chosen her.

Maybe Taranos chose her because she would give birth to the real *Hero,* she thought, *maybe it is me, but my mother didn't realise*. Even as she thought it, she knew it was wrong. But a part of her lit up, and she desperately wanted it to be true.

She got to her quarters, thinking about Taranos and the Heroes. Aerene had mentioned hearing the voice of her God, and so had her mother. *Maybe I can communicate with Taranos too*. Praying never worked for her before, but maybe she was doing it wrong.

She knelt on the ground, bowing her head and clasping her hands together. *I don't know where to start,* she thought, *but here goes nothing*. She pictured the flashing yellow lightning she used to see in her dreams as a child, the yellow that was now as familiar and comfortable as a home. Though she'd never felt a connection with Taranos, her magic was born of the God of Power; magic had to help her commune with it.

The magic in her mind flashed and grew, and she brought it to the surface; it buzzed on her skin, covering her entirely. Closing her eyes, she focused all her attention on Taranos. *Hear me,* she thought, *please hear me*.

"Taranos," she said, "I don't know if you know me, but please, I need a sign from you. I need to know that my mother is really the Hero you wanted. Why can't it be me?"

Eliza waited. She tried to imagine what a God's voice would sound like. Her magic pulsed around her, sparking and alive. No voice arose from the crackling energy. She listened as intently as she could. *Please hear me, Taranos*. But no matter how much she focused, or how often she repeated herself, she heard nothing at all.

Aella

1794

Aethos was much like Omatus, except a solemn integrity filled the air, unlike the pretentious atmosphere that pervaded Kerberos' city. There was no hint of Sithares in Aethos either, other than what she brought with her and her army. The Circle of Shadows already knew of Kerberos, had in fact fought him themselves; though they were still keen for any information she could give them.

"He wields Shadow Magic now," Aella said, "as well as Fire Magic, of course."

“Yes,” Zeera said, “we are aware. We believe he possesses every kind of magic now but Air Magic. And that is guarded closely by the Austris Arans.”

“And he fought all of you,” Aella said, “and won?”

“Yes.”

She knew he was powerful, but she had no idea how much power he held. He said to her she would have defeated him if not for his new talents; but even then, he only showed her one new kind of magic. *How is it even possible for one person to possess that much magic?* She thought, *surely, he can’t maintain that much sheer power for long.*

“Has anyone wielded more than one magic at a time before?” she asked Zeera.

“There are legends. Stories, really. Nothing we can confirm with any certainty.”

“Like Darkfire?” the young Ermoori woman said before blushing and looking at the ground, “Mathys told me that story a few times.”

“That is one of the more famous stories, yes,” Zeera said, “but historians never agree on whether it really happened.”

Aella heard the story when she was younger too. A warrior with the power of Shadow and Fire, powerful enough to destroy Pandeia itself. It reminded her dimly of Dakesh; he had been talented, though unfocused, and he wielded Fire Magic as a Shenza. But as far as she was aware, he’d only carried the sword of one of their Shadow

Magicians; he didn't possess the magic himself. Besides, she remembered the story of Darkfire being an ancient prophecy, rather than a legend that had already happened.

"Kerberos was one of the most dangerous people in Pandeia," Aella said, "even before he gained control of other magic. Not just because of his strength and power, but because of his mind. He's ruthless. Bloodthirsty. He'll do anything to achieve his goals."

"Well," Lashek said, "what *are* his goals?"

"I don't know."

"You know him better than anyone here," he said, "surely there's something you can tell us."

"At the time I knew him, his goal was to take Omatus. He never told anyone in his tribe, not even his most trusted Commanders. There was no clue that would have given his true intentions away. Trust me, if he has a new plan, we won't discover it until it's too late."

"He obviously desires power," Zeera said, "the question is whether he wants it for its own sake, or if he wants to use it for a specific purpose."

"It's not just power," Aella said, her voice low, "he has something else, too."

"I'm sure we all love the suspense," Lashek said, "but out with it. What more could he have?"

"He made himself immortal," Aella whispered, "him and a group of his most talented warriors. He sold our souls to Sithares in exchange for immortality."

“He’s immortal?” Lashek said, “all that magic, *and* he can’t be killed? He’s getting awfully close to just being a God himself.”

“You said ‘*our* souls’,” Zeera said, “are you the same as him?”

“I’m nothing like him,” Aella snapped, “but… yes, he made me immortal too. No one but him had a choice. He made the deal without our knowledge or consent. I haven’t aged in twenty years… neither has Kerberos.”

Lashek grunted, and Zeera shook her head in shock. The two Ermoori women simply stared, pale and wide-eyed. Kerberos’ smug smile appeared in Aella’s mind, sitting on his throne in Omatus. Killing him was going to be the biggest challenge she’d ever faced; but she had the Circle of Shadows on her side now, as well as the armies they controlled.

“How many of his warriors are immortal?” Zeera asked, “other than yourself?”

“I’m not sure exactly,” Aella said, “but it’s a large group. Hundreds, possibly.”

“And they can’t die?”

Aella hesitated, her mind cast back to the first battle of Omatus, when she tried to stop Kerberos. She’d jumped from the great bridge, and death had consumed her. It felt like an eternity, the Fires of Sithares’ kingdom devouring her flesh endlessly. When she finally came back, her mind had been broken.

“We can die,” she said, “but then we come back. It does something, to our mind. Fractures it. I think because Sithares takes a piece of our soul each time. We stay dead for around a day, I think. But it feels like forever to us."

The Circle stared at her, then exchanged looks with each other. Zeera's eyes never left Aella.

"So, could we kill them," Zeera said, "and then bind them before they come back?"

"Depending what you use. When they come back, there is a burst of Fire Magic. Most ties would be incinerated."

"Shadow Magic would do it," Zeera said.

Aella nodded. The binds that Kerberos created to imprison her had certainly worked.

"Wait a minute," Lashek said, "that's the best we can do?" Tie Kerberos up and just… leave him somewhere?"

"There is a weapon that can kill him," Aella said, "forged by Sithares itself. It's called the Soul Blade, and Kerberos carries it on him wherever he goes. If we can take it from him, we can kill him."

"That's great," Lashek said, "if any of us are alive after the Ermoori invade, we'll pick a fight with him then."

Zeera sighed, closing her eyes briefly. Aella felt her frustration; Lashek was already getting on her nerves. But his words cut through, and she frowned as their meaning settled in her mind.

"You're really planning on letting the Ermoori invade Aethos?" she said, "why not take the fight to them?"

“The only way that would work,” Zeera said, “is if Kerberos could be trusted to join forces with us. And even then, I have little faith in him or his followers.”

“We can’t trust him,” the young Ermoori woman said, “no matter what.”

“I agree,” Aella said, “but we have several armies at our disposal right now, and other than Kerberos himself we have the most powerful magicians in the world. We don’t need Kerberos or his Thearans.”

“You have no idea what the Ermoori are capable of,” Zeera said, “this is about more than just how many warriors we have. Our priority is Sithares, but the Ermoori are almost as much of a threat as the God of Fire. If we have any hope at all of defeating them, all of Pandeia need to work together.”

Arthor

1794

Arthor stared at the disc in his hand. Its smooth black surface was marked by thin gold plating, a technology Arthor would never understand. The war raged on, Riffolk leading his troops an ocean away. The disc reflected his study's lighting; pure orange candlelight flashed from its surface as he turned it between his hands.

Ermoor's people were still celebrating; even at this late hour, Arthor heard laughter and music from his neighbours. *If they only knew,* he thought, *there would be mourning and shocked silence*. The

Shenza were their enemies, there was no denying it; but if Ermoor knew the truth about their people, and about the war, the atmosphere in the city would be decidedly different.

Not for the first time, Arthor wondered what other secrets Riffolk kept. As the Lord Commander, Arthor should have had access to all information Riffolk did; he was in charge of safety and security for all of Ermoor, after all. *I know there are secrets Riffolk keeps from me,* he thought, his eyes stuck on the access disc he held.

He checked the old clock against his study wall; it was just after midnight. *Surely Riffolk's lab assistants have gone home by now,* he thought. This was the chance of a lifetime; access to Riffolk's lab while he was out of the country. He had to know what other secrets Riffolk was keeping. Almost a year without the voice in his head, and his old sense of justice was fully restored. He felt like a new man; a better man. *I can't do anything with Riffolk staring over my shoulder, but in his absence, maybe I can start to make things right.*

Despite celebrations going in many houses, the streets were empty. Arthor walked on his own; getting a cart carried too much of a risk of people knowing where he was going. Luckily, the rain had mostly stopped, though ominous clouds still blacked out the night sky.

It took him a while to arrive at the lab, but when it came into sight Arthor breathed a sigh of relief; the building sat in total darkness. His authorisation disc lay against his chest on its lanyard. It occurred to him that Riffolk's lab assistant—while he may have been against

Lucius—was ultimately loyal to the Prime Overseer. *This could be a trap*. Suddenly, he felt like a fool.

He'd come too far to walk away. Besides, without Riffolk around, Arthor was technically the highest-ranking person in all of Ermoor. *Even if they saw me,* he thought, *what would they do?* Riffolk would find out, but it could be years before he returned from the war.

Breathing slowly, Arthor stepped up to the security console next to the door. *I'm doing it,* he thought, *I have to*. For the first time he could remember, he was thinking clearly. Justice would never happen without people standing up to the Prime Overseer. *Who better to stand up to him than the Lord Commander?* The security console beeped as he swiped his disc through the slot, and the door's lock clicked.

Beyond the main door, the corridors shined with their same brightness as always. Once the door closed behind him, it was impossible to tell what time of day it might be outside. He'd taken hours to find Riffolk's office storeroom. Filing cabinets filled the space, along with drawers and a table. He knew he was alone, but he moved as quickly as he could nevertheless. *Even if no one shows up until the morning,* he thought, *Riffolk's lab isn't exactly the safest place to go snooping around.*

He wasn't sure exactly what to look for, or where it might be. But eventually, he found it; a single-drawer cabinet under the desk. It was almost hidden, painted black and nestled against the underside of the desk drawer itself. Inside, Arthor found folders tied closed, thick and almost overflowing with loose papers. Opening one of them, he scanned through the contents.

"Riffolk..." he murmured, "what have you done?"

Experimentation. Torture. Murder. Shenza spies had infiltrated Ermoor on at least two occasions, and Riffolk caught them. He'd used their bodies to test weapons, and subjected them to any number of other atrocities, before killing them in cold blood. According to the files he kept, the Shenza had been instrumental in several of his advancements in weapons and defensive technologies.

What was worse; after the Tyran uprising, one of their people was also murdered by Riffolk in his own lab. *If only I could bring this to someone,* he thought, *and bring Riffolk to justice*. But even if there was someone other than Riffolk, the injustices he'd found were secrets only known by Riffolk himself. No one would believe him, and no one would dare go against the Prime Overseer.

At least I'll know. Even if no one else ever will. The more he read, the angrier he became; at Riffolk, of course, but also at himself. He knew how evil Riffolk was, even before tonight. But now, he saw more than just a plan to take control of Ermoor. He saw specific and premeditated torture. Using people as though they were pieces of some sick machine. *I don't know how I lived with myself before,* he thought, *but no more. Riffolk must be stopped.*

The problem was Riffolk's secrecy. The Shenza infiltrating, the Tyrans, Riffolk's coup against the Twelve; none of it was known. Arthor could do nothing about the Shenza spies or the Twelve. There was far too little evidence and it was too far in the past. But the Tyrans still toiled below Ermoor. *If I can show Ermoor what's happening under their noses,* he thought, *I can plant the seeds of doubt against Riffolk.*

Centuries of propaganda had poisoned the Ermoori against the Shenza, and even Arthor himself found it difficult thinking of them as anything other than military opponents. Trying to convince the citizenry that the invasion was wrong would be futile. But the Tyrans were a people in and of themselves, a people who'd done nothing wrong. If the Ermoori saw an entire community of innocent people being forced into slave labour, it might be enough.

Heart thumping, Arthor snatched as many folders as he could from the secret cabinet and left the lab. He had to know all of it, but he couldn't sit here reading all night. *There'll be time to return these later,* he thought, *as long as no one tries to get into that cabinet while Riffolk is away*. He didn't think it likely that Riffolk would allow any of his staff to read files this secret; but all the same, he promised himself he would return them the instant he'd finished reading them all.

Mattias

1794

Victory. Even months after they'd won, the word reverberated in Mattias' mind, strange and uncomfortable, but thrilling nonetheless. *We actually did it,* he thought, *the Shenza are defeated*. They were melting back into the forests. Reports came in of the Shenza fleeing up the giant mountain in the country's centre, and further south. The forest of Shanaken finally belonged to Ermoor.

For the first time in a long time, Mattias felt confidence. Even standing in the dark forests where he'd spent more than a year being in constant danger, he suddenly felt brave. There were still Shenza hidden in the trees, but they'd stopped attacking, and seemed to be trying to sneak their way to safety.

Their current orders were to hunt down any remaining Shenza, and to level as much of the forest as they could. Only their tanks had firepower strong enough to fell the mighty trees of Shanaken, and with most of the Shenza gone or successfully hiding, there wasn't much else for his men to do.

Despite their victory, Mattias and his unit had remained in the forest for months after the fighting stopped. After a while, they found no more Shenza. They'd been there long enough to recognize the worst of the plants and animals, and could avoid or destroy anything dangerous. Mattias grew exhausted. *We're not even fighting a war anymore,* he thought, *we're just sitting in a rotten forest while our enemies escape and regroup.*

Mattias' unit had survived fairly well over the months; from fifty men, they were now twenty-two. Though the men who'd died would remain in his mind and heart for the rest of his life, his unit had killed hundreds of Shenza; perhaps even thousands. *Surely even the Prime Overseer would be proud of that ratio,* he thought.

"Captain Sterling," Commander Liford said, approaching from the direction of a temporary headquarters they'd set up, "we're receiving new orders. Come with me."

He gestured for his men to stay put, and kept pace with the Commander. *We've taken the forest,* he thought, *what more could the*

Prime Overseer want from us? But all he could do was wait; the Commander was silent as they marched back to the makeshift headquarters.

When they arrived, he guided Mattias to his own tent, where a teleradio was set up along with a map of Shanaken and a pile of written notes. Commander Liford stared at the map for a moment, then finally acknowledged Mattias' presence again.

"Captain," he said, "We have taken Shanaken faster than even the Prime Overseer foresaw. It's excellent news, and I can tell you that he is aware of your involvement, and he's pleased with you. Our next goal is twofold, and you will be involved in both parts."

"I see," Mattias said, "I wasn't aware of any goals beyond Shanaken, Commander."

"No, the Prime Overseer likes to keep things on a need-to-know basis."

"And now I need to know?"

"Correct. Our next goal is to begin construction on the foundations of a new city here in Shanaken. After enough trees have been knocked down, that work will begin immediately. You are assigned as Captain of the project. As soon as the foundations are secure, you and your unit will move on to take Tarsium."

"We're... waging war on the *Tarsi*, as well?"

"Ermoor is the most powerful, and the most civilised, of all of Pandeia's people. We would not be doing our greater duty to Pandeia if we didn't spread that power and civility as far and wide as possible."

"Of course," Mattias said, "of course. I suppose I just didn't expect two wars so close together."

"It's one war, Captain. Tarsium is merely the second battle."

More fighting. Mattias knew almost nothing about the Tarsi, except that they were as Godless as the Shenza. Rumours surrounded them, but nothing confirmed by the Prime Overseer or the Twelve Crowns before him. The one thing he'd heard consistently was that they were passivists, but that they somehow enforced a strict no violence law throughout the country by making perpetrators simply disappear. *I doubt it's true,* he thought, *but what if it is? How do we fight a war against people who can make their enemies disappear?*

"Your unit will be merged with another," the Commander was saying, "to make up the full fifty men. Enjoy your time overseeing construction, Captain… it will be as close to peacetime as we're likely to get until the entire war is over. In a few months' time, you'll be restocked with ammunition and equipment, briefed on the battle plans, and then shipped out."

"Who else knows? Can I tell my men?"

"Only the captains for now. I wanted to inform you first, but feel free to tell your men whenever suits. I'll let you know when we've found the rest of your new unit."

He returned to his men, mind reeling as he tried to imagine yet another brutal battle. *We were lucky to have survived the last few months,* he thought, *now we have to face another enemy*. Even worse, their new enemy was fresh and not run down by months of fighting.

Plus, all the Shenza who fled to Tarsium will join their fight too.

"What's the news, Captain?" Gabriel said, "we finally going home?"

"Well," Mattias said, "not exactly. We'll stay and handle construction for a while first. Then... we're being shipped over to Tarsium."

"What in God's name for?"

"The war is not over. We're taking Tarsium now that Shanaken's ours."

"Are you serious?" Ernest said, "we don't even get to go home first?"

"No. We're getting merged with another unit so we're at full strength again, and we'll get a break from fighting while Shanaken is rebuilt into a city. Then it's on to another battlefront."

His men looked at each other, then at him. He saw the victory drain from their eyes, replaced by a resigned hopelessness that he completely understood. *There is no end,* he thought, *we're going to just keep fighting for the Prime Overseer, until we die.*

Danel

1794

Months after arriving at the southwest shore, Danel's turn finally came. The vessels available were few and only held so many Shenza each; if an Ermoori warship had come down the ocean channel between Shanaken and Tarsium, the thousands waiting for boats would have been totally vulnerable. Luckily, it seemed the Ermoori were preoccupied with the forests, and weren't intent on chasing the Shenza.

He had let others before himself, especially the children. They piled into barges and fishing boats, anything that would fit them, and left Shanaken as soon as possible. There was no energy for ceremony, or emotion; nothing but escape. *I hope the Tarsi have space for us,* he thought. He wasn't certain they would even be willing to take the Shenza in, let alone let them live in Tarsium indefinitely.

Danel sat in cold, silent defeat as the barge he'd boarded plowed through the ocean. Countless Shenza surrounded him, packed tightly together and just as silent as him. Now that the fighting was behind him, all that remained was grief and rage. He never would have admitted to feeling so much anger; the Shenza were supposed to be calm at all times. But for the first time in his life, Danel felt that rage was a reasonable response. *They've taken everything from us,* he thought, *why shouldn't we be angry?*

The journey took a long time; at least, it felt that way to Danel. With no space, the Shenza simply had to sleep where they sat, leaning on each other and trying not to fall. Danel ate sparingly, once or twice per day; he had no idea how or where he would obtain food in Tarsium.

Finally, they arrived at the port outside Carmerth. By the time he left the barge, he was so exhausted and empty that he couldn't think. He followed the other Shenza in a daze, too tired and hungry to even think about where he was going.

Carmerth was a ground-based city, like Ermoor; but from the stories Danel had heard about Ermoor, they had nothing else in common. In Carmerth, every street was sprawling and lively, where Ermoor was grey and as perfectly organised as a machine. The Shenza wandered through Carmerth, sticking together, searching for somewhere they could stay. Danel knew even before he'd looked at more than a handful of places that nowhere was big enough to house all of them.

There are thousands of us, he thought, *we'd need to split up and spread across all of Tarsium to find enough beds for us all.* As they walked, a Tarsi approached and waved them over.

"Greetings, Shenza," he said, "we know of your struggle. I'm so sorry for your loss."

A *Kaizeluun* stepped up to her, speaking loud enough for a lot of the Shenza to hear.

"Thank you for your sympathies, Tarsi. But we need beds and food, not pity. And we need a way to defeat the Ermoori and take back our land."

The Tarsi nodded.

"We will do what we can. Come with me. I will send for the other Shenza as they arrive."

They followed the Tarsi woman, who took them to a strange ancient-looking building. It was no bigger than the room of an inn. She waved them in, and the entire crowd of Shenza disappeared into the tiny building. When Danel crossed the threshold, he understood how; immediately inside the door was a flight of stairs that stretched down into the ground.

After hours walking down endless stairs, they reached a massive tunnel with a narrow but deep river running through the centre of the floor. The Shenza milled together at the base of the stairs, and the Tarsi woman addressed them all.

"This place is a secret known only to the Tarsi," she said, her voice echoing through the tunnel, "and it will be a safe place for all of the Shenza. This network of tunnels spans the entire underground of Tarsium. It may not be as comfortable as an inn, but there is enough space for all of you, and it will keep you hidden from the Ermoori."

The *Kaizeluun* thanked her, and all the other Shenza muttered their thanks as they walked past into the tunnel proper. *We'll have to sleep on the floor,* Danel thought, *there can't possibly be enough bedding for everyone*. Shenza were trained to survive and live a very simple life, without the luxurious comforts most other cultures enjoyed. Still, the tunnel floor was jagged stone and filthy mud, and he didn't look forward to trying to sleep.

For all its cold, filthy darkness, there was somehow a familiar comfort to be found in the tunnels. The Shenza stayed close, and after a while their silence changed to low conversation. Food was brought down from stalls above ground. Gradually, the energy in the tunnels shifted from grief and defeat, to a kind of stubborn optimism. There was still much to grieve, but for now they were safe, and fed. *And we still have each other,* Danel thought.

Once they'd been underground for several hours, exhaustion took hold. With no bedding, as Danel feared, all they could do was huddle up together on the filthy ground. Uneven rocks and other protrusions forced them into uncomfortable positions. But once he'd found a place to lay down, Danel was surprised at the comfort the soft mud provided. As long as he avoided the jagged rocks, lying down wasn't as bad as he'd first thought. *The filth is another matter,* he thought, *I don't think I'll ever get the mud out of my clothes or hair again.*

Quiet conversation echoed all around him even as Shenza began falling asleep. Most talked about the Ermoori, and what the future might hold, but some were reminiscing about Shanaken. The kitchens, training platforms, and the forest in general all came back to him, and Danel drifted to sleep with peaceful visions of his home. His last thought before he fell asleep, as sweet as it was bitter, was *I miss the sound of the forest.*

Riffolk

1794

The war in Shanaken lasted months; when the fighting was done, and the country finally belonged to him, almost a year had passed. His Commanders reported after they stormed the canopy cities and drove the last groups of rebels away.

Riffolk watched them spread through the forest, updating his map to show the ground they'd gained. According to his reports, a relatively large percentage of the Shenza were dead; almost a third of them. Those who weren't had fled, some up the giant mountain in the country's centre, but most across the sea to Tarsium. *Without their trees and feral wildlife to protect them,* he thought, *they'll be far easier to kill*. He looked forward to destroying them in Tarsium.

When the last of his Commanders had reported their success, Riffolk sent out his congratulations. His army suffered many casualties, but the Shenza suffered far more. Besides, he hadn't even deployed half his troops. However many he lost in Shanaken, there were thousands more ready to fight.

After Shanaken was taken, the next several months were to be spent levelling the trees. A city would be built in Shanaken, and civilization would finally be present. *Shanaken will be renamed,* he thought, *and folded into my rule*. Riffolk used the time to plan and strategise. It meant the Shenza also had time before they had to fight Ermoor again, but that was a small price to pay.

His plan for Tarsium was even more difficult than Shanaken. Other than a few small mountain ranges, Tarsium was a flat and easily traversed country, but that meant there was no protection, and they couldn't use any stealth. The Tarsi possessed no military force, but their reputation for enforcing their laws was formidable, and Riffolk still had no idea how they earned it. Added to that the Shenza joining them after they fled Shanaken, the Tarsi would potentially be able to put up a real fight. Riffolk never took unnecessary risks; his entire army would be deployed to Tarsium, other than a full unit which would remain in Shanaken. To maintain order.

Though Shanaken was empty for now, Riffolk planned on allowing the Shenza back after the war. *Assuming they can follow*

Ermoori law, he thought, *instead of acting like savages*. He didn't believe the propaganda about them, of course; but their culture was inarguably less evolved than Ermoor's, and he planned on changing that.

Riffolk looked at the map of Pandeia. While there were only two points of entry at Shanaken, one of which was a trading port to Tarsium on the far south, Tarsium could be invaded from every direction. It was perhaps their only real advantage other than the sheer power of Riffolk's weaponry. He would send two warships to Carmerth in the south, and the rest around to Sarnia on the north western coast. From there, his army would converge on Azar once the other two districts were taken.

Changing pace from military tactics, Riffolk checked his Detector. He gasped as he noticed an immediate difference; the book that previously lay underneath Azar now sat in Omatus. In fact, Azar was now a magical dead zone compared to the last time he'd checked the detection device.

Riffolk also noticed a concentrated collection of extremely powerful magic on the map. It sat in Aethos, made up of a collection of separate but powerful magic sources; it didn't take long for Riffolk to realise they were people. He didn't know who they were, but of one thing he could be certain. *Mara,* he thought, *she will be with them.*

Though he hated to admit it, Mara's magical capacity matched his own. If she was surrounding herself with equally powerful magic wielders, killing her might prove more difficult than he'd first hoped.

I'll need my army with me to face such a threat. If he could obtain the other forms of magic, destroying a group of powerful people would be more of a fair fight.

With the book of Water Magic in Omatus, Riffolk's hopes of retrieving it dropped dramatically. Kerberos was an opponent to be careful of, and not to be underestimated. By Riffolk's count, Kerberos now possessed four forms of magic; Fire, of course, Power and Shadow from Riffolk's lab, and now Water from the book he'd taken from Azar. Only one remained, the one that sat so far south on his map that no explorer had ever charted the area.

He couldn't afford to divert more resources that way. As much as he needed the magic, winning the war was his priority. It was difficult for him to set aside his mission to gain magic, but it was only a matter of time. Once he owned Pandeia, he could focus everything he had on collecting the remaining books.

The war would be fairly straightforward, if not easy; the only variables were Kerberos, and the mysterious group of magicians in Aethos. *They must have a purpose,* he thought, *I'll need to keep an eye on them.* Whether they were planning to stop his invasion, or achieve some other mission, Riffolk would deal with them eventually. No matter how benign such a group might be, they posed a threat to Riffolk and his goals.

His teleradio beeped as a Commander hailed him. Riffolk jerked out of his thoughts with a sharp exhale; he hated being interrupted.

"What is it?" he said, checking the code that identified the teleradio; Commander Liford.

"Prime Overseer," Liford said, "I'm sorry to bother you, but our men have been waiting on our orders, and we're not sure what to tell them. What are the next steps?"

Riffolk kept the troops out of his long-term plans. It was a decision Arthor disagreed with, which came as no surprise to him. But if his army knew they were to ship straight from Shanaken to Tarsium, how could they be expected to focus completely on the current objective?

Adjusting the settings of his teleradio, Riffolk opened the channel to all Commanders.

"Attention all Commanders," he said, "new orders are as follows: Any units who have suffered casualties will be merged with others to create whole units. Level as many trees as possible, and oversee construction of the foundations of a new city. Construction workers, resources and blueprints are enroute. Once foundational construction is finished, one unit is to remain in Shanaken. All other battle-ready troops are to be deployed to Tarsium."

A scattered chorus of acknowledgments cut through the teleradio's static. He had already dispatched a massive shipment of tools, resources and technology. Once it arrived, construction would properly begin on the new city. *It will be glorious,* he thought, *perhaps even more beautiful than Ermoor itself, and certainly more impressive than the wild forest.*

His tanks had been remarkably effective at bringing down the giant trees; though it shouldn't have come as a surprise, given he'd designed them with that purpose in mind. In the short term, however, he'd need the tanks on the front lines. They would destroy shields and walls with ease, and possessed firepower unmatched by any other city or ruler in Pandeia. With them at hand, there would be no need for siege tactics; Riffolk could simply destroy whatever defenses lay in his path and invade every city at will.

Riffolk dictated the rest of his plan for Tarsium to the Commanders. When they each acknowledged and signed off, Riffolk resumed musing over the group of magicians that had moved to Aethos. *A pity they left Azar,* he thought, *I would have liked to face them sooner*. He wondered briefly what their mission might be; but trying to guess something with no information was an exercise in futility.

No matter what they want, he thought, *eventually they will be destroyed.* As much as he wanted to be done with it and wipe them out, Riffolk was a patient man when he wanted to be. He'd waited almost two decades for this war, after all; he could wait a little longer.

Arthor

1794

The day after taking files from Riffolk's lab, Arthor brought them to his office. He had nothing real to do, no reason to be at his office in the first place; but it paid to keep up appearances, and he didn't feel the need to be anywhere else. The files lay strewn over his desk, haphazardly organised in piles correlating to the folders they came from. *If there's a chance I can get away with this without Riffolk realising I know his secrets,* Arthor thought, *I have to be careful.*

He poured through everything. Every paper listed and explored yet another horrifying experiment or new weapon design. Arthor had seen most of the weapons already, but every now and then, something truly disturbing covered the lined work paper. Riffolk had worked in various kinds of weaponry, most of which were guns or close-quarter combat weapons. Buried within the papers he'd found, however, were schematics for chemical weapons; acids, poisons, and things Arthor didn't understand.

"There's war, Riffolk," Arthor said to himself, "and then there's *this*."

It was disgusting. Even in war, there were lines that could not be crossed. A fair fight involved both sides having access to weapons, and being able to attack and defend on an even field. The types of weapons Riffolk was working on could be deployed against an enemy without their knowledge or ability to defend.

"I hope you haven't finished these," he said again, imagining Riffolk's cold smile, "there is no justification for using these against anyone."

All he could hope for was that Riffolk had a long way to go; that they wouldn't be finished in time to be used in the current war. The weapons he'd designed for the invasion were more than powerful enough to take control of Pandeia. Chemical warfare was not only barbaric, but entirely unnecessary.

This is why he didn't allow me in his lab in the first place, Arthor thought, *he knew I would have a problem with these weapons.*

His message receiver dinged, its red light flashing as a new transmission came in. Settling the paper he read down onto its pile, Arthor approached the machine. He pressed the buttons and flipped the switches he needed to, and Riffolk's voice filled his office.

"Operations to level the forest are well underway," he said, "Tarsium is our next target. I'm altering our strategy for Tarsium and Omas. It will be far more difficult and take far more time than Shanaken. Once I have a sound strategy, I'll send it through as a message on this system. I look forward to your input."

The message ended, and the machine clicked into silence. Arthor sighed. *It won't be long before Tarsium is taken down.* It felt like a decade since their army departed, but he knew it was just over a year. Still, time felt slow and stretched. He was alone, not just literally but in his own head.

A part of him wished to be with his men, fighting and planning with the army he'd trained. He was a far better leader than Riffolk, at least where military matters were concerned. Besides, as Lord Commander, leading his men in battle was supposed to be his responsibility. He'd been involved in countless battles on the Shanaken north shore, and combat always gave him a sense of purpose.

Sighing once again, Arthor returned to his desk. There were many more papers he hadn't read; they were disheartening and disturbing, but he was intent on reading everything. Some of the files were updates to existing technology, many were new designs for the war, and some were things he'd never seen before.

He read for hours; the sunlight spearing in through his window slipped across the room as the day passed. Outside his office, he heard distant teleradio announcements every now and then. His assistant brought him food at meal times, but other than that he spent all day in his office with no contact from the outside world.

As he read Riffolk's secrets, he thought about Tyra. He thought about what it might take to reveal their existence to the rest of Ermoor. Words alone would do nothing. He had to *show* them. He needed the people to see what their lifestyle cost. What supporting Riffolk really meant. *Only another uprising can work,* he thought, *anything smaller than that will go unseen by the majority*. At least with the military gone, an uprising would be achievable. The last attempt by Tyrans resulted in a swift and unceremonious defeat by the soldiers in Dreadhold. *And the capture and torture of a Shenza by Riffolk.*

It's possible, he thought, *though even if I succeed my career will be over. Probably even my life*. Riffolk had certainly killed people for less. *If it means ending his rule and removing his power, it will be worth it*. If Riffolk remained in power, unchecked, he would put all of Pandeia under the same ruthless regime as Ermoor. The people may not know how evil he really was, but if they found out, they'd see Ermoor in all its ugly truth.

Just as the thought ran through his mind, he picked up a new blueprint. It took a few moments for the implications to settle into his mind. *No,* he thought, *this makes no sense*. He read through it again, trying to find another meaning to what he was seeing. No matter how he looked at it, the same glaring fact echoed in his mind.

Some years ago, Riffolk had designed an independent power source capable of powering all of Ermoor. Every factory, government building and household. Arthor's mind swirled with confusion and rage. *Why wouldn't he implement it?* A power source like that would have meant an end to the slavery of Tyra. An entire group of people could have been freed years ago, and Riffolk had even built it; but, for no discernible reason, he'd left it as nothing more than an automatic back-up in case of an emergency that stopped the Tyrans from performing their 'duties'.

Maybe he just enjoys the fact that he owns those people, he thought, *or maybe it's that he takes pleasure from their suffering*. Whatever the reason, it filled Arthor with a cold, sharp fury that left his hands shaking. He'd always been uncomfortable with the idea of Tyra, though before Riffolk left for the war, it somehow hadn't bothered him as much as it did now. *Riffolk must be revealed to Ermoor as the evil he truly is*.

Paca

1794

Half a lifetime passed Paca by, the Tyrans working in silent rage the whole time. Their situation was hopeless; everyone in Tyra knew it. Paca spent every waketime switching between boiling rage and cold, quiet resignation. It was almost as exhausting as turning the Wheel. The mood over all of Tyra was an echo of Paca's; sometimes furious, sometimes low. All Paca wanted was to go back to the way things had been before; when Tyrans had never heard of the world above, and the Wheels of Life were their sole, glorious purpose.

Before the first outsider appeared, their lives were technically no different. But their purpose had been stripped, and now all they had was the hard work and the knowledge that their lives were meaningless. She could have lived happily believing that they were doing the work of the Creator. Now, there was no escaping the fact that they were simply workers forced to labour for someone else's benefit.

Conversations among the Tyrans outside of the Wheel Rooms had mostly dried up; they each knew how the other felt, and there was nothing more to say. They ate in silence, filed into the sleeping quarters in silence, and the few Tyrans who still wanted to train did that in silence too.

Despite the quietness, Paca felt a deeper connection to her fellow Tyrans. It was as though, through the pain and grief put on them, their oppressors had forced them to unite, in a strange way. Regardless of the fact that every Tyran knew they couldn't fight back, there was a shared, unspoken knowledge that they *would* fight, together, if they ever had to. Paca was becoming old, but she knew she'd fight along with everyone else.

The few conversations that were had focused on simple, inconsequential things. Eventually, though, the rage they felt rose to a level that couldn't be ignored; conversations eventually turned once again to fighting, and revolution. There were still many weapons in Tyra that the demons apparently didn't know about. The temptation to use them grew every time the Tyrans spoke about it.

“There has to be a way to open the portal from inside Tyra,” Cara said after a group of Tyrans finished talking about another uprising, “they have to be able to get out if they’re here.”

Paca nodded, frowning. It made sense.

“But how could we find it? Provoking them doesn’t work, and they wouldn’t make it easy to find.”

Cara hadn’t done much training with Zailen, but she did take a weapon. There were almost enough weapons in the barrels Zailen brought with him for everyone to have one. How he’d dragged them through pitch black tunnels alone, Paca would never know.

“I didn’t say it would be easy,” Cara said, “I just said there has to be a way. And they have to have more than one portal, otherwise they couldn’t have taken people from every other region without someone spotting them.”

“More portals,” Paca mused, “means more chances of finding one.”

“Exactly.”

Slowly, talk of an uprising became more common again. The Tyrans were training; not as many of them, and not as hard as they had with Zailen, but just as often. The energy that spread through Tyra’s tunnels grew into a frenzy. Paca noticed after a while that people were talking about the uprising as though it would definitely happen; no longer as a hypothetical, or a fantasy to quell their fury.

She would never admit it out loud, but the talk scared her. If they kept up at this pace, the Tyrans might actually go looking for another fight. Or worse, provoke the demons outright again. The last time had been her fault; she never wanted to see that happen again.

A while ago, Paca began training her fellow Tyrans. She took everything Zailen had taught her, and kept it alive, making sure as many Tyrans as possible would know how to fight. Her hope, unlike those talking about revolution, was that the Tyrans might be able to fight for their freedom in the future; but trying to force an opportunity against such a powerful enemy would be futile. They had to wait, and be patient, and hope that an opportunity would present itself naturally.

Though she felt the same rage as the rest of her people, Paca had decided long ago that she preferred training for its own sake rather than for any misguided hope that she could overthrow the demons. Perhaps it reminded her of Zailen, or perhaps she'd simply grown to enjoy the feeling of learning. Either way, teaching others was certainly something Paca enjoyed.

Cara was a talented warrior now. She was younger than Paca, and when Zailen first appeared she'd only barely been old enough to train in the first place. But in the time since, she improved enough to almost rival Paca. They grew close, and she was one of the few people Paca enjoyed being around.

She humoured Cara every time she spoke about revolution; but for Paca, it would never be something she genuinely considered. Cara knew it, but had the good grace to pretend otherwise. Sooner or later, though, Paca knew pretending wouldn't be good enough. *We deserve a better life,* she thought, *we need it*.

Arthor

1794

Dreadhold, Ermoor's military district, was silent as the grave. Arthor walked through the still streets, glancing everywhere. *Not a single soldier.* As Lord Commander, Arthor had been in Dreadhold countless times. But he'd never seen it utterly empty before. The silence held a strange power; as though there were spirits in place of the missing people.

Arthor knew where he had to go. He knew what he had to do. His plan would work, and if it went the way he thought it would, it could topple Riffolk from his pedestal. Days, weeks of planning had gone into this one action. *May God help me complete my mission.*

Though there were several entrances to the tunnels underneath Ermoor, there was only one door into Tyra itself that he was aware of. All he had to do was get to that door. Almost every soldier was overseas, but Arthor wasn't sure if there was a light guard remaining for Tyra. He would have left a team behind, but then again, he would have left a full battalion behind, and Riffolk refused that.

One of the streets of Dreadhold held each of the barracks; every branch of the Ermoori military had its own barracks. They were massive buildings, and walking past them took what felt like at least an hour. He reached the barracks for the Tyran Guard. Though his plan was based on secrecy, the Lord Commander wasn't exactly out of place in Dreadhold; *it's worth checking who might have stayed behind,* he thought, *just in case*.

He knocked on the thick barracks door. The silence sat for long enough that Arthor began to think the entire district truly was empty. But just as he turned to leave, the door handle gave a small squeak and click as it pulled open.

"Wha- Lord Commander?"

A young soldier stared at him from the doorway. Arthor smiled, nodding to the young man. Remembering himself, the soldier saluted Arthor and opened the door wider.

"I'm so sorry, Lord Commander," he said, "forgive me. Would you like to come in?"

"No need for stress, soldier," Arthor said, "I'm simply taking a stroll through Dreadhold to see how things are going without the army."

The man smiled, what looked mostly like relief. He didn't look familiar to Arthor.

"Things are quiet here, Lord Commander. There's almost none of us. We're just waiting for the end of the missions."

"How many men were left here?"

Arthor watched the young man's reaction before he answered; there was no hesitation or guilt on his face.

"There's only three of us in this entire building," he said, "and I think that's only because we guard Tyra. I don't think the other barracks have any soldiers at all."

"Three in the barracks plus the guard underground?" Arthor prompted.

"No, sir. Three total, we take turns patrolling Tyra one at a time."

Three men, he thought, *for all of Tyra. All of Dreadhold.* It was almost too good to be true. Then again, any men at all presented an obstacle. He had to get past them, and he couldn't afford witnesses. *Strangely enough, now I wish Riffolk really had taken every man with him.*

There was an entrance from this barracks, and if he could get past these men, he could find the door into Tyra more easily. *There is a chance I won't be able to sneak past them.* He never wanted his men to die, even on the battlefield; if it had to be by his own hand, he would never forgive himself. But he was done standing idly by while Riffolk corrupted Ermoor. For the first time, he could see how badly astray his country had gone.

"No problems in Tyra, I trust?" Arthor said.

"No Lord Commander, it's quiet as a shadow down there. As always"

"Good. I hope you and the other two aren't growing too restless with so little to do."

"Of course not, Lord Commander. Doing our duty is excitement enough."

"I'm glad to hear it," Arthor said, "so tell me. Where are your fellow soldiers now?"

"Wickham is in the mess hall, sir. I was sitting with him when you knocked on the door. Brewer is patrolling in Tyra."

"Very well, let's get some food then, shall we?"

The young man led him down a wide corridor to the mess hall. His colleague, Wickham, looked up and dropped his cutlery when he saw Arthor.

"By God himself," Wickham said, "what are you doing with the Lord Commander, Yardley?"

"He's visiting to see how we're holding up."

"Brewer's likely to have a fit when he finds out. He won't believe us at all."

"Don't worry, son," Arthor said, "my plan is to go down there myself. I'm sure I'll run into Brewer."

"Just don't sneak up on him, Lord Commander," Yardley said, "it's easy to get spooked in those tunnels."

"I'll be careful."

Yardley sat next to Wickham, and picked up his own cutlery. Neither soldier seemed to remember that their Lord Commander didn't have his own food yet. *Not that I planned on eating anyway,* he thought.

His gun sat in its holster, perfectly balanced and weighted to his hand. He didn't want to use it, but now that he was here, there was no way to disappear into the tunnels without the men wondering where he'd gone. They would most likely report it to their superiors, even though he was the Lord Commander. Besides, his plan was to let the Tyrans free, and he couldn't do that while Ermoori soldiers guarded the barracks.

Finally, Yardley looked up from his food, his face flushed and wide-eyed as he stared at Arthor.

"Oh, forgive me, Lord Commander," he said, "I forgot to offer you food. Our kitchen is against that wall there, the cold room is through that door in the corner. I can make something, if you'd like."

Arthor turned to look at the kitchen as Yardley pointed it out, turning his holster out of their view. He settled into combat, his senses rising with his heartbeat as he prepared himself. While turned, he moved his arm casually as if adjusting his belt. The comfortable grip of his gun slipped into his hand effortlessly, and he pulled it free of its holster without a sound.

"Oh, don't worry about that, boys," he said, keeping his voice even, "I'll prepare something for mys-"

while talking, Arthor spun around, levelled his gun at the closest soldier's head, and fired. Without a pause, he took aim and fired at the other soldier barely a second later.

He holstered his gun, and strolled out of the mess hall without looking at the dead men. The guilt would be bad enough without having to see it in his mind's eye. Breathing slowly, Arthor headed towards the entrance to Tyra. His mission was almost done. The people of Tyra would be free, and Riffolk would be exposed as a monster. *Whatever I do here today,* he thought, *it's for the good of Ermoor. For the good of all.*

Paca

1794

The Tyrans worked themselves into a fury; once the idea of an uprising took root again, it spread and grew like sickness through the entire city. Their weapons, which had remained hidden and almost forgotten since the last attack, came out once more. Though Paca disagreed, the Tyrans began bringing their weapons to each shift, laying them on the floor in a concentric circle parallel to the Wheel.

It became a constant routine that fit perfectly into their lives. Paca saw weapons everywhere; carried by people to and from their shifts, placed carefully next to beds in the sleeping quarters, and surrounding the Wheel of Life during their work time. She understood why they did it. After a while, every single Tyran had caught on; even she joined in.

She'd always believed that their best chance was to wait for an opportunity to present itself, then pounce. *But we can't take an opportunity to attack if our weapons remain hidden*, she thought, *so having them with us is the best way*. So, even Paca kept her weapon with her at all times.

Eventually, though no one predicted it, their habit paid off. It happened during a shift; Paca was pushing the Wheel around for the thirtieth time when the room exploded with blinding light. A moment of shock and fear passed, and then Paca snapped into action.

"Go," she screamed over the sudden chaos, "weapons, now!"

The Tyrans moved almost before she'd finished the sentence, Paca with them. They snatched whatever weapon was closest to them, and sprinted to the portal. Paca's heart pounded as she fought to see past the light and into the portal beyond.

One man stood in the cold brightness; Paca and her people still called them demons, but they knew better. He stood by himself, no weapons, not even in a combat stance. *He doesn't even wear armour*, she thought with a surge of fury, *they have grown far too arrogant*.

Paca screamed and rushed at the man. Her fellow Tyrans followed. They reached him before he could react, stabbing and kicking and hitting. He was dead before his body fell to the oddly smooth ground beyond the portal. Paca stepped over the threshold, squinting through the glare and holding her weapon ready.

There were no more demons. No people at all. Just beyond the man, another corpse lay in a pool of blood. Paca frowned at the lone man who'd opened the portal. *Was he another saviour,* she thought, *or is this some sort of trap?*

Tyrans filed into the hallway, then stared at Paca.

"There will be more of them," she said, "we need to be ready to fight hundreds of them, if that's what it takes."

Murmurs of agreement spread through the crowd. *It's really happening,* she thought, *we're finally fighting back*. Somewhere deep in her gut, Paca knew they wouldn't be successful. *Maybe some will escape,* she told herself, *but not everyone. We'll either die, or be forced back to Tyra yet again*. Still, she pushed herself on.

Paca found a way out, after some exploring. The entire time, she waited for more demons to appear; none did.

"Keep ready," she said, "this has to be a trap."

They went up, climbing to another portal; this one was already open. Paca went through first, forcing the fear and dread away. On the other side, she helped Tyrans come up after her. The room was empty. Beyond it, Paca saw a bigger room, lined with tables; two more dead men sat slumped at one of them, but otherwise it was empty as well.

It occurred to Paca again that the demon who opened the portal might really have intended to help them escape; but she couldn't have taken the chance, and what was done was done. Whoever he was, he'd helped them escape anyway.

Paca kept the Tyrans in a close group, weapons ready. They swept through every room of the new place; it was deserted. Far smaller than Tyra, too. Then they found a larger door, and when they opened it Paca finally understood what the world above was.

The first thing she noticed was the space above their heads; there was nothing, absolutely nothing, as far as it was possible to see. She stared straight up, forgetting to breathe. Far above her head, everything faded into white nothingness. Paca had never imagined so much empty space in her life; let alone that it might exist right above her. For a terrifying moment, she felt a sickening lurch in her stomach; it felt to her as though she might simply fall into that endless abyss without a tunnel to stop her.

"How… how far up do you think it goes?" someone said.

Paca swallowed, blinked hard, and forced herself to focus.

"I don't know," she said, "but we can't think about that now. We need to make sure there's no more demons."

They ran along the smooth ground, searching everywhere for more of the demons. The open spaces, though they left Paca feeling sick and vulnerable, helped a great deal in their search. Lining both sides of a wide-open walkway were enclosed groups of rooms like the one they'd come from. Paca told several groups of Tyrans to search them while she led the larger group further along.

She almost *wanted* to find them. Just to have something to do with the rage and fear screaming through her body. But at the same time, every moment that passed without any demons appearing increased her excitement. Every step she took that carried her further from Tyra, the freer she felt.

After what felt like a long time to Paca, the walls on either side of the walkway changed. What used to be repetitive patterns and unbroken grey gave way to colours, shapes and textures Paca had never even imagined.

They traveled what had to have been the entire length of Tyra without seeing a single demon. Paca reminded her group every few moments to stay vigilant; though unlikely, they might still be walking into a trap. Her energy started flagging, but Paca still urged her people on. *We need to find somewhere safe,* she thought, *somewhere we can protect ourselves if they attack again.*

As they traveled further into the world above Tyra, Paca only saw more things she wanted desperately to learn. How did it all work? There were lights above them, and lights coming from inside the walls. Music and speaking blared occasionally from some hidden source, without any hint of people to cause it. The walls and ground were smooth and perfect, and there was no trace of mud or filth anywhere.

She'd almost forgotten to be on the lookout for demons, when Paca and her group came face to face with several people. They stared at her and the rest of the Tyrans, looking as shocked and wary as Paca felt.

"What do we do now?" Cara said.

Danel

1794

He didn't know how long they'd been underground for; months, at least. They could only venture to the surface a few at a time, or the risk of being noticed was too high. Even then, most of the Shenza didn't bother. Even in small numbers, they were perpetually filthy now, and they drew attention.

Every day, the Tarsi brought food for them. Danel never would have expected such hospitality; though the Tarsi and Shenza were close allies in ancient times. He didn't realise at the time of fleeing, but there were hundreds of wounded Shenza among them, and the

Tarsi also tended to them. Most died, but many fought through and survived.

Over the time he spent down there, Danel grew accustomed to the tunnels. The constant sound of the babbling river became almost as soothing as the ambient forest noise back in Shanaken. It was clean water, and despite the mud that covered the entire tunnel floor, it tasted pure. Though he was hesitant at first, the Tarsi showed him that it was drinkable, and after that the tunnels felt far more welcoming.

The darkness was all that bothered him; and the lack of trees. Living in the forest canopy meant an abundance of shade, but there was always dappled sunlight. As a fisher, Danel also spent a lot of his time out on the ocean, where there was nothing but light and air.

Underneath Tarsium, the network of tunnels was seemingly endless. They stretched all the way from the southernmost edges of Carmerth to Sarnia, and possibly even the mountains north of there. According to the Tarsi, they were usually full of water, but could be drained if needed. He assumed the Tarsi could flood the tunnels just as easily, and though they'd earned the trust of the Shenza, the idea still left him uneasy.

More Tarsi visited them every day, and it wasn't long before Danel considered many of them his friends. They shared a distrust—not to mention dislike—for the Ermoori, and they asked questions about the invasion all the time. They were convinced the Ermoori would invade Tarsium after Shanaken. *I don't blame them,* Danel thought, *the Ermoori certainly have the strength to do it if they wanted to.*

A group of Tarsi and Shenza sat together next to the river, Danel with them. Speaking about the invasion was becoming easier, and now that they were recovering in relative safety, a lot of the Shenza felt bolder.

"If they don't attack Tarsium by the time we're all recovered," a fellow Shenza said, "we'll go back and end this fight."

"No," said another, "we won't. They beat us the first time, why would the second be any better?"

"How many of those vehicles did they have?" one of the Tarsi said.

"I saw three," someone said.

"Me too," Danel said, "but who knows how many more they might have that weren't sent into the forest? And you weren't in my group, so who's to say we saw the same three?"

"Damn, you have a point."

The Tarsi looked at both Shenza, frowning with his giant eyes.

"So, no one knows their strength? Their numbers?"

Danel shook his head.

"They stormed into the forest after the shore. They killed so many of us that we had to split into groups to make it more difficult for them to track us. A lot of us haven't seen each other since. We each only saw a fraction of their army."

“And even setting aside their numbers,” a Shenza woman said, “their armour is almost impenetrable. We managed to kill some of them, but half the time they could simply stand together and remain unhurt."

Nodding, the Tarsi remained silent. But his eyes glowed with frustration, and the frown never left his face. Danel found himself wondering if the Tarsi had an army themselves. *They've never been at war,* he thought, *that I can remember. Can they even help us against the Ermoori?* He didn't think the Tarsi stood a chance, if the Shenza couldn't stop them. *I'm not sure anyone can,* he thought.

"Their number aren't even the part that scares me," another Shenza said, "it's the weapons they have. We can't defend against that."

Danel's mind flashed back to the fighting. Deafening booms and streaks of light sizzled through the forests, wreaking terrible damage on any Shenza unlucky enough to be caught in their wake. The image of Lenai's body being shredded into nothing came back to him, and he closed his eyes.

"They have made some technological advances, that is true," the Tarsi said, "but there is always a way to win."

"Does that mean you'll help us?" Danel asked; he couldn't help it.

"We will do our best."

Paca

1794

Are they those tree people?" someone in the crowd in front of Paca said, "I thought we just defeated them in the war?"

Paca didn't fully understand, but the last sentence forced the rage within her to the surface.

"War?" she shouted, "there was no war. You people controlled our lives, but that's over now. You haven't won… we're taking our lives back."

A cheer rang out through the Tyrans, thunderous and powerful. Before Paca could say any more, dozens of Tyrans ran at the crowd in front of them. They hacked at the people with their weapons, and Paca felt the same swell of excitement as when they killed the demon earlier. Something deep down told her they would never go back to Tyra again.

Paca joined her people in the attack, pushed on by her resolution that Tyra was in their past forever. The people died as Paca attacked, and as she watched her fellow Tyrans attack.

It didn't take long for something to switch in her mind as she killed another of them, and finally she saw the people without rage clouding her vision; they were scared, unarmed, and helpless. They reminded her of the Tyrans themselves, before Zailen appeared. *These aren't the ones who controlled us,* she thought, *these aren't the demons*.

"Wait," she said, quietly at first, then shouting; "wait!"

It took a long moment, but finally the Tyrans stopped attacking. Most of the people had fled by then, and only a handful stayed behind. The rest were dead. Paca looked at the surviving people; they looked paralyzed, as though they desperately wanted to run but couldn't.

Dozens were dead around her. They looked so vulnerable, and Paca was suddenly overwhelmed with guilt. She looked again at the survivors.

"I'm… sorry," she said, her voice breaking, "we thought you were the demons."

One of the survivors frowned, her arms folded over her chest as she glanced between Paca and the corpses on the ground.

"Demons?" she said, "what demons?"

"The people who kept us underground."

The woman's frown grew deeper.

"So, they're people?" she said, "why do you call them demons, then, if you know they're people?"

She didn't know what to say. There was no simple way to say that for countless generations, the people who controlled them dressed themselves to look like demons, and that her people hadn't known any better. That their religion revolved around not just their Creator, but those demons too. And that her people had no idea that there was an entire world above their heads.

"I don't know," Paca said instead, "and it's a long story. If you're not with them, then who are you?"

"We're Ermoori," the woman said, "citizens of the greatest city in Pandeia."

She seemed to grow taller as she said it, her chin lifting in defiance as though she dared Paca to say a word against her. Paca said nothing; she'd never heard of Ermoori, and knew nothing of the 'city' or Pandeia.

"Well," Paca said, "we are Tyrans. I don't know what this place is, but it can't be that great if it's sitting on top of Tyra."

"What do you people *want*?" the woman said, "why are you here, killing us?"

"This was our only chance to escape. We had no idea there

were people up here that weren't demons. All we want is somewhere to live, somewhere where we don't have to work in darkness our whole lives."

Shouts and murmurs of agreement filled the crowd on Paca's side. The people in front of her didn't respond, and after her own people fell quiet again, silence filled the space between the two groups. Paca had no words left; it seemed the woman facing her felt the same.

"What do we do now?" one of the Tyrans in the crowd asked.

Paca looked into the eyes of the people opposite her. It was a good question; these people weren't their enemies, but they clearly couldn't trust each other either. The Tyrans had thought about their escape for such a long time, but knowing nothing about the world above meant they couldn't actually plan it beyond getting out of Tyra. Now they were here, Paca was at a loss.

"Is there anywhere we can go?" Paca asked.

"We barely have enough space for ourselves," the woman who'd spoken for them so far said, "The city is big, but there are too many people in the poor districts already."

"Poor districts?" Paca said, "what does that mean?"

"We are the workers of Ermoori. We work in the factories, and work as maids and servants. We aren't paid much, but living expenses keep going up. Especially with this war."

It sounded to Paca as though these people lived almost just like the Tyrans. *And we killed them. The people in charge of them must be the demons,* she thought, *and it sounds like they have far too much power.*

Mattias

1794

Near the end of the year, months after their victory in Shanaken, Mattias' unit received the order to deploy to Tarsium. They sat in the same room of the warship as when they'd shipped to Shanaken. It looked exactly the same, but felt completely different. It was cold, sterile, and utterly still. After spending the better part of two years in a forest that teemed with life and noise, the warship's silence felt somehow oppressive.

His team, back up to a full fifty-man unit, sat in uneasy silence as the warship streaked along the ocean. The distance between

Shanaken and Tarsium was far less than the distance between Ermoor and Shanaken. *It won't be long before we're fighting again*, he thought, *hopefully our luck is just as strong in Tarsium.*

"Captain," Martin said, "how long before we reach Tarsium?"

"No more than a couple days, I'd say," he said.

Martin fell silent again. The battle would be completely different again. New terrain, new opponents. There was no telling how it would go.

"At least we won't have to deal with those giant trees anymore," Mattias said.

A murmur of agreement spread through his unit, almost breaking the tension pulling at each of them. The trees, and the forest in general, had been far too difficult to fight in. Although Ermoor won the battle, it was brutal and harrowing the entire time they'd been there. Mattias knew he would have nightmares about it for the rest of his life. *If I even survive this war.*

For as long as he could remember, the teleradios all around Ermoor announced the evils of Shanaken, how they had refused to listen to the light, how the only option was that they be destroyed. The rest of Pandeia was Godless too, they said, but no announcements that Mattias could remember mentioned an attempt to share God's love with countries other than Shanaken.

Were there ever attempts to teach Tarsium the right way? He thought, *or is the Prime Overseer simply not willing to try after such a long time fighting for Shanaken?* He wanted to believe that everyone deserved a chance to accept God's will, but their orders were to attack the Tarsi on sight. Just like Shanaken, they were taking the country itself; the Prime Overseer wanted to rule over it. *I suppose that's an easy way to bring God's love and civilization to the rest of Pandeia,* he thought.

Is that really what God wants? Or is it what the Prime Overseer wants? For the first time in his life, Mattias considered the possibility that those might be different things. A cold chill ran through his body, made worse by the cold of the metal warship around him.

"Sir," Gabriel said, "is it true the Tarsi can turn invisible? Or change their face to look like anyone?"

"That sounds awfully like magic to me," Mattias said, "what do you think, soldier?"

"No, of course," he said, stammering as he shook his head, "just a stupid rumour, I shouldn't have said anything. Sorry, sir."

Mattias smiled, trying to look reassuring. But in his mind, all he could think was *I really hope rumour is all it is. If they're anything like the Shenza, they'll have some kind of magic too*. He only hoped the Prime Overseer had given them weapons that could work well against Tarsi; like their proximity-triggered explosives against the Shenza. At least their rifles were incredibly powerful regardless.

"Anyone have any dice?" Mattias asked, desperate to lighten the mood.

"Aye, over here, captain," one of the new men said, "anyone

for a game of Spectre's Bluff?"

A few other soldiers had their own dice, and several games began throughout the room. Mattias simply watched, content with the noise and laughter as the games grew more competitive. The looming battle never left his mind, but watching his men get even a few hours of respite from the horrors that awaited them did wonders for his own morale.

Finally, after being goaded by a handful of his men, he joined in a game. They didn't bet real money, but push-ups instead, and after each round the winner could demand anyone within the team perform the amount they'd won that round. Gabriel won the first round Mattias joined. When it was over, he cast a sly glance at Mattias, and a series of disbelieving howls rose up from the unit.

"Give us twenty, Captain," he said.

Mattias shook his head, smiled, and lowered himself into push-up position. *Any Commander would lose his mind seeing me obey a soldier like this,* he thought, *but if it raises morale and helps us bond before this next deployment, it's an easy price to pay.*

They played up until the moment the red glow filled their room, washing over all of them as smiles disappeared from their faces. They all looked at Mattias, trust and loyalty on the faces of his old team and fear and helplessness on the faces of the new men.

"Okay, men," he said, his voice almost wavering as he fought to keep it still, "it's time. Weapons ready."

Paca

1794

It took a long time for the word to spread around the world above about the Tyrans, and an even longer time for enough of them to agree to help house Paca's people. They slept in clusters on the paved streets in the meantime, shivering and breathing out plumes of condensation. It was even more miserable than sleeping in Tyra, and dozens of Tyrans died from the cold.

The people they met were called Ermoori, and they had a lot in common with the Tyrans. Eventually, they brought Paca and the Tyrans to their homes, which were buildings made of smooth stone with separate rooms inside them. Although the Ermoori complained about having no space, Paca almost laughed out loud when she saw their sleeping quarters.

"Why is it only in one room?" she asked, "if you're really running out of space, you could use all these other rooms to sleep in too."

At first, she didn't receive an answer. She had to explain that in Tyra, the sleeping quarters were shared by as many people as could fit without doubling up on the narrow stone benches. In Ermoor, by contrast, each person had a separate sleeping room. Only the people who were in dedicated relationships shared a bed; even then, the beds were large and luxurious.

Though the two groups shared a lot in common, tension lingered between them. Paca tried as hard as she could to understand them, to try and bring the two people together. There was a sense of desperation among their people, something even the Tyrans never felt. It made it difficult for the Tyrans to settle in anywhere, though the Ermoori at least seemed to be trying.

Paca regretted the way they'd met more than anything; her people killed dozens of Ermoori, and the Tyrans had no reason to trust the Ermoori even after they stopped attacking. She knew the violence wouldn't be easily forgotten, and she didn't blame the Ermoori for that. But it felt as though the responsibility for both groups coming together lay solely with her.

The woman who'd spoken for the Ermoori when they first met

was named Talia, and she was working on building trust among her own people. Paca was grateful, but the Ermoori were stubborn. *All we need is somewhere to live,* she thought, *somewhere where we're not controlled by monsters.*

A lot of her people had to sleep in the rooms the Ermoori didn't use for sleeping, piled next to each other. What shocked the Ermoori was how comfortable the Tyrans were sleeping on the floor; the floors of their homes were lined with a soft, shaggy material even softer than the clothing the Tyrans wore. When Talia said something to her about it, Paca smiled.

"Our beds in Tyra were made of stone," she said, "these homes you have are beautiful, and more comfortable than anything in Tyra."

It was a little uncomfortable having to sleep in the same buildings as the Ermoori, but in the short term it was the only option. Paca had no idea what she would do in the future. Cara was just as worried; all of them were. She spoke to Paca whenever she could, usually immediately after she'd stopped talking with Talia.

"Why does she care how we sleep?" Cara said, "it's not like we have an option anyway."

"Don't worry about it, Cara. She's just not used to our culture, like we're not used to hers."

"She was laughing at us for sleeping on the floor."

"It's strange to them that to us, their floor is comfortable. That's all it is, Cara. They're not the enemy."

Cara's mouth drew into a hard, tight line. She peered into

Paca's eyes, searching for something.

"Are you sure? Even you said the demons might be laying a trap, when we first escaped."

"Yes, I'm sure," Paca said, "they may be more comfortable than we were, but they're still suffering. Their people control them as much as the demons controlled us. And remember, we killed dozens of them when we first met them. Trust will take time."

Cara nodded slightly, frowning deeply as she looked away. It seemed to convince her, eventually, and her face smoothed out into a satisfied expression. Paca knew it wouldn't be the end of things, but it was a huge step in the right direction. Even better, the conversation gave Paca an idea.

"Talia," she called, "can you ask the Ermoori to tell the Tyrans about these rich people? We need to know more about your situation."

The Tyrans listened intently, over many conversations, and by the time they'd learned all about the Overseers and nobility of Ermoor, trust began to grow. After she heard it all, Paca was almost certain that the Overseers and the demons were one and the same.

They controlled every aspect of the Ermoori's lives. Though they didn't dress as demons, they did rule through fear and intimidation. Even their religion was similar to the Tyrans'; they believed in a God who created everything, and who rewarded faith and punished evil. The Ermoori didn't call Him the Creator, they simply called Him God. But everything else about it felt far too familiar to Paca.

After their talks, Paca knew what they had to do. The Overseers were evil; she knew that now. And they were connected to the demons that controlled Tyra. Both had to be destroyed. The only problem was that the Ermoori had no combat ability, and no weapons. They also weren't as close a group as the Tyrans; though they lived in houses that crowded together, and worked together in factories, they seemed to have no sense of community beyond their God.

We need to join them together, she thought, *and rise up against the Overseers*. Of course, it was far easier to think such a thing than to make it actually happen. But Paca knew it was possible, and she wouldn't give up.

The word spread, and Paca felt the same sense of energy building that she'd felt in Tyra when talk of a second uprising began. The Ermoori were far less brave than the Tyrans, but her people were passionate and fearless, and it caught on. The biggest problem would be training the Ermoori. It took a long time for Paca to learn anything of value from Zailen, and the Ermoori didn't have him to train them.

She decided to train them anyway; even if it would take years, Paca had to make sure they could fight when they needed to. There were other Tyrans who had become skilled fighters, as well; Paca tried to recruit them as additional trainers. *I'm getting too old to fight now,* she thought, *if it takes too long to organise I'll be too weak.*

Ermoor was a strange place, but eventually Paca became used to the sheer empty space above her head. Some of the other Tyrans didn't quite adjust, but they did their best; though they spent most of their time indoors. The Tyrans who grew used to Ermoor did so slowly, and Paca tried to be patient with them. Any behaviour the Ermoori didn't understand made them uncomfortable.

At first, she only trained a few at a time. It was all she had the energy for, though she knew it was nowhere near enough. Once the Tyrans who knew how to fight well enough to teach it were comfortable in Ermoor, they could train many more. *This will work,* she thought to herself, *we will do this, and the ones who control Ermoor will be destroyed.*

Danel

1794

For months, the Shenza lived underneath Tarsium. They trained, and shared everything they knew of the Ermoori with their gracious hosts. The Tarsi worked with them to understand the strategies and technology of the Ermoori. Danel told them everything he could think of, everything he'd seen and experienced since the invasion. All the Shenza shared their memories, as traumatic as they were.

Living in tunnels underground slowly became a new normal for the Shenza; Danel knew nothing could replace Shanaken, but as a temporary home it was comfortable. He went above ground whenever he could, though they still stuck to a few at a time. Walking in the sun left him refreshed and peaceful. Not far out of Carmerth, thick forest took up much of the land, and Danel strode through the trees at every opportunity.

Though they were eager for information, the Tarsi never shared their own plans with any Shenza. As far as Danel could tell, the Tarsi had no military of their own. He had no idea how they would use the information the Shenza gave them. *All I can hope for is that the Tarsi have a secret army,* he thought, *like these secret tunnels.*

Kala, one of the first Tarsi to befriend the Shenza, joined Danel after he returned from his latest above ground stroll. She sat with him next to the river, a patient smile on her face as always. *I've told her everything I know,* Danel thought, *what else can she possibly want to know?* Instead of asking a question, Kala called the attention of all the Shenza nearby. When enough of them had gathered, she stood and addressed them.

"We think the Ermoori will invade Tarsium soon," she said, "and now that we have a good understanding of their abilities, we want to begin training and preparing."

"Do you have an army to fight with us?" Danel asked.

"Of sorts," Kala said, "but we want to prepare with you so that we can fight together. So that Tarsium becomes as familiar to you as the forests you came from."

"Kala," someone in the crowd said, "if the forests of Shanaken did nothing to stop them, how can we hope to defeat them on open land?”

Kala gestured around them, the same patient smile on her face.

“Does this look like open land to you, Shenza? Tarsium holds many secrets. We helped you to become familiar with these tunnels so that you could use them with us in the coming battle. The Ermoori will be exposed, and we will be hidden.”

A wave of murmurs swept through the Shenza. *They do have a plan after all.* Danel tried to imagine what fighting the Ermoori would be like in Tarsium. *No tree cover, except those tiny trees outside Carmerth.* At their tallest, they could only have been about five metres tall; they were barely even trees by Shenza standards. But if the tunnel network was as extensive as Kala implied, surprise attacks in Tarsium might be just as effective as they were in Shanaken.

There were technically mountains in Tarsium, but they were more like hills, low and gently rolling over the countryside. With the vehicles the Ermoori used, they’d be able to travel at speed throughout Tarsium without obstacle. Even in the dense and dangerous landscape of the Shanaken forest floor, the Ermoori moved far too quickly, and possessed far too much strength to be stopped.

The Tarsi better have some pretty powerful secrets for them to be planning to stop Ermoor, he thought, *either that or they haven't been listening to us at all.* He'd tried, along with all the others, to impress upon them the sheer power of Ermoor. *Our best barely put a dent in their ranks, and the skills of the Kaizeluun are beyond any other warriors in Pandeia.*

"We are willing to share some of our secrets, anything that helps to defeat the Ermoori."

"With all due respect," Danel said, "the Shenza couldn't stop their army, and we had giant trees to slow them and the *Kaizeluun* fighting with us. What secrets could you possibly share that would help defeat them?"

"These tunnels will give us an advantage," she said, "and the Tarsi possess a unique kind of magic that will come in handy against an enemy like the Ermoori."

The crowd stared at her, their expectation palpable throughout the massive tunnel. After months of living in Tarsium, the Shenza still knew next to nothing of the Tarsi; Danel was beginning to think they just enjoyed being mysterious. *Surely, they'll actually share some secrets at some point,* he thought.

"We will need to separate into groups, the way you did in Shanaken," Kala said, "each group will be led by several Tarsi, and we will spread out through the tunnel system. There are hidden entrances above ground all over Tarsium, and our plan is to surround and surprise the enemy in quick attacks, and then disappear before they can react."

Another wave of mutters spread through the crowd, and Danel knew the others were thinking the same thing he was; *surprise attacks won't be as effective as the Tarsi think. Those Ermoori vehicles move much faster than their size indicates, and their weapons fire at speeds even the* Kaizeluun *can't match.*

"The Ermoori won't be overwhelmed so easily," one of the *Kaizeluun* said, "they learn and adapt too quickly. Their weapons and armour are too powerful."

Kala nodded, her smile never wavering.

"We are aware. However, they cannot adapt to an attack they never see. Have faith in us, Shenza. You will see in time."

Danel sighed; *can't Kala just give us a straight answer?* The reaction of the crowd covered the sound of his sigh, but their voices contained just as much disappointment as he felt. *At least we know part of the plan, for now.* None of them knew when—or even if—the Ermoori would invade Tarsium, but Danel would have bet all his remaining coin on sooner rather than later. *If the Tarsi are really going to fight, they better let us in on these secrets before it's too late.*

Conversation blossomed in the tunnel, every Shenza trying to have their voice heard. As much as the Tarsi seemed in control, they hadn't lived through an invasion. They didn't know what it was like to try to fight back against the Ermoori. Even surviving was unlikely; let alone victory.

He still had trouble sleeping. The Ermoori never stopped shooting into the tree trunks, and deep booming explosions had rung out into the night. Danel still heard them when he tried to sleep, even in the tunnels below Tarsium. *The Tarsi just don't understand what it's like to fight against an enemy like that.*

Kala held her hands up, and the crowd died down again. Danel looked around; *they all want answers. The secrets of the Tarsi need to be shared now, or they lose us as allies*. He could see their doubt and frustration, and he knew Kala could too. *Like it or not, they have to share their knowledge with* us. *We have to join forces against the Ermoori, or we die*.

"I understand your frustration," Kala said, "but there are certain things the Tarsi need to do without your knowledge. We are fighting a different kind of war now, with new rules. The Tarsi will be fighting in complete secrecy, while the Shenza confront our enemy directly. We-"

A strange sound filled the tunnel, cutting Kala off as everyone turned towards the disruption. Water swept towards them in a wave, filling the width of the river. It stopped when it came alongside the centre of the group, and a Tarsi stepped out of the water as it fell back into the river.

"It's happening," the Tarsi said, "Ermoor is invading Tarsium."

Mattias

1794

The warships slammed into Tarsium's flat beaches, doors opening and ramps falling simultaneously, in a rush of chaotic noise and motion. Mattias ran down the ramp onto the soft sand, his men behind him.

Low hills rolled over the countryside beyond the beach. There was no army to greet them, no hint that their presence had been noticed at all. No giant trees hid their enemies, and Mattias let his men form up on the sand as they'd been trained. Along the beach, warships ran aground and soldiers stormed out into organized units. The northern shore of Shanaken was tightly packed compared to the long beach of Tarsium, and Mattias hadn't seen as many Ermoori soldiers in one place since they gathered in Ermoor itself.

In Shanaken, the trees cut off every unit from each other, and even within units, soldiers often couldn't see their fellows. Now they could maintain formation and even move in unison with the units next to them. In between the units, Ermoori tanks rolled to a stop, looming over the soldiers.

They marched beyond the beach, crested the nearest hills, and cast their eyes over the Tarsium countryside. It was beautiful. Mattias knew they were there to fight a war, but he couldn't help his eyes going wide as they took in the lush green grass and gentle hills. Further away, the hills disappeared in a thick forest, and beyond that, the hills turned into proper mountains.

Tarsium was split into three districts, each spread out across the entire country. Azar was closest, but fell on the other side of the forests and mountains he looked at now. The other two districts lay on the north and south points, much further away. Azar was the largest, and was to be their first target.

"Captain," Ernest said, "our path to Azar… is it straight through those mountains?"

"Yes," Mattias said, "or as straight as we can manage, anyway."

"Nothing compared to the trees in Shanaken," Gabriel said from behind Mattias, "this will be easy compared to that."

“The frogs haven’t even gathered an army to meet us,” one of his new men, Michael, said, “we’ll win this one without even a battle.”

A spatter of laughs rose up among those close enough to hear. Mattias didn’t particularly support calling the Tarsi ‘frogs’, but it brought the soldiers closer together and helped morale. They’d taken to calling the Shenza monkeys back in the forests, and he let it go then as well.

Without ceremony, the Commanders each gave their signals, and Mattias’ unit advanced alongside the others. The trees ahead of them were laughably small, and Mattias almost looked forward to how much easier combat would be in Tarsium’s landscape. If anyone had suggested a few short years ago that he'd be looking forward to combat because of the landscape, he would have laughed in their face.

The march took the better part of two hours, and then the Tarsi trees were metres from them. Once again, they stopped, peering into the forest and awaiting the orders of their Commanders. For the entire march, there were no Tarsi soldiers to oppose them. If he didn’t know better, Mattias would have believed Tarsium to be entirely uninhabited.

Not only were the trees far smaller than in Shanaken, they were small enough that Ermoori tanks could simply drive over them, snapping the trunks and flattening them against the soft earth. They advanced, Mattias scanning the forest ahead as they moved. Fighting in Shanaken had taught him to never let down his guard, even in times of total quiet.

Mattias' armour was comfortable, but heavy. The weight of it was a worthy sacrifice to make; the armour was so strong and covered so much that it almost felt like a man-shaped tank he could walk in. It spoke to the sheer skill of their Shenza enemies that they managed to kill any Ermoori at all, let alone as many as they did.

The passage between the mountains was barely wide enough to fit a tank. They shifted to a column, one unit in between each tank, marching four soldiers at a time across the gap. On either side of them, the mountains rose steeply.

"Eyes up, men," Mattias called, "this is a great place for an ambush."

He'd barely finished speaking when a scream echoed from somewhere in the soldier's ranks. Another rose up, and then another, and then their neat marching column erupted into chaos. Mattias scanned the mountains around them, but saw nothing. An Ermoori soldier nearby fell to the ground with a heavy thump, screaming, blood flowing from his eyes as he clawed at them in desperation. Seconds later, his screaming stopped, and he lay still.

What in God's name, he thought, *what kind of weapon can do that?* Mattias switched his rifle to its lightning cartridge, aiming near where the soldier had fallen. There were no enemies he could see. His men followed his example, raising their weapons and scanning everything in sight.

Finally, he saw movement in the trees that grew from the mountains; he fired, and heard a scream. Whether it was the enemy or one of his own, he couldn't tell, but he had to act on instinct. He glanced at his men; they turned in every direction, not firing, breathing heavy as panic threatened to overtake.

"Men," he called, "fire on my mark!"

He fired twice more at the same place, and a second later dozens of lightning bolts slammed into the mountainside. *Give them a target*, he thought, *and they have somewhere to put all that fear*. No more screams rose up after that, but when Mattias motioned for his men to stop firing and looked around the path, he saw no less than five of his Ermoori soldiers dead on the ground.

It wasn't only his unit; he could see beyond the tanks that other units took casualties as well. He still didn't even know where the enemy had been; he fired at where he'd seen movement, but it could've been anything.

They waited for what felt like hours for any sign of the enemy. No movement caught Mattias' eye after that. They piled their dead onto the tanks; they couldn't afford the enemy taking armour and weapons that powerful. When they were done with that, they marched on.

A while later, Mattias didn't know how long exactly, they entered a valley just large enough to fit their army, tanks included. Tents were set up, a perimeter organized, and guards assigned to patrol. It wasn't perfect; they were surrounded by mountains on every side, and the enemy could have been anywhere among the trees and rock formations. But it was a good enough place to stop in the short term.

Mattias' men shared a few tents, clustered together like the pale mushrooms that grew in the rotted leaves on the forest floor. The attack left them quiet, not as shaken as they'd been in Shanaken, but quiet nonetheless. To give them something to do, Mattias ordered the men to check their weapons and armour. When they started, he began a game; it was called liar, and required no dice or cards to play. For the first time in a long time, as he listened to his men calling out the beats of the game, Mattias relaxed.

The sounds of boots marching around the base was like music to his ears. They couldn't take their armour off in case of sudden attack, but Mattias removed his helmet for a short time. It felt strange; as heavy as the armour was, he'd grown used to its weight, and without it he felt naked. He felt exposed, the back of his head itching as though he could sense the enemy taking aim.

He didn't know how long the war would last, but as he put his helmet back on and sighed as its comforting weight settled on his head once more, he almost didn't care. He did, somewhere deep down, know that as soon as the fighting began again, he would desperately wish to be back in Ermoor. But for now, he had his armour, his rifle, and the men who fought for him. And for now, that was enough.

Danel

1794

They let the Ermoori march into the mountains. Danel crouched among shrubs and tree trunks, waiting for a signal from the Tarsi. He'd been told the Tarsi would handle most of the attack; the Shenza were mostly there as distraction, and to cause some extra damage once the real attacks began.

Watching the powerful army march so close to him left his lungs almost empty of air; he couldn't help but hold his breath. Their eyes and weapons roamed over Danel, over the trees, over everything. But they never saw him.

When the army was far enough along, a scream pierced the silence; the attacks had begun. Within seconds, more screams rose up along the entire line of marching soldiers. Their tanks rolled to a stop, the large cannons on top swinging around as they searched for a target. Danel watched, trying to see the Tarsi; he saw nothing, even knowing that they were attacking made no difference. The Ermoori soldiers simply screamed and collapsed, as though their life was being ripped from them by the Gods themselves.

On a whim, Danel motioned to a *Kaizeluun* next to him to draw her *Kaizuun*. She did, and stared at the Ermoori soldiers with new eyes. Finally, she saw what was happening; her eyes went wide, her mouth dropped open, and she simply stared.

"By Amalus," she said.

"What?" Danel asked, "what is it?"

Over the screams of the Ermoori, she described it to him.

Barely visible, even with a *Kaizuun* in hand, were dozens of razor-thin shards of ice, floating at eye level along the path. As a soldier neared them, they would remain in place, slicing effortlessly into the Ermoori soldier's eyes. Once they were in place, the ice shards thrust all the way into the soldier's head.

Danel listened to her description, his heart stopping painfully as he watched it happen below.

The Ermoori began firing randomly into the mountainside, lightning bolts sizzling from the barrels of their weapons. Danel had no idea if they hit Shenza or Tarsi or nothing, but the Ermoori shouted and fired nonetheless. A rogue lightning bolt arced into the ground near Danel; it took everything he had to remain motionless. The Ermoori who'd fired the shot screamed and clawed at his eyes, dropping his weapon, before his voice choked into silence and he collapsed.

It was devious, and brutal, and Danel felt a chill down his spine as he watched another soldier die screaming. *Lucky the Tarsi are on our side,* he thought, *I can't imagine suffering through that.*

After several dozen Ermoori were dead across the entire army, the attacks stopped. The soldiers gathered their dead as quickly as possible and marched on, faster than before. When they were out of the pass, the Shenza and Tarsi cheered.

Danel sought out Kala after the Ermoori were completely gone. He still felt shaken watching how the enemy had died; Shenza were deadly warriors, but they didn't inflict the kind of suffering Danel had just seen. Wherever possible, the Shenza chose mercy. Even the Ermoori would get a quick death when facing Danel, or any other Shenza.

"That was…" Danel started, then gave a shaky sigh, "wow. I've never seen anything like that."

"We fight a different way," Kala said, "the Ermoori chose to wage war on the world, and the Tarsi plan to show them the error of their ways."

"But that," Danel said, "that was akin to torture. Why not simply kill them?"

The Tarsi woman smiled. It was without mirth, an empty smile that spoke of the burden of knowledge.

"This is not a matter of killing them all, Shenza. Even if we could, this enemy will not back down in the face of death. They must face worse. Doubt, fear, and pain must greet them at every turn."

Danel thought again about the no violence law in Tarsium, and how anyone who broke that law simply disappeared. He wasn't sure if anyone had broken that law in his lifetime. The Tarsi really knew how to use another person's fear as their weapon. He only hoped their plan worked, and that Ermoor could be dissuaded from continuing the war.

If not, there was going to be far more suffering than he'd seen today.

"What about making them just disappear?" Danel asked. He assumed that was painless, since the rumours never mentioned torture.

"That will not be enough," Kala said, "they must witness the consequences firsthand. They must fear this place, fear the war itself. They must believe that every time they attack, or march, or sleep, they might die screaming. They must believe that they are in danger of a horribly painful death, every moment of every day."

Aerene

1795

The massive land mass that was Omas loomed on the horizon. *Not long left,* Aerene thought, *and I'll be meeting the Circle of Shadows*. It felt strange to her, and her mind still hadn't quite accepted it. *I have no idea what to say to them. Are they expecting Austris Ara to swoop in and save the world, or are they already prepared to fight themselves?* She would be expected to behave the way the ancient Austris Arans did; regal and poised, graceful, proud and self-assured. But she wasn't of royal blood, and she had no idea what she was doing.

They have not summoned you to judge your etiquette. They have summoned Austris Ara to help defeat Sithares.

Aurath's voice always came as a shock to her; she often forgot she was being listened to by a God.

"True," she said, "I guess I'm just nervous."

"Who are you talking to?" Shaela said, stepping up to her balcony and glancing out at the distant continent before them.

"There's no one here," Aerene said, "who do you think?"

"Aurath? Really?"

Aerene nodded, and Shaela shook her head in awe. She'd never bothered to hide her jealousy that Aerene could speak to Aurath; but unlike Aelis, her jealousy never turned to bitterness.

"I'm just being reassured," Aerene said, "because I was thinking about how scary it is that I'll represent all of Austris Ara."

"That's it? Reassurance? You get to speak to a God, and you don't even try to learn the great mysteries of life and magic."

"Aurath really doesn't talk much. I just hear its voice sometimes, when I'm thinking to myself."

Shaela's lips twitched into the briefest frown. *She still thinks being the Hero is all glory and being best friends with Aurath*, Aerene thought, *like it's not about leading our city into a war of the Gods*. The royal guard did know better than that, of course; but she acted as though the real responsibilities were less important than just being able to commune with Aurath directly.

"I'm really scared, Shaela."

"About speaking to the Circle?"

Aerene nodded, staring hard at Omas as it gradually grew on the horizon.

"I'll be there with you," she said, "I can speak for you, if you like. I may not be of much use other than that, but at the very least, I can help you talk to them."

She will play a pivotal role in the war to come.

"That would help a lot, I think," Aerene said. *I would have said yes anyway,* she thought.

"Perfect," Shaela said, "as soon as I tell them all I'm the Hero's bodyguard, it's sure to keep them properly humble."

Aerene laughed.

"They'll already see you as one of the mythical Austris Arans, Shaela. No need to lord it over them too much."

"Why not? If we're going to be revered, we might as well enjoy ourselves."

Her smile was dry, full of the kind of humour that Aerene sometimes couldn't understand. Half the time, when Shaela made comments like that, she wasn't joking; *I can't tell if she means it this time*. Shaela had always enjoyed bossing the Aethans around. As descendants of the original inhabitants of Aethos, the Aethans still looked like Omasi, and Aerene knew Shaela would jump at the chance to throw her authority around. The royal guard never abused her power, but she certainly enjoyed it.

Aerene, on the other hand, had never been comfortable with the inherent difference in power between the Austris Arans and the other people of Pandeia. She knew Austris Arans were above any other people in station, but she'd never really enjoyed knowing that her life was automatically more valuable than somebody else's.

"Aerene," Shaela said, "what's wrong? You're being even more quiet than normal."

"What's wrong? Really? I'm responsible for representing all of Austris Ara, for the first meeting between our people and the rest of Pandeia in two thousand years! I'm terrified, Shaela. I wasn't meant for this."

"Clearly, Aurath believes you were. Are you questioning our God?"

"Of course not."

"Then have faith, Aerene. You were chosen for a reason. Besides, I guarantee the other Heroes will be just as nervous as you are. They'll probably be intimidated by you. And they'll *definitely* be intimidated by me."

Aerene tried to believe her. She felt a little better looking at Shaela's smile; but the feeling grew cold and heavy as she turned her gaze back to the massive country in the distance. It looked dangerous, like the dark silhouette of a giant shark looming just under the surface.

"I hope you're right, Shaela," Aerene said, "I really do."

Zeera

1795

Zeera settled into focusing her time and energy on training the Circle. They, for the most part, joined in willingly. The only exception was Mara. As much as she cared for the Ermoori woman, Zeera desperately wished to be able to change Taranos' mind; Eliza would make a far better Hero, even Mara agreed on that.

But the choice was out of her hands. There was nothing she could have done; the Gods made their own choices, and for their own reasons. All Zeera could do was try to train Mara as much as possible. She was speaking more now than when they first arrived in Aethos.

For that much at least, Zeera was grateful.

News continued to come in from her agents about the war. Tarsium had been attacked, though the Ermoori progress through her homeland was slow. She struggled every day with the knowledge that her people were being besieged by such a powerful force. But there was nothing she could do about it; her responsibility lay with the Circle, and destroying Sithares was more important than Ermoor.

Life in Aethos began to feel stifling to Zeera; she felt stuck, and all she could do was wait for either the book to be found, or the Austris Arans to show up. Neither happened, and so she did what she could. She researched the spells, going over them countless times. There would be almost uncontrollable destruction when she cast the spell for real; half the difficulty lay in focusing the spells into Sithares' book.

It wouldn't be like the summoning spell; that was a single spell Zeera cast by using magic drawn from the Heroes. Destroying Sithares would take many layered, separate spells; and Zeera only knew part of them, thanks to the original Circle of Shadows. Each spell had to be cast by every member of the Circle, which meant she had to teach them all. It also meant they each needed to be able to hold and wield enough magic to cast all the spells.

Before she taught the Heroes, Zeera wanted to know the spells so well that she could cast them in her sleep. The magic was familiar to the Tarsi, but to no one else in Pandeia. What most didn't know was that the elemental magic of the Gods was not the only type of magic that existed. For millennia, the Tarsi had practiced another kind of magic, what they called Deias.

Deias was an ancient language that carried power within its words, whether written or spoken. Every being in Pandeia could use Deias, with some training and practice; in that way, it differed greatly from elemental magic. The spells were written on ancient scrolls by the original Circle; whether they invented them or simply wrote them down from some other source, Zeera would never know. Zeera possessed one of the scrolls, and the other was said to be with the Austris Arans.

As she read the spells for perhaps the thousandth time, one of her agents rushed into her training room.

"Zeera," he said, "you need to come and see this."

"What is it?" she asked, following the agent's lead.

"They're coming," he said, sprinting through the hallways that led to the city square, "they're finally coming."

Once they were outside, the agent rushed to the centre of the square, and pointed out at the ocean. In the distance, a bright white mass sat on the horizon. The day before, there had only been sky. A rush of powerful emotion erupted within Zeera; hope, relief, excitement, and a strange kind of panic. *They really are coming here,* she thought, *the Austris Arans*.

After she saw them on the horizon, waiting for them to arrive felt like torture. Day by day, the floating city grew larger. After a week, she saw people as tiny as insects, and could make out details on the buildings. Another week later, they were close enough to see their facial expressions. Then, finally, the city set down on Pandeia's soil for the first time in thousands of years.

At the edge of Aethos, overlooking the water, massive circular indentations marked a perfect pattern. At the edge of those patterns, an ancient arch sat empty, as though a gateway had been erected to nowhere. It was where Austris Ara had originally been built, and served as a dock of sorts to the city. When it landed, the edge of Austris Ara fit perfectly within the indentations, forming a bridge between the two cities.

On the Austris Aran side of the bridge, a large and ornate arch had been built that matched the Aethos one. Standing underneath it, waiting until their city settled into stillness, was a small group of Austris Arans. They were exactly how she'd imagined; majestic, powerful, and almost God-like. Zeera waited to greet them along with the Heroes. She felt Mara's fear from metres away.

They walked slowly, serene expressions on their chiseled faces. Zeera bowed as they approached, and introduced herself and the other members. At first, an unmistakable air of tension sat between the Austris Arans and the Circle. They spoke as though they thought themselves to be Gods, and as though all the people of Pandeia were merely their subjects.

“Aethos,” the royal guard said, “is much as the records state. I expect quarters have been organized for the chosen and myself?”

“Of course,” Zeera said, “atop the temple, as tradition dictates.”

The temple, though used by the original Circle, was in fact built to worship Aurath and Air Magic. Built on top of its roof was a wind tunnel to channel Air Magic. Next to that lay the sleeping quarters of the original Austris Aran Hero. As far as Zeera was aware, the quarters had remained unchanged since the first Hero stayed there.

“Good,” the royal guard said, “have your people bring Aerene’s things to her quarters. Mine too.”

Zeera nodded and bowed again. In ancient times, when the Austris Arans lived in Aethos, they ruled over the Omati. They were seen as deities, powerful benevolent rulers who could do things the Omati only dreamed of. To Zeera, it seemed as though the Austris Arans still saw themselves in the same way; and expected Pandeia to treat them as such. As much as she respected them and their assistance, their arrogance bothered her.

The Circle would have to be patient with their newest members, and Zeera was nothing if not patient. Already, however, she foresaw disagreements and clashes of personality between the Austris Arans and the other Heroes; particularly Lashek. He thrived off of mocking others, and knew no method of communication other than sarcasm. Zeera didn’t look forward to keeping the Circle in line over the coming months.

Eliza

1795

Aethos was a strange but wonderful place. Eliza's mind kept returning to her first day there. The people were different; olive-skinned and muscled, and always busy. They seemed to tolerate the Circle's presence, but kept a cold distance. Even if they hadn't, Eliza didn't have much chance to get to know them. She was brought to a beautiful old building that the Circle used as their new headquarters. It looked like a temple; ornate and ancient, and made of a unique marbled stone.

Eliza knew that most of Omas was inhospitable desert, but

Aethos was more like Tarsium than she expected. There was certainly more sand and dust than she was used to, but not enough to called it a desert. She spent most of her time in the building they'd made their headquarters, comforting her mother and trying to listen in to the other Circle members discuss their plan.

"We can't start until Mara is better," someone was saying, "and who knows when that'll be. Plus, we need the guardians here."

A little while after they arrived in Aethos, the Circle performed some kind of ceremony. It was supposed to summon 'guardians', whoever they were. So far, no one had shown up. Zeera assured them it wouldn't be long, but the guardians sounded like a made-up story to Eliza.

"They'll be here," someone else said, "and Mara is getting better every day. She's talking and eating, and she's accepted Mathys' passing. It won't be long."

It sounded like Zeera and Lashek, but Eliza couldn't be sure. She sat in the hallway outside a room the Circle met in. They'd lived in Aethos over a year, and yet the Circle still mostly kept Eliza out of their affairs. She knew she was younger than all of them, but she wasn't a child anymore. *I deserve to know what's happening,* she thought, *I'm a part of this too*.

"You said that when we first summoned the guardians," the first voice said, "and it's been over a year."

"Have patience. Killing a God takes time and planning. This is no simple assassination."

"I wish it was. I hate waiting around like this. The Ermoori are taking more of Pandeia every day. Destroying Sithares won't mean anything if Ermoor slaughters everyone before we're done."

Eliza had kept up with news of the invasion as much as she could; but it was just another thing the Circle kept from her. Perhaps they thought she was too fragile to learn about such things. *I can handle it*. What scared her was that the Ermoori were her own people, and that they were led by her father. *Does he want to take me back to Ermoor? Or does he want to kill me? Does he even know I exist?* She shouldn't have known about him, but his face had been in her dreams ever since she was a child.

He still appeared in her nightmares. And she knew how terrified her mother was of him. Part of her was disgusted that her own people were invading and destroying the entire world; but another part of her, a secret part, felt a strange sense of power. *He's perhaps the most powerful man in the world,* that part whispered, *and I'm his daughter*.

She hated him for the pain he caused her mother, of course, but if he took control of all of Pandeia... *It might all be mine one day. Then I can make things better*. The thought was strange, uncomfortable. She didn't actually want that much power. But if it came upon her, she could at least try to use it for good.

"Ermoor will not win their war," the voice that sounded like Zeera said, "but you are right. Time is running out. You need to be patient, everything that can be done is being done."

Footsteps drew close to the door. Eliza leapt into a sprint, using the training Mathys gave her to remain silent even at full speed. She was well beyond the hallway by the time the door opened behind her, and slowed to a normal walking pace as she approached the main shared space. It was a large room, with benches spaced around the walls at regular intervals. Eliza sat on one just before Zeera and Lashek entered.

"Eliza," Zeera said, "how is your mother doing today?"

"She's well, thank you. She even smiled this morning."

"Lovely."

Zeera was always kind to Eliza, but she spoke to her as though she was a child. All of the Circle members did, even the agents who performed errands for them. She was sick of it. *I'm an adult, why does no one see that?*

Lashek sat next to her as Zeera left the room. He was completely healed, and had been for some time now. It was about two years since Kerberos attacked the Circle in Tarsium. The only person who seemed to be still affected by it was her mother.

"Did you learn a lot just now?" he asked.

"What... what do you mean?" Eliza said.

"You were listening in to Zeera and I."

How could he possibly know that? Eliza thought, *I was so careful, just like Mathys taught me.*

"*Kaizeluun* can see the life force of all living things," he said, "an aura. It lets us know what kind of creature, whether it has magic, all sorts of things."

It's like he can read my mind, she thought.

"Sorry," she whispered, "it's just… no one tells me anything."

"I understand. I'm not mad, Eliza. I'm frustrated too. I know it seems like everyone's hiding things from you, but the truth is none of us really know what's happening right now. We're all just waiting."

Eliza nodded, and Lashek let silence settle over them. She felt restless; usually she would train with Mathys when she felt this way, but no one else seemed willing to train. So, she sat with Lashek instead, trying to control her patience. *I could train on my own,* she thought, *or ask Lashek to train with me*. But as restless as she felt, those options didn't appeal to her as much as training with Mathys used to.

She tried to think; *I need to do something, instead of just sitting around.* But nothing came to mind. Lashek was still, peaceful, and she envied his ability to be content with doing nothing. She'd seen him train before, and had actually trained with him. From what she knew of the Shenza, they trained every single day, harder than most warriors. *How does he just sit here if his people are used to working so hard?*

As Eliza tried to think of a tactful way to ask him, one of the Circle agents ran into the room. He waved at them to follow him, urgency shining in his massive eyes. Eliza and Lashek looked at each other, frowning, and then back at the agent. *Ermoor is invading,* Eliza thought, *we're going to die*. But there was no fear in the agent's eyes, just a polite insistence.

"Come with me, please," he said, "the guardians have arrived."

The guardians were amazing people. Tall, blue-skinned and possessing massive golden wings, they looked like living myths. Two of them entered Aethos, one the Hero and the other a royal guard. The Hero was young, and when her and Eliza met, they got along immediately.

"I'm Aerene," the blue-skinned girl said, "you're Ermoori, aren't you?"

Eliza nodded, smiling.

"My name is Eliza. I'm Mara's daughter. She's Taranos' Hero."

Aerene's smile grew warmer.

"I'm glad she has family with her. You must be so proud."

"Well, yes," Eliza said, "but really I wish I could be Hero instead."

Aerene frowned, looking at her for the first time in a different way. *As though she thinks I want the power for myself,* she thought, *and she misjudged me.*

"I mean because I want her out of danger," Eliza said in a rush, "because I know how scared she is."

Something changed in Aerene's eyes once again; this time it was a sort of relief, and a genuine warmth.

"Hey," Aerene said, "would you like to train together?"

Eliza grinned; she couldn't help herself.

"I would love that," she said.

Aerene

1795

For the first time since its creation, the great city of Austris Ara settled onto the grey dirt of Omas. For her entire life, Aerene never noticed that Austris Ara constantly emitted a low, subtle vibration. Once the city landed, a stillness settled over the entire city that left her feeling sick.

The ground was level with the city's edge; something about seeing it pushed at the edge of her mind. *It feels like a dream*, she thought, *like a really strange dream*.

Shaela had joined her in her quarters, and they now stood at the edge closest to Aethos. The city was built in the exact spot it landed in; there was a huge archway built at the edge of Austris Ara, and a matching archway built in Aethos to line up with it. The archway was a familiar sight to Aerene, but seeing it as the other half of a portal between two cities made it look utterly different.

"Are you ready?" Shaela asked.

"Not really," Aerene said, "but let's go."

Behind them, the people of Austris Ara stood in silence, watching their Hero pass through the giant archway and into Aethos. Later on, there would be a joining of the countries, a celebration as the estranged cultures became reacquainted. But for now, Only Shaela and Aerene were allowed to cross the threshold.

A small delegation met them just beyond the archway. It seemed to be a member of each country, and Aerene looked at each one carefully. She knew at a glance where they were from, what magic they would use. The God who chose them. Looking from one to the other, she could tell they each were sizing her up the same way. Though there was something more in their eyes; a look of confusion or shock, or both. *It's as though they didn't know what Austris Arans look like,* she thought, *except the Tarsi. There's no surprise in her eyes at all.*

"On behalf of the Heroes of the Circle of Shadows," the Tarsi said, "welcome back to Aethos."

Aethos wasn't as big as Austris Ara, but there were countless people packed into every street and building as they passed. Not just

Aethans and other Omasi, but Thearans too. Every single one of them looked desperate and exhausted; but on each upturned face, Aerene also saw a fierce hope.

The delegation that met them walked ahead, guiding them to a place they could meet properly. No words were exchanged between them other than the Tarsi Hero's initial greeting. Shaela shot her a reassuring glance, and Aerene tried to calm herself before she had to talk to the other Heroes.

They walked through what felt like most of Aethos before they reached an ornate building that Aerene knew was an ancient temple to Aurath. Shaela and Aerene were led into the temple, and finally they were away from the stares of countless people. The temple itself was massive, with windows high up just under the ceiling that allowed the air to flow freely. They were large enough to allow Austris Arans to fly in and out, but high enough that no one could see in or out through them.

After passing through the main room, the Heroes guided them to a wide staircase which curved upwards, to what Aerene assumed would be a wind tunnel room like the one on top of the royal palace. She hadn't seen it from outside, but the walls of the temple were too high to see anything on the roof.

Finally, they stopped walking, and Aerene smiled as her assumption proved correct. The wind tunnel's design matched the one in Austris Ara exactly, and she felt at home again for a brief moment.

Seats were set up around the inside of the wind tunnel in a

circle, surrounding a large circle table. The Tarsi who greeted them sat, and the others took her lead. Aerene was the last to sit, just after Shaela. For a tense moment, the Heroes all looked at each other with sober expressions. *They feel the same way I do,* Aerene thought, *they understand the weight of this meeting, of the war. We're all as scared as each other.* Though the thought didn't lighten her mood, it was a slight comfort.

"I know everyone here quite well," the Tarsi started, "but our new guests have yet to meet us, and it would be best for everyone to introduce ourselves. I am Zeera, Hero of Asheilos."

She gestured to the woman next to her, an Ermoori who looked even more terrified than Aerene felt. *Can the Ermoori be trusted in the Circle of Shadows this time around?* Aerene thought, *and does this one know about the scouts Shaela killed?* Of all the people they saw in Aethos, the Ermoori made Aerene the most nervous. Even two thousand years ago, the Ermoori were a violent and corrupt people.

"I'm Mara," the woman said, "the... well, Hero, I suppose... of Taranos."

"My name's Lashek," the Shenza said, "Hero of Amalus. I love the wings, by the way. They'd make things a lot easier."

Aerene frowned at the man’s tone; he sounded friendly, but there was an edge of tension in his voice. He spoke Oman fluently enough, but his Shenza accent was still thick, and Aerene wasn’t sure what to make of him.

"I am Aella, queen of Theara. I'm not the chosen, but I have communed with Sithares. It must be stopped."

There was no Thearan Hero last time, Aerene thought, *I'm certain of it. How can we trust them to fight against their own God?* She said nothing, and kept her face still. Her and Shaela would have plenty to talk about after the meeting.

"I am Aerene, Hero of Aurath."

Others were sat at the table too, but only the Heroes and the Thearan Queen introduced themselves at first. Something about having a worshipper of Sithares with them felt off to Aerene. *Our purpose is to destroy her God. If she really worships Sithares, why would she be here?* Even more concerning was Aella's story; she hadn't been chosen, by her own admission, and yet had the gall to appoint herself as representative of Sithares in the Circle. There was no way to voice her suspicion without bringing more tension to the meeting, so Aerene simply sat and watched as Zeera began. *I don't have a good feeling about any of this,* she thought.

Shaela

1795

In the hours leading up to reaching Aethos, Shaela spoke with Aelis. He was as cold as ever, as though forty-five years hadn't passed since Aerene was chosen instead of him. *He'll never be a good King,* she thought, *if he holds grudges like this*. Though publicly, Aelis supported the Hero, everyone knew of his hatred. The people made their mind up shortly after Aerene was chosen that she was a far better authority figure than he could ever hope to be.

Aelis sat in his quarters, as he so often did of late. He barely reacted when Shaela entered. She strolled to the table where he sat, and took a seat across from him.

"We'll be arriving soon," she said, "Aerene and I will go into Aethos. If you'd like to see the city, Aerene says you can come once the reunion ceremony has begun."

Aelis' eyes darkened.

"I have no interest in those *people*," he said, practically spitting the last word, "I will remain here, where I belong. You and your Hero can live among those tiny lives, if you choose; but Austris Arans will always be the superior people."

Shaela hadn't expected any less from him; in fact, she was relieved. *He would have caused more problems by venturing into Aethos,* she thought, *and we need things to run as smoothly as possible*.

"As you wish, your majesty," she said, "Aerene and I will endeavor to represent Austris Ara as best we can."

Shaela hated having to watch her words so carefully; Aelis was the type to be offended by any little thing. *I shouldn't have to talk this way at all,* she thought, *Aelis isn't even King yet*. But, as frustrating as it was, Shaela had to placate the prince. It was either that, or try to deal with the disaster that would inevitably occur if he made a scene in Aethos.

After speaking with Aelis, Shaela went to the King and Queen. They were also happy to wait in the city; but unlike their son, they were looking forward to the reunion ceremony. Aethor was born only shortly after Austris Ara left Aethos. Lorae was younger by a few centuries, but both were excited to see the city.

Finally, with the royal family ready, Shaela returned to Aerene. Together, they watched Aethos grow closer. It was strange to her to realise that her people were returning to their home, instead of visiting a strange city. *I've never been there,* she thought, *but it's where my people come from.*

Arriving at Aethos was a confusing but exhilarating experience for Shaela. She was just over seven centuries old; far too young to have seen Aethos with her own eyes. But she knew a lot about it, and seeing it gave her a strange sense of what the Austris Arans called empty echoes; memories of an event that never happened. Aerene's nerves were palpable as they walked over the threshold into Aethos. Shaela tried to be a reassuring presence for her, but it didn't come naturally.

The Tarsi who greeted them was fairly powerful, but nowhere near the level of some of the other people in the group she led. There was a representative from each country there, and Shaela felt every type of magic rolling from the group in waves.

Shaela looked over every member of the Circle; Her job was to protect Aerene, and as far as she was concerned, none of these people could be trusted until they proved themselves. As much as she hated to admit it, some of them were powerful enough to pose a real threat if they chose to fight.

Two of them in particular were of concern to Shaela; the Thearan and the younger Ermoori. Their power was formidable, and both of them exuded a restless kind of energy, as though they might take any excuse for a fight. The others were less aggressive, though the Shenza gave off a low, mostly dormant rage. *He doesn't trust us,* Shaela thought, *and I don't trust him*.

The Thearan, who stood with a regal authority in her stance that reminded Shaela of Aelis, swelled with endless Fire Magic. Her power was unbelievable, and Shaela found herself almost fearing the woman. It was a feeling she'd never experienced before. *If she wants a fight,* Shaela thought, *there won't be much we can do to stop her*. Fire Magic was the most powerful and destructive form of magic, except maybe for Power Magic; an exceptionally powerful Fire Magician could face entire armies alone, and still emerge the victor.

Next to her, the young Ermoori girl watched them with unabashed awe on her face. Though she looked innocent enough, the magic crackling within her body gave away her sheer power. The older Ermoori was powerful too, but the younger existed on an entirely different level.

Shaela glanced at Aerene; the Hero looked overwhelmed. She wasn't paying attention to the Circle, or to anything the Tarsi woman said. *She wasn't trained to provide security,* she thought, *so she's simply experiencing this as any young girl would*. Aethos was a strange place, and Aerene was nervous beyond her ability to manage.

That's my job anyway; ensuring Aerene's safety, so she doesn't need to think about it.

Aethos brimmed with people; hundreds of thousands of Omati and Thearans filled the streets. Shaela was used to feeling magic around her. Austris Ara was perhaps the most magic-filled place in all of Pandeia. What she wasn't used to was the different types of magic surrounding her. It felt as though she'd stepped through a portal into a whole other world.

As they followed the Tarsi woman through the streets, Shaela thought about the war to come. Though it would require massive amounts of magic, it wasn't a war in the traditional sense. There would be no combat, no weapons, no strategy. *In fact,* she thought, *that will probably be the safest time for Aerene*. It was a strange thought, but true; Aerene knew the necessary spells fluently, and had more than enough magic to complete them. Sithares would fight back, but that was a battle of wills more than anything else. *And the other Heroes will be fighting together.*

The faces of people followed them through Aethos. Every face stared with awe and shock; Shaela smiled as they walked. Aerene, who was already uncomfortable enough being Hero in Austris Ara, looked even less happy having the stares of the people of Aethos pointed at her.

Eventually, they reached a temple, and the Tarsi woman ushered them inside. It looked to be the same design as the Sky Temple, and Shaela smiled again. *It's not too different from home, after all,* she thought.

Zeera

1795

After a shaky start, Zeera invited the Austris Aran Hero and her royal guard into the temple with the other Heroes. She knew the first step was communication; making sure they knew what the Circle required of them, and making sure they could become a part of the team. She at first only invited the Hero, Aerene; but the royal guard invited herself with such conviction that there was no option but to let her come too.

All she wanted was for them to be able to work well together; if they failed to connect well enough as a team, their spells wouldn't bond properly. If that happened, Sithares could never be destroyed. Most likely, in that scenario, their magic would backfire and turn against them. The destruction that might be caused was something Zeera didn't want to think about.

After the Heroes introduced themselves, Zeera stood and addressed them all.

"Heroes," she said, "Sithares has risen again. We must destroy it, and we can only do that together. You will need to use all of your magic, all of your skill, and all of your courage."

Mara's face turned paler the longer Zeera spoke. Lashek kept shooting side-long glances at the Austris Arans. Aella's face was as still as stone, staring at the wall behind Zeera. Surprisingly, the only one who seemed to be genuinely paying attention to her was Aerene.

"Most importantly," Zeera continued, "we need to bond as a team. The strength of our bond will determine how effective the spells are against Sithares."

"So, what you're saying," Lashek said, "is that we have to be best friends… or all of Pandeia gets destroyed?"

Aerene looked at Lashek with a mix of amusement and confusion. Her mouth twitched, and then turned down; *she's trying not to laugh,* Zeera thought, *maybe it won't be so hard for them to connect after all.*

"Are you complaining, Lashek?" Zeera said, "I would have thought it easy for you to make friends, with your… interesting sense of humour."

Lashek frowned, and hunched down into his seat. Zeera realised her tone had been harsher than she intended.

"What it really means," she said, "is that we need to train together as much as possible, and spend as much time together as we can. I will teach you the spells we will need soon. We need to learn them together."

"Wait," Shaela said, "you're the Heroes of the Circle of Shadows, and you don't even know the spells you need to cast?"

"This is ancient magic, Shaela," Zeera said, "it has been forgotten for millennia."

"How old it is has nothing to do with anything. This is the magic that keeps Sithares at bay. It should have been taught to all the members of the Circle, generation to generation. What has the Circle been doing all these years, if not preparing for Sithares' rise?"

Zeera couldn't believe it. Shaela spoke as though the Circle should have remained active, for thousands of years, practicing and training despite Sithares being dormant for entire eras. It had been difficult enough to start the Circle up again; maintaining it for thousands of years would have been almost impossible.

"The Circle disbanded," Zeera said, "a little while after Sithares was imprisoned. I built it back up again, when the time came."

Shaela's face was the picture of shock. On the face of a God-like being, it was almost comical.

"Dis… disbanded?" she said, "who made that decision? The

Circle is Pandeia's only line of defense against Sithares. Disbanding it is the most irresponsible act I have ever come across."

As she spoke, the comical effect of her shock dissipated with jarring speed. Her words were harsh, but her tone was worse; it took on a vicious edge, a low and deadly whisper undercutting each word.

"The people of Pandeia do not age the way you do, Shaela," she said, "to us, thousands of years is simply too long to keep memory. The Tarsi recorded as much as we could, and if not for us, the Circle would not exist at all."

Shaela scoffed, and Zeera noticed Aerene's expression; she looked like she wanted to be anywhere else in that moment. *She is embarrassed,* Zeera thought, *that Shaela is treating us as lesser beings*. It gave her hope that the chosen Hero was a far more reasonable being than Shaela. That maybe Aerene didn't possess the same sense of momentous self-importance the other Austris Arans displayed.

"If not for your failure," Shaela said, "Sithares would not have been allowed to remain active so long after its reawakening. How long as it been? Decades? Were you properly prepared, you could have acted as soon as Sithares surfaced again."

"Wait a minute," Lashek said, rising from his chair fast enough that it slid backwards on the stone floor, "Zeera is putting everything into this mission. Who are you to tell her she failed? What have you done for Pandeia lately?"

Turning to face Lashek, Shaela brought her full size to bear;

her wings spread out across the room, she stood taller, and her hands bunched into fists.

"How dare you?" she said, "Who are *you*, to question the wisdom of Austris Ara?"

"I don't recall a time," Lashek said, "that disappearing into the sky for thousands of years, to leave us mere mortals with our problems, was considered wise. If you cared about the Circle so much, why did you bail? If anything, you're the ones who disbanded it in the first place."

Shaela raised a hand, and Lashek was yanked up into the air instantly. His hands went to his throat, clawing and grabbing at something that wasn't there.

"I was led to believe you Shenza were far more… obedient," Shaela said, "I cannot imagine what Amalus sees in you."

"Shaela," Zeera said, her voice turned harsh and loud, "release him. Now."

Lashek crashed to the floor. He recovered quickly, rubbing his neck and staring at Shaela with undisguised malice. Shaela turned to Zeera, her wings folding back into place. She pointed a finger at Zeera.

"That is the last time you order anything of me," she said, "I serve no one but the Hero of Austris Ara."

"I serve the Circle," Zeera said, "and all its Heroes. We are on the same team, Shaela. Remember who our enemy is, I beg you."

Lashek opened his mouth, but Zeera shot him a glance that stopped whatever snide remark he'd prepared in its tracks.

“This is exactly what I wanted to avoid,” Zeera said, “when I told you all that we have to work together. The more we fight each other, the easier Sithares wins.”

Shaela

1795

Shaela stormed from the meeting, frustration flowing through her body. Aerene kept pace, confusion mixing with genuine fear on her face. Their quarters had been assigned and prepared, and Shaela headed straight for them. *I've had enough of talking with these silly little beings for one day,* she thought, *if I hear of one more failure from them, I'm going to lose control.*

The Circle being disbanded was bad enough; the fact that it happened almost as soon as Sithares was imprisoned only served to agitate Shaela even more. The Circle came about in the first place to destroy Sithares, to stop it before it could destroy the world. But for the last two thousand years, no Circle even existed.

"Shaela," Aerene said, "did you have to attack that Shenza man? We're supposed to be a team."

"Yes, we are," Shaela said, "and they disbanded their team. For two millennia, they've done nothing but grow weak and ignorant, knowing Austris Ara would come to their rescue. I didn't attack him. I gave him a small but necessary punishment."

"Shaela-"

"Aerene, these people have failed us. Their responsibility was to keep the Circle ready. Now, we have to train them and teach them until they're ready… while Sithares grows stronger by the day. You have seen the smoke coming from Sitharkos, yes?"

"Zeera knows the spells," Aerene said, "she'll teach them."

Shaela scoffed and picked up her pace. It was infuriating; Aerene desperately wanted to see the best in everyone. But the Circle, good intentions aside, were far from the best. Two thousand years had weakened the people of Pandeia. Some of them were powerful, it was true; but even they were nothing compared to the magicians of old. Even King Aethor's power was something to behold. Aelis would grow to be powerful as well, though nowhere near as powerful as the chosen Hero.

As well as the lack of knowledge of their Heroes and the Circle in general, what confused Shaela was the mood. Everyone looked low, defeated; desperate. As though they didn't think stopping Sithares was possible at all.

"Why are they all so miserable?" Shaela said, "being a Hero is the greatest honour a person can have. Destroying Sithares is the most noble fight it's possible to be a part of. What happened to this place, these people?"

Aerene shook her head; she looked as concerned and confused as Shaela felt.

"They only live a handful of decades," Aerene said, "to them, the original Circle was nothing but myth. It's so far in the past for them that most don't even know it existed."

"But it shouldn't matter," Shaela said, unable to keep the frustration out of her voice, "the importance of the mission is what matters. Sithares threatens all of Pandeia, and all it took for these people to forget that is… *time*?"

They reached their quarters. Their rooms were right next to each other, in the Sky Temple that had been built in Aethos. The other Circle members were given quarters in separate buildings, some underground, and all with their own training rooms. Shaela and Aerene were to train on the temple's roof. The building was massive, beautiful, and familiar. It struck Shaela that the temple they now stayed in was older than Austris Ara itself.

"Shaela, please," Aerene said, "please promise me you'll be more patient with the Circle. They're doing their best. We're here to help them. We're all on the same team. I know it's frustrating, and confusing, but… please, do it for me."

With a heavy, drawn-out sigh, Shaela closed her eyes. *Aerene is a far better person than I am,* she thought, *Aurath chose wisely*. In that moment, Shaela wished Aerene was of royal blood. With her as legitimate ruler of Austris Ara, the city would prosper like never before.

She's right, she thought, *these people can't help that two thousand years is too long for them*. It still bothered Shaela, but Aerene's words made sense; they had to be patient.

"I'll do my best," Shaela said, "but only if they do, too."

Aerene smiled, and Shaela tried to bury her anger and smile back. *Destroying Sithares was never going to be easy,* she thought, *but the hardest part might be pretending the Circle doesn't annoy me beyond reason*. As long as they could learn the spells, Shaela was willing to at least try. But looking at the sorry group, she didn't believe the Circle could do what they needed to. *They should have learned these spells decades ago,* she thought, *and should have been practicing every day since then.*

"Shall we train?" Aerene said, her face showing nothing but calm and contentment, "the temple roof looks like a great place."

Shaela nodded, sighing again. As bad as her mood was, training with Aerene might cheer her up.

"Sounds good," Shaela said, "I need to unwind anyway."

Aerene beamed at her, and they walked up to the temple roof together.

Lashek

1795

Lashek had heard stories about the Austris Arans. The specifics in those stories were uncertain at best; but nothing he heard prepared him for the moment he first saw them. They were tall, and although far taller than anyone in Pandeia, their height was the least incredible thing about them. Vivid blue skin glowed in the sunlight. Their eyes were completely white, with no pupils or irises. The hair on their heads was a shining, pure gold. But most shocking of all were the giant golden wings that arched from their backs, taking up space even when they stood on the ground.

When they walked into Aethos, Lashek drew his *Kaizuun*. It showed him their power, and their aura, more clearly than perhaps anyone else could have seen it. Their magic was deep, so powerful that it lay almost solid around them. But unlike most other powerful magicians, their magic was utterly calm. Lashek had never seen such control. It was almost as intimidating as Kerberos; perhaps even more so.

The chosen Hero of the Austris Arans was Aerene, a woman who looked about the same age as Eliza. She was quiet, and humble, and Lashek noticed her and Eliza bonding almost instantly. The woman with Aerene, who Lashek understood to be some sort of bodyguard, was named Shaela. She was far more serious, and Lashek couldn't help but feel suspicious of her.

They were called the Guardians of Pandeia. When Lashek first heard the term, something hot and sharp boiled up from within him; an unfamiliar kind of rage that made his hands shake. The Austris Arans were so powerful, and were given the name Guardians; and yet they'd kept distant from Pandeia for thousands of years. There were so many times they could have helped the people of Pandeia. Nothing stopped them but their own arrogance, as far as Lashek was concerned.

Lashek thought about the countless times Ermoor had tried to invade Shanaken. So many times that Austris Ara could have fought with them against evil. He thought about the last attack; when Shanaken fell for the first time in history. The ancient trees that had stood for millennia, crashing to the ground. Now, with the Ermoori arriving in Tarsium and gaining more and more of Pandeia by the month, the Austris Arans finally decided to grace them with their presence.

Zeera was grateful, even excited, to have them in Aethos. The other Circle members felt the same, or were distracted by their otherworldly nature. Lashek seemed to be the only one who harboured any resentment towards them. If they didn't care enough to intervene before, why could they be trusted enough to be loyal now?

After they'd been in Aethos a little while, Lashek finally got to speak with Shaela alone. He led her into his training room, breathing deep and even to control the anger that bubbled in his chest.

"Why are you here?" he asked, "why now?"

"We were summoned, Lashek," Shaela said, "the summoning spell was the only connection we had with Pandeia."

"Surely you could have known if there was trouble, some other way? Pandeia has been suffering a long time. Ermoor has been attempting to invade constantly. I've lost so many friends on the northern shore, and knowing you were out there, and couldn't be bothered helping us, is just-"

"Lashek," Shaela said, "I understand. I do. But you need to trust me when I say that we had no idea what was happening in the rest of Pandeia."

"How can that be true?" Lashek said, "you're the most powerful beings I've ever seen. You had to have felt *something*."

“We were halfway across the planet, Lashek. Magic does not work that way.”

Lashek sighed, taking his eyes off the blue and gold being in front of him. She projected calm, and certainty, and strength. Though he still felt off, it was difficult in that moment not to trust her. He couldn’t have felt anything that happened in Tarsium, or Omas, after all. It still bothered him that they would have stopped hundreds of Shenza from dying if they’d been around during the attempted invasions; but hearing her say they couldn’t have known helped a little.

“Are you and your people invested in this war?” Lashek asked, “I mean, really invested? Will you die for Pandeia, if it comes to that?”

Shaela looked at him, holding his gaze with her own. Her calm remained unchanged. She put her hand on his shoulder, and Lashek felt a wave of cool relaxation spread over his body. Her eyes were so strange, but even despite the lack of pupils, he knew she was staring into his own eyes. There was a kindness in her stare, a compassion that overwhelmed and humbled him.

“If that is what it takes,” she said, “I will die for Pandeia, and I will do so gladly.”

Mara

1795

Once the Austris Arans arrived in Aethos, Mara slowly became more comfortable with their presence. They mostly remained in their own city, and the two who did come into Aethos proper were quiet and respectful. Still, Mara couldn't help but feel like their appearance heralded the final stage of their mission; sooner rather than later, Mara would be required to help destroy Sithares. After that, they'd have to fight in a real war.

Even though seeing the Austris Arans in person helped to calm her fear of their arrival, it did nothing for her fear of using magic again.

At least for the summoning spell, she'd only lended her magic to Zeera; though it was uncomfortable, she didn't have to use magic herself. With every day that passed, Mara's fear grew. Her nightmares became worse. Power Magic crackled in the depths of her mind while she slept, distorting the dreams that came to her. Riffolk's face plagued her.

She couldn't stop herself; after a little while of the Austris Arans living with them, Mara needed to talk with Zeera. With every day that passed, Mara knew the time drew closer to when she would need to join the Circle properly. She searched through the temple for almost an hour, finally finding Zeera in Shaela's training room with the Austris Aran.

"Mara," Zeera said when she reached the doorway, "I did not expect to see you exploring the temple."

Mara tried to smile; she didn't feel as though she succeeded.

"I need to speak with you," she said, "if… if that's okay."

Shaela glided to the ground, and they both silenced their magic. They'd been training, though it looked to Mara like neither had been trying particularly hard.

"Of course," Zeera said, "what would you like to discuss?"

Mara shot a glance at Shaela; she didn't know how to say that she didn't want Shaela to be a part of the conversation. Though the Austris Arans were technically called the guardians of Pandeia, Mara still didn't know them; and even if she did, Shaela herself wasn't even one of the Heroes. Despite that, Zeera made no effort to send Shaela away, and Mara couldn't summon the courage to ask her to leave.

"Well…" she said, "I was just wondering if there's a way that I could…"

She faltered, the words escaping her mind as she chased them, her panic growing. Zeera's eyes were trained on her own, patient and kind. Mara took a deep breath and shook her head.

"Sorry," she made herself say, turning to Shaela, "can I talk with Zeera privately?"

Shaela stared at her for a second, then left the room without a word. After a few more steadying breaths, Mara forced herself to ask the question.

"Is there some way to make someone else the Hero… instead of me?"

"You mean Eliza?"

Mara nodded, ashamed that it was what she wanted, and embarrassed that Zeera could read it so easily.

"Honestly," Zeera said gently, "I am not sure. Before I met Aella, I would have said no. Now, I cannot say with certainty."

To Mara, it felt like an explosion of hope bloomed suddenly in her chest. Where she expected Zeera to say no, she instead said maybe; it *could* be possible, after all. For a brief moment, Mara embraced the hope. After that, a stark reality settled on her with cold claws: if they were successful, it would mean all the danger that Mara faced would fall to Eliza.

"The only time the Gods have chosen new Heroes," Zeera

said, “is when the original Hero died. I have heard of one occasion where a Hero was swapped for another without the first dying, but I do not know the full situation.”

“How do we find out how to do it?” Mara asked.

“I will do my best to discover how it can be done. You must be patient, Mara, and in the meantime, I have a favour to ask.”

Mara nodded, cold spreading through her body as her mind worked to show her the worst-case scenarios.

“I need you to train, and practice,” Zeera said, “so that if this fails, you will still be able to help the Circle.”

Once again, tears welled up in her eyes. She tried to ignore them, nodding at Zeera to show her agreement. Zeera seemed satisfied, and she turned to leave the training room.

“Wait,” Mara said, “there’s… one more thing.”

“Yes?”

The nightmares were getting so bad that Mara almost never slept anymore. She was certain that Riffolk’s constant hatred and dark thoughts were beginning to change her own thoughts and feelings. It was becoming unbearable.

“I can feel someone else,” she said, “in my head. I wanted to know if that’s ever happened before. With the other Heroes, or something.”

Zeera smiled, reassurance emanating from her in pleasant waves.

“All Heroes hear the voice of their God,” Zeera said, “it can be strange, and sometimes scary. But I assure you, it is completely normal."

"No," Mara said, "this isn't Taranos. I mean someone else. He's… evil. He was there when I was touched by Taranos. He was… he was touched as well."

In an instant, Zeera's face changed from calm and friendly to focused and fearful. It was a shocking difference, and Mara found herself panicking all over again.

"Someone else was touched by Taranos?" Zeera said, "who was it?"

She didn't want to say his name. Even thinking his name felt like too much of a risk. But she had to answer Zeera, even if it scared her.

"Riffolk," she said, barely able to say it out loud.

Zeera's eyes shot wide, taking up most of her face.

"Riffolk *Hayne*?" she said, "the Prime Overseer of Ermoor?"

Nodding, Mara stared at a spot on the floor, trying to keep her panic at bay long enough to finish the conversation.

"How did we not know this earlier?" Zeera asked, her massive eyes roaming the room, "the Circle knows everything."

"So… this isn't normal, then?" Mara asked.

"I have never heard of it happening before, no. But if Taranos touched you both, especially at the same time, then it would make sense that you both share a connection. You are technically *both* the Hero."

Mara was openly weeping now, letting the tears fall down her cheeks as she stared resolutely at the floor. She'd never wanted to be Hero in the first place, and swapping with Eliza would have been complicated enough before; if Riffolk was also Hero, it became impossible. If she wasn't Hero, the title fell to Riffolk by default.

"He can't be," she said, shaking her head, "he's not a Hero, he's a monster."

Zeera looked at her with a depth of sadness that Mara had never seen before. She looked as though she saw everything Mara had been through; simply by staring into her eyes. Everything Riffolk did to her when she lived in Ermoor; all of the fear, the isolation, the hopelessness she'd felt, was reflected back at her in Zeera's eyes.

Finally, Zeera's eyes shifted away. They snapped in several directions, as though making quick calculations. Then, she looked back at Mara once again; except her expression was full of dawning horror.

"He's the father," she said, "isn't he? Eliza's father?"

Mara sobbed, nodding her head as the tears doubled. Admitting it, especially to someone who knew how dangerous Riffolk was, broke her heart all over again. She loved Eliza with all her heart, but the fact that her father was Riffolk hurt her more than she could say.

"I'm so sorry," Zeera said.

She let Mara cry for a few moments, until the sobs died down. When Mara's breathing had returned to normal, she looked at Zeera;

the Tarsi woman was looking at her with gentle kindness.

"We won't let him near you, or your daughter," she said, "I promise."

Mara nodded, but a small part of her knew that Riffolk couldn't be stopped. Not even by the Circle. When he wanted something, he took it. The cold certainty that she would die still sat within her mind, unmoving.

"There are legends," Zeera said, "about the Heroes of ancient times. Have you heard the legend of Xanthe?"

Words felt too difficult for her, so Mara shook her head instead. Zeera smiled gently in acknowledgement, and went on.

"I thought as much. Xanthe was the first Thearan touched by Sithares. The first to gain Fire Magic as we know it today. What most don't know, is that Xanthe's children were more powerful than herself. Her daughter was Roxane; the most powerful Fire Mage in history. Though both women are revered among Thearans, even most of their own people do not know the two are related."

"What are you saying to me?" Mara said, "I don't understand."

"I am saying that Eliza's power makes sense now. Magic that strong grows by generation, with the creation of new life. Riffolk may seem indestructible to you, but Eliza is immeasurably more powerful, I guarantee it. Roxane was the child of one Hero; Eliza is the child of two."

Eliza

1795

The guardians were unlike anything Eliza could have possibly imagined. Incredibly tall, with bright blue skin and large golden wings, they looked like Gods to her. Furthering their Godly image, they arrived at Aethos on a gigantic floating city. In her wildest dreams, Eliza would never have believed that an entire city could float through the sky. Even after witnessing it with her own eyes, she still struggled to believe it.

Eliza learned after they arrived that they were actually called Austris Arans, and that they used to live in Aethos thousands of years ago. One of them, Aerene, looked to be about Eliza's age. Aerene was the chosen Hero of her people, but she acted as humble as if she didn't even know it. Eliza immediately liked her. After the two groups met each other and all the formalities were done with, Eliza and Aerene sat together in the open roof of the temple. They'd just trained together, both going easy on the other. Eliza still marveled at the way Aerene looked.

"I never thought I'd see Aethos," Aerene said, "I mean, other than paintings."

"There are lots of things I never thought would happen," Eliza said, "these are strange times."

Aerene smiled, a look of knowing shining from her eyes. They said *I know exactly what you mean,* without Aerene saying a word.

"What was it like?" Eliza asked, "living on a floating city?"

"I could ask you the same question," Aerene said, laughing, "about living on the ground. I didn't even realise it would feel different until we landed."

"I can't imagine being so high above the ground... I would be terrified."

Aerene laughed again.

"The wings help a lot with that," she said, "being in the sky is very natural for Austris Arans, anyway."

For a moment, Eliza tried to imagine what it felt like to have wings. *How do they fly? Does it feel like having two extra arms, or totally different?* Her mind couldn't make sense of it. She couldn't help glancing at Aerene's wings as she thought about it. They joined to her body at the shoulder blades, and they moved and twitched with Aerene's movements like any other limb. Looking too long made her shoulder blades feel strange, and she looked away again.

"I don't mind you looking, Eliza. It's something you've never seen before. I feel curious looking at the people here every now and then too."

"What would you feel curious about?" Eliza said, "we don't have any extra arms or anything."

"I mean, we do have Omati descendants living in Austris Ara," Aerene said, "but I still can't imagine what living without wings is like. I'm not sure I could handle it. I hate walking unless my wings are sore."

Eliza shook her head, still trying to wrap her mind around it. *Being without wings to her is just as strange as having wings is to me*. Everything about Aerene and her people was strange, not just her wings. Her blue skin looked unreal, as though it had been painted. Her hair, like her wings, was gold. It shone like the sun, flowing and perfect in the breeze rushing through the wind tunnel where they sat. Perhaps strangest of all, her eyes contained no visible colour, not even the black dot in the centre; the entire eye was just white. It was strange, but fascinating.

There were Omasi people living in Austris Ara since the floating city departed Aethos. Generations of them, living for thousands of years surrounded by these God-like beings. They were treated like servants, but they seemed happy. Eliza knew that her mother and other wealthy Ermoori kept servants; but they were simply other Ermoori people, and they were paid for their work. The Omasi living in Austris Ara were allowed food and clothing, and given their own places to sleep, but had no money. They didn't seem to even understand the concept. Instead, they simply lived to serve the Austris Arans.

Mathys taught her how to look after herself from a very young age, so the idea of servants made Eliza uncomfortable. The fact that the Omasi servants were happy still didn't quite assuage her discomfort; *I don't understand how someone could be happy if their entire life was dedicated to someone else's whims*. Aerene was a kind person, and the rest of the Austris Arans didn't strike her as cruel, but there was something about keeping servants that sat wrong in her heart.

Aerene stirred beside her, and Eliza's thoughts snapped back to the present. They glanced at each other, and Eliza's eyes wandered back to Aerene's wings again.

"Can Austris Arans fly when they're first born?" Eliza asked, "or does it take a long time to learn?"

"I don't know," she said, "that was a long time ago. I've been able to fly for as long as I can remember, though."

"It couldn't be that long ago. I still remember things from when I was three or four, and that was almost twenty years ago now."

"Oh, I can remember twenty years ago with no problem,"

Aerene said with a smirk, "but when I was three or four years old... that's a very long time ago."

"I thought you were around my age?" Eliza said.

"Austris Arans live far longer lives than any other people in Pandeia. I may look young… and in terms of our lifespan, I'm the equivalent of a twenty-year-old, I suppose. But I'm three hundred and seventy-three years old."

Mara

1795

A while after the meeting Zeera hosted with the Heroes, Mara's fear grew out of control. She knew that Zeera was simply trying to do her job. But after hearing everything that was said, Mara couldn't contain her panic any longer. Her nightmares were growing worse, and still no one listened to her fears.

One day, after watching Eliza train with the Austris Aran girl, Mara's heart felt as though it would explode. She left the building in a daze, and when she was finally alone, her heart continued thumping against her chest, her lungs struggling to take in any air. The walls and floor twisted in her vision, blurring together as she tried to keep walking.

Aethos pressed in on her, loomed over her, until there was nothing else. The city seemed to scream in her mind, the way Riffolk did in her nightmares. It laughed and crawled in her head, dragging itself over everything until even the sky above her disappeared. She couldn't breathe, couldn't think or see. She knew, in that moment, that Aethos would be where she died.

Some part of her knew that her connection with Riffolk was related to their magic; that same part knew that it couldn't be broken. Asking Zeera had been a desperate attempt to explain it away as something simpler, something less terrifying. The only piece of solace she'd gained from their talk was that Eliza was more powerful than Riffolk. If it was true, it meant her daughter might survive the coming war.

Even the idea that Eliza could be fine failed to calm the raging chaos that threatened to swallow her mind. *There is no escape,* she thought, *the Circle, Riffolk, Kerberos... no matter what happens, I will be facing too much danger*. There was simply no way to come out of all the coming obstacles; fighting a war and attempting to kill a God, almost at the same time. Both were impossible, even as separate tasks. And no matter what she did, Mara would be drawn into both.

She could think of only one way out; she ran. Though her vision still swam, and her body screamed as her heart pounded, she made her way to the main gates of Aethos. The people around her barely reacted as she stumbled through the square.

Riffolk's face flashed into her mind. His evil smile spread wide, his bright blue eyes crackling with sparks of yellow lightning. She actually heard him laughing, somehow, in her head. Even though it had been more than two decades since she heard his voice, she still knew the sound intimately.

There were so many people in Aethos; Thearans, Omati, and Austris Arans milled around the square. She saw the main gates, swimming in her vision. White clouded the edges of her eyes, her thoughts just as faded. Guards stood near the gates, and Mara approached one of them.

"Let me out," she said, "I need to leave."

"Are you okay?" the guard said, though no trace of concern came through in his voice, "do you need help?"

"No," she said, "no help. Just please, let me out of Aethos."

The guard stared for a moment. While he looked her over, Mara forced herself to stay still. It was all she could do to wrestle against the panic that overwhelmed her.

"Alright," the guard finally said, "just don't go too far. Aethos needs you safe. All of Pandeia needs you safe."

Even the guards know who I am, Mara thought, *I can't go anywhere anymore without the Circle knowing about it*. Soon enough, she knew, Zeera would find out that she'd left Aethos. After that, it wouldn't be long before Circle agents tracked her down and brought her back again.

The gates slowly opened, creaking and groaning as the massive doors turned out. Mara’s breathing sped up, her lungs taking in almost no air. Finally, when the gates were wide enough for her to walk through, she ran.

Lashek

1795

After he spoke to Shaela, Lashek felt slightly better about the Austris Arans. His suspicions weren't completely abated, but he'd at least been given the opportunity to confront one of them directly. With both them and the Thearans in Aethos, however, Lashek's fears never quite faded.

He watched them train, watched them interact with the other Circle members, and watched them on their own. Other than talking with an air of superiority, they gave him no indication of being untrustworthy. Shaela became friendly towards him after their talk, and Lashek returned the warmth as best he could.

Lashek spoke to Eliza one day, just after they'd sparred together. Her immediate bond with Aerene worried him.

"Do you really think they're committed to this fight?" he asked, "they seem to think they're better than everyone. Maybe once they destroy Ermoor, they'll take what's left of Pandeia for themselves?"

Eliza scoffed, shaking her head and looking at him as though he'd been talking about mice taking over Pandeia.

"They came when we summoned them, didn't they?" she said, "it would've been just as easy for them to wait and watch until the war was done, if that's what they wanted."

"They haven't been seen in Pandeia for thousands of years," Lashek said, "no one knows what they want or what they're capable of. All we have is ancient stories. Myths."

Again, Eliza scoffed. She smiled, half exasperation and half amusement.

"Lashek, you're being paranoid. You were worried about Aella, too, and look at how well she's settled in."

"Maybe I am a little paranoid," he said, "but you're too trusting. So is Zeera. We're letting all these people just march on in to Aethos, with no idea who's loyal to who. I'm telling you, someone is going to stab us in the back. Then you'll believe me."

This time, Eliza actually laughed. Lashek almost shouted at her, but held his tongue with all the effort he could muster.

"I'll watch your back for you then," she said, "does that help you feel a little better?"

After Eliza, Lashek went to Zeera. He knew she was even less likely to listen to him, but he had to try. She sat in her own quarters, meditating, when he walked in. He didn't say anything at first, and for a moment she didn't react to his presence. Several minutes passed, and finally Zeera muttered something to herself and stood to greet him.

"Lashek," she said, "are you well?"

"Better than ever," he said, "can't you tell?"

She smiled, but it was a knowing smile full of resignation; he knew Zeera only put up with him because he was Amalus' chosen Hero. Still, despite his constant sarcasm, they got along fairly well.

"Something is bothering you, Lashek," she said, "just tell me, and be done with it."

Lashek thought about how to phrase his suspicions. As far as Zeera was concerned, the newest additions to Aethos were perfectly trustworthy. Even after their experience with Kerberos, she was quick to trust and open to all. Convincing her that Aella might be a problem, and that the Austris Arans barely cared about Pandeia at all, would take verbal skills that Lashek didn't possess. All he could do was say how he felt.

"Since Aella and her Thearans appeared," he said, "I've felt as though something is off. They worship Sithares, and some part of me can't help but think they could be in league with Kerberos."

Zeera remained silent a long while, the tired smile that was on her face slowly fading. By the time she spoke, her expression had settled into a careful, controlled blank.

"Kerberos needs no more allies than he already has. I've spoken to Aella, and I assure you, Lashek… she wants Kerberos dead more than anyone in Pandeia."

"Even so," Lashek said, "she does worship Sithares. Our entire mission is to destroy the God she worships. How can we trust that she will follow through with the Circle's goal?"

She shook her head, slowly, her face unchanged.

"We must have faith."

"That's it?" Lashek said, "you're leaving the fate of Pandeia in the hands of a Thearan based on blind faith in a stranger?"

Zeera didn't answer. They stared at each other, neither willing to concede their point. Zeera's faith was unshakeable, and Lashek's suspicions refused to give way to mere hope. He decided to drop it for now; she was, after all, the leader of the Circle. But for a brief moment, Lashek wondered *why* she got to be the leader. What had she done to earn such a title? Breathing slowly, and reciting the three tenets of the Shenza, he forced the questions out of his mind. Suspecting strangers was one thing; suspecting Zeera would achieve nothing. Lashek sighed.

"I'm just worried, is all," he said, "there's so much that could go wrong."

"Of course there is. But the original Circle of Shadows was created out of strangers, to stop a threat to all of Pandeia. This time is no different. If we hope to succeed, we need to trust each other."

He knew she was right. But the knowledge did nothing to soothe his fears about the Thearans. Even if Aella herself hated Kerberos, any of her warriors might have been loyal to him. Or to Sithares. And then there was the Austris Arans; if they were so powerful, and if they were the Guardians of Pandeia, where had they been? Why not protect Pandeia before now?

Zeera stared at him, seeing the emotions pass over his face and waiting for him to voice them. Again, he didn't know how; and again, he decided to just forge ahead.

"I'm not sure I can trust them completely. The Thearans, nor the Austris Arans."

Her eyes shot wide, the effect glaring after its steady stillness. *It never even occurred to her that they could be anything other than totally trustworthy,* Lashek thought, *even though they've never once used their power to help us.*

"You question the Guardians now, too?" she asked, "I know you and Shaela had your disagreement, but do you really think they would respond to the summons, only to betray the Circle?"

"Yes," he said, "I do. For thousands of years, Shanaken has faced the brunt of Ermoor's wrath. We've fought them, died fighting them. They've only grown stronger. These Guardians of yours could have stopped them decades ago, *centuries* ago, if they'd wanted. They could have stopped thousands of deaths, could have stopped this war before it even began. But they didn't. Why would I trust people like that?"

Zeera had nothing to say. For the first time since Lashek had known her, she was speechless.

Mara

1795

Outside of Aethos, Mara slowed down a little. She'd been running for what felt like an hour. The path she followed was unfamiliar; she didn't even know what direction she was headed. All she knew was that mountains lined the horizon in front of her. *Just go,* she thought, *get away. If I find somewhere to stay, maybe I can live a simple life*. Her life in Saford had been beautiful; quiet, peaceful, and full of love. *I just want that back. It's all I've ever wanted.*

When she was far enough out of the city, a strange kind of

relief settled over her. Although she knew she wasn't out of the Circle's reach, the open air and lack of people helped to calm her panic.

Eventually, Mara came across a cliff; next to the path on the left, the ground simply fell away. Beyond that, the ocean stretched endlessly into misty shades of blue and white. Though the view was beautiful, Mara couldn't help but stick to the right side of the path as she walked.

Several hours after she ran through the gates of Aethos, Mara saw a camel-drawn carriage ahead. Two large Omati men sat in the wide driver's seat; she saw them turn in her direction when they noticed her. Between them, the path jutted out to the left, on the cliff's edge. A series of steep hills and ridges lined the right side of the path, blocking any escape. Putting her head down, Mara sped up, angling away from the carriage. The men's voices carried to her as they drew closer.

"Hey, hey, pretty Ermoori girl," one of them said.

Her heart wrenched in her chest at the words; they'd spoken in Ermoori.

"Come on now," the other said, "he gave you a compliment. Don't be rude. How about giving us some company on the road?"

Mara couldn't summon the courage to reply. Instead, she increased her pace once again. The carriage veered in her direction. As it neared her, it crossed the path, rolling to a stop in front of her. The two men jumped onto the ground, approaching her from both directions.

"Stupid Ermoori whore," the first man said, "thinks she's too good for the likes of us."

Tears flowed down Mara's cheeks; her voice had gone. The two men were each at least a full head taller than her, and broad across the chest and shoulders. If Mathys had still been alive, she would have felt safe even standing so close to such brutes; alone, she didn't know what to do. It had been a long time since she trained, and equally as long since she'd used magic.

"No," she finally said, "please. I just need to… to get away from Aethos."

The men ignored her, staring over her body as though she was for sale in a shop.

"Come here, girl," the man on the right said, "it's been too long since I had a pretty girl."

"You've never had a pretty girl, Silas," the first man said, "except the ones you've paid for."

Silas laughed.

"Exactly," he said, "so I'm overdue for my share. You can have her when I'm finished."

Behind the two men, the carriage door on the far side opened and closed. A third man called out from out of her sight.

"The bickering is pointless, you two," he said, "since she's Ermoori."

The third man emerged from behind the carriage, and a scream caught in Mara's throat as her heart froze. His hair was dark, almost jet black. He was tall, slim, and might have been handsome were it not for the situation. What stopped her heart, however, were his eyes; bright, icy blue. Just the same as Riffolk's.

"And she *is* beautiful," the Ermoori man continued, "which means… she's mine."

Riffolk's face exploded in her mind's eye, as the Ermoori man smiled at her. Sheer, absolute terror overcame her. Her world disappeared in a flash of hissing yellow; magic rose from somewhere deep within her, reaching for the men and the carriage in eager bolts. A shockwave ripped from her as the men and carriage were eviscerated; a deep crack sounded from below her and the ground shook beneath her feet.

Mara fell as the ground slid under her; it crunched and grated as a massive chunk of the cliff tore away from the path. The huge piece of earth and rock halted in its slide, for just long enough that Mara thought she might make it off. She was halfway onto her hands and knees when another crack arose from below her; the cliff lurched again, and Mara toppled.

The cliff slipped to the side, and Mara scrabbled at the ground for purchase, but it was no good; she began sliding down the path she'd been walking on barely a minute before. *I'm going to die,* she thought, *because of my magic. I knew it*. She finally found a small jutting rock, and grabbed onto it for dear life. There was no relief to be had, however; the entire chunk of cliff Mara clung to was still sliding towards the ocean far below.

She couldn't speak, couldn't even scream. Still clinging to the hand-hold she found, Mara squeezed her eyes shut and tried to keep breathing. The world twisted around suddenly, and in the chaos, Mara lost all sense of direction. She knew she was falling, but with her eyes closed there was no telling which way was up.

As she fell, the massive rock she held on to smashed into the cliff face and spun out of control. Her hand-hold disappeared, and Mara slid along the twirling rock, caught inexorably in its momentum. She felt the force of its spin shoving her against it even as she slid. Keeping her eyes shut, praying for something to save her, Mara lost her breath as she was flung off the huge chunk of rock and sent spinning into the air.

For a wild moment, it felt to Mara as though she was flying. A strange kind of desperate acceptance filled her mind. *I'm just about to die,* she thought, *there's nothing I can do about it now*. She spun through the air, twirling as she tried to catch her breath. *Any second now,* she thought, *I'll hit the water, or that big rock, or the cliff face*.

As she fell, it wasn't Riffolk that filled her mind, as she'd expected; it was Eliza. Her beautiful smile, her strength and confidence. She was the best of both Mara and Mathys, and though the fear that filled her in her final moments was overwhelming, the pride and love she felt for Eliza then was almost just as strong.

Mara smashed into a hard but somehow slightly yielding surface; the air ripped from her lungs. It was rough, but nothing like what she expected. Her eyes were still closed, but air began rushing around her once again. Eventually, distantly, she recognized the feeling of being held in someone's arms. It didn't make sense; *is this what death feels like?* she thought, *an angel of God, carrying me away?*

"You're alright, Mara," a voice said over the wind in her ears, "I've got you. It's okay."

A little while later, the voice spoke again. Her voice was beautiful; musical and kind, with a depth that spoke of wisdom and patience.

"I was scared too, you know. When I was chosen. But we're in this together."

When Mara finally gained the courage to force her eyes open, she saw the perfect face of Aerene smiling down at her.

"You found me," Mara said, "you… you saved me."

"Well, yes," Aerene laughed, "you're one of us. Even if you weren't a Hero, you're Eliza's mother."

She said it as though that settled the matter. As though their friendship meant more to her than anything else. As Aerene carried her back to Aethos, Mara thought again about Eliza. Her daughter never failed to surprise her. Though the Austris Arans hadn't been seen for thousands of years, Eliza had somehow created an unbreakable bond within weeks of their arrival. *She saved my life,* Mara thought, *just as much as Aerene did.*

For the rest of the flight back, Mara's fear left her. Tears flowed from her as a strange feeling filled her instead; for the first time in a long time, Mara felt seen. Understood. Most of all, she felt hope. *This perfect being was scared,* she thought, *just the same as me. If she can get past it, maybe she can help me to do the same.*

Eliza

1795

Once the Austris Arans settled in, life returned mostly to normal; though now there was a palpable sense of purpose and urgency felt by everyone in the Circle. Everyone continued training, and the Heroes continued their secret meetings to discuss destroying Sithares. The way they'd spoken before arriving at Aethos gave Eliza the impression that things would move quickly from this point. But other than the strong feeling of urgency in the air, it felt to Eliza like nothing had changed.

After running away and then being saved by Aerene, her

mother was mostly better; but still quiet. She'd started going to the Circle meetings with the other Heroes. It gave Eliza more time to train and relax on her own, which she was glad for; but she wished more than anything to be included.

She sat on a bench in one of the training rooms, catching her breath. The Heroes were meeting now, talking about the future of Pandeia itself, while Eliza practiced combat moves. It felt almost pointless to her. *They're going to save the world and all I'm doing is punching these stupid training dummies*.

"Would you like to train with me?" a cold voice called from the doorway, forcing a gasp from Eliza.

Shaela walked into the room. *How can someone so big move so quietly,* she thought, *I almost screamed.*

"I'm… not sure I could keep up with you," Eliza said.

"Don't worry, I won't hurt you."

It's better than training alone, she thought. Her and Aerene had trained together several times now, but Aerene was a Hero, and had to be at the meetings held by the Circle. The only other person she enjoyed training with was Lashek, and he was a Hero too.

"Okay," she said, "let's go."

Shaela's combat pose was intimidating; her wings were spread wide and low, angled aggressively to give her perfect balance. She looked more like a mythical predatory beast than a person. Aerene was powerful, and Eliza had learned a lot about Air Magic; but she still didn't know what to expect from Shaela.

She waited, not quite brave enough to make the first move. Power Magic crackled through her body. A ready stance Mathys taught her kept her bodyweight centred and mobile. On the balls of her feet, hands raised, she locked eyes with Shaela. *Your opponent's eyes tell you more than their stance will,* Mathys had always told her, *focus on their eyes during combat, not their limbs.*

They stared each other down, impatience bubbling under the surface as she waited for Shaela to attack. Shaela's eyes narrowed a fraction, and Eliza saw her muscles tense slightly. *There.* Barely a second later, Shaela leapt straight towards Eliza. With her wings spread, she was able to streak across the room without touching the ground. Eliza ducked low, tensing for impact.

Shaela's feet cannoned into her, just barely blocked by Eliza's crossed forearms. She almost fell from the strength of the attack, but kept her footing as Shaela flipped over her. Taking the chance, Eliza dived as far forward as she could, twisting out of the dive to face Shaela as she rolled to her feet. Shaela was already sweeping across the training room floor towards her.

Eliza dived to the side at the last second, sending a bolt of electricity into one of Shaela's wings in midair. She heard it connect, heard Shaela's grunt and the thump of her hitting the floor and rolling. Eliza was on her feet again in an instant, hands up and ready for more.

Shaela took a second longer to roll back to her feet; *I hit harder than I thought I would,* she thought, *whoops*.

"I wasn't expecting that," Shaela said.

"Sorry."

"Not at all. Let's keep going."

Shaela shook off the attack, settling back into a ready stance. Eliza brought more magic to the surface, pooling it into her hands to strike quickly. She'd barely used any magic the first time; *I need to be careful if that was enough to hurt her,* she thought. Holding back was something she learned from a young age, to control the destructive power within her. She'd never used even close to all of her magic, even when she trained alone. Shaela was powerful, but if one tiny bolt threw her that badly, Eliza needed to be mindful.

For a moment, they stood opposite each other as they had at the beginning of the sparring session. Shaela's eyes were narrowed, her brow furrowed in cautious concentration. *She's learned,* Eliza thought, *she won't let her guard down so easily again*. As quickly as she could, Eliza scanned Shaela with a glance. *The wing is injured near the shoulder. It'll be more difficult for her to glide. She knows my attacks come from the hands, so she'll avoid them or try to restrain them. I still don't know what kind of fighting technique she uses, but for now I have to assume it's the same as Aerene's*.

Aerene's style was fast, based more on accuracy than brute strength; but she mixed her physical attacks with Air Magic to add power to each blow. If Shaela fought the same way, Eliza would have to move fast and focus on dodging instead of blocking. Her forearms were already sore from the one attack she'd blocked. Combat between experienced fighters always became a rhythm, and once that rhythm settled in Eliza would be able to exploit it the way Mathys had taught her.

This time Shaela didn't attack first; she waited the way Eliza had. Moments passed in palpable tension, Shaela completely still, until Eliza finally attacked. Pointing her hand slightly to Shaela's left, she let electricity flow from her into the wall, missing Shaela by barely an inch. As she knew would happen, Shaela swayed to the right, and Eliza leapt to meet her dodge with a flying kick.

Shaela slid under her kick, and Eliza sent another bolt straight down as she passed overhead. She landed, twirled, and saw Shaela coming at her fast. *It's time,* she thought; she'd discovered a new technique while training by herself. Aerene always held back, but Shaela was genuinely trying to win. If she couldn't unleash her magic in attacks, she could at least use it to do something else.

In the split second before Shaela reached her, Eliza poured all of her focus into magic. Closing her eyes, she threw her hand to the side, bringing her magic to bear and letting it flow from her fingers. As happened when she tried it alone, she felt her body writhe and move with the electricity. The rush of movement and sound was unlike anything else. Within a second it was done, and the electricity faded to show Shaela's back as she passed through the point where Eliza had been.

Shaela paused, then turned to follow the path Eliza's magic had taken. Her eyes bulged as she saw Eliza standing ready on the opposite side of the room, still buzzing with magical power.

"I've never seen... anything like that," she said.

"I discovered it by accident," Eliza said, "I'm still learning how to control it."

"No one taught you this?"

"No. My mother doesn't have as much power as me, and even if she did, she wouldn't use it. Mathys trained me for a while, but he had no magic at all. I had to teach myself."

"Mathys?"

"Oh," Eliza said, *I forgot they've never met,* she thought, "he's... he *was*, our… protector, I suppose."

"What happened to him?"

Eliza tried to keep her voice from wavering, but failed.

"He was killed by a man called Kerberos."

"Zeera told me of him. How dangerous he is."

"He's a monster," Eliza said, "and he could destroy the entire Circle of Shadows by himself."

"Not with us here," Shaela said, cold certainty shining from her eyes, "Sithares will fall, and Kerberos too."

Zeera

1795

There was one thing that had to be done as soon after the Austris Arans arrived as possible; putting together the spell that would destroy Sithares. The Austris Arans had been in Aethos a little while now, and Zeera was feeling the pressure. In ancient times, the Circle had kept half of the powerful runes, and Austris Ara took the other half with them into the southern skies of Pandeia.

Zeera knew her half well, as she knew Aerene and Shaela did their own. All that remained was combining the halves into the full spell.

The three of them sat together, in a private antechamber of the temple; Zeera, Shaela, and Aerene. Though the Austris Arans knew their runes by heart, Shaela carried an ancient scroll that matched Zeera's. Ordinarily, such runes would disappear a short time after being drawn; but the ancient Circle had discovered a way around this. How they did so, Zeera would never know.

Shaela and Zeera laid their respective scrolls onto the stone bench they sat before, side by side. They both cast their eyes over the runes, taking in the full spell. *This hasn't been seen by anyone for over two thousand years,* Zeera thought, *not put together like this*.

As the scrolls came to rest beside each other, Zeera could have sworn she felt a soft pulse of energy emanating from them. She glanced at Aerene; the Austris Aran girl stared hard at the ancient paper with a look in her white eyes that said she felt it too. Shaela simply frowned, scanning over the scrolls repeatedly.

When the time came, the Heroes were each going to have to cast the spell simultaneously, which meant all of them had to learn it by heart. Zeera and Aerene each knowing half was a good start, but they had a long way to go.

Zeera's attention went to the second scroll; she read the runes from start to finish multiple times, trying to burn them into her mind's eye. She would be in charge of teaching the other Heroes to cast the spell, so she had to know it as well as she knew Water Magic.

"Wait," Shaela said, her frown deepening as she snatched

Zeera's scroll from the bench. Zeera watched, unable to stop a frown of her own.

"Is that…" Aerene said.

"I believe so," said Shaela, "but I don't know why…"

"What?" Zeera asked, "what's happening?"

Shaela put the scroll back down, next to the other, and motioned between them.

"Do you know how a spell like this would work?" she asked.

"Well, only in theory," Zeera replied, "it's not exactly a common type of spell."

"Well, we have a problem," Shaela said, "a really big problem."

"What?" Zeera looked between the two women, trying to gauge their thoughts and getting nowhere. "What's wrong?"

Shaela finally sighed, and looked Zeera directly in the eyes. She pointed at the bottom of Zeera's scroll, where the runes would lead into the Austris Aran half of the spell.

"Right here," she said, "there is a piece of the spell missing."

Shaela

1795

Knowing how much training would need to be done, Shaela assumed the role of teacher alongside Zeera. Though things were tense between the two at first, they eventually grew closer. Shaela had to force herself to respect the Tarsi, and the Circle in general. They shared a mutual goal, after all.

The one thing Shaela was grateful for was that she'd agreed to train Aerene and Aella. The two were incredibly powerful, and though Aella was learning from scratch, she was intelligent and talented enough to learn quickly. The spells required for their mission were known by all members of the royal family, as well as royal guards and priests-in-training. Aerene knew them already, which meant Shaela need only focus on Aella.

As well as teaching her the spells, Shaela trained Aella in general magic use. For a Queen, Aella showed a surprising amount of humility. Her attitude was cold, but she listened to everything Shaela said and practiced diligently.

Zeera faced a far larger challenge; training people who'd never even heard of Deias, when she herself had barely learned its uses. Shaela didn't envy her. *I should just teach them all,* she thought, *if only I had the patience for such a task.* But as well as patience, Shaela had to maintain the reputation and standing of the Austris Arans; they were above the people of Pandeia. They weren't mere teachers.

Her conversation with Aerene helped to take some of the anger from Shaela at the Circle for neglecting their duties; but it wasn't entirely gone. It still bothered her that such an important mission could be utterly forgotten. *Why create the Circle in the first place,* she thought, *if it was to be disbanded at the first opportunity?* Austris Ara had been against making the Circle a secret organization from the beginning; but they were outvoted, and the Circle was kept hidden from the general population. It had been one of the reasons the city was designed and built to leave; Austris Ara was intent on teaching their people the full history of the Gods' war, and the rest of the Circle was intent on teaching only the chosen Heroes.

Austris Ara's wisdom was ignored back then. Shaela's only

goal now was to destroy Sithares completely, so that the Circle need not exist at all anymore. *These people don't deserve our help,* she thought, *if they can't even begin to help themselves.*

Aerene threw herself into the Circle with her entire being; she was already close friends with Eliza, and she seemed to be wholly in support of everything the Circle did. It infuriated Shaela almost as much as the Circle itself. *As wise and compassionate as she is,* she thought, *Aerene is far too naïve.*

Shaking herself out of her thoughts, Shaela checked on Aella's spell. Aerene practiced next to her, but as usual, her spell casting was perfect. Aella, on the other hand, struggled with some of the symbols. Shaela corrected her as patiently as she could. They couldn't practice the actual spell that would destroy Sithares, so they practiced far simpler spells instead.

"The runes are so similar to each other," Aella said, "I keep getting them mixed up."

"It is an intricate language," Shaela said, "it can take years to learn fully. Elemental Magic can be self-taught, and used by feel. Deias is different… it requires real knowledge, and finesse."

She was teaching Aella a simple spell; an orb of light. The Thearan Queen hadn't managed to produce one yet. With a quiet sigh, Shaela drew the runes on her palm slowly, so that Aella could see. When the word had been finished, each letter drawn over the last, Shaela pulled the spell off her skin. It grew and inflated into a sphere. Once it was the right shape, soft light gradually emanated from its smooth surface.

Aella's eyes never left the spell as Shaela cast it. When she was finished, Aella tried again. She almost got it, but several of the runes were still off.

"It feels like I'm not improving," Aella said, "I thought I would pick it up faster than this."

"This will take time," Shaela said, "none of the people in Pandeia even knew Deias existed. Keep practicing."

Aella nodded, drawing a new set of runes on her palm. Again, it was off; but Aella's dedication didn't wane. Every time the spell failed, the drawn runes burned brightly for a moment before dissipating into thick white smoke. The smoke drifted up into the training room's still air, eventually dissolving into nothing. It was a gentle failure; by comparison, the spell they'd need to perform to destroy Sithares could destroy all of Aethos if they didn't cast it perfectly.

Shaela drew the runes again, in a row on the training room's wall so as to stop it being cast. There was magic within the language itself, but only when drawn the correct way. Aella looked at the runes intently as Shaela drew them; as with the failed spells, each only lasted moments before it burned and disappeared. She tried again, and finally pulled a completed spell off her palm. It grew and lit up just as Shaela's had.

"There it is," Shaela said, "good. Again."

Aella complied, drawing the runes once again and succeeding.

Shaela nodded, and Aerene smiled at them both. For a while longer, Shaela made Aella keep practicing. Aerene practiced right alongside her, despite already knowing the spells by heart. She encouraged Aella, watching and nodding with a supportive smile. Aella's expression never changed from intense concentration; Aerene's encouragement seemed to have no obvious effect.

After the orb of light spell, Shaela taught Aella several more spells. Although she'd learned the orb spell after a lot of attempts, she was going to have to practice consistently to maintain the ability and knowledge. Aerene practiced as well, though she didn't need to.

Every now and then, Shaela and Zeera talked, comparing their experiences training the Heroes. As Shaela predicted, Zeera struggled far more than she did.

"Lashek and Mara will take a long time to learn this magic," Zeera said, "how are your Heroes going?"

"Better," Shaela said, "Aerene is already accomplished when it comes to using Deias. Aella is a fast learner."

"Luckily, we seem to have time before we're able to retrieve the book of Sithares. I will need that time."

Shaela nodded; she was pleased Zeera knew her own limitations, instead of assuming she could teach Deias flawlessly with no problems. Shaela agreed very deliberately to train Aerene and

Aella; despite Mara's sheer power and the reputation of the Shenza as magic-wielders, Shaela had seen Aella's potential immediately.

As much as the group's bond did affect their ability to successfully cast the spells, they still required a huge amount of magic and dedication from each individual caster. *If the Heroes I train can successfully cast the spells,* she thought, *and Zeera can do it too, that might be enough to destroy Sithares*. The other two Heroes were up to Zeera's ability as a teacher. Shaela didn't have much faith in them, but if Zeera was even remotely competent, the Circle had a chance.

The only remaining problem—and it was a considerable one—was that the spell itself remained incomplete. Shaela still reeled from the revelation. She had no idea what the old Circle had done to the information; but without it, regardless of how much training the Circle did, the spell would be impossible.

Zeera

1795

With Shaela finally on board with the Circle, Zeera left some of the training to her. They split the Heroes between them to teach the spells they needed; Zeera taught Lashek and Mara, and Shaela taught Aerene and Aella. Shaela knew all the spells offhand, as though they were common knowledge. Aerene seemed to be familiar with them, though she still needed to be taught.

Zeera felt confident enough with her knowledge that she could teach Lashek and Mara; but Mara's confidence was another issue entirely. She was still fragile, easily frightened, and withdrawn. Zeera found herself wishing once again that Taranos would change its mind, and make Eliza its Hero.

Their lessons started off slowly, with Zeera trying to explain the way Deias worked; it was an unknown to almost every being in Pandeia except the Tarsi.

"Deias is a language that uses your natural life energies to create magic," Zeera said in their first lesson, "it works differently to elemental magic, but you can channel your unique magic into it, as a sort of fuel."

Mara stared at her, pale and wide-eyed. Lashek frowned, blinking as he tried to make sense of what she said.

"It is a spoken language," she continued, "but the runes can be traced on the palm of the hand or on inanimate objects to create physical spells. We will need to do both."

"We need to learn a whole other language?" Lashek asked, "I'm still getting the hang of Oman."

"You only need to learn the spells, Lashek," Zeera said, "nothing else."

Lashek nodded, but he didn't look convinced. *Teaching these two is going to be almost as difficult as actually performing the spells,* she thought, *Asheilos help me*. The worst part was that they had to stick to simply learning the theory; performing the spells before it was time wouldn't end well. They were specific in design, and without the book and the podium, there was no knowing what effect they could have.

After explaining Deias as thoroughly as she could, Zeera began describing the specific spells they needed to learn. She saw Mara's eyes glisten with emotion the longer she listened, and knew the Ermoori woman was overwhelmed. Lashek, to his credit, focused more than she'd ever seen him in the past.

It was the beginning of what Zeera knew would be a long and arduous process. Finding the book of Sithares still sat at the top of her priorities list; as urgent as learning the spells was, the magic without the book became redundant.

They spent a few hours every day learning Deias. Zeera first taught them a couple of simple spells, things they could practice to get the hang of using a new magic. Even those spells took a long time, and Zeera's patience was tested daily. Mara seemed unable to learn anything new. She was powerful, and when pushed could unleash a storm of destructive magic; but other than emergencies, she refused to use her magic.

Zeera knew that Eliza was equally as powerful as Mara; if not even more so. It made her wonder if there was a real reason only the Heroes could destroy Sithares. If she taught Eliza the necessary spells, wasn't it possible that the young Ermoori could perform the magic instead of her mother? She decided to ask Shaela about it; the Austris Aran knew more about the Circle and their history than anyone Zeera knew.

She found Shaela shortly after they'd both finished teaching their lessons. Pulling her into a side room, Zeera lowered her voice and leaned close.

"Mara is unable to learn the spells," she said, "and she can barely even use her magic, even though she is incredibly powerful."

"I have noticed her failings," Shaela said, "why are you bringing them to me?"

"Well…" Zeera said, "is there any chance Eliza can become the Hero for Taranos, instead of Mara?"

"No."

Shaela's face was set, her eyes unforgiving.

"Sithares chose a new Hero even though Kerberos still lives," Zeera said, "why can Taranos not do the same?"

"It should not be possible. I do not know the details or how powerful Sithares may have become, but I can tell you it has never happened before."

"But it has now," Zeera said, "so it can happen again."

Shaela looked at her, the expression on her face unchanged.

"If it was at all possible," she said, "it is something that the Hero would need to discuss with their God. But I warn you now: trying to persuade the Gods is a dangerous path. They do not take to mortals interfering with their plans lightly."

Zeera took a long breath. Shaela's gaze never wavered.

“What about the spell, then?” Zeera said, “why can’t someone other than the Heroes participate in the spell to destroy Sithares?”

“I thought you had studied it?” Shaela said, her voice cold, “if you had you would know that it opens a channel directly to each Hero’s God, pouring their power into a joint attack. Only the ones who have a direct link to their God, the chosen, can wield the spell.”

All she could do was ask Mara to pray to Taranos; and possibly Eliza too. Beyond that, it was in the hands of the Gods. She knew they were both willing to make the change, but that meant very little if Taranos wasn’t willing to enact it. If Mara had to be the Hero, Pandiea’s fate would depend on her ability to perform spells she couldn’t even learn.

Lashek

1795

While the Circle prepared and trained together, word reached them of the Ermoori invasion. They were spreading through Pandeia at a slow but constant pace, and were now in Tarsium. The fighting had been devastating for months, though the Ermoori were stalled. All Lashek could think about was the number of lives lost every day; lives that they could be saving if they took the fight to the Ermoori.

It wasn't just Tarsi that Lashek thought about; his fellow Shenza were in Tarsium as well. The agents who worked for Zeera reported on the war as often as they could. Their news was that most of the Shenza who survived the attack fled to Tarsium and went into hiding. Now that Ermoor had invaded Tarsium as well, it was only a matter of time before they either fled Tarsium, or died.

He knew he was where he needed to be. The Circle needed him, and Amalus had chosen him. But something within him called out to the Shenza; he longed to be with them, fighting alongside them against the Ermoori. Their home, Lashek's home, was already destroyed.

It was doubtful he could make as much of a difference as he wanted to, but a part of him needed to try.

After a few days mulling over the war, Lashek decided he'd had enough. *The Austris Arans won't do anything until the Ermoori arrive in Aethos,* he thought, *and neither will Zeera. By then it will be far too late. It's time for one of us to actually do something.*

He started packing his things. Shenza didn't own much, but he still took his time. Since leaving Shanaken and living with the Circle, Lashek had built up more of a collection of belongings. Nothing compared to outsiders, but Shenza would have considered it shameful that he owned so much.

Eliza caught him before he was finished. She was halfway through asking if he wanted to spar again, and cut herself off as she saw him kneeling in front of an open travel pack. She looked over him and the pack, her eyes darting between the two as her face grew dark.

"Where are you going?" she asked.

“My people are dying,” he said, “and it’s only a matter of time before the Ermoori wipe them out. I can’t stay here, Eliza. I can’t.”

“Don’t you think the Circle knows that? We’re here to stop them, Lashek.”

“No, we’re not,” Lashek said, his voice rising, “we’re here to stop Sithares. Our mission has nothing to do with those… those monsters. They just happened to invade at the same time as Sithares became a threat.”

Eliza’s eyes fell to the floor. She knew he was right; he watched the realization dawn on her face. Since the war started, the Circle had only rarely talked about stopping the Ermoori; to most of them, the two causes had become one, but the Circle’s real goal was only ever Sithares.

“We are going to stop them, though,” she said.

“Yeah, sure,” Lashek said, “once they reach Aethos. After my people are dead. I’ll make sure to tell them who came to their rescue when I finally join them in the Eternal Mountain.”

He stood, tying the pack closed and grabbing his *Kaizuun*.

“I’m sorry, Eliza,” he said, softening his voice as much as he could, “but I need to leave.”

She rushed from the room before he did. If she was crying, Lashek didn’t know how to stop it; and couldn’t spare the time regardless. Now that he’d made the decision, getting to Tarsium suddenly felt far more urgent.

Lashek was outside the headquarters, close to the main gates of Aethos, when a powerful shout rang through the air.

"Lashek!"

He stopped, shooting a glance over his shoulder. Zeera stood in the centre of the wide street, her massive eyes glaring. Lashek had never seen a look of such fury on a Tarsi's face before. If he didn't know any better, he would have thought she wanted to kill him. Eliza stood behind her, staring at him with a desperate kind of sorrow.

"Are Circle members no better than prisoners?" he said, "unable to leave Aethos of their own accord?"

"Circle members can come and go as they please," Zeera said.

"Well then," Lashek said, continuing his stride to the gates.

"However," Zeera said, her voice even louder now, "the Heroes of the Circle serve Pandeia. You are not free until your mission is accomplished. Until Sithares is dead, you will remain in Aethos."

Eliza

1795

After their sparring session, they talked for a while longer. Shaela was surprised that Eliza wasn't Taranos' chosen Hero instead of her mother.

"I'm surprised too," Eliza said, "mother is far too shy and fragile to be a Hero."

"She was chosen for a reason," Shaela said, "we just don't see it yet, I suppose."

The Austris Arans were intensely devout. Eliza's mother and Mathys both had been, before Eliza was born. They'd both told her of the Ermoori and their false God. When she was old enough, they told her about Taranos. But she never felt the same kind of faith as the Ermoori or the Austris Arans seemed to feel. Even though she *knew* the Gods were real, she didn't feel any kind of connection to them. *Except my magic.*

Shaela was right, though; her mother was Hero, chosen by a God, and she wouldn't have been chosen for no reason. Still, the rest of the Circle felt the same way as Shaela and Eliza, according to Aerene. Her mother barely spoke at their meetings, and wasn't willing to practice the spell to destroy Sithares with them.

Aerene walked into the training room, waving and smiling at both of them. The meeting ran longer than usual, but Aerene had come straight to find Eliza; she always did. They always talked about the meetings afterwards, too, though there were some things Aerene refused to tell her. Eliza's mother refused to talk about all of it. *I'm not even sure she understands all of what's happening,* she thought.

"Eliza!" Aerene said, "you've been training with Shaela?"

"She is far more powerful than I realised," Shaela said, "powerful enough that she could be Hero."

Aerene nodded. Eliza blushed; *I thought I was crazy for wanting to be Hero,* she thought, *but they see it too.* They left the training rooms, and as soon as Shaela was out of earshot Aerene turned to her.

"We're still trying to figure out this ancient spell," she said, "we've tried so many things but some of it is missing. Zeera is furious.

None of the Circle realised the spell was incomplete until after Austris Ara arrived."

"I thought you were just practicing?" Eliza said.

They'd already spoken about how complex the spell was, but from what Aerene had said previously, it sounded like it would just take practice. *But if some of it is missing,* she thought, *they might never even figure it out*.

"It seemed like that before," Aerene said, "but Zeera finally told us all a little while ago that she doesn't know the Circle's half. Shaela and I assumed the spell would be ready when we got here. We thought a lot of things would be different."

"Don't the Austris Arans know it? I thought they knew everything?"

Aerene frowned.

"We left some information to the Circle for safekeeping. We didn't realise how time would change things for people who don't live as long as us. This spell is the most dangerous piece of magic ever created, so it couldn't be left in just one place. Austris Ara took half, and the Circle was left with half."

Aerene's eyes were bright, glowing with an intensity that scared Eliza.

"It seems", Aerene continued, "that somewhere along the way, some of the Circle's half was lost."

"Why are you telling me now?"

Eliza tried her best to leave the things Aerene couldn't tell her alone; it was difficult to pretend she didn't desperately want to hear it all.

"Because," Aerene said, "I think you deserve to know, and I can’t keep it secret anymore. I’m scared. There’s a good chance we’ll never be able to destroy Sithares at all.”

After their talk, Eliza sought out Zeera. Aerene and Eliza would both get in trouble if Zeera found out that Aerene was telling her what happened in the meetings, but she needed to anyway. Her mother was clearly struggling, becoming more withdrawn, and if any more tension arose in the Circle she would only suffer more. It wasn't fair. Zeera sat in the dining area near the kitchens, thankfully alone.

"Zeera," she said, her voice wavering and quiet, "can we talk please?"

"Of course."

Eliza sat next to her, trying to form the words she needed.

"I really want to be a part of the Circle," she said, the words falling from her mouth gracelessly, "I really think I can help. My mother needs to stop. She needs rest."

"I want you to be a part of the Circle, too," Zeera said.

She... she does? Of all the things Zeera could have said, Eliza never expected that.

"But you don't understand," Zeera continued, "it *has* to be the

Heroes. No one else can do this."

"But I'm more powerful than my mother," Eliza said, "if there's anything that takes magic, it should be me in her place."

She tried not to say anything specific. *If I mention the spell they're working on,* she thought, *Zeera will know I've been talking with Aerene about their meetings*.

"Your mother was chosen, Eliza. It's done."

"But if Taranos chose in the first place," Eliza said, "can't it choose again?"

"The magic it takes to make someone a Hero is complex and powerful," Zeera said, "and the Gods have limits, just as mortals do. A new Hero can't be chosen unless the current one dies."

They really just don't want me involved at all, do they? she thought. She could help, she knew it as well as they did. *I'm stronger than mother, more powerful, and I have more control of my magic than she does. Why doesn't she let me in to the Circle*?

"Can I help without being a Hero? Isn't there *anything* I can do?"

"You need to support Mara. She was chosen and she needs to play her role. Like you said, she's not as strong as you, and she will need your help."

That's all I am, then, she thought, *moral support. It's better than nothing, I suppose*. Her biggest fear was that her mother would be hurt, traumatised, or killed for the Circle's sake. If that happened, and if Eliza could have avoided it by taking her place, she would never be able to forgive the Circle. *Or myself.*

"Can I at least join in the meetings?" She asked.

"I'm sorry, Eliza," Zeera said, "no."

Lashek

1795

Lashek had never felt more trapped in his life. While his people died in a foreign country, the Circle kept him in Aethos until they successfully killed a God. It seemed impossible to him. Zeera insisted they could do it, but Sithares was the most powerful God in Pandeia, according to the information he'd gleaned from the Tarsi and the resources in Aethos.

The plan itself made no sense to him; there was a book that gave whoever read it the power of whichever God it belonged to. Destroying the book, according to Zeera, killed the God. He didn't know how she'd learned this, but his mind simply couldn't accept the idea. His understanding of the Gods was that they lived in a spiritual realm inaccessible by people; if that was the case, how could anything in the real world affect them?

He wanted to trust Zeera; he really did. But with everything that happened, he found it next to impossible to trust anyone, let alone the leader of the Circle. She never shared secrets, she never told them her full plan, and she was keeping him away from his fellow Shenza.

Even worse than this, the spell they were supposed to learn was missing the last runes. Even the Austris Arans, who lorded their knowledge over everyone else, didn't know the finished spell. They thought they knew everything, but it was as much their failure as it was the rest of Pandeia's.

Trying his best to be at peace, Lashek performed the Zuunshai in his training room. He went through the dance several times in a row, increasing his speed each time. By the time he was done, the things worrying him settled into a low background noise in his mind. His heart was calm, though he knew it wouldn't take much for him to become worked up again.

In this state, he could think more clearly. He remembered feeling this way most of the time back in Shanaken; at the time he hadn't realised, but looking back, the forest really did bring out his best. Being so far away from home was beginning to take its toll.

Focus, he told himself, *things aren't as bad as you think.* Many Shenza had survived, and though they'd fled their country, winning the war against Ermoor might mean they could take Shanaken back again. Though he wanted more than anything to be with his people now, he had to put faith in their ability to survive against the Ermoori on their own.

Besides, though the Ermoori were formidable opponents, the Shenza weren't alone. Lashek tried to remind himself that the Tarsi were helping and defending his people in Tarsium. Zeera was secretive, downright mysterious even, but her people were compassionate and honourable.

His mind seemed to swing wildly between trusting that things would turn out, and raging against everyone around him for not doing enough. Latching onto the calm he'd gained from his *Zuunshai*, Lashek sat on the soft dirt of his training room and closed his eyes.

Reaching out to the trees and plants around him, Lashek fell into Shadow Magic. He felt the comforting cold spread through his body, the tingle of magic as it entered his body from the life surrounding him. It was nothing compared to Shanaken, but he pushed beyond the limits of the room his body sat in; the life that flourished throughout Aethos came to him, and all of it was connected.

He let go of his conscious mind, the way Amalus taught him all those years ago; it was called Shadow Meditation, and it led to either vast knowledge, or madness. Most Shenza, even talented Shadow Magicians, didn't realise; but life itself held memories that could be experienced by those who had the patience to listen. Lashek was open, his body simply a channel of Shadow Magic through which life connected to everything.

There was a great deal of information, ancient memories and more recent events that the life in Aethos had stored away. It all flashed through Lashek at the same time. He caught as much of it as he could, but there was far too much for one person to process. His soul was still too troubled to absorb much of anything.

Among the chaos, Lashek felt a common thread, something he'd felt in Shanaken too; *no matter what happens,* it said, *life will continue. There will always be Shenza, and there will always be Amalus*. Lashek wasn't sure if it was the voice of Amalus, or Shadow Magic, or if it was simply life itself talking to him. But either way, in that moment, he breathed a shaky sigh of relief.

He still wanted to fight beside his fellow Shenza, but at least he could feel assured that somehow, life would go on. The war that loomed on the horizon would be vicious, and many would die; but there would be survivors. The Shenza were not going to end.

Slowly, Lashek came back to his body, feeling thousands of years and thousands of perspectives melt away from his mind. The anger that he'd held onto dissipated along with his connection to the life around him; he was left with the serenity that emanated from the ancient trees and plants that grew around the city. They'd seen war, death, famine, and countless other difficulties; and yet at their core, they were utterly calm.

Finally, Lashek stood. He breathed, feeling his body respond to his mind. After being connected to so many other forms of life, being alone in his body felt strange. The trees in his training room had been transplanted from several gardens around the city; the memories still sat fresh in his mind. He looked at them, seeing them with new eyes now that he knew them properly. Reaching out his hand, he felt their leaves, their bark, the life that coursed through them.

"Thank you," he said.

Aella

1795

The Shenza, Lashek, reminded Aella of Dakesh; not just because of his jet-black hair and pale skin, but the anger and aggression that emanated from him in waves. He was particularly cold towards Aella. Other than her, he was quite friendly, especially towards the young Ermoori and the Tarsi leader.

For a time, her mind kept swapping the two Shenza; as though it couldn't tell the difference. Every now and then, memories from before she'd died pushed their way into her mind; but they remained broken and scattered. She'd known Dakesh well, and the new Shenza was a stranger. Aella decided to get to know him, even if he seemed to want nothing to do with her. As a Thearan, Aella had one way to get to know anyone: combat.

She challenged him to a sparring match. He looked as though he was about to refuse, but something changed in his eyes as he watched her. She noticed his hand lay on the hilt of his sword while he considered her offer.

"You know what?" he said, "that sounds great."

His Oman was a little off, and he spoke with a thick Shenza accent, but they could still talk. They strolled in silence to one of the training rooms. Aella used the short swords she'd had made for her in Theara; she still missed her Fire Blades. One of the reasons she wanted to destroy Kerberos, other than revenge, was to get those swords back. *He has to have them,* she thought, *somewhere*. She couldn't remember what happened to them, or where she'd last seen them. Her memory failed her, but she knew she wielded them sometime before she died. *It was on the bridge,* her mind suddenly dredged up, *just before I jumped. They disarmed me, and I had to jump without the blades*.

Lashek took up a combat stance that showed calm, his blade balanced in both hands. His face was relaxed, though his eyes shone with a strange energy that Aella didn't recognise. She met his stance with one of her own; a variant of Ero's Fangs she developed herself. His eyes scanned over her body quickly, searching for information; Aella did the same.

He rushed at her, fading into a blur of Shadow her eyes could barely follow. Aella fell into the magic coursing through her body, letting it take over. Trusting its power. The rush of strength and speed felt as familiar to her as breathing, and she twirled to face Lashek as he came around behind her.

His blade was everywhere, but so were hers. She met every attack, and countered every one with her second sword. Though he was fast, Aella was faster. In the glory of combat, Aella let herself enjoy toying with him for a moment; she could win at any time, and she thought she could see him realise it as they fought.

Aella let loose a torrent of Fire from one of her fists as she swung the blade simultaneously; Lashek growled as he dove out of the way. Watching his dive, she aimed a fireball at the place he would land. He twisted mid-dive, bringing his blade into the fireball's path and landing heavily on his shoulder.

The fireball exploded against Lashek's sword, and he grunted as the heat and force of the blast slammed into his body. Aella leapt over him, rushing to meet his clumsy roll as he recovered from the fireball. He came up exactly where she thought he would, barely ready for her next attack.

She decided to let him recover a little, skipping backwards to allow him time to return to his feet. He attacked immediately, but Aella was more than prepared. She let the fight go on a while longer, pushing him as far as she thought he could go. When she knew him properly, knew his style and movements, she aimed a solid kick at his sternum.

Lashek landed heavily on the floor, blade still in his hand. For a moment, it looked as though he was about to continue attacking; but he stood, shaking his head, and smiled at her.

"You're dangerous," he said, "I really do hope you're on our side."

"I am," Aella said.

Lashek sheathed his blade, and sat on the bench, no longer looking at her.

"That's what *he* said, too."

"Who?"

He sighed, staring intently at the ground.

"Kerberos."

Aella felt rage and fear explode in her chest. Mingled with that was confusion; *why does this man think I'm anything like Kerberos?* She breathed through the intense emotion, mindful that Sithares used emotion to control its followers. With a gentle sigh, Aella forced herself to see things from the Shenza's perspective. It was understandable; Kerberos had tricked them, causing massive damage to them and their mission, so now the Circle refused to trust her until she proved herself.

"He's on no one's side but his own," she said, "no matter what he says."

"Other than Sithares, you mean?" Lashek said, a bitter smile on his face.

"I'm not so sure, anymore."

"What do you mean?"

Aella mulled over the words she needed. She had to be careful; if she admitted that Sithares had chosen her over Kerberos, she would lose all of the trust she'd fought for since arriving in Aethos. But she had to let them know that Sithares no longer favoured its prodigal son. It meant he could be weaker, and if the magic that came with being a Hero remained with her long enough, it could also mean Aella's strength might make all the difference.

"Ever since he took over Omatus," Aella said, "his goal was achieved. That meant he stopped serving Sithares. He still oversees fighting and death from within Omatus… but Sithares wants all of Pandeia to burn, and, it seems, Kerberos doesn't."

"Are you saying Kerberos is no longer Sithares' Hero?" Lashek said, understanding and excitement battling each other in his voice.

"As far as I know, that's right."

Lashek stared at her, even more intently than before. His eyes narrowed, though there was no real threat in his stance or expression.

"And how do you feel about Kerberos," he said, "and Sithares?"

"I want them both destroyed," she said.

Sithares screamed again in her mind, its white-hot rage flashing through her thoughts.

"Wouldn't that mean you lose all your magic?" Lashek said, "I thought you'd worship Sithares like the rest of them."

"I do," she said, "I mean… I did. I want the magic to stay. But there has always been a part of me that doesn't really believe in Sithares' goals. I don't want Pandeia to burn. And Kerberos? I hate him more than you could ever know."

Eliza

1795

Zeera called everyone together after one of their secret meetings a few weeks after their talk. The mood had been declining steadily, and Zeera's expression as she regarded them all didn't help.

"We've received news from Tarsium. The Ermoori seem to be taking the advantage. Our forces stalled them for as long as they could, but they are gaining ground."

Eliza glanced at her mother straight away; her face had turned pale, her eyes shining and wide.

"They're coming," Mara said, "they're coming closer. They're coming for me."

"Mother, we'll stop them," Eliza said, "it's okay."

"No, they're going to find me. *He's* going to find me."

Her mother kept muttering the same things over and over, shaking her head and breathing rapidly. Zeera gestured to the group, and they silently left the room. She sat next to Eliza's mother, and they both comforted her.

"You are part of the Circle, Mara," Zeera said, "we will protect you. Nothing bad will happen to you while you're with us."

"You don't know him," Mara said, "he won't stop. I've felt his rage. I know what he wants. How bad he wants it."

Eliza knew who she meant; *Riffolk. My father*. She'd seen him in dreams since she was a child. Her dreams were never particularly disturbing, nothing compared to the nightmares her mother had. But she knew exactly what Mara meant when she said she felt his rage. Even though she never felt scared by his face, her dreams always showed it twisted into fury and covered in crackling yellow lightning.

"He's not more powerful than the Circle, mother," Eliza said, "we can stop him."

Mara shook her head. Her face pale, lips pulled into a tight grimace, she stared straight into the dining table. Eliza still didn't know all of what happened in Ermoor before she was born, but seeing the fear in her mother's eyes started a cold terror burning within her own stomach.

"It's not just him," her mother said, "it's his whole army too. They've taken Shanaken, now they're taking Tarsium. It won't be long before they're here."

It was true; Eliza heard reports of the damage they'd left in their wake. The forests of Shanaken remained impenetrable for thousands of years, and had now been levelled and destroyed by the Ermoori. Tarsium had no army, according to Zeera; just the Circle and its agents. Eliza couldn't imagine how Tarsium was standing up to an army that breached Shanaken.

She looked at Zeera. The Tarsi woman stared at her mother, unreadable and still. *It's impossible to know what she's thinking,* Eliza thought, *even with those giant eyes*.

"Your daughter is right, Mara," Zeera said, "we can stop him. The Shenza pulled back into Tarsium, and when Tarsium falls they will come with our people to Omas. We are working on a final plan, as you know. In the meantime, I need your focus to be on destroying Sithares. If the God of Fire still lives when Ermoor reaches us, all is lost."

Her mother sobbed at the last word, as though it was a certainty. Eliza held her close. In that moment, after Zeera's words, Eliza struggled not to believe all was already lost. She knew there was a chance at victory, of course; but it seemed such a slight chance. *According to Aerene, they're still not even close to figuring out the spell to destroy Sithares*. Meanwhile, Ermoor came closer to them every day.

"Do you want me to help you with the spell, mother?" Eliza said.

Zeera shot a look at her; a brief but bright flash of anger. *Well, now she knows I know*. But her mother nodded, and Zeera's anger disappeared as quickly as it appeared. *Now she just looks exhausted,* Eliza thought, *and disappointed*. It was better than anger, but not by much. *I just hope Aerene doesn't get in trouble for telling me*.

"She needs my help," Eliza said to Zeera, "you all do. You can't keep me shut out any more, the Circle has to work together. If we don't figure out this spell, Sithares wins. Ermoor wins."

"Fine. But from now on, the only information you get comes directly from me. No talking in secret."

The Circle is entirely secrets, Eliza thought, *what about all the secrets you've been keeping from me?*

"Of course," she said instead, "I promise."

Zeera

1795

Word continued to come in about the Ermoori. Zeera tried to keep most of it out of the ears of the Heroes; they couldn't afford to be distracted. But the Heroes trained and spoke with others, and there was no avoiding the news. As awful as it was, Ermoor was winning the war.

At the speed they were going, it was possible they could reach Aethos before the Circle found and destroyed Sithares' book. If that happened, their mission was doomed. With Ermoor's sheer power, there was no way to fight them and try to destroy Sithares at the same time.

Zeera called on Shaela once again. Their situation was becoming desperate, and the time had come for Zeera to at least attempt to use their greatest resource; the Austris Arans.

"We need your people," Zeera said, "to either locate the book of Sithares, or help fight the Ermoori to slow them down. Or both."

"We are not your personal army, Zeera," Shaela said, "we are here to destroy the God of Fire. Not to fight against pathetic little beings who cannot even wield magic."

"Forget about the Ermoori, then," she said, "but will you help to find Sithares' book?"

Shaela stared at her, face blank, her white eyes giving away nothing. The lack of pupils made her eyes look endless, as though they were portals into an eternal, magic-filled abyss. Zeera knew she had been alive for centuries, and she saw every year of it in those eyes.

"My people belong in Aethos," she said, "while Austris Ara is attached to it, it is our home. We do not fetch items for the Circle."

Zeera fought against the frustration that threatened to overtake. *She knows how important this is,* she thought, *how is it so easy for her to refuse?* The Austris Arans could travel faster and further than any other being in Pandeia; if anyone could track down and bring the book back to Aethos in time, it was them.

"This is not some game of fetch, Shaela," she said, forcing her tone to be as neutral as she could, "the book of Sithares is the most important item in all of Pandeia. We need it to complete our mission.

If not for that, why did you come at all?"

"Our mission is to provide a Hero, chosen by Aurath, to lend their magic towards destroying Sithares. That is the extent of our contract with the Circle of Shadows."

Maybe Lashek was right after all, she thought, *they do not actually care about the people of Pandeia. They are simply fulfilling an ancient promise*. Lashek didn't trust them, had never trusted them, and now Zeera saw what he'd seen when they first arrived. Still, the Austris Arans had at least displayed some honour and loyalty by coming back when summoned; for that she respected them.

"When the Ermoori reach Aethos," Zeera said, "what happens then?"

"As I said, my people belong in Aethos. The Ermoori do not. If they attack, we will retaliate."

"Will you stay until the war is done?"

Shaela glanced away at nothing, a slight frown on her face, as though genuinely considering whether she wanted to fight in the war.

"We have no immediate plans to leave Aethos," she said, "ask me again after we have destroyed Sithares."

Zeera sighed, nodding in resignation. *We cannot rely on their help in the war against Ermoor,* she thought, *that will complicate things if they leave before Ermoor invades Aethos*. It sounded to Zeera as though the Austris Arans would most likely still be around, given how quickly Ermoor was spreading through Pandeia. But Shaela also made it clear that she didn't care about the war, or who won; as long as Sithares was destroyed.

"I expected more of the Austris Arans," Zeera said, "it saddens me that you care so little about Pandeia and its people."

Shaela's shoulders rose, her wings spreading a little as she drew herself up. Her brow furrowed, though her expression changed far less than when Lashek had provoked her.

"You expected more of *us*?" she said, "you are the ones who have failed the Circle. You let your own history slip through your fingers, and forgot the magic you needed."

"Your people don't know the full spell either," Zeera said, "you cannot put the blame for that solely on us."

"Your people are the ones who insisted on keeping it secret from the rest of the world," Shaela said, "if you hadn't, the knowledge would have been too well documented to lose so easily. Add to that your inability to keep the Circle active and to remember the mission itself, and the failure is clearly your own."

"Time is a different beast for the rest of Pandeia," Zeera said, "I told you that before. To us, thousands of years is simply too much time. But at least we care about the people of Pandeia. We are fighting to save them… you are fighting for your own reputation."

Again, Shaela stood taller, indignation plain on her face. Her expressions were subtle, but Zeera was learning to read them. *She was so much friendlier lately,* Zeera thought, *but that was obviously no more than an act*. They'd been getting along well, but Zeera saw now that Shaela's attitude towards the people of Pandeia had never changed after all.

Instead of responding, Shaela simply stared at Zeera. Finally, she exhaled, her shoulders dropping again. The anger drained away, leaving something Zeera thought looked like sadness.

"You may be right," she said, "we have been away from Pandeia for a long time. Perhaps the time affected us, and our attitude, as well."

It was more than Zeera expected; not quite an apology, but an admission of fault nonetheless. She supposed being alive for as long as Shaela had been had to result in some level of wisdom. *I hoped they would be wise and benevolent,* she thought, *but up until now, they have not shown either*.

"All we can do now," Zeera said, "is agree to work together. The time our people spent apart is simply a bridge we must cross. But to do that, we both need to walk across it together."

Shaela took a long, slow breath. Her face still barely changed, and a deep sorrow emanated from her eyes.

"You are a good leader, Zeera," she said, "and you have taught me a valuable lesson."

That was far easier than I thought it would be, she thought, *perhaps the Austris Arans are a great people after all*. It remained to be seen whether they'd join the fight against Ermoor, and it may still have been an act, but Zeera still left the room feeling a weight drop from her shoulders.

I still need to get the Book of Sithares, however, she thought, *as soon as possible, and at any cost.*

Karak

1795

When he first arrived in Aethos, Karak had avoided Zeera until Aella was introduced to the Heroes, and her warriors settled in to their new home. She knew he was there, and that he didn't have the book. There was no avoiding that; if he'd brought the book back, he would have brought it straight to her, and she knew it. But with an entire army showing up, and the Circle's training to attend to, she'd been far too busy to look for him, and Karak used the time to try to gather his courage.

Once things were settled in Aethos, and Zeera finally had the time, she sought him out, as he knew she would. It took a surprisingly long time. *She's had a lot to focus on,* he thought, *but still, I thought she'd come after me immediately*. Somehow, sneaking around Aethos and avoiding her had been worse than if she'd simply come to him. Many times, he'd been tempted to approach her; but owning up to his latest failure was far more difficult than he'd expected. When she appeared, he was sitting alone in some temporary quarters shared by Tarsi agents.

"Karak," Zeera said, "you returned without the book. Again."

Karak nodded, forcing himself to look her in the eye. Fury blazed in her cold eyes, but there was more; a sadness, so deep it was almost mourning. As though she was already grieving the fall of Pandeia.

"I'm sorry," he said, "Kerberos is formidable. His warriors are powerful, and he keeps the book under constant watch."

"I know. I sent another team while I let you recover. They are monitoring the book, and Kerberos, so we may formulate a successful plan."

"We need far more than just a plan," Karak said, "we'd need an army to retrieve it. Especially after already making two attempts."

Zeera was utterly still as he spoke, staring into his eyes with an intensity that unnerved him. For a long moment, she didn't speak or move. Karak fought against the panic that threatened to rise in his throat.

"If it takes an army," Zeera finally said, "then we will send an army. Correct me if I'm wrong, Karak, but it seems to me as though you don't understand the seriousness of the situation."

"No," Karak said, "I do. I do, I swear. But Kerberos is a monster unlike anything we've faced before. Even before he gained the other forms of magic, he was almost unstoppable."

Again, Zeera simply stared at him. *She doesn't understand how powerful Kerberos is,* Karak thought, *or she just doesn't care*. A thought he'd had before came back into his head, ugly and terrifying; *she's going to keep sending me back there, until I either get the book, or until I die*.

"We must get the book, Karak," Zeera said, "it is the only way. There is no alternate plan, no other way to save us. I know Kerberos is powerful, and we will deal with him when we can. But for now, however we can, we *must* get that book."

"Please don't send me back there," Karak said, unable to stop the words, "please. I'll do anything else. If I go back there, I'll die. Kerberos is going to kill me; I just know it."

"If you die in the service of Pandeia," Zeera said, "that is a noble death. We all die, Karak. What matters is what we do with our life before that happens. If there is even a chance you can bring that book back to us, you have to take it. I'll send a team with you again."

Karak sighed, tears sliding down his face. *I knew it,* he thought, *there is no escape. My death will be at Kerberos' hands*.

"You say it will take an army," Zeera continued, "but I disagree. I think there is a way to take it with a small team. We just need a better plan. And we will have one before long."

Though he managed to nod in agreement, Karak's entire body shook. *She's sending me to my death,* he thought, *and we both know it*.

"How many agents will you allow me to take?" he asked.

"I think a team of six will suffice."

Some of the tension in his body rushed out. Six was far better than four. It meant at the very least they could fight the warriors Kerberos left to watch the book. Their last attempt had required three Tarsi to be in the arena; but without needing to worry about the Thearans, Karak's team would be able to focus all their time and energy on the book.

"Okay," he said, speaking more to himself than to Zeera, "alright. I can work with six."

Zeera nodded; a short, sharp movement that spoke of expectation and impatience.

"Good," she said, "we will begin planning then. In the meantime, train and prepare, Karak. I have been patient with you, given you many chances. I've even let you rest and heal from your last mission. This is your last chance."

She left the training room, and Karak sighed. With Zeera out of the room, his fear finally rose up, and Karak wept; there was no escaping his fate now. With a huge effort, he pushed past the fear and forced his tears to stop. *I need to train,* he thought, *Zeera is right. Everything depends on this last mission. This time*, he promised himself, *I will be ready. I won't give up. I won't fail.*

For now, however, Karak was utterly exhausted. Fear and humiliation had coursed through his veins ever since returning to Aethos. Though there was much for Karak to do, he could think of nothing but sleep. That, and the inevitability of his death. He knew the only reason he survived the last attempt to steal Sithares' book was because Kerberos himself hadn't been in the room when Karak showed up. *Even then,* he thought, *I barely survived.*

With a team of six, his chances were far better than alone. But far better than nothing still wasn't much. Karak tossed and turned as he tried to sleep, pain and fear rushing through his mind and body in equal measure. Kerberos waited in Omatus, and Karak was going to have to face him again. Nothing scared him more than the King of Omatus. *I can do nothing now,* he thought, *but wait, and pray.*

Eliza

1795

They sat together in one of the Circle's meeting rooms, facing each other on the floor, a metre or so apart. Both of them fell silent as they focused again.

"Let's go again," Eliza said, "but this time I want you to watch where I focus my power, and add your own to it."

Her mother nodded, and Eliza let lightning flow from her hands into a controlled sphere between them. She held it, crackling and rotating, as her mother gathered her own magic. They'd been practicing several hours a day for weeks now; her mother had a lot of power, but nowhere near the control that Eliza possessed.

Mathys trained Eliza to be in control. He never used magic and didn't understand how it felt, but his training was still incredibly useful. Her mother trained with Mathys when she was younger, but her training was cut short because she'd been pregnant with Eliza at the time. Afterwards, she was more focused on raising Eliza than on practicing magic.

She felt magic pooling around her mother. They shared a connection that was deepened when their magic was active, and she could see in her mother's eyes that she felt it too. The sphere grew slightly as both focused their energy on it. Its crackling became wilder, and Eliza fought to control it as her mother poured even more power into it.

"That's good," she said, "but try to focus on the shape as you add magic to it. We both need to keep it under control."

Her mother's eyes narrowed, but for a while nothing changed. Eliza gritted her teeth as the sphere of magic pulsed and warped. She struggled to keep it under control, trying to wrap her own magic around her mother's to contain it.

Finally, the sphere calmed again, and her mother's magic became one with her own. The crackling disappeared almost entirely; in its place, a soothing hum filled the room. Between them, the sphere floated in total stillness, a perfect balance of both their magic.

"I can feel it," Mara whispered, "the control."

Eliza nodded. She'd come close a few times, but this was her first success. There was a spark of joy in her mother's eyes, but her exhaustion dampened any celebration she would have showed. Eliza felt the same way; she was relieved and proud, but so exhausted that she couldn't give more than a weak smile. Throwing a bolt of lightning was one thing, but holding a controlled sphere of pure magic for an extended period of time was utterly different.

"I'm going to let go now," Eliza said, "slowly. You need to take control as I do."

Her mother barely reacted; only a grim smile touched her lips as she stared at the sphere. As slowly as she could, Eliza eased her concentration from the magic between them. The amount of power they held now could have decimated the entire room and several beyond that. *She can do this. I trust her*. Mara gasped as the weight of the magic shifted to her.

Eliza watched carefully. The sphere wavered, an occasional crackling sound splitting the smooth hum. Sweat beaded on Mara's face and she bared her teeth. *She's got almost all of it now,* Eliza thought, *I'm barely doing anything*.

"Hold it, mother," Eliza said, "you're doing it."

Her mother didn't respond. Her eyes were fixed on the magic, narrowed and shining with intensity. A spark leapt from the sphere and cannoned into the ceiling above them. The humming disappeared, replaced by constant crackling, and the sphere lost its shape.

Eliza tried to take control back, but it was too late. The magic twisted and warped, sparks lashing out at the ceiling and walls. Her mother grunted with effort; hands balled into fists. Eliza reached out, adding more magic around the warping sphere and forcing it inward, wrapping it around like a net to keep it contained. *I don't even know if this will work,* she thought.

She held to the wrapping spell with all her strength, adding it to the sphere and forcing it to take the right shape again. But as she forced the magic into a ball again, it absorbed the spell and erupted into flashing bolts. The room around them filled with explosions and pulses of yellow light.

Desperate, Eliza pulled as much of the magic back into herself as she could, letting it flow through her instead of the room. The rest of it exploded, knocking them both against opposite walls. She felt the magic within her buzzing violently, as though it longed to leap out of her and destroy more of the room. For a long moment, its power felt as though it would overtake her; as though she herself would explode.

Across the room now, her mother groaned as she slowly rose to her feet. Eliza felt paralysed by the powerful magic coursing through her body; she couldn't so much as make a sound. Footsteps thudded into the room, and Eliza heard Zeera's voice.

"What happened?"

Mara groaned again. Eliza tried to stand, but the magic flared into vicious, tingling pain where she touched the floor. She tried to speak, but no words would come. All she could do was wait for the magic to dissipate properly. She heard Zeera move to help her mother.

"What happened?" Zeera asked again.

"Eliza was helping me," her mother said, "teaching me control. It was a little too much."

"Eliza, are you okay?"

Zeera's footsteps approached her, and Eliza forced herself to speak through the buzzing electricity flowing through her.

"Don't touch me," she said, grunting with the effort, "too much magic."

After the magic finally wore off, they sat together at one of the dining tables.

"So, Mara controlled it herself?" Zeera said.

"Yes," Eliza said, "for a while. It was a huge amount of magic. I would have struggled with it too."

"That is a good sign." Zeera smiled at her mother. "I'm pleased with your progress."

"I'll get better at it," Mara said, "Eliza is a good teacher."

"She certainly seems it. Eliza, I misjudged you. I apologise. But there is still a long road ahead of us."

Eliza nodded.

"The spell."

"That's right, the spell. We know how to capture Sithares, as the Circle did in ancient times. But Sithares has grown far too powerful to simply capture… and the spell to destroy it completely is another matter. A far more secret spell."

"How do we find the missing parts?"

Zeera hesitated, shooting a look at Mara. *She thinks my mother told me what the Circle has been talking about*. It made sense, but Eliza didn't want to get her mother in trouble. *I don't want Aerene in trouble either*. Hopefully now that Zeera was including her it wouldn't be much of a problem anyway.

"It is our belief that the key to destroying Sithares is hidden somewhere in the book. Each God has a book which contains everything its worshippers need to know. The only problem is we still don't have it."

"Why would the book tell us how to destroy the God it belongs to?" Eliza asked.

"It's only a theory," Zeera said, "but, for the moment, it's our only hope. Shaela has her people researching their history books, and I have my agents doing the same."

"There has to be a way," Eliza said, "the original Circle wouldn't have let such a small mistake happen… would they?"

"They may not have known, Eliza. There's no way to tell what happened. But I promise, we will find a way to destroy Sithares."

Aella

1795

Shaela was an incredible being; all of the Austris Arans were. They were unlike anything Aella could have imagined. She felt magic flowing from them freely, as though they were constantly holding their magic at full power.

She watched Shaela's stance, as well. The Austris Aran woman moved with precision and grace at all times. Aella read a hundred lifetimes of intense training in Shaela's body. There was strength, too; not just because of the magic coursing through her body, but pure, non-magical muscle power.

Aella couldn't help but feel a subtle but palpable sense of threat from the Austris Arans. They may have been fighting to save Pandeia, but there was a feeling of disconnect from the ancient beings; as though no matter what happened, they knew they would still be fine. It scared Aella almost as much as Kerberos' relentless brutality had. *I'm giving up Fire Magic and probably everything else I have to destroy Sithares,* she thought, *and these people's lives won't change even if we don't succeed.*

So why are you fighting with them?

The voice was an almost constant presence in her mind now. She didn't bother to answer it most times; it could read her thoughts anyway. Instead, she simply let it whisper and rage in her head, doing her best to ignore it.

She sat with Shaela in one of the training rooms, talking about Austris Ara and Air Magic. Aella knew nothing about them or their culture; she never even knew they existed until she came to Aethos. The most interesting thing to her, other than the fact that their city floated above the clouds, was their lifespan. They could live to almost two thousand years of age; sometimes longer. Knowing she was immortal, Aella felt intrigued by the possibility of other beings living as long as she might.

They talked about Thearans, too. Shaela was particularly interested in Aella's past, and Aella was happy to recount what she remembered. There wasn't much, but what little of her memory remained unfractured, she told to Shaela.

After a long conversation, they trained together. Aella didn't see much power in any of the other Circle members, except perhaps the young Ermoori girl. But Shaela was both powerful and knowledgeable, and Aella found herself comparing the Austris Aran to Kerberos. The one difference between them was stark, however; though Shaela didn't seem emotionally invested in Pandeia, there was no malice or evil in her eyes.

Despite her benevolent nature, Shaela fought as viciously as Aella had ever seen. Most of the time, she floated in mid-air, attacking and blocking from above. It was a whole new kind of fighting, which made weighing her capabilities far more difficult. Still, Aella held her own, and the longer they fought, the easier things became for her.

Every warrior had habits. Every warrior had weaknesses. To the observant, both became clear in time. Shaela, like most warriors who possessed a clear and innate advantage, came to rely on it in combat. Her wings, while difficult to get around, could be used against her; especially for someone wielding powerful Fire Magic.

Aella aimed a fireball at Shaela's right wing. She slowed herself down, taking longer to aim than she normally would; Shaela took the bait. As soon as she swerved to avoid the fireball, Aella launched another one, much faster this time, at her other wing.

Shaela looked caught, just for a second; but the fireball exploded and the fire that should have burned her wing veered instead to the floor in a controlled rush. Aella changed stance, staring at Shaela's wing. There was no sign of damage at all. *I saw it explode,* she thought, *there is no defence against that*.

With a small but satisfied smile, Shaela landed across from Aella. She didn't bother with a combat stance, instead simply standing, relaxed and smiling.

"How did you do that?" Aella asked.

"Air Magic can do a lot more than you may think," Shaela said, "and fire is strongly reliant on air. Air can build or break fire."

She spoke slowly, as though she had all the time in the world. Aella supposed it was natural for someone who'd been alive for such a long time. Technically, she *did* have all the time in the world. What took up space in Aella's head most in that moment was Air Magic. They'd spoken about it earlier, but Shaela kept to the basics. Aella had no idea how effective it could be.

When Karak first told her about the Circle, Aella thought it might be the best chance she had of destroying Sithares and Kerberos. After training with several of their members, she'd come to the conclusion that she was the best of their warriors. The young Ermoori girl was surprisingly powerful, but other than that, she knew she could kill them all if she had to. And if she could do that, they didn't stand a chance against Kerberos. But Shaela was different. She wasn't even the chosen Hero for Austris Ara, and yet she could wave Aella's magic away like it was nothing.

"Is there any way that Fire Magic could get through your

defences?" Aella asked.

"If I was unprepared," Shaela said, "definitely. Or if the magician was sufficiently powerful, I suppose."

"Sufficiently powerful?" Aella said, "am I not *sufficiently* powerful?"

Shaela laughed, her voice musical and light. There was a depth of calm that lay within her presence, the way Aella sometimes felt looking over the desert from Sitharkos. Though she was more used to rage and passion, the calm felt nice.

"You would be more than powerful enough, Aella," Shaela said, "if you didn't hold back. I would enjoy watching you fight for real."

She knew I wasn't really trying, Aella thought, *but she can still see how much power I have*. Watching the ease with which Shaela manipulated Air Magic, all that Aella wanted was to live as long as the Austris Aran had. If she could keep Fire Magic, her immortality would have meant her knowledge and power could grow exponentially.

As things lay, Aella wasn't even sure what would remain of her after Sithares was destroyed. Would she still be immortal? Would she have Fire Magic? Would she die immediately? If Sithares was the reason she came back from death, was it the only thing keeping her alive now? No one she knew could answer her questions; and even if Sithares knew the answers, it wouldn't ever be honest with her. Either way, Sithares had to be destroyed, and the Austris Arans were their only chance.

Eliza

1795

Over the next few months, Zeera told her more and more about the Circle's activities. There was so much more to their mission than she would have believed. Several of their agents were out searching for the Book of Sithares, more were looking for ways to beat the Ermoori, and still more were keeping contact with the survivors in Shanaken. Most of the Shenza and Tarsi remained in hiding in Tarsium, underneath the ground. They fought against the Ermoori still, but according to Zeera it was likely they would have to fall back to Omatus soon.

Eliza didn't know much about warfare, but Zeera's plan seemed too reckless to her. They were leaving everything until the last possible moment to strike with all their strength. She knew Mathys would have agreed; there was too much that could go wrong. They were too desperate, and Ermoor was too powerful.

She'd tried telling Zeera, but the Tarsi were used to being right, and it seemed to Eliza that even when they were wrong, they assumed their view was correct. With the Circle's plan, the final battle for all of Pandeia would take place either in Omatus or Aethos. The idea terrified Eliza, and her mother too. It relied on the Shenza and Tarsi escaping Tarsium and reaching their destination before the Ermoori. And it relied on most or all of them surviving.

They needed to be in Aethos to perform the spell; but only the Heroes were required for that. Aerene's army, along with the Omasi and Circle agents with them, should have travelled up to Tarsium along with the Omati. It made sense to Eliza to bring the battle to the Ermoori before they could take any more ground. But when she tried to explain it, Zeera and the others always had a counter to her arguments.

So, we're just sitting here, she thought, *waiting for the Ermoori to swarm in and kill everyone*. Unless their plan worked perfectly, of course. In the meantime, all she could do was help her mother practice magic, and train herself.

Aerene's foot swooped just over her head, and she blinked, bringing her mind back to the present. She had been thinking about the war again. *Almost got knocked out just then,* she thought, *I need to focus*. She spun and dove away from Aerene, rolling to her feet and aiming a bolt of lightning just next to her target. It forced Aerene to her left, and Eliza's right; her stronger side. Before Aerene finished dodging, Eliza kicked at her knee.

The attack connected mid step, and Aerene crashed to the floor. *Lucky I pulled the kick,* she thought, *if I'd given it all my strength her leg would have broken*. Eliza remained in a ready stance, magic tingling in her hands. *No matter what you see,* Mathys had always said, *never drop your guard. The enemy is not dead until you confirm their heart is still*. Aerene may have fallen, but it could be a trick to lure her into a vulnerable position.

She took the opportunity to back away, keeping Aerene in her sight. But when Aerene finally rose, her pain was apparent. *She wasn't tricking me*. She stood with her wounded leg up to keep the weight off it, and took a ready stance again.

"Are you alright?" Eliza asked.

"My knee isn't, you really hit hard. But I have a perfectly fine pair of wings."

With that, her wings spread and her legs straightened as all her weight was taken off them. *So much for taking the advantage,* Eliza thought. Mathys had always taught her to strike weak points first, and making the final strike when the enemy was weakest. Or, if possible, striking hard and fast right at the very beginning to take the enemy down with as little fuss as possible. Eliza preferred the latter, but in a practice match against Aerene that tactic was pointless; *if I just rushed her, we wouldn't be able to practice technique properly.*

Aerene floated, her wings barely moving. *How does she do that?* Eliza thought, *I've seen her do it before, but I still don't understand.* She thought wings needed to move to make someone fly, but apparently the Austris Arans could float. When she'd trained against Shaela, a well-placed bolt to the wing had grounded her effectively. But Eliza and Aerene trained together often, and Aerene was beginning to learn her tricks and tactics.

She brought her magic to the surface, crackling between her fingers as Aerene floated above her. The next move was up to Aerene; Eliza was ready. As she suspected, Aerene swooped over her head, kicking with her good leg as she passed. Eliza shot a bolt at her thigh and rolled in under Aerene's wounded leg. *That's both legs now,* she thought, *she'll have to use magic or try to hit with her hands or wings to hit me.*

Her wings were large, which meant she had long range; but she needed them for balance. Punches could be dodged or blocked with relative ease, but if Aerene got close enough to punch, her wings would be a bigger problem. They could wrap around her, sweep her off balance, or simply bludgeon her. Eliza brought more magic to her fingertips, and waited for another attack. *If you let your opponent attack first, it can play with their mind,* Mathys said, *depending on who they are, it can make them overconfident. Or it can even put doubt in their mind, making them think you're in control. And if your enemy thinks you're in control, you are.*

But Aerene didn't attack. She simply floated, staring at Eliza with a tired look in her eyes. Eliza felt the same way; it wasn't just the training; it was the constant news coming in from the Tarsi. Ermoor was approaching, and nothing they could do was slowing the invasion down.

Aerene's shoulders slumped, and Eliza knew it wasn't a bluff. She relaxed as well, and they shared a look that said everything. Earlier that day, Zeera had reported the casualties of Tarsi and Shenza in Tarsium. Though they'd still wanted to train together, neither of them could keep their minds off how many had died. *And they're still dying every day.*

It was difficult to focus on training lately, as much as Eliza loved it. She and Aerene spoke about it often. They both felt the same way; helpless, able to do nothing but talk and train until the Ermoori reached them.

Aerene lowered gently to the ground, wincing as her legs took her weight again. Eliza felt her cheeks flush; although she knew how strong Aerene was, she always felt guilty after their training was done.

"Let's get some food," Aerene said, "I need to sit down for a while."

"Sorry," Eliza said, "I thought you could handle it."

Aerene shot her a dangerous look, and Eliza laughed.

"It's difficult to take that look seriously when you're waddling around like that," she said, laughing harder.

Aerene let out a frustrated groan.

"I'll get you next time," she said, "you'll see."

Epilogue

1795

The command deck of Riffolk's warship had become a second home, a makeshift lab where he tracked and planned the progress of the war. No soldiers were allowed in; the quiet isolation helped him focus. His soldiers were spreading through Tarsium slowly, but steadily. The Tarsi fought in unexpected ways, but his designs were holding up against even unseen enemies. They took casualties, of course; but that was to be expected in war.

What interested Riffolk most on his electronic map, rather than the movements of his soldiers, was the bright lights clustered in

Aethos. Barely a few months after his forces moved into Tarsium, a massive concentration of magical power had drifted from south of the map and connected with Aethos. He'd already been tracking the powerful gathering there, but now their numbers had spiked threefold. There were scatterings of magic-users throughout Omas, and Tarsium, and Theara; but nothing anywhere near what was in Aethos.

His search for the books of magic had come to a standstill, but along with the new group in Aethos, he knew must have come another book. If Kerberos wasn't already aware of it, it could mean an advantage to Riffolk. Kerberos was already ahead; he possessed all the forms of magic except whichever now lay in Aethos. It only gave Riffolk more reason to join his army when they reached the city.

He was already aware that Mara had to be there. *I still don't know their purpose,* he thought, *but I'll know soon enough*. It would be the final battlefront of the war, and unless they made a move before he got there, it would be where he found her.

The soldiers were fighting well. His warship, still at anchor on Tarsium's east coast, worked as a base of operations. Once enough of Tarsium was taken, Riffolk would join his army himself. After that, it was on to Omas. His army would take Omatus first, and then go straight to Aethos. Another branch of his army, fresh men who had been held in reserve until now, would sweep down the western coast of Omas, taking the smaller cities. They would meet his main force in Aethos. He looked forward to finally reaching the ancient city.

I will gain new magic, he thought, *decimate the remaining forces of Pandeia, and then... Then I will finally come face to face with Mara.*

THE END

If you loved this book (or even if you didn't), please leave a review on Amazon, Goodreads, or anywhere else that hosts reviews.

It really makes a huge difference to me being able to share my books with the world.

www.ingramcontent.com/pod-product-compliance
Lightning Source LLC
Chambersburg PA
CBHW020718310726
48979CB00004B/976

9780648429487